Hippocrene Companion Guide to the

SOVIET UNION

Lydle Brinkle

Hippocrene Books
New York

Acknowledgments

I am indebted to those students, teachers, and others who made trips to Russia with me during 1973 and 1976. They helped to provide much useful information that was incorporated into this book. Also I wish to acknowledge the assistance of the Faculty Senate and the College of Humanities of Gannon University, Erie, Pennsylvania, for their financial support of this endeavor. Finally, I wish to thank these contributors:

—Dorothy Lyons, Jill Chelko, Joanne Carlson, and Margie Hudak, who typed the final version of the manuscript.

—Pam Fuccaro, who typed the original version and corrected grammatical errors in it.

—The Reverend Robert G. Fin, Associate Professor of Russian Language at Gannon University, for his encouragement of this project.

—Verna Desko of Atlanta, Georgia—friend, teacher.

—Doctors Martin F. Larrey and Phil Kelly, former Deans of Humanities of Gannon University.

—Carolyn Brinkle, who endured with me while I worked on the manuscript, and headed the household while I was running about in Russia gathering information for this book.

—Aeroflot, Intourist, and the many Russian guides who contributed information and materials for the manuscript.

—*Soviet Life* and *Ukraine,* monthly magazines published by the Soviet Union.

All photos in this book were taken by the author, including the cover photos.

For information, address: Hippocrene Books, Inc.
171 Madison Avenue, New York, NY 10016.

Library of Congress Cataloging-in-Publication Data

Brinkle, Lydle.
   An American's guide to the Soviet Union / Lydle Brinkle.
     P. 328 cm. 15¼x23
   Bibliography: p.
   ISBN 0-87052-554-9
   1. Soviet Union—Description and travel—Guide-books.
I. Title.
DK16.B75   1988   88-5087
914.7′04854—dc19   CIP

ISBN-087052-635-9

Printed in the United States of America.

Contents

Preface to the Third Edition

The Soviet Union is the essence of adventure in travel. It is the largest nation on earth and consists of a diverse geography. It has had a long and multicolored history; many of its writers, artists and scientists are well known in the West; its elegant palaces, architectural works of art, historic museums and monuments match those in other parts of Europe or elsewhere. Moreover, the Soviet Union today is a country experiencing radical change. Due to severe economic pressures in the Soviet Union, Kremlin officials have decided to shift the country's centrally planned economy to a market economy. This momentous decision means that the Soviet people must brace for a series of far-reaching reforms. The big question of *Perestroika* (economic restructuring) is how fast should and will the proposed reforms be implemented. President Gorbachev has advocated a gradual economic transition to be carried out in stages. Some other Soviet officials are pressing for more rapid economic reform. Under Gorbachev's plan, an economic and banking system based on a market economy would be the first stage in the transformation of the depressed socialist economy. It would be followed by greatly increased bank interest rates, price reforms, a new system of taxation, and joint-stock ownership by individuals and companies of as much as sixty percent of all state enterprises. Most food (including bread, meat, and fish) is expected to double in price at least and higher unemployment and a decrease in wages are forecast. Price reform will likely also bring about further inflation.

Mikhail Gorbachev and the economy are in a desperate situation. Soviet consumers have been unloading their rubles, buying up food and any available consumer goods in a frenzy before their currency loses its value further. The shortage of consumer goods in the past led Soviet citizens to hold onto their rubles. Now, a doubling or tripling of prices would absorb most of those rubles, and this is a major reason for the panic buying. According to a *Wall Street Journal* report (May 16, 1990), the average Soviet family had purchased enough laundry detergents to last them for seven years. In 1989, the Soviet Union imported $1 billion worth of detergent, only to have it grabbed from store shelves by hoarders. Consumer items like salt, matches, detergents, and soap which resist spoilage or loss by insects and rodents, quickly disappear from stores.

Under the old fixed price system of the Soviet economy, farm commodities were largely sold to the state at prices set by the government. Farmers now sell many of their surplus commodities for cash. It is ironic that at a time when the government is importing grain, Soviet farmers are feeding large quantities of their stored grain as well as potatoes and bread to their livestock. This waste is related to the fact that the Soviet government heavily subsidizes the price of food.

The open air markets common on Soviet streets, generally have a higher quality of produce (vegetables, fruit, potatoes, chicken, eggs, etc.) than the State stores. Small, private farm plots supply much of this produce. The produce sold to State stores at fixed prices is usually lacking in quality, since farmers can sell their best commodities at higher profits in the open markets. It is a simple matter of economics.

The U.S. not only feeds its people with about two million farmers, but exports millions of tons of food and grain to help feed other countries, including the Soviet Union. The U.S.S.R. has twelve times as many farmers and produces seven times as many tractors as the U.S., but still cannot adequately feed all its people. Soviet farm output is less than one-quarter of that in many Western countries. The absurd system of state and collective farms and their mismanagement and failures are directly linked to the woeful state of the Soviet economy. Large quantities of vegetables, fruit, potatoes, grain, and other produce never arrive in Soviet markets due to inadequate storage facilities, poorly organized and inefficient transport, frequent shortages of labor and its poor coordination at harvest time, equipment failures and lack of spare parts, etc. Crops may rot in the field at harvest time while other produce is pilfered by corrupt managers and officials. Black marketeering is common and constitutes a sub-culture of its own in the Soviet Union. Privatization of agriculture may be the only hope of reform.

Besides agriculture, other sectors of the economy that have experienced hardships include industry, transportation, and the construction trades.

Furthermore, energy production has fallen resulting in a decline in oil exports needed to raise hard currency. Oil is the leading Soviet export, with natural gas and then gold constituting the country's other main assets. But, if these resources were sold in larger quantities on the world market, this would tend to lower their prices and undermine the Soviet economy. In 1989 the U.S.S.R. registered nearly $1.5 billion trade deficit. Inflation has been running between six and ten percent annually.

Standards of living in the U.S.S.R. differ considerably from those in the U.S. and most Western countries. In Soviet society slightly more than eleven percent of the population comes under the American or European label of middle class, whereas sixty percent of the U.S. population falls in this category. Wealthy or high-consumer families make up only 2.3 percent of Soviet society. At the top of the Soviet social pyramid is a very rich group of persons (less than one-half of one percent of the population) that include diplomats, scientists, well-known athletes, high ranking party officials, and wealthy black marketeers.

The Soviet welfare system is another example of social inequality. According to Soviet economist Andrei Kuteinikov (*Wall Street Journal*, January 26, 1990), the state spends twenty percent of its GNP on welfare. However, the wealthy Soviet elite dip heavily into these expenditures. They receive their medical care in the best health facilities, send their children to top educational institutions at no cost, utilize the most sought after recreational and resort facilities, and receive inflated pensions upon retirement. The upper crust of Soviet society also frequently own separate apartments or *dachas* in the countryside or along the seashore, drive the best cars, possess more than their share of appliances, eat the best foods, and have bank accounts.

The huge mass of the Soviet people languish in austerity with little hope of improving their lot. Shortages are everywhere, but hardly affect the party hierarchy who enjoy a privileged access to goods, housing, cars, etc. Party members import shoes, clothing, liquor, perfumes, etc. from abroad. *Perestroika* has promised much to Soviet citizens, but to date has delivered little to the average consumer. Meanwhile, discontent is brewing amongst the masses, and could bring violent revolutionary change to the whole Soviet society. The current changes in the Soviet Union may only be a prelude to more radical changes to follow. Russian history relates that its people can endure many hardships and sufferings, but their patience may be wearing thin.

Waiting in line, or queue, is a way of life in the Soviet Union. It is a cult the Soviets have developed to a high degree. Besides queues for sugar, meat, fruit, and the like, drivers and cars frequently queue for a turn at the gas pumps. Gas stations are few, even in large Soviet cities, and the gas supply often runs out while one is waiting in line. Attendants may close their pumps abruptly for lunch or for some "emergency", leaving customers angry and confused.

Perestroika has also brought more entrepreneurship to the U.S.S.R. Individuals and cooperatives are engaging in more private enterprise, such as car repair shops, plumbing services, restaurants, open-air markets, medical and health services for fee, etc. However, private enterprises, are heavily taxed, limiting their growth. Foreign enterprises are slowly making inroads into the Soviet market. McDonald's, Pepsi Cola, and Baskin-Robbins serve customers there, and other Western enterprises such as General Electric, sell aircraft engines, plastics, power generation systems, and medical equipment. Western owned hotels are also being built in the Soviet Union.

With his economy in shambles, Gorbachev has had to face yet other far-reaching problems in his country. One of the most serious is ethnic unrest, especially in the Baltic Republics, Kirghizia, Uzbekistan, Armenia, Azerbaijan, Moldavia, Georgia, and Tadzhikstan. Not only have some of these ethnic groups fought each other, but on occasion they have fought Soviet troops and policemen. Hundreds of Armenians and Azerbaijanis have died in ethnic clashes in Nagorno-Karabash, an area in Azerbaijan peopled mostly by Armenians. The Armenians are mainly Christian in belief, while the Azerbaijanis are mostly Shiite Moslems.

Ethnic Russians have fled the Central Asian Republics of Uzbekistan, Tadzhikistan, and Kirghizia by the thousands after facing violence there. Ethnic clashes in Kirghizia and Uzbekistan left over one hundred dead in June, 1990. The Kirghiz and Uzbeks are both Sunni Moslems, but have hostile feelings for each other over contested claims to land and housing rights. General poverty, high unemployment, and a shortage of housing characterizes Soviet Central Asia.

In the Baltic states, the Lithuanian declaration of independence from the Soviet Union on March 11, 1990 led to an economic embargo by the Kremlin of oil and natural gas, industrial goods, and other raw materials to the republic. Latvia also declared its independence, and Estonia received a pledge from the Supreme Soviet parliament that full independence would gradually be restored. In June, 1990 the parliament of the Russian Soviet Socialist Republic (the bulk of the country) declared its laws to have more weight than the country's federal statutes. Gorbachev then proposed that the fifteen republics of the Soviet Union should be formed into a loose federation of sovereign states. As power continues to gradually shift from the Kremlin to the republics, local organs of power will have to assume more responsibility for activities and unrest in their backyards.

The terms "Russia" and the "Soviet Union" are often confused. Russia is the largest and most important of the fifteen republics which comprise the country as a whole, the Soviet Union. Even those aware of the difference frequently use the two interchangeably, as is case in this narrative, except when making a distinction between them.

This book is more than a standard tourist guide to the Soviet Union. Descriptions of monuments, places and landscapes are interwoven with the narrative to tell a story. While it is largely intended as a readable guide and ideal companion for travelers, scholars and researchers will doubtless find some morsels of knowledge as well. The book is written also with the purpose of urging a better understanding of the Soviet Union, its people, culture and history. It is hoped that the reader will find it both informative and stimulating.

--Lydle Brinkle

Preface

The following is a narrated account of four visits by the author to the Soviet Union: the first in 1973, followed by others in 1976, 1985, and 1988. An attempt is made to relate to the reader the way this writer experienced the Soviet Union, what was seen and heard about it, and some of the impressions of the day-to-day conditions under which the average Soviet citizen must operate.

Essentially, the content of this book consists of information drawn from the logs of three separate journeys to the Soviet Union. For the purpose of continuity the information has been integrated from the three logs to read in a sequential manner. Logs are important firsthand impressions since they relate eyewitness accounts. Unfortunately, logs have largely become a lost form of art in the twentieth century.

Numerous Russian guides were utilized as sources in writing the notes for this book. Nevertheless, there were some inaccuracies and inconsistencies in the information they provided. When possible, this writer attempted to verify their information against that of more authoritative and scholarly sources. Additional sources of information used to supplement that provided by my guides came largely from pamphlets and guide books provided by Intourist, the Russian national travel agency. The author has also frequently taught the course "Geography of the Soviet Union" at the university level, thus enabling him to enhance his talent for description, explanation, and overview of the subject matter.

This book is more than a standard tourist guide to the Soviet Union. Many tourist guides are simply a litany of long lists of hotels, restaurants, consulates, and other such information with little background material on the areas about which they are written. This book goes well beyond that by incorporating both practical information of use to the tourist as well as a historical and geographical narrative to explain the significance of what is seen and observed. Descriptions of monuments, places, and landscapes are interwoven with the narrative to tell a story. Indeed, the book is largely intended as a readable guide and ideal companion for travelers to Russia. On the other hand, there are doubtless tidbits of information in the narrative that will serve as morsels of knowledge for the scholar or researcher. This book is written also with the purpose of urging the need for a better understanding of the Soviet Union, its people, culture, and history. It is hoped that the reader will find it factual, informative and stimulating.

The object of this book is to present to its readers an easy-to-understand and knowledgeable description of the three most frequently visited and toured areas of Russia, namely Moscow, Leningrad, and Kiev, in addition to a number of secondary cities that are also frequented by tourists. All the cities in the Soviet Union are of secondary importance, from a tourist standpoint, to the "big three" of Moscow, Leningrad, and Kiev. However, the author is confident that the reader will also find the chapters on Odessa, Novgorod, Volgograd, and the others similarly appealing and interesting.

An appendix briefly describes and provides pertinent information on more than three dozen Soviet cities not considered in the main body of the text. Tourists or visitors to the Soviet Union are permitted entry to all these cities and should one or more of them be on an individual's itinerary, the appendix should prove useful in this regard. Each chapter contains (when appropriate) a general information section on local tours, restaurants, museums, and so forth. Before the editor and publisher approved the final version, the author tested its appeal and utility by requesting that a number of his students, colleagues, and some individuals planning trips to the Soviet Union read the manuscript and comment on its worth, or value, and general interest. Some of those who read the manuscript preferred the personalized narrative account of it without the supplemental information on lists of hotels, museums, city tours, and restaurants. However, those planning a trip to the Soviet Union thought the supplemental information was relevant and could prove of value. Thus, while the original version of the manuscript did not contain the appendix and practical information sections, these parts have been added to enable the traveler to make his journey easier to plan and, perhaps, more enjoyable.

The reader need not be a student of Russian history or geography to follow the narration in this book. The author has taken some pains to explain to the reader of the narrative the historical significance of the various landmarks. Important personages and events, as they fit into the context of the narrative, are also described in some detail.

The terms "Russia" and the "Soviet Union" are often confused by many tourists and individuals. The two terms are frequently used interchangeably, even by persons knowledgeable of the differences in their definitions. The term "Russia" refers to the largest and most important of the fifteen republics that comprise the country as a whole, which is known as the "Soviet Union." In this narrative the terms are used interchangeably, unless it is necessary to make a distinction between them.

It is a bit surprising to this author that more tourists and travelers do not opt to visit the Soviet Union when they make plans for travel abroad. The Soviet Union has a long and multicolored history; it is the largest nation on earth and consists of a diverse geography; many of its writers, artists, and scientists (past and present) are well known in the West; and there are elegant palaces, architectural works of art, historical museums, and monuments to match those in other parts of Europe or elsewhere.

It is my hope that this book will not only enhance its readers' knowledge of the Soviet Union, but also will stimulate some of them to visit that country and see it firsthand.

The Soviet Union is the essence of adventure in travel. It is an unusual and fascinating place to visit. You can visit legendary cities or see new developments such as enormous hydroelectric facilities and vast collective farms.

How many people do you know who have been to the Soviet Union? Why not make it your next adventure? See this land of many mosaics and experience the wonder of an exciting journey. In a country so vast as the Soviet Union there is a great diversity in the texture and rhythm of life of its more than 130 ethnic groups of people. It is a gem for the traveler lucky enough to visit there. If you have never been to the Soviet Union, you have missed a land of surprises. But travel is not possible to all, and for those who cannot avail themselves of this opportunity, this book will serve as an interesting and revealing armchair guide to a penetrating look at the U.S.S.R.

For those who have not visited the Soviet Union this book will supply one of the best means of gaining at home a personal acquaintance with that country and its wealth of historic remains.

The conversational tone of the text—a feature lacking in most guide books—will render the experiences obtained definite and real to the reader.

—Lydle Brinkle

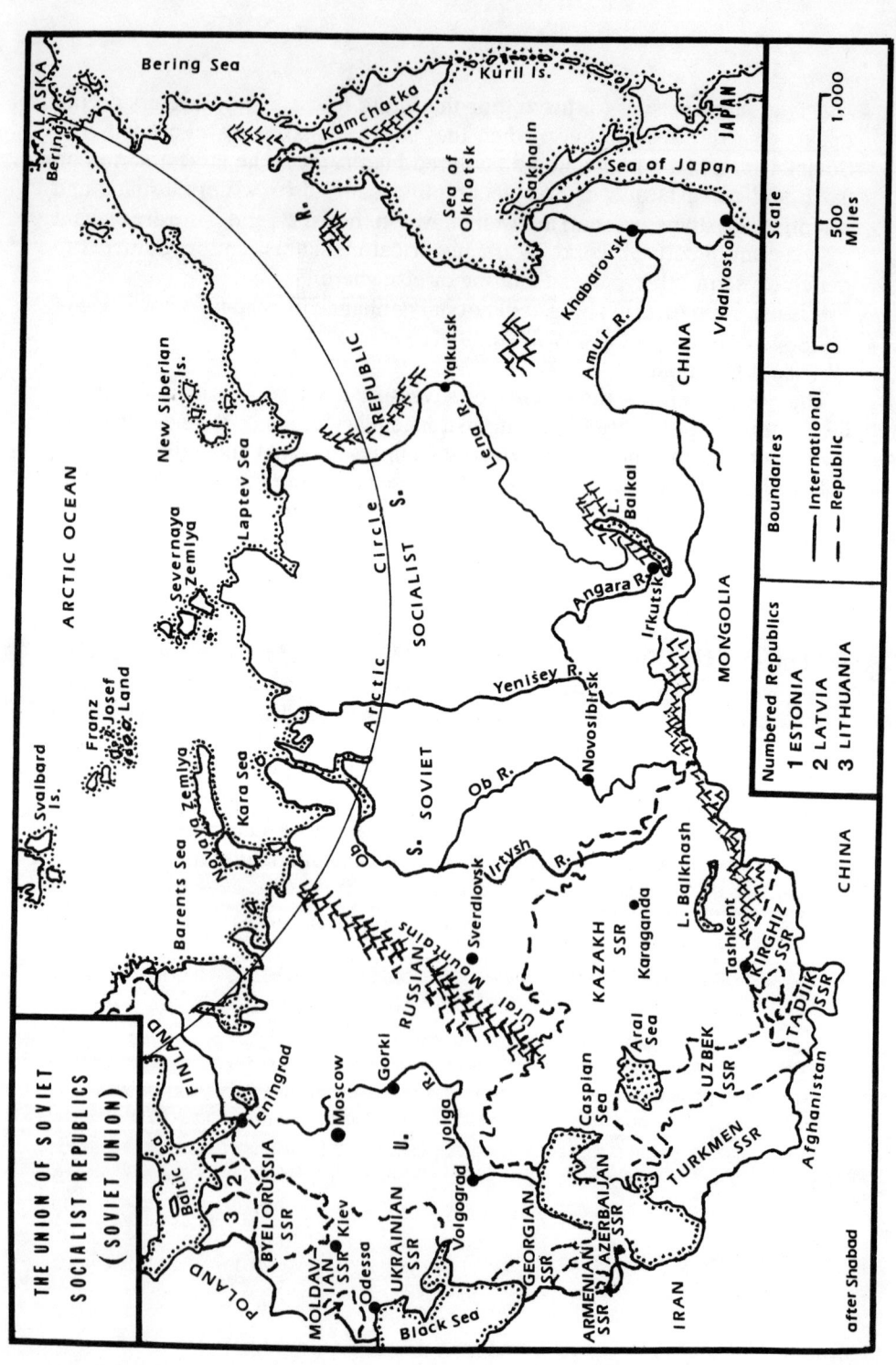

THE UNION OF SOVIET
SOCIALIST REPUBLICS
(SOVIET UNION)

Scale

1,000

500
Miles

0

Boundaries

—— International
--- Republic

Numbered Republics

1 ESTONIA
2 LATVIA
3 LITHUANIA

after Shabad

Bering Sea

ALASKA
Bering

Kuril Is.

Kamchatka

Sakhalin

Sea of Japan

JAPAN

Sea of
Okhotsk

Khabarovsk

Amur R.

Vladivostok

CHINA

R.

REPUBLIC

Yakutsk

Lena R.

L. Balkal

Angara R.

Irkutsk

MONGOLIA

SOCIALIST

Arctic Circle

S.

Yenisey R.

Novosibirsk

S. SOVIET

Ob R.

Irtysh R.

L. Balkhash

CHINA

Tashkent

KIRGHIZ
SSR

TADJIK
SSR

New Siberian
Is.

Laptev Sea

Severnaya
Zemlya

ARCTIC OCEAN

Franz
Josef
Land

Svalbard
Is.

Novaya Zemlya

Kara Sea

Barents Sea

Sverdlovsk

Ural Mountains

RUSSIAN

Ob

KAZAKH
SSR

Karaganda

UZBEK
SSR

Aral
Sea

Caspian
Sea

TURKMEN
SSR

Afghanistan

FINLAND

Baltic Sea

Leningrad

Gorki

Moscow

U.

Volga R.

Volgograd

IRAN

POLAND

3 2 1

BYELORUSSIA
SSR

MOLDAV-
IAN
SSR

Kiev

Odessa

UKRAINIAN
SSR

Black Sea

GEORGIAN
SSR

ARMENIAN
SSR

AZERBAIJAN
SSR

INTRODUCTION

Those who consider the human soul as a fixed
and concrete object will never understand the
mutability of the human character: they will
easily resort to false remedies which only
aggravate the evil.

—Herbart

The U.S.S.R. (Union of Soviet Socialist Republics), also known as the Soviet Union, is the largest country in the world in area. It covers 8.65 million square miles (compared to the United States area of 3.67 million square miles) and extends some 6,000 miles from the Baltic Sea on the west to the Bering Sea on the east. From north to south the U.S.S.R. extends more than 3,000 miles from frigid Arctic waters to the lofty Pamir Mountains along the China-Afghanistan frontiers. The Soviet Union is over two and one-half times the size of the United States. Colossal is an appropriate term for such a giant.

This multinational state, comprising between one-sixth and one-seventh of the world's land mass, includes within its borders more than 40 percent of the area of Europe and Asia. Over 75 percent of the Soviet Union lies in Asia.

Russia's neighbors, beginning with those on the west and extending southward and eastward, include Norway, Finland, Poland, Czechoslovakia, Hungary, Romania, Turkey, Iran, Afghanistan, Communist China, Mongolia, and North Korea. On the east, in the Bering Strait between the U.S.S.R. and Alaska, two tiny islands known as Little Diomede (U.S.) and Big Diomede (U.S.S.R.) lie only a few miles apart. The Soviet Union lies on two continents, covering the eastern half of Europe and northern third of Asia. The boundary between the two continental portions of the U.S.S.R. follows the crest of the Ural Mountains. The distance between Moscow and the Ural Mountains is over 1,000 miles.

A large portion of the U.S.S.R. is comprised of a huge plain that stretches from Poland and the Baltic Sea on the west to the Yenisey River in the east. From Finland on the northwest to the vicinity of the Black Sea this plain extends southward through the heart of European Russia. The Ural Mountains separate both this immense plain and the U.S.S.R. into two large plains regions, that of European Russia and the area of western Siberia.

About 10 percent of the land area of the Soviet Union is *tundra,* a frozen, treeless wasteland stretching across the northern part of Russia largely in the area north of the Arctic Circle (66½°N). Most of the tundra is a plains area covered by moss and underlain with permafrost, a permanently frozen subsoil. The growing season in the tundra is extremely short, averaging about two months in most places.

Nearly one-half of Russia's soil is underlain by permafrost. Over wide areas of Russia the permafrost is measured to depths of hundreds of feet in thickness. When frozen the permafrost provides a solid base for railways, roadbeds, and buildings, but when its surface thaws for several inches in the summer its strength is lost and structures built upon it tend to become displaced, buckled, or disclose settling in their foundations.

South of the tundra lies an immense, almost unbroken, stretch of forests extending from the Baltic Sea area on the west to the Pacific Ocean on the east. This forested region is known as the *taiga.* Almost one-third of the Soviet Union's land area is covered by forests and nearly one-third of the world's forests are found in the Soviet Union. About 90 percent of the U.S.S.R.'s timber reserves lie in the Russian S.S.R. The principal tree is the pine, which accounts for roughly one-half of all trees in Russian forests. Most of these forests stand east of the Urals on the Asiatic side of Russia, but extensive areas have been reforested in the Volga-Don region in recent years.

In northern Russia the *izba,* or Russian log house, is commonly seen in both the countryside and city alike. The izba is made of whole trees, one piled on top of the other and interlocked at the corners of the house. Izbas are traditional houses in the rural landscape. The floor of the izba is usually made from planks cut from trees. Also in northern Russia many village churches are built of logs and timber similar in design to that of the izbas.

Most of the Soviet Union's people live in the area of that country lying south of the taiga, stretching to the shores of the Black Sea and eastward to the vicinity of the Caspian Sea, then crossing the Urals north of that sea and stretching in an arc to Lake Baikal in Siberia. This zone of Russia is a composite of meadowlands, tilled farmland, forests, and *steppe,* which for the most part is a treeless plain relatively flat in topography.

The steppe is an illimitable feature of southern Russia. From Hungary and Central Europe it stretches into European Russia, thence to the Caspian Sea and southern Urals, and on across Asiatic Russia to Lake Baikal. To say that it has had an important influence on the development of Russian history is perhaps an understatement. This vast steppe-frontier of Russia has no counterpart, unless the Great Plains of North America can be considered its cousin. Through past milleniums, wave after wave of people have wandered and invaded across its surface. These tribes kept mainly to the southern portion of the steppe, especially around the Black Sea area. They seldom penetrated the forestlands to the north. Some of the early tribes are lost in antiquity and legend, others are but a mere remembrance in the passage of time, and still others have become so assimilated into the local inhabitants that their original identities and culture are obfuscated by the moving tides of history. These included the Goths, Huns, Avars, Ugres, Khayars, Pecheniegs, Polovtsky and the Tartars. The steppes have an overwhelming sense of awe about them. As one stands in their midst and peers into the distance there is a distinct impression of loneliness about the land; its void is pervasive, and traveling from one horizon to the next does little to alter the geography of its features. Time seems unimportant here. The passage of a century would probably matter little in the configuration of the landscape.

Towns and cities have risen and disappeared on the steppe. Others still stand but their names have changed over the course of centuries. It is perhaps a contradiction to describe the steppe as monotonous in one breath, and in the next say the nomenclature of its land often baffles even scholars. The many peoples who have occupied the steppe have each contributed their own terminology and names to the thousands of villages, towns, and other features scattered across its surface.

From the area of the Caspian Sea, running across the extreme southern part of Russia to the Aral Sea and Lake Balkhash, is a mostly desert region. Oases relieve the monotony of this desert in places. The desert region stretches across the Turkemen, Uzbek, Kazakh, Tadzhik, and Kirghiz republics of the Soviet Union.

The bulk of the Soviet Union lies north of 45° north latitude, with only some of its extreme southern portions dipping below the parallel. In crossing the United States the 45th parallel runs through central Maine; the extreme northern tip of New York State; northern Michigan; St. Paul-Minneapolis, Minnesota; then westward across northern South Dakota; central Idaho; and northern Oregon. Thus even the more southern portions of the U.S.S.R. lie largely in latitudes of the northern parts of the United States.

Distances in Russia are great. The longitudinal extent of the country from east to west laces it in eleven time zones. When the people in Moscow are arising in the morning, the inhabitants of Vladivostok in the east are preparing for bed.

There is hardly a time in a 24-hour period when the sun is not shining on some part of this colossal country. Moscow time is eight hours ahead of U.S.

TABLE 1
TEMPERATURES (Fahrenheit)

All temperatures shown are averages. Days of rain are averages per month.

CITY	JAN. HIGH	JAN. LOW	JAN. RAIN	FEB. HIGH	FEB. LOW	FEB. RAIN	MAR. HIGH	MAR. LOW	MAR. RAIN	APR. HIGH	APR. LOW	APR. RAIN	MAY HIGH	MAY LOW	MAY RAIN	JUNE HIGH	JUNE LOW	JUNE RAIN	JULY HIGH	JULY LOW	JULY RAIN	AUG. HIGH	AUG. LOW	AUG. RAIN	SEPT. HIGH	SEPT. LOW	SEPT. RAIN	OCT. HIGH	OCT. LOW	OCT. RAIN	NOV. HIGH	NOV. LOW	NOV. RAIN	DEC. HIGH	DEC. LOW	DEC. RAIN
Alma-Ata	24	14	5	27	17	5	35	24	6	56	46	5	66	56	4	74	64	4	79	69	2	77	67	3	67	57	3	54	44	4	35	25	4	30	20	4
Brest	49	39	11	50	38	8	53	40	9	58	44	10	63	48	10	68	53	11	71	56	12	72	57	12	69	54	13	61	49	11	55	44	10	50	41	11
Dushanbe	38	25	4	42	30	4	54	44	5	65	53	4	75	63	3	83	72	2	87	74	1	83	70	1	73	60	1	62	50	2	52	40	2	43	41	3
Erevan	29	15	7	34	18	5	50	30	7	66	42	9	76	50	11	87	57	2	95	63	1	92	64	3	83	55	3	69	45	4	50	34	6	38	26	7
Irkutsk	0	11	3	7	6	3	21	8	2	36	27	4	52	41	8	67	52	7	70	58	9	66	54	11	52	40	8	38	26	6	3	9	4	4	8	4
Khabarovsk	13	0	3	23	6	6	33	19	5	46	34	7	54	43	10	63	52	13	70	60	13	76	64	12	68	55	10	55	42	6	36	24	4	20	8	3
Kharkov	28	17	10	31	19	8	38	26	7	51	39	9	65	53	8	70	58	9	74	62	11	72	60	10	63	51	7	52	41	7	39	28	9	32	20	7
Kiev	27	16	10	30	18	8	37	25	6	50	38	9	64	52	8	69	57	9	73	61	10	71	59	10	62	50	7	51	40	7	39	27	9	32	20	7
Leningrad	23	12	8	24	12	8	33	18	6	45	31	7	58	42	6	66	51	9	71	57	10	66	53	13	57	45	10	45	37	10	34	27	10	26	18	10
Moscow	14	5	11	19	8	9	29	15	8	43	29	9	60	42	9	67	50	10	71	54	12	68	51	12	56	42	9	44	33	11	28	21	10	17	10	9
Odessa	36	17	7	38	19	4	45	32	5	56	40	6	69	54	6	77	60	7	81	66	6	80	66	5	72	53	4	61	42	5	50	31	5	42	21	6
Rostov	23	10	7	25	13	4	32	19	6	45	32	6	52	45	5	64	53	6	68	58	6	66	53	5	57	45	4	44	34	5	34	22	5	27	14	6
Sochi	44	34	7	45	35	8	48	36	6	56	44	5	68	56	5	76	62	3	81	69	1	80	68	1	73	61	5	64	54	6	57	44	8	48	36	8
Sukhumi	45	35	7	46	37	8	49	37	6	57	45	5	68	58	5	77	63	3	82	70	1	81	68	1	74	61	5	65	55	6	57	45	8	48	37	8
Tashkent	36	24	4	40	28	4	52	40	5	64	52	4	74	62	4	82	70	2	86	74	1	83	70	1	72	60	2	60	49	2	51	39	2	42	40	3
Tbilisi	32	16	7	35	18	5	53	33	7	67	43	9	78	51	9	88	58	8	96	64	3	93	65	3	84	55	1	69	45	4	51	35	6	38	26	7
Volgograd	20	9	7	23	11	4	30	18	6	43	31	6	51	45	5	62	50	6	66	55	6	64	52	5	55	43	4	43	33	5	32	20	5	25	13	6
Yalta	39	30	9	41	32	5	45	36	7	54	42	6	65	52	4	74	60	5	78	65	4	79	64	4	71	57	5	63	50	6	50	39	7	43	35	11

TABLE 2

Country	Population
Communist China	1,200 million
India	720 million
U.S.S.R.	285 million
U.S.	241 million

TABLE 3
THE SOVIET UNION

Union Republic	Capital	Republic Pop. (millions)	Area (sq. miles)
Russian Soviet Social Republic	Moscow	145.1	6,590,500
Ukrainian S.S.R.	Kiev	52.4	232,000
Uzbekistan S.S.R.	Tashkent	19.0	154,000
Kazakhstan S.S.R.	Alma-Ata	16.5	1,067,600
Byelorussia S.S.R.	Minsk	10.8	80,300
Azerbaijan S.S.R.	Baku	7.1	33,600
Georgian S.S.R.	Tbilsi	5.5	27,800
Moldavian S.S.R.	Kishinev	4.4	13,100
Tadzhikstan S.S.R.	Dushanbe	4.9	54,800
Kirghizia S.S.R.	Firunze	4.6	76,400
Lithuania S.S.R.	Vilnius	3.8	25,100
Armenia S.S.R.	Yerevan	3.6	11,600
Turkemenia S.S.R.	Ashkhabad	3.5	188,400
Latvia S.S.R.	Riga	2.8	24,700
Estonia S.S.R.	Tallinn	1.6	17,400

Eastern Standard Time.

Environmental influences strongly affect the lives of humans everywhere and play a significant role in historical events which ultimately shape the destinies of nations. To understand how the widely divergent areas and regions of the Soviet Union have an impact on and influence the mental attitudes of that nation requires a close look at Russia's physical characteristics. The broad monotonous plain of the U.S.S.R. stretching from Europe to northern Asia manifests a wide range of vegetation, climate, and soil types. Nearly one-third of Russia is too cold or too dry to support any productive agriculture. As Boyce notes in *Geographical Perspectives on Global Problems,* "agricultural problems are equally as much a reflection of the harsh continental conditions as the failure of Soviet collectivism."[1]

The continent of Europe is a very different land in the west than it is in the east. Western Europe is peninsular and maritime in character, whereas the eastern portion of the continent stretching into the vastness of Russia takes on a continental appearance and characteristics. European Russia is mostly warm and sunny in summer. Humidity is generally low, but rains are frequent in October and November. In Siberia, winters are usually long and snowy. East of the Caspian Sea rainfall is negligible, but in Western Georgia it may rain for weeks at a time. In winter, high pressure systems generate icy winds that blow across Russia's huge land mass.

The Soviet Union has every major type of climate on earth, except that of tropical. In the far north is found the land of the midnight sun, while in the far south of Russia palm trees grow. While the temperature drops to nearly 90° below zero in northern Siberia, roses are in bloom in Batumi in the Georgian Republic along the Black Sea. When wheat farmers in the south of Russia are gathering their grain, it is already snowing in the north. Moscow and central Russia are warm in the summertime, averaging about 62°F. in July (see Table 1). Winters in Moscow are cold, with January averaging 10°F. Winter is the dominant season in Russia. Winter clothes comprise a large part of one's wardrobe. Russia's climate is a major handicap to the U.S.S.R.'s ability to feed its people adequately. The harsh climate helped to defeat both Napoleon and Hitler.

Siberia, the coldest place in Russia, has more than 53,000 rivers and over one million lakes. Lake Baikal, in southern Siberia, is the world's deepest freshwater lake (5,315 feet in depth). The lake is more than 426 miles long and could hold all the water of the five American Great Lakes. The name Siberia is derived from two Tartar words "sib" (to sleep) and "ir" (land). Siberia makes up one-tenth of the earth's land area.

Twelve seas border on Soviet territory. Russia's Arctic seacoasts are frozen over in the winter, with the exception of the coastline around the port of Murmansk on the Kola Peninsula. In that vicinity the warmer waters of the

Gulf Stream/North Atlantic Drift mix with Arctic waters, enabling the port to remain ice-free in the winter. Aside from Murmansk, Russia's other seaports on the Arctic Ocean are relatively insignificant for shipping. Even in the summer, icebreakers are needed to help keep them open. Aircraft and satellite photos are also helpful in determining shipping lanes in the Arctic Ocean. Russia's Pacific coastline has milder weather by contrast to the Arctic coastline, but even it is icebound in the winter. Vladivostock, Russia's major seaport in the Pacific, is ice-free in summer, but its cold winter with nearly 100 days of snow cover freezes over its harbor in that season.

The Baltic Sea on the western side of Soviet territory is also icebound in winter for several months. The Baltic is a relatively small sea (163,000 square miles), resembling more a large lake than a sea. From their Baltic seaports, Soviet ships can reach the Atlantic Ocean only after passing narrow straits between Denmark, Sweden, and Norway, and then navigating the North Sea.

The Black Sea, on the southwest of the U.S.S.R., is the Soviet Union's warmest sea. It covers 175,000 square miles and remains unfrozen in winter with the exception of a few gulfs. Like the Baltic, the Black Sea is also similar to a large lake. It connects via the Turkish straits with the Aegean Sea, which opens into the Mediterranean. Odessa, the main seaport on the Black Sea, has ice in its harbor approximately one and a-half months during winter.

The U.S.S.R. abounds in rivers and waterways and has an enormous hydroelectric potential, which is claimed by the Russians as the largest in the world. The largest inland body of water in the world, the Caspian Sea, is located in the southern portion of the U.S.S.R. The Volga, Europe's longest river (2,300 miles in length), has its source in the Valdai Hills northwest of Moscow, then flows eastward north of that city before it finally turns southward where it flows through the southeast part of European Russia until it reaches the Caspian Sea. The Moscow Canal connects Moscow with the Volga on the north of the city. The significance of the Volga River system for transportation purposes exceeds that of the combined importance of all other Soviet rivers. The U.S.S.R.'s major rivers in flow and length are the Siberian rivers Yenisey, Lena, Ob-Irtysh, and Angara. From the standpoint of transportation, these great rivers are of little value to the Russians since they all flow into the Arctic Ocean to the north of Russia. Their value is further diminished for shipping because the main transport routes from the Urals to the Pacific run east-west rather than north-south as do these great rivers.

Many rivers flow across and drain Soviet soil; they number over 100,000. The continent of Asia has the largest number of the world's longest-flowing rivers.

The Ob-Irtysh river system in Siberia is Asia's and the U.S.S.R.'s longest river, measuring approximately 3,461 miles in length. Another huge Siberian river system, the Yenisei-Angara, is only a bit shorter at 3,100 miles. Most of the water in Siberia's rivers comes mainly from melted snow, rather than rainfall. The same is true of Russia's European rivers, the Volga, Dnieper, and Don. The rivers of the Soviet Union supply more than one-third of the world's hydroelectric supply.

In spite of Russia's vast river network only a handful of rivers play a prominent role in its economy, trade, and transportation picture. The Volga and its tributaries alone handle nearly two-thirds of all freight traffic on the rivers of the Soviet Union.

More and more freight and passenger traffic in the Soviet Union is being moved by railroads and airlines. Russia has more than 110,000 miles of railway lines, enough to stretch around the earth nearly four and one-half times. Its lines make up more than 11 percent of the world's total track mileage. Soviet railways carry more than ten million passengers daily. The world's longest railway route, the Trans-Siberian, stretches 6,700 miles from European Russia to the Pacific Ocean. Trains carry about two-thirds of all passengers traveling intercity in the Soviet Union.

Aeroflot is the world's largest airline. It flies to about 90 countries, and some 3,600 towns and cities in the Soviet Union. Aeroflot was founded in 1923 and carries more passengers than any other airline in the world.

Another form of transportation in the Soviet Union is the horse. The U.S.S.R. has millions of horses. In the 1920s there were 35 million horses in Russia, or approximately one-third of the world's total. Today the numbers are far fewer, but proportionately Russia still retains a large share of the world's total horse population. The countryside is full of horses. One can see them pulling wagons along roads, working in the fields, or roaming the meadows and pasturelands.

Transportation and population complement one another. The Soviet Union houses a large population that is quite unevenly distributed. Most of the Soviet Union's large cities and the majority of its population are found in European Russia, the area west of the Ural Mountains. About three-fourths of all people in the Soviet Union live in the European part of that country.

If measured by population, the U.S.S.R. is the world's third most populated country (see Table 2 below):

Soviet population numbered 241 million in January 1970 and reached 262 million in 1979. Yet, the population growth rate was slower in the 1960s and 1970s than in the 1950s. In 1970 there were only 87 males per 100 females in the Soviet population. Cities at that time contained about 55 percent of the people. In 1986, males comprised 46 percent of Soviet population, which is two-thirds urban.

The present population of the Soviet Union numbers about 285 million people living in 15 republics (see Table 3). The Russian S.S.R. accounts for 145.1 million of the Soviet people, distributed over six and one-half million square miles. Thus, this republic has about 52 percent of the Soviet population and approximately 75 percent of the U.S.S.R.'s total area. The Russian republic also produces about 66 percent of Soviet industrial output and 50 percent of the Soviet Union's agricultural produce. Both Moscow and Leningrad, the two largest cities in the U.S.S.R., are located in the Russian republic.

The birthrate has been declining in most areas of the Soviet Union. Further complicating the labor and economic situation is the high death rate for men. The birthrate has been reduced by more than one-half since World War II. A related problem in the demographic picture is that the birthrate decline is not equal in all Soviet republics. The two most highly industrialized republics, Russia and the Ukraine, have the lowest birthrates, which is affecting manpower needs and creating labor shortages.

Industry and agriculture are competitors in the labor market. There is a general shortage of manpower in most sectors of agriculture due to the fact that industry drains off large numbers of rural population to sustain its operation. However, some rural areas actually have a surplus of labor, but many of these people refuse to leave their traditional homesites and settings, preferring them instead of uprooting and moving to employment in a city. Yet, in other rural areas, notably the Georgian S.S.R., many thousands of rural residents seasonally migrate to other republics to take jobs in industry and construction, thus creating labor shortages at critical times in farm operations and harvesting. Harvesting may be delayed and some crops lost as a result.

Women continue to outnumber men in both urban and rural areas of the country. The female population exceeds that of the male by about 12 percent. Women account for over 70 percent of all doctors, more than 50 percent of all students, over 35 percent of all lawyers, and 30 percent of all engineers in the U.S.S.R.

The Soviet Union contains some 130 different nationalities and ethnic groups. More than 40 of these have their own written language. The largest language family of people in the Soviet Union is the Slavs, who comprise the Russian, Ukrainian, and Byelorussian peoples. Slavic speaking people make up about three-fourths of the Soviet population. The ethnic Russians, found mainly in the Russian Republic, comprise about 51 percent of the U.S.S.R.'s people.

The homeland of the Slavs was originally in the area of the northern slopes of the Carpathian Mountains. Later they branched out in different directions, heading south, east, and west. The eastern branch became the Russian Slavs, who reached the Dnieper River around the seventh century. The Eastern Slavs comprised a number of tribes, some of which settled on the eastern bank of the Dnieper, while others took up residence on the left bank. The

Slavs quickly spread over the low, flat plains of Russia. The rivers flowing across these plains enabled the Slavic tribes to maintain contact, trade, and communication with one another. The social intercourse spurred between these tribes proved to be a strongly unifying factor, both religiously and politically; it united them into one nation under one church.

The Soviet Union considers itself a modern country. From a scientific standpoint it is one of the more advanced nations on the earth. Russia was the first Communist government on a large scale. The country is a vast human experiment in an attempt to prove the theories of Marxism-Leninism.

Large areas of the geographical landscape of Russia have been reshaped by science and technology. Rivers have been diverted from their old courses to bring water to dry areas; forests have been cleared for new towns and settlements; geological explorations have opened up new mining centers; Siberian swamps have been drained for habitation; and the climates of some areas reportedly have been altered.

Tourist facilities and their development in the Soviet Union have been greatly expanded in the last two decades. Many new hotels have been built, and the Soviets have gradually opened up more of their cities and other areas to tourists that were formerly closed to them.

More than two million foreigners visited the Soviet Union in 1970, with more than 66,000 of these coming from the United States. During 1985 more than five and one-half million foreigners visited the U.S.S.R., including more than 100,000 Americans.

GENERAL INFORMATION

Passport

A U.S. passport valid one month past the date of your departure from the Soviet Union is required. Two photos (2½" × 2½") and proof of citizenship are required to apply for a passport.

Visa

Required for visiting the Soviet Union. The cost for a visa is $35, which is required prior to departure. Your travel agency or tour operator will assist you in applying for a visa.

Tourist visas for travel to the Soviet Union should be obtained via U.S. or Canadian travel agencies arranging travel to the Soviet Union.

In order to obtain a tourist visa, the following documents must be submitted to the Soviet Consular Office no less than 14 days prior to arrival in the U.S.S.R.:

—a valid passport for foreign citizens permanently residing in the U.S.A. or Canada or xerox copies of pages 2 and 3 of American passports. (Stateless persons residing in the U.S.A. have to present a Reentry Permit to the U.S.A.)

—four black and white $1\frac{3}{4}'' \times 1\frac{1}{2}''$ photographs of face made on matte or dull paper with white background. Pictures on glossy paper or vending machine photos are not accepted. All four photos must be identical and made during the last 12 months.

—one copy of visa application duly filled out, typed, and signed; date of departure from the U.S.A. or Canada must be indicated on application form as well as complete travel itinerary (cities) in the U.S.S.R.

—Intourist reference number (confirmation number).

—travel agency voucher number.

All visa documents must be accompanied by a letter from a travel agency arranging travel to the U.S.S.R. If the traveler has a family passport, the application forms and photographs must be submitted for each family member traveling to the U.S.S.R. In peak travel season it is recommended that one apply for visas as far in advance of the departure date as possible in order to avoid delay in issuing. However, applications should not be submitted any earlier than 3 months prior to the date of entry into the Soviet Union. In case of even earlier departure from the U.S.A. or Canada to any other destination abroad, the date of departure should be indicated in the top right-hand corner of the visa application form. Tourist visas are valid for the duration of the tour booked, plus the time required for travel from the Soviet border to the first point of service on tour, and from the last point on tour to the border. Tourist visas must include all the cities on the confirmed itinerary indicating the dates of stay there. Foreign tourists can visit only those cities in the U.S.S.R. that are included in the tour. Tourists can enter and leave the country through any border points of the U.S.S.R. open for passenger traffic, unless otherwise indicated in the visa. A Soviet tourist visa is granted free of charge in the form of an enclosure without stamping the passport.

Tourists who come to the U.S.S.R. and wish to extend their tour or their stay in some town on the tour can request the purchase of an additional tour and visa extension at the Intourist Service Bureau of the hotel where they are staying.

Customs

The Soviet customs office asks travelers coming into the country to answer in writing a few simple questions contained on the Customs Declaration form.

Travelers are allowed to take into the country duty free and without special license any articles intended for personal use. There is no limit to fur pieces, precious metals and stones, pearls and articles made thereof, that may be brought into the U.S.S.R. by travelers. However, such items should be declared and registered at the point of entry into the country by the traveler and upon departure from the Soviet Union.

HELPFUL HINTS ON ARRIVAL AND DEPARTURE PROCEDURES

For Arriving Passengers

On arrival in the Soviet Union all tourists must pass through Passport and Visa Control. After finishing with this control, it will be necessary to fill out a Customs Declaration. Blank forms will be found at a series of properly marked desks, just outside the Passport/Visa Controls area.

At the Customs desk submit your Customs Declaration to the person in charge. In turn you will receive a Customs Certificate. Please remember that you must show this certificate each and every time you exchange money. Upon presentation of this form when leaving the country, you can then exchange any unspent rubles for foreign currency.

Keep this Customs Certificate in a safe spot. If lost, it will not be replaced, thus preventing you from exchanging currency when and if needed.

When you have finished with customs procedures, proceed to the Intourist Desk, where you will be asked to show your vouchers and also learn at which hotel you will be staying (if you do not already know it). The person on duty (at the Intourist Desk) will also assign you a car for the transfer from the airport to your hotel.

If you arrive at the airport late at night, it is recommended quite strongly that you exchange money at the airport exchange bureau. The bureau at the hotel where you will be staying will probably be closed (exception: the exchange bureau at the Hotel Intourist, where 'round the clock service is available).

For Departing Passengers

At least five hours before departure (preferably on the day preceding departure), order your transfer car from the hotel to the airport at the Intourist Desk.

On arrival at the airport, check in immediately at the Flight Departure Desk. From here, go to the currency exchange desk, where you will be able to exchange all unused rubles for foreign currency. Please remember that rubles can be exchanged only upon presentation of the Customs Certificate and all of the money exchange receipts accumulated during your stay in the Soviet Union.

You are next requested to go to the Customs area, where your baggage may be inspected. The officer on duty will take the Customs Certificate from you here. After you have finished with customs formalities, you must pass through Passport and Visa Control. These are all the formalities you have to go through to leave the country. Next, proceed to the departure lounge and wait there until your flight is announced over the loudspeaker.

Currency

There is no limit on the amount of foreign currency that can be brought into the Soviet Union, however the amount and denominations must be declared with the Soviet Customs at the time of entry. The Customs Declaration certificate on which this information is listed must be retained and presented on departure from the U.S.S.R. At that time a new declaration is filled out and the two are customarily compared by customs officials.

Cash and traveler's checks which the traveler wants to bring into the Soviet Union must be registered at Customs upon arrival. A special Customs Certificate, on which the amount of currency brought into the country is noted, will be issued to the traveler at Customs.

While in the country, travelers can exchange their own currency for rubles at the Exchange Bureaus of the State Bank of the U.S.S.R., which are conveniently located at all border crossings, in hotels, at international airports and seaports.

When converting foreign currency into rubles, travelers must show the Customs Certificate to the Exchange Bureau representative. In turn, they are given State Bank Certificate #F377 *(spravka),* against which they can exchange unused rubles for foreign currency at departure. Travelers cannot exchange unused rubles into foreign currency without first submitting State Bank Certificate #F377.

It is not permitted to take rubles into or out of the country. The State Bank of the U.S.S.R. and its branch offices honor and accept traveler's checks issued by American Express, Bank of America, Barclay's Bank, Citibank, Thomas Cook & Son, Perera Express, and Republic National Bank of Dallas.

While in the Soviet Union, travelers may also charge all tourist services on the following credit cards: American Express, Carte Blanche, Diners Club, Eurocard, VISA (Bank Americard), and Access. Should the traveler need additional funds during his trip in the Soviet Union, he can arrange for a cable transfer from his bank to Vneshtorgbank, Moscow, U.S.S.R., utilizing the services of a Vneshtorgbank correspondent abroad.

There is a currency exchange bureau of the State Bank of the U.S.S.R. at all Intourist hotels.

It is against the law to engage in any foreign currency transactions (i.e., sale, exchange, etc.) with anyone except the State Bank of the U.S.S.R.

Vaccination Requirements

None.

Hotels—Accommodations

All accommodations are at the discretion of Intourist.

SOME REGULATIONS AND USEFUL HINTS FOR FOREIGN TOURISTS MOTORING THROUGH THE SOVIET UNION

1. Tourists may only travel along Intourist routes, in accordance with the tour purchased. On entering the Soviet Union, they must obtain an Intourist road map.
2. While traveling in the Soviet Union, the tourist must carry the following documents with him at all times:
   A passport with the Soviet visa; a driver's license complying with the provisions of the 1968 International Road Transport Convention or a driver's license with a special Russian insert, obtained at the entry border point into the Soviet Union, or an international driver's license; an international certificate of car registration, issued by the country of departure; voucher or Intourist service coupons, received in exchange for it; a Motoring Tourist Memo showing the tourist's name, citizenship, car plates, itinerary, stopover points and dates (such a memo is issued to the tourist upon entering the Soviet Union); a declaration stating that the tourist will take the car out of the Soviet

Union on his departure, certified by Customs upon entering the country.

3. The Motoring Tourist Memo is not issued to foreign tourists traveling through the Soviet Union in groups by motorcoach. Such groups will follow their prescribed itinerary, accompanied by an Intourist guide, and have a prearranged program for their stay in towns along the itinerary, indicating dates of arrival and departure from such towns (out-of-town campsites, motels).

4. The car must display prominently its license plates (from the country of origin), as well as distinguishing marks from the country of departure, in compliance with the traffic regulations and the 1968 International Road Transport Convention.

5. Any change in the selected motor route may be made by the tourist only after confirmation at the nearest Intourist office along his route.

6. For offenses against public order, traffic violations or noncompliance with the rules of motoring through the Soviet Union, tourists will be held responsible under the laws of the Soviet Union.

7. Motoring tourists must keep their cars technically fit and must refrain from using them in the event defects develop that constitute a danger to traffic safety.

8. The speed limit in cities, towns, and other populated areas is 60 km. per hour (37 miles).

9. Horn-blowing is permitted only on highways in nonpopulated areas or, out of necessity, to avoid an accident or collision.

10. The motorist must always give the right-of-way to motor vehicles using special acoustic or light signals, such as ambulances, fire engines, and police cars.

11. Driving a vehicle under the influence of alcohol or drugs is strictly prohibited.

12. Foreign tourists may travel along Intourist routes/itineraries either in their own car or in cars rented from Intourist (passenger cars may be rented with or without chauffeur, motor coaches with chauffeur only).

13. Tourists are advised to insure their cars with "Ingosstrakh" against breakage and damage, as well as Third Party Liabilities, while in the Soviet Union. "Ingosstrakh" also issues accident insurance. The company pays out insurance premiums and meets possible claims in the currency in which the insurance was effected. Tourists can obtain insurance at the border entry point in the Soviet Union as well as in Moscow. Cars rented from Intourist are insured against breakage (breakdowns), with motoring tourists protected against Third Party Liability arising from the use of the car while in the Soviet Union (insurance rates are included in the cost of car rental).

14. Extra gasoline and car service may be purchased through Intourist.

Important: All tourists traveling in their own cars or a rented car through the Soviet Union are strongly advised:
1. to follow their Intourist itinerary.
2. to pay a road tax of 10 rubles for each car and 5 rubles for each trailer to a representative of "Sovtransavto" upon entering the Soviet Union.
3. to obtain (a) a Motoring Tourist Memo and (b) road maps covering their itineraries upon entering the Soviet Union.

Cameras

Soviet Customs permit you to bring into the U.S.S.R. one still and one movie camera. Bring your own film. American film may be difficult to find inside the U.S.S.R. and is usually more expensive there. Also, Soviet film usually cannot be processed in the United States and it frequently suffers early fading. Photographing from airplanes is forbidden over Soviet air space, as is the filming of airports, military installations, and many bridges and transportation facilities. If in doubt, ask your guide.

Photography and Films

Throughout the Soviet Union tourists will find many sites which they might like to photograph. There are no restrictions placed on travelers in this regard, except the standard ones imposed by any country concerning military installations, etc. As anywhere in the world, there are always certain people who do not like to be photographed without their consent.

Black-and-white as well as color films are made available in the Soviet Union. However, it is recommended to have Soviet-made color film developed and processed there. Such film can be processed by the Agfa developing process but it is not suitable for Kodacolor or Kodachrome processes.

Shopping

Items frequently purchased by tourists include caviar, vodka, balalaikas, fur hats, hockey sticks, wooden dolls, jewelry, "palekh" boxes, stamps, toys, abacuses, etc. "Beryoyka" shops that handle these items are usually found in hotels, airports, sea terminals, and other locations.

Mail

Mail from the Soviet Union to the U.S. or vice versa usually takes about twelve days. Hotels customarily have a postal service at which stamps are sold, as well as a mail chute for departing letters and cards. Hotels usually provide services for registered mail, cables, and long distance calls. Poste Restante (General Delivery) facilities are available for travelers staying in Moscow and Leningrad.

Moscow: Poste Restante, K-600, "Intourist" Hotel, 3/5 Gorky Street, Moscow, U.S.S.R.

Leningrad: Poste Restante, C-400, "Otiabrskaya" Hotel, Leningrad, U.S.S.R.

Mail to tourists visiting other cities should be addressed as follows: Traveler's name, c/o Intourist, the city in the U.S.S.R.

There are cable and telephone communication facilities between the Soviet Union, the United States, and Canada. The rate for postcards to the United States or Canada is 4 kopecks; for letters, 6 kopecks, when sent via regular mail. For airmail postcards the rate is 14 kopecks; for letters by air, 16 kopecks.

Electrical Current

The electrical current in the Soviet Union is 110-220 volts, 50 cycles A.C. American appliances such as electric razors, hair dryers, and electric curlers require a transformer to use. European plug adaptors are also necessary.

Medical Regulations and Service

Medical service in the Soviet Union is available in any city or town throughout the country. First aid, if hospitalization is not required, is provided to tourists free of charge.

In case hospitalization is required for first aid, the expenses for stay in the hospital should be paid for by the tourist at the rate of 20.00 Rbs. per person per day. A tourist can be hospitalized only with the approval of the Soviet Medical Institution(s), except in emergency cases.

Medical Treatment

Medical treatment is available for tourists at the following health resorts:

—in the Northern Caucasus: Essentuki, Kislovodsk, Pyatigorsk, Zheleznovodsk.
—in the Southern Caucasus: Tskhaltubo
—on the Black Sea Coast: Sochi
—on the Baltic Sea Gulf: Repino

The Black Sea area of the Soviet Union is the major center of the health resort industry in the U.S.S.R. Located along the Black Sea and in its vicinity are the important health resort centers of Odessa, Yalta, Sochi, Kabardinka, Pyatigorsk, Essentuki, Kislovodsk, Zheleznovodsk, Borzhomi, Bakuriani, and Tskhaltubo. The Black Sea coast of the U.S.S.R. is an almost unbroken chain of resorts. It is the warmest sea bordering the Soviet Union. The Black Sea has a variety of climates, including Mediterranean and Humid Subtropical, and waters with medicinal qualities, all of which are important factors favoring the bathing and resort and health-treatment institutions. Preventive medicine establishments, known as *sanatoria,* are an important facet of the resort and health enterprises in the Black Sea area.

The 285 million people of the U.S.S.R. have full comprehensive health service, with the exception of medicines and drugs, for which the patient must pay on his own. During Tsarist times most employed urbanites enjoyed compulsory social insurance, but the rural areas of Russia derived few benefits from the medical services and were generally inaccessible to such services.

Private practice does exist in the Soviet Union, however the practice has to be licensed and proper equipment is required for consulting rooms. In reality, the state discourages private practice through penal taxation. During the 1960s, the U.S.S.R. permitted the establishment of fee-paying outpatient facilities. Doctors, dentists, and nurses working in government owned and operated hospitals are paid civil servants. Abortions are free of charge, as is pre- and postnatal care, and treatment for infertility. Sanatoria, clinics, and hospitals are also owned and maintained by the trade unions and state and collective farms.

The number of sanatoria and holiday homes grows each year in the U.S.S.R. Everyone in the country has the right to an annual vacation. On the average, a voucher to a sanatorium for 24 days costs 121 rubles. Only one-fifth of them are sold at full price, another 20 percent are issued free, and the remainder are discounted at 30 percent of the actual cost. The remaining 70 percent of the cost is covered by the trade unions' social insurance funds. Every tenth voucher to a sanatorium or holiday home is issued free of charge.

Vouchers for two to four family members are sold at a reduced rate. For example, a 12-day rest for a whole family costs about 40–50 rubles. A voucher to a plant's preventive medical treatment spa for 12 days costs 7 rubles, while one to a holiday home for 16 days is 22 rubles. The majority of resorts are run by trade unions, while some of them come under the Ministry of Health, various industrial enterprises, or agricultural cooperatives. Vouchers are distributed by trade union committees as well as state bodies of public health and social security.

The Lviv Railroader Holiday Home in Sudak in the southeastern part of the Crimea annually accommodates 6,000 residents of the Lviv region. In addition to living quarters, its vacationers are customarily provided with food service, showers, cinemas, laundry service, children's playgrounds, and sports fields.

Over 2,300 holiday sanatoria, capable of accommodating nearly 600,000 persons were located at resorts in the Soviet Union in 1982. Large industrial enterprises also had provisions for handling an additional 235,000 people in their 2,800 overnight sanatoria where minor disorders can be treated. Additionally, the trade unions operated more than 1,200 hotels, capable of handling more than 375,000 of their members. In 1982 nearly 43,500,000 Soviets used the facilities of rest homes and sanatoria.

Types of Medical Treatment

Essentuki: Treatment of the digestive system, metabolism, urological diseases.

Kislovodsk: Treatment of the cardiovascular and nervous systems, lung and windpipe diseases of a nontubercular origin, endocrine gland disorders, metabolism.

Pyatigorsk: Treatments of muscle, bone and joint diseases; digestive, nervous and cardiovascular systems; women's (gynecological) disorders; skin afflictions; metabolism.

Repino: Treatments of the cardiovascular system; blood circulation; lung and windpipe disorders of nontubercular origin; muscle, bone and joint diseases.

Sochi: Treatment of muscle, bone and joint diseases; nervous and cardiovascular systems; women's (gynecological) disorders; cardiovascular system; skin afflictions.

Tskhaltubo: Treatment of muscle, bone and joint diseases; women's (gynecological) disorders; cardiovascular system skin afflictions.

Zheleznovodsk: Treatment of urological diseases, digestive system, metabolism.

The duration of treatment at health resorts is 24 days (in Tskhaltubo, two weeks). Tourists coming to the Soviet Union specifically for medical treatment must carry an up-to-date medical history from their physician with them. Medical histories may also be obtained in the Soviet Union at an authorized clinic, for an additional fee of 50 rubles per person. Services include:

—accommodation in a sanatorium or a hotel

—full board

—porterage of two pieces of hand luggage in a sanatorium or hotel upon arrival and departure

—transfers for therapy or other treatments

—services of interpreter during doctor's examinations and treatments

Notes: (1) medical treatment is not available for children. (2) For tourists coming to the Soviet Union by plane, train or sea, transfers upon arrival and departure are to be included in the tour cost for additional charge. See section on independent travel. (3) For the tourists staying and undertaking treatment in a sanatorium, refunds are not made in case of contradiction to the treatment and for unused days of treatment.

Insurance

All necessary trip insurance in connection with travel to the Soviet Union may be arranged through American International Group (AIG) with corporate offices at 70 Pine Street, New York, New York 10270, (212) 770-5004. AIG is the Intourist approved insurer for North Americans traveling to the Soviet Union and maintains full claim facilities in the U.S.S.R. through an arrangement with Ingosstrakh (The Insurance Company of the U.S.S.R.).

Automobiles may be insured through AIG in the United States or Canada prior to departure or at the point of entry into the U.S.S.R. Liability and physical damage insurance for motorists is advisable.

Some travel agencies in the U.S.A. arranging travel to the U.S.S.R., in cooperation with AIG, are selling an all-inclusive travel insurance plan which includes complete coverage of trip cancellation, baggage loss, accident (including repatriation), airline bankruptcy and cancellation for political reasons. For details, please refer to AIG.

Entertainment

Tickets for the ballet, opera, circus, or concert performances for tourists traveling in a group are reserved ahead of time with the travel agent.

Individual tourists who desire such tickets over and above the group allotment may obtain them through the Intourist Service Desk at the hotel where they are staying.

The regular theater and concert season in the Soviet Union runs from September through May.

Evening performances generally start at 7 or 7:30 p.m.
Dress is optional.

Holidays

New Year's Day	January 1
International Womens' Day	March 8
International Labor Day	May 1–2
Victory Day	May 9
Constitution Day	October 7
Anniversary of the Great October Socialist Revolution	November 7–8

Hunting, Fishing, and Photographic Safaris

Intourist provides arrangements for hunting, fishing, and photographic safaris in the U.S.S.R. Hunting is available for the following species: European deer, Manchurian deer, stag, Caucasian brown bear, elk, European roe, Siberian roe, Daghestan fur (mountain goat), chamois, boar, game and water birds.

Fishing is available for: zander, bream, gudgeon, carp, pike, perch, trout, rudd, roach, chekhon, bullhead. For all details on hunting, fishing and photographic safaris (location of hunting and fishing preserves; hunting and fishing seasons; conditions of services) please, contact your travel agent or Intourist.

Hunters should present all sporting rifles for customs inspection and declare the rifles' serial numbers on the Customs Declaration form. Sporting rifles brought into the Soviet Union must be taken back when the hunter leaves the country.

Skiing

Cross-country skiing is available in Moscow, Leningrad, Kalinin, Irkutsk, and Minsk from January 5 till March 10. Services rendered by Intourist are:
—hotel accommodation
—ski rental
—toboggan rental
—sled rental
—skate rental
—sauna

—ice fishing
   Down-hill skiing is available in Armenia (accommodation at Sevan motel, 30 km. from down-hill sports complex Tsakhkadzor) from December through March.
Services rendered by Intourist are:
—motel accommodation
—ski boots and rental
—motorcoach transfer to/from down-hill area
—ski lifts
—lessons by ski instructor

ART FESTIVALS

"Moscow Stars," Moscow, May 5–13
"White Nights," Leningrad, June 21–29
"Russian Winter," Moscow, December 25–January 5
                    Leningrad
                    Novgorod
                    Irkutsk
                    Vladimir/Suzdal
"Kiev Spring," Kiev, May 18–30
"Farewell to Moscow," February 19–March 5
Russian Winter," Leningrad,

USEFUL ADDRESSES

INTOURIST
Main Office: 16 Marx Avenue, Moscow 103009, U.S.S.R.
Telephone: 203-6962
Cable: Intourist, Moscow
Telex: 871 411211-A, 411211-B, 411211-C

INTOURIST
630 Fifth Avenue, New York, New York 10111
Telephone: (212) 757-3884

STATE BANK OF THE U.S.S.R.
12 Neglinnaya Street, Moscow, U.S.S.R.
4 Brodski Street, Leningrad, U.S.S.R.

VNESHTORGBANK
8 Serpukhovsky Val, Moscow, U.S.S.R.

INGOSSTRAKH (Foreign Insurance)
Pyatnitskaya Street 12, Moscow, U.S.S.R.

HOUSE OF FRIENDSHIP WITH PEOPLES OF FOREIGN COUNTRIES
14 Kalinin Prospect, Moscow, U.S.S.R.

SPUTNIK (Youth Travel Organization)
15 Vorobjevskoje Shosse, Moscow, U.S.S.R.

AEROFLOT (Soviet Airlines)
4 Fruzenskaya Nab., Moscow, U.S.S.R.

MORAGENTSTVO (Soviet Steamship Lines)
11/1 Marx Avenue, Moscow, U.S.S.R.

MAIN CUSTOMS HOUSE
1-a Komsomolskaya Square, Moscow, U.S.S.R.

AEROFLOT (Soviet Airlines)
37 Leningradsky Prospect, Moscow, U.S.S.R.

ACADEMY OF SCIENCES
14 Leninsky Prospect, Moscow, U.S.S.R.

ACADEMY OF MEDICAL SCIENCES
14 Solyanka Street, Moscow, U.S.S.R.

SPUTNIK (Youth Travel Organization)
4 Lebyazhi per., Moscow, U.S.S.R.

Items to Bring With You

The tourist should bring along his/her own shampoo, toothpaste, detergent to do laundry with, bath soap, aspirin and medications, hygiene supplies, Kleenex, washcloth, and extra batteries for cameras and radios.

TABLE 4
FLIGHT TIME BETWEEN SOCIET CITIES
Approximate Duration in Hours

Moscow–Alma-Ata	4¼	Moscow–Baku	3
Moscow–Bratsk	6¾	Moscow–Dagomys/Sochi	3
Moscow–Donetsk	1½	Moscow–Dushanbe	4½
Leningrad–Dagomys/Sochi	3	Leningrad–Erevan	3½
Leningrad–Kiev	2	Leningrad–Lvov	2½
Leningrad–Minsk	1½	Leningrad–Odessa	2½
Leningrad–Tallinn	1	Leningrad–Tashkent	4¾
Leningrad–Tbilisi	3¼	Leningrad–Volgograd	3
Alma-Ata–Dushanbe	2	Alma-Ata–Tashkent	1½
Baku–Erevan	1¼	Baku–Rostov-on-Don	2
Baku–Tbilisi	1½	Bratsk–Irkutsk	1¾
Bukhara–Samarkand	1	Bukhara–Tashkent	1
Moscow–Erevan	2¾	Moscow–Irkutsk	7
Moscow–Kazan	1¼	Moscow–Khabarovsk	7½
Moscow–Kiev	1½	Moscow–Leningrad	1
Moscow–Lvov	2¼	Moscow–Minsk	1½
Moscow–Odessa	2	Moscow–Rostov-on-Don	1¾
Moscow–Samarkand	3¾	Moscow–Tashkent	3¾
Moscow–Tbilisi	2½	Moscow–Vilnius	1½
Moscow–Volgograd	1½	Moscow–Yalta	2¼
Moscow–Zaporozhye	1½		
Leningrad–Alma-Alta	5	Leningrad–Baku	3¾
Bukhara–Urgench	1¼	Dagomys/Sochi–Kiev	1¾
Dagomys/Sochi–Rostov-on-Don	1¼	Donetsk–Kiev	1¼
Dushanbe–Samarkand	1¼	Dushanbe–Tashkent	¾
Irkutsk–Khabarovsk	3	Kherson–Kiev	1
Kiev–Kishinev	1½	Kiev–Minsk	1½
Kiev–Odessa	1	Kiev–Volgograd	2
Kiev–Yalta	2	Kishinev–Lvov	1¾
Minsk–Rostov-on-Don	2	Riga–Tallinn	1
Riga–Vilnius	1¼	Samarkand–Tashkent	¾
Shakhrisabz–Tashkent	1¼	Tashkent–Urgench	1½

Chapter I.
MOSCOW
Under the Kremlin's Stars

Don't forget these prophetic words,
My brothers, my friends:
Only great Moscow
Holds us in its embrace.
                    —Mikhail Popovich

Members of a tour group commonly meet at J.F.K. or some other international airport for their flight to Moscow, often departing late in the afternoon between four and six. For the most part, tour members are strangers to each other though they are participating in the same tour. However, friendships and feelings as a group soon remove the role of strangers from their midst.

A typical flight might leave at 6:20 p.m. New York time destined for Copenhagen, Denmark, or Frankfurt, Germany, where one would switch to another jet and proceed to Moscow. To quote an old Russian proverb: "Pushed off from one shore, and not yet landed on the other."

By 6:58 a.m. European time, after a six-hour flight across the Atlantic

Ocean, you may land in Copenhagen, switch planes and be off for Moscow at 7:45 a.m. En route from Copenhagen you soon fly over the Baltic coast of Lithuania or Latvia. The land below will depict a primarily agricultural scene. The farmland in some areas will appear laced with woods. Some plots will look very mathematically divided and many dirt roads can also be seen. No cars will appear visible. Once over the Soviet landscape, you are not allowed to take any photographs of the landscape below for reasons of Soviet national security. In general, the landscape below will appear checker-boarded with colors of brown, green, and gray. A winding river or two will appear visible to the eye as the plane approaches and passes over these.

Approximately two hours and five minutes after leaving Copenhagen your jet will land at Sheremetevo airport near Moscow, and you will begin your adventure. Immediately after your plane comes to a halt several Russian soldiers and officials will likely gather on both sides of the jet, accompanied by maintenance personnel and perhaps a medical attendant. Several Aeroflot personnel are usually in the vicinity of the cockpit area of the jet. As soon as you walk off the plane you are likely to sniff the air, to sense a certain odor about Moscow. The odor is indefinable, or perhaps because you are in Russia now your senses may seem more acute. The soldiers will look over everyone departing the aircraft. Following a brief delay you will be ushered aboard a bus to take you to the terminal in order to go through a passport control area of square cubicles lined in a row and each occupied by a Russian soldier wearing a loose-fitting khaki green uniform, brown boots, and a military cap. Next, each person will be required to fill out a declaration form listing all belongings of value to include money, traveler's checks, currency, gold, platinum, jewelry, baggage, and other such articles as brought into the country. When departing the Soviet Union, the process is repeated. Shortly thereafter you will meet your Intourist guide. The odds are that your guide will be a short, pretty, dark-haired young lady named Natasha, which is a common female name in the Soviet Union.

In spite of all the hoopla about Russia's space program, little of its effi-ciency has crept down to its airports at Moscow. For a city as large as Moscow, its airports have few of the gift shops and restaurants customarily seen in Western airports. The restrooms leave a lot to be desired, and women try to keep them clean with large handmade whisk brooms.

Customs is the last gauntlet left to run before formally entering Russia. There all of your luggage will be opened and checked. One must fill out a Customs' Declaration form listing all types and amount of currency brought into the U.S.S.R. Personal items are not usually scrutinized or questioned unless they appear excessive in amount. Rubles cannot be brought into the country. One still camera and one movie camera are permitted to enter Russia with the tourist. All film for personal use is allowed entry; customs officials rarely question the number of rolls of film, probably due to the fact that Western-made film is difficult to locate in the Soviet Union, and Russian film is not easy to have developed when the tourist returns home.

The entire ordeal will seem drawn out; it doesn't appear necessary to take so much time, but the experience reveals that the Russians are not hasty in such matters. Thus, the waiting in line, complicated by the lack of sleep and the after-effects of a long flight, finally enervate each individual. In time, customs is reduced to spot checks, but at random an occasional visitor may have his luggage reopened after proceeding through some stage of the inspection.

Customs in most East European bloc countries is annoying. Members of tour groups, however, may experience less lengthy customs checks than individuals traveling alone. Visas for the Soviet Union indicate if a traveler is a tour-group member. Interestingly, if one's name is Russian in origin, even though born in America, it might mean a thorough inspection for that person.

Having successfully completed customs, you next board an Intourist bus for a forty-minute ride from the airport in the outlying rural area to Moscow. Your guide will give you a rundown of your activities while visiting Moscow and a mini-tour along the route to the hotel.

Near the airport on the west side of Moscow, tank traps mark the site of the halting of the German army in World War II. The Germans reached within 23 kilometers of Moscow.

The route from the airport to town bears signboards in both English and Russian promoting products of Aeroflot, Stanko Imports, Prodintory, and other Soviet foreign-trading organizations. The commercial promotion seems a significant sign of the times, a symbol of the Kremlin's preoccupation and need for trade and tourism. Trade may in time serve as a catalyst for more freedom in the Union of Soviet Socialist Republics. Experimentation with new technology, new concepts of management, and more flexible economics may ultimately lead to greater freedom of thought and expression; however, Communist leadership manages to stifle the germ of change.

Your first impression as you ride along is one of disbelief. It is difficult to imagine actually being in Russia; it will seem as if it is all a dream. But it will not be a dream; shirtless Russian soldiers may be seen working in the hot sun cutting grass with sickles along the roadside. You may observe people swimming and sunbathing near man-made ponds and small creeks. Others may be seen walking along or waiting for a bus. They are all real, alive and happening. When you think of Russia, what does your mind conjure? You think of the threat of communism, Lenin and Stalin, world domination, the Cold War, military might, and so forth, all negative. But do we ever realize that people like us live and work in Russia just as we do at home, that we both share so much of the earth's environment and other basic interests as well? Maybe if we did realize this on more occasions, our world might be a better place to live.

During your visit to Russia you are under the auspices of Intourist, the Russian national tourist agency. Your Intourist guide will seem indoctrinated and very socialist minded. Most of the Intourist guides in Russia are females. Your guide will likely introduce her country as the *first* Socialist Republic in the world. She will proudly announce that the majority of the people have Saturday and Sunday off from work.

The ride from the airport is about 34 kilometers down Gorky Street to your hotel. Gorky Street is the "Main Street" of Moscow. It is the principal shopping street of the city. Enroute, your guide will give you a briefing on Russia and points of interest in Moscow and its environs. The Soviet Union covers about one-sixth of the land surface of the entire globe. The bulk of the population, now at 285 million, and most of the large cities are in the original core area of the Russian state stretching from Kiev to Moscow and Leningrad. Moscow is over 800 years old. It was founded within dense forests in 1147 by Prince Yuri Dolgorusky. His name means long arm, which is an apparent reference to the arms of the prince. A statue of him stands in the center of Sovietskaya Square. It was erected in 1954. In 1156 he built a small wooden fortress on Borovitsky Hill at the juncture of the Neglimnaya and Moskva rivers. The walls of the wooden fortress covered an area about one-third of the size of the Kremlin grounds today. Later, Moscow became the capital of the Russian people during the time of their struggle against Tartar invaders. Moscow was sacked and burned in 1382 and 1571. In 1611 the Poles also burned the city.

Ivan III (1462–1505) made Moscow the capital of Russia. He used the plans of Italian architects to transform the city into a modern capital. Ivan IV (the Terrible, 1553–84) extended Russia's territory by conquest, and ruled with despotic authority. In 1613 the Romanov dynasty was established when Michael Feodorovich (1596–1645), an aristocratic merchant, was crowned tsar. The word *tsar* means supreme authority or throne.

When the Metropolitan Peter moved his residence from Vladimir-on-the-Kliazma to Moscow in the 14th century, the city attained a significant measure of importance. Ivan III cast off the Tartar yoke in 1480, solidifying the power of the Moscow princes. The princes further strengthened their power and that of Moscow in 1547 when they reserved the title of tsar for themselves. In these ways Moscow gained not only political but ecclesiastical power as well. By the end of the 16th century, the Muscovite state had become very powerful.

In the 18th century Peter the Great moved the capital to St. Petersburg, now Leningrad. However, in 1918 the capital was again transferred to Moscow, which became the headquarters of the Russian Communist party (the Bolsheviks). Today the Kremlin ("Citadel" in Russian) is the administrative heart of the U.S.S.R., but was for many centuries the residence of the ruling family. Many places of historical interest are connected with the Kremlin. Moscow currently boasts a population of nearly nine million people. The city is built on seven hills. Moscow is one of thirteen cities in Russia designated as a "Hero City" by the Communist party for its stand against the Germans in World War II.

Moscow is located at 55° 45' north latitude and 37° 37' east longitude. In terms of North America, Moscow lies at approximately the same latitude as Ketchikan, Alaska; Thompson, Manitoba; and Hopewell, Labrador.

Moscow time is calculated at Greenwich time plus three hours. When it is 6 p.m. in Moscow it is 9 a.m. in Chicago and 7 a.m. in Los Angeles. At midnight on March 31, all clocks and watches in the U.S.S.R. are put ahead one hour. At midnight on September 30 the clocks are put back one hour.

In November 1961 all towns, streets, schools, and so forth, that bore the name Stalin were renamed. At that time Stalin's remains were also removed from Lenin's Tomb on Red Square.

The climate of Moscow has an average high temperature of 14°F. and an average low of 5°F. in January (the coldest month). July (the warmest month) in Moscow has a high average temperature of 71°F. and a low average of 54°F. January in Moscow averages eleven rainy days, while July averages twelve days with rain.

Moscow is the economic hub of the Soviet Union. The city is a major manufacturer of lathes, ball bearings, automobiles, electronic and aviation products, communications equipment, textiles, steel, locomotives, scientific instruments, and candy. Eleven major highways and eleven railroads converge on the city.

The U.S.S.R. Academy of Sciences was established in Moscow in 1934, and nearly one out of every three Soviet scientists lives in the city. The Academy of Sciences is located at 14 Leninsky Prospect. The Academy of Medical Sciences is located at 14 Solyanka Street.

Moscow is located on the Moskva River, a tributary of the Oka. The Moskva River joins the Oka southeast of Moscow at the city of Kolomna. The Oka joins the Volga west of Gorki. Moscow is also connected with the Volga north of the city by the Moscow-Volga Canal (8.8 miles long), which was constructed in 1937. Consequently, Moscow is a port itself, due to its river and canal connections, through which ships can traverse on their journeys to the Arctic Ocean, Baltic Sea, Black Sea, and Caspian Sea. However, in the vicinity of Moscow the waterways are frozen and iced for five months each year.

The present-day layout of the city of Moscow developed from four rings of fortifications built in concentric circles around the city. These fortified rings were built over the centuries following the founding of the city in 1147, and consisted of walls, towers, ditches, and ramparts. The walls surrounding the Moscow Kremlin were the first defensive ring built. The city added the other three rings gradually. The second ring of walls was built around the trade area known as the Kitai-Gorod, which enveloped the Kremlin. A third wall was later constructed in what is now the Boulevard Ring, enclosing the Bely Gorod or "White City." The fourth and last wall built extended around Sadovoye Koltso, the present Garden Ring Road. Thus, the current design of Moscow reflects the medieval growth of the city and the defensive walls erected to protect it.

On arrival in Moscow you will be told your place of residence, perhaps the National Hotel on Marx Street overlooking the Fifth of October Square with Red Square beyond it. Unlike virtually all other countries where a traveler knows where he will be staying when on tour, Intourist seldom informs the tourist of the hotel in which he will stay until his arrival. The National is an old but fine hotel. Lenin lived in it a while in room 107. Upon arrival you may think of a nice hot bath, fresh clothes, and a rest from the long trip. Such may not be the case. Once checked in at the desk, where you surrender your passport and Russian visa, you proceed to your room to receive your luggage. Then you may be whisked away on a tour of the city by your guide.

A city excursion may cover many streets and squares, a number of which display historical monuments. A get-acquainted tour of the city usually circles around the inner part of Moscow or the center of the city for a look at Red Square, the Kremlin, Lenin's tomb, St. Basil's Cathedral, the Moskva or Russian Hotel, Lenin Library, Bolshoi Theater, Pushkin Square, Moscow City Hall, and other sights. This is usually an orientation tour; you will return to each of these sights on other occasions while visiting the city. Moscow is huge; it is one of the world's ten largest cities. The city is a meeting place between East and West. Here Europe and Asia mingle their nationalities.

One-third of Moscow is greenery. This serves as a natural air-conditioning system for the city. More than 300 industrial enterprises have been removed from the city for environmental reasons.

In addition to monuments, churches, and museums, a tour of the city would not be complete without a walk through picturesque Red Square. Red Square got its name in the seventeenth century. The word "Red" in Old Russian means "beautiful." Approaching this square, you are likely to observe many military personnel gathering in the vicinity of Lenin's mausoleum. The Russian soldier is very rigid, stern-looking, and has an eye for looking over the foreigner. The people flock to Lenin's tomb on the hour. They literally run for the changing of the guard. Lenin is not only the Soviet's George Washington but also something greater in their eyes—he is their god. His mausoleum occupies the highest place of honor and has held the coffin with Lenin's body since 1924. Russian and foreign tourists line a queue along and around the Kremlin wall three days a week in order to view his body. The Russians will stand in line for hours come rain or shine to go inside the tomb. The people marvel at the changing of the guard at Lenin's tomb, which is a very impressive ceremony. The soldiers are super rigid, and very stiff. They look and act like mechanical men, and what is more, they goose-step in much the same way that the Nazis did.

Red Square is a very busy place, with people literally covering the sidewalks. The sidewalks are wide and spacious, but the most interesting part of them are the underground crossways which make it unnecessary to walk across the busy street intersections. St. Basil's Cathedral, now a museum, is a focal point in the square, along with Lenin's Tomb, and the nearby Gum Department Store.

In tsarist times Red Square was a place of public punishment. Here criminals and others sentenced to death were burned in cages, hanged, buried alive, dismembered, impaled, had molten lead poured into their mouths, or some other cruelty enacted upon them. The low, circular stone platform on Red Square in front of St. Basil's is the oldest structure on the square. It was from this platform that the tsar's proclamations were announced to the public. The square was also the marketplace in medieval times.

After arrival at their hotel most tourists go to a nearby money exchange to get rubles and kopecks, the currency that is used in the Soviet Union. At the money exchange, declaration forms are needed to record the exchange. When departing Russia, no one is permitted to take Russian paper currency abroad.

On each hotel floor is located a desk, behind which is seated a Russian woman in charge of that floor. She is available to assist you with any desired room service. She normally keeps watch on all persons leaving and entering her floor. It is a good idea to make her a gift of a pack of gum and cigarettes, then if you need some service performed you are more apt to get a quick response.

A typical supper may consist of Chicken Kiev, french fries, and fried cabbage. Ice cream is a favorite Russian desert. The Russians make good ice cream. It tastes like it has been made from pure cream.

After dinner you may decide on a walk to the Moscow River Bridge beyond Red Square, or some other locale. Red Square is cool in the evening, well lighted, and there are always guards on duty. The square always seems busy. There is virtually no fear of anyone harming you on the streets, even late at night. One feels safer on Russian streets than on most streets in America after dark. Perhaps the punishment would be too severe for anyone molesting, attempting robbery, or assaulting another person.

The tongue spoken by Muscovites is the standard form of the Russian language which is basically divided into a northern and southern dialect. People in the area of Moscow speak a median form of the two major dialects. The word formations of Russian, including its composition, derivation, and inflection, as well as its phonetics, are different in each of the two main dialects. An individual's social and economic origins also affect the dialect which one speaks. The Moscow dialect is also the basis of literary Russian. Old Church Slavonic has greatly influenced the southern Slavic tongue and written Russian since at least the eleventh century. The Russians are fond of proverbs and like to play with their language, especially by shortening long compounds. Russians use the Cyrillic alphabet in writing their language.

The architecture of Moscow developed more through wood than stone, since the early city was surrounded by dense forests. It was not until the late fourteenth century that stone made its appearance in Moscow buildings. Between 1480 and 1516 the wooden walls around the Kremlin were replaced by red bricks.

One evening as I was retiring, Mike, a young man in my group, said he wanted a picture of a statue of Karl Marx opposite the Bolshoi, two blocks from our hotel. He persuaded his roommate, Jim, to accompany him, and they were off. Mike got the pictures he wanted of Marx and the Bolshoi and then decided he and Jim might as well explore. The next day Mike and Jim related the following story to me. After leaving the Bolshoi, they headed toward Red Square and GUM Department Store. Arriving at their destination, they observed some window displays in GUM and then walked across Red Square to Lenin's Mausoleum.

As they stood there, they met a Russian citizen whose name he later gave as Arthur. He had been standing next to Mike and Jim in front of the mausoleum and just started talking to them. Arthur offered to show them around a little, as the next changing of the guard was not for another twenty minutes, till eight o'clock. Mike and Jim discovered that their Russian companion was a schoolteacher in geography and history, but at the time was working in another area of education. He was a tall man, well over six feet in height, brown hair, broad shoulders, and wore a red shirt and plaid pants. He had a surprising knowledge of rock music and knew quite a lot about certain recording stars like Elvis Presley, the Beatles, Simon and Garfunkle, and others. Arthur said that he had listened to British pirate radio stations in the late 1960s, and was anxious to know about the present top groups and individual male and female rock singers. He went on to hail a certain British rock magazine as the best for overall rock information and indicated that Russia has had some rock groups visit to do concerts. Arthur stated that records were available through Yugoslavia, where they are manufactured, and he went on to recommend certain albums. According to Mike and Jim,

Arthur knew more about the subject than either of them.

They proded Arthur with some questions and found he owned and drove a car. He said he would like one with a diesel engine and good gas mileage. He showed his driver's license: a folded red card with black print and his photograph. Mike and Jim in turn took out theirs and showed them to Arthur.

They then asked Arthur how he found Russian students were to teach. Arthur said that he wasn't teaching anymore, and by his reaction, Mike and Jim ascertained that he hadn't enjoyed it too much, though he never came out and said so.

The trio then returned to Red Square for the changing of the guard. Arthur explained about the plaques on the wall behind Lenin's Mausoleum and said that these were the graves or monuments to party and state officials, cosmonauts, important figures, and the like.

After the ceremony they walked back toward the hotel. Arthur revealed that he believed that the four most important things America had given the world were: 1) Elvis Presley, 2) Mickey Mouse, 3) baseball, 4) the H-bomb. Mike and Jim found this amusing, and even Arthur laughed a little. Still, along this vein, Arthur didn't want to hear anything about America per se.

The next subject of discussion was sports, particularly the popular sports in Russia of hockey and soccer. Arthur, it was discovered, was quite a hockey fan; he told of training schools that were held for ice hockey during the winter, then seemed amazed that hockey equipment for boys was on sale at GUM, but it wasn't too clear why.

Arthur was curious as to how the Soviet National Hockey team was received by Americans. Mike and Jim replied, saying Americans were impressed by the Russian victories over our pros, though they were tempted to use the excuse that except for a few pro teams, the others were mediocre in quality. Arthur gave his thoughts on the rough style of play of some American teams, which was negative, because the Soviet style is less physical and involves more finesse; a Soviet player may yell words of anger and names but won't customarily physically attack and strike another player. Arthur mentioned the Soviet national team that walked off the ice rather than play the rough style of the Philadelphia Flyers.

On the Olympics (1976) the discussion was brief. Arthur mentioned the Soviet girls' basketball team that beat ours, but on any subject it proved futile to contradict him. He did comment that the United States was very good in basketball.

Education crept in once again and Arthur said eight years was compulsory for schooling, or until a student reached age 14. After that it is either normal or trade school. Arthur tried to persuade Mike and Jim to read certain newspapers that were more "truthful" about his country, but Jim commented that all newspapers were opinionated, or less than honest.

Most city tours include a visit to the Exhibition of the Economic Achievements of the U.S.S.R. Intourist will likely furnish you a special guide in addition to your assigned guide for the tour. On the way to the exhibit grounds your attention will be directed to various points of interest such as the huge Ostankino TV Tower and 320-foot high Monument to Conquerers of Outer Space. In front of the entranceway to the exhibition grounds is located a huge stainless steel sculpture of the "Collective Worker and Farm Women" designed by Vera Mukina, a sculptress. The statue was designed in 1937. Upon arrival at the exhibit area you will board an open-air three-car minibus by which to travel to see the various pavilions and sights. In all there are seventy pavilions, each one representing a facet of the Soviet Union: agriculture, industry, construction, science, food, the arts, and so forth. Some of the popular pavilions include those of "Soviet Culture," "Atomic Energy," "Health," "Education in the U.S.S.R." and "Cosmos."

A visit to the Exhibition of Economic Achievement of the U.S.S.R. is a must. This is an exhibition of Soviet progress for approximately the last thirty years. Upon entering the grounds you pass through a high arch that will remind you of the Arc de Triomphe in Paris. The exhibition grounds cover 500 acres. The various pavilions are built in the architectural styles of the fifteen different Soviet republics. At the center of the grounds stand golden statues representing each of the fifteen republics comprising the Soviet Union. The 300-foot monument to commemorate Soviet space explorations can be seen from the open-air bus as you ride through the exhibition grounds. A tour of the grounds will include the Friendship of Peoples Square, many beautiful fountains, Industry Square, the sports grounds, flower gardens and orchards, and a stop to visit the Science Pavilion, "Cosmos." Inside are largely mock-ups of space hardware and technical devices pertaining to the Russian space program. Pictures are allowed to be taken inside. If you have a suspicious mind, it will tell you that some of the models on display are outdated or no longer used. Inside "Cosmos" are man-made earth satellites, including an original *Sputnik* which made its appearance in the sky in 1957. There is also the model "Salyute," in which the Russian and American astronauts shook hands in space. One can enter inside a model of "Soyus," the Soviet spacecraft which joined with the American space lab. Also in the science pavilion, there is a replica of the dog "Laika," which lived seven days in space in 1958. This gave Soviet scientists the impetus to push ahead since men could then apparently live in space. Simulated models of the first manned spacecraft, Yuri Gagarin's Vostok I, and Titov's spaceship Vostok II, are also on exhibit. These exhibits make the visitor see why the Russians are so very proud of their space program. Some other notable achievements of the program include:

(1) *Sputnik 1*—Launched Oct. 4, 1957. First artificial satellite around the earth.
(2) *Sputnik 2*—Launched Nov. 3, 1958. First inhabited space capsule (dog, "Laika").
(3) *Luna 2*—Launched Sept. 12, 1959. First spacecraft on the moon (moon impact).
(4) *Luna 3*—Launched Oct. 4, 1959. First circumnavigation of the moon.
(5) *Luna 9*—Launched Jan. 31, 1966. First successful lunar "soft landing."

A short walk from the Space Pavilion will bring you to a theater for a cyclorama of the Soviet Union. This is a circular movie hall with screens 360 degrees around. Approximately 14 to 18 projectors are used at any one time, presenting the picture as one complete totality. Inside, it is usually warm and crowded with everyone standing and their heads tilted backward watching a travelogue on the Soviet Union.

From the cyclorama as you walk back in the direction of the "Cosmos" pavilion are beautiful fountains that decorate the grounds. The "Friendship of Peoples" fountain has jets of water shooting into the air. Surrounding it are golden statues of people, all with their arms outstretched. The park and grounds of the Exhibition of the Economic Achievements also merge with those of the U.S.S.R. Academy of Sciences, on whose grounds are botanical gardens, greenhouses, and diverse flora from around the world.

In the distance can be seen the new television tower that rises over 1,700 feet. In the middle section of the tower is the revolving Seventh Heaven Restaurant, which offers a splendid view of Moscow. The restaurant slowly rotates around the tower's axis.

Russian meals are an experience and a treat in themselves. Restaurants are often crowded, and unless you are there with a group, you will usually be seated with one or two other persons. A typical lunch in a good restaurant might consist of strips of beef, chicken in brown sauce, Russian beans, cheese, Georgian bread, and a number of drinks: sweet apple juice, and that Russian treat, vodka! Even in a small amount, vodka packs a mean kick. Water makes a good chaser to put the fire out. One must drink vodka with "respect"; at first you don't feel its effects but gradually it affects the senses. The Russians like to drink it "bottoms up."

Vodka is made from the fermented juice of potatoes. It is close to being pure alcohol. The Russians consume it in large quantities. One should never drink it on an empty stomach, lest it surge quickly into the bloodstream. Russian diplomats are said to drink several glasses of milk before consuming vodka, since milk helps both to dilute the effect of the alcohol and to delay its absorption into the circulatory system.

The peculiar thing about a Russian meal is that just when you think that the meal is over, a waiter comes up and takes away the empty plate and replaces it with some other exotic delight. A meal might be served in this sequence: Borscht, chicken, shish kabob, a second serving of chicken, then ice cream and coffee, all topped off by Russian champagne. When dining in Russia, one can never be sure that the meal is over until everyone stands to leave, so eat and drink a little at a time, for more may be coming. Menus are printed in Russian and foreign languages, and prices are quoted in rubles and kopecks.

While in Moscow, don't pass up the opportunity to take a tour of the famous Moscow Subway. Throughout the entire system no two stations are exactly alike in design. All are clean and there is no sign of graffiti on the trains or on the cars. No advertisements are visible on or in the trains or in the underground stations. Women in blue uniforms with red caps stand on the platform to help travelers get to their destinations.

To reach the subway it is necessary to take a long but swiftly moving escalator from just below ground level to an underground station. Be mindful to stay on the right when descending so that people in a hurry can descend around you quickly. No matter how many times you ride the subway in Moscow, you will continue to marvel at its beauty and efficiency. The subway carries more than five million people in Moscow daily.

The first line on the subway was opened in 1935. The subway system is tremendous and one that has been studied and copied by other countries. The fare is five kopecks. The system is laid out like a wheel, and carries more passengers than any other metro in the world. One of the most beautiful stations is Komsomolskaya Station with its eight mosaics illustrating Russian victories. The different stations exhibit crystal chandeliers, mosaics, and frescoes for the viewer to behold. Each station shines with marble, bronze, and crystal. The walls are covered with numerous sculptures, mosaics, and stained-glass compositions. The rides are fast, quiet, and very comfortable. The entire system is modern, efficient, and supposedly the finest in the world. There were 110 stations in operation in 1979.

Another experience that the tourist will encounter is an Intourist store, the Berioska, to shop for souvenirs. The Berioska is also called a "Dollar Store" because only foreign currency, not rubles, may be spent in it. American dollars are desired currency in these stores. The Russians need foreign exchange to purchase wheat, electronic equipment, computers, and other goods abroad. Outside the Soviet Union the ruble has little value. The Soviet Union is not a place where foreigners customarily look for purchasing automobiles, refrigerators, and other consumer goods.

On the first floor there are usually busts of Lenin, wood carvings, buttons, records, tapes, a variety of liquors, and more. The second floor has fur coats and hats, jewelry, postcards, cameras, printed slides, radios, rugs, and other such items. The shops are not very large according to Western standards, but they do have some variety and specialties of Russia. If you were a Soviet citizen, you would be unable to shop there, unless the Intourist guide gave permission to you, a Russian relative, to enter the shop. Rubles are not accepted, and any purchase must be made in U.S. or some other foreign currency or traveler's checks.

Everyone will likely experience the Russian purchasing game firsthand. It goes like this: The customer must wait for the clerk behind the counter, who may be occupied with another customer, preparing a purchase, or just standing there. In any event, you must wait for the clerks to come to you. The important thing is that when you are waited on you have the clerk's undivided attention. Having made your selection, the clerk writes up a purchasing form specifying the price of the merchandise in Russian and foreign currency, such as U.S. dollars. Then you take the forms to the cashier's booth and pay for the item, return to the clerk with the forms and pick up your purchase. It is not surprising when you receive change from the cashier for it to be in the form of another currency if change can't be made in yours. Your change may come in an assortment of Swiss, German, and French coins. The system is very time consuming and confusing. Clerks are few so you wait for your turn at the counter. Merchandise is displayed behind the counter so that one cannot make his selection ahead of time.

An evening visit to the Moscow Circus will present the viewer an outstanding performance. The Moscow Circus is a spectacle that is known worldwide. In fact it has been televised in the U.S. on a number of occasions. To begin with, all the performers are introduced before the show begins. Clown acts, the high wire, a juggler, acrobats, performing dogs and horses, and a trapeze act are presented to the delight of the audience. As each performer completes his or her act, a matron presents a small bouquet of flowers. In the finale, all the performers come out for one last round of applause, and on occasion special presentations are made to outstanding members of the circus. Finally someone will thank the officials on hand and the audience, and the curtain will descend.

Viewing the circus in Moscow is exciting. It is held in an old, modest-size building and is a one-ring circus. The program is spectacular, with Popov, the famous clown, as one of its mainstays. There are other circuses in Moscow, some of which are held outdoors.

Mail sent from the Soviet Union does not seem to have any regularity in reaching its destination. Take precaution with postcards. After addressing them individuals often find out that the large Russian stamps cover most of the address. Then many persons end up having to rewrite the cards.

A visit to the Kremlin is a must. Within the confines of its walls are many buildings and objects associated with Russian history. Before entering, you will be asked to deposit any flight bags, packages, etc., in a locker area, as these items are not allowed within the Kremlin walls. A small rental fee of ten kopecks is required.

Known as the heart of the Soviet Union, the Kremlin contains within its fortress walls the Grand Kremlin Palace (1838–1849), the Armory (1815), the Arsenal (1936), the Senate Building (1776–1788), the Palace of Congresses (1961), and Cathedral Square. The Kremlin is essentially a 69-acre walled-in area built in the fifteenth century. It was given its name by Grand Prince Ivan Danilovitch. The Kremlin rises in the heart of Moscow and is an embodiment of the history of the Russian people. The Socialist Revolution ushered a new era into the ancient Kremlin. The less than three-quarters of a century of existence of the Soviet state is inseparably linked with the Kremlin. It was here that Lenin mostly lived and worked while in Moscow, and it is in adjacent Red Square that the Lenin Mausoleum stands. The Kremlin stands on a hill that is largely imperceptible except when facing it from across the Moskva River. Moscow derived its name from this river.

The wall surrounding the Kremlin is about 65 feet high. The Kremlin has a circumference of slightly over a mile. It is to Moscow what the Eiffel Tower is to Paris and the Colosseum is to Rome. The history of Moscow centers on the Kremlin.

The Kremlin Wall has nineteen towers. Party officials and their autos enter the Kremlin from Red Square through the Gate of the Redeemer, built in 1491. In 1625 a clock tower was built above the gate. The gate faces and stands opposite St. Basil's Cathedral. Atop the gate is Savior's (Spasskaya) Tower with clocks protruding from it. This tower is the tallest of the Kremlin's towers, standing 220 feet high. The melodious chimes of this beautiful clock tower are broadcast by Radio Moscow to many parts of the earth. The pinnacle of the tower has a huge five-pointed ruby-red star mounted above it.

The Communists proclaim the five-pointed stars which tower above the Kremlin as symbols of the unity of the five continents. But which five? There are, in fact, seven continents, so it is a mystery which five the star represents. It would be far more apprporiate to say the five-pointed star represented the five seas to which Moscow has access by inland water transport. By river and canal connections, boats can reach the Baltic, Black, Caspian, Barents, and Azov seas.

The Presidium of the Supreme Soviet and the U.S.S.R. Council of Ministers is housed in the Kremlin as well as the most recent building, the Palace of Congresses. Various conferences and meetings are held in the auditorium of the Palace, which seats 6,000. It was built in 1961 and contains a huge banquet hall.

In the southwest corner of the Kremlin, facing the Moskva River, is the Grand Kremlin Palace. The palace was built by the architect Ton in 1838–1849 on orders by Tsar Nicholas I. A former palace belonging to Tsarina Elizabeth stood on its site. The tsars lived in the Grand Kremlin Palace while in Moscow. It contains paintings, a throne room, and the banquet hall of the tsars. Connected to the palace is the celebrated Red Staircase, a long tier of steps entered by way of a huge archway at ground level. It was on this staircase that Ivan the Terrible greeted the Polish ambassador to Russia and then drove a spear through his foot.

The Kremlin was the place where all the tsars were crowned, married, and sanctified by the church. When a new tsar was crowned, the bells of the Kremlin announced his ascension to the throne of Russia. The Russian Church was also headquartered in the Kremlin.

An excursion through the grounds of the Kremlin will bring you to the Assumption, Annunciation, and Archangel Michael cathedrals that now serve as museums. It is said that Napoleon stalled his horses in these churches when he invaded Moscow. Moscow contains numerous churches. Bulbous domes can be seen rising above the skyline of the city. The huge domes remind one of inverted onions. Gilded spires radiate the sun beaming down on them. Over 300 gilded domes, mostly of Byzantine origin, rise above the roofline of Moscow.

Inside the Annunciation (Blagoveshchenski) Cathedral, the ceiling of the entrance hallway is decorated with a genealogy in picture form of Russian tsars. Its 16th-century murals of Theodosius are artistically exquisite. Within the cathedral is a gallery of icons, many of which were made by the monk Andrei Rublyov. One of the icons is a large representation of St. John with arms outstretched, made by Theopanes the Greek. A mural portrays Jonah being swallowed by a whale.

Icons are basically paintings on boards depicting a religious figure(s) or scene. It is not unusual that any two icons might have the same name for each represents its creator's intentions. On the main wall of the Annunciation Cathedral icons are displayed on as many as five or six different levels. The second icon to the right of center on the lower level gave its name to the cathedral. At one time women were not allowed in the main area of the cathedral because they were considered too sinful. Consequently, special galleries were constructed for the women. In one of the cupolas is a portrait of Christ. A staircase connects the cathedral with the Grand Palace.

The original Annunciation Cathedral was burned, but after the fire it was rebuilt in 1564 with nine gilded cupolas, and is known as the "Golden Topped." This cathedral served as a private chapel to the tsars. The chapels in the cathedral are very small. It was built by Pskov architects in 1482–89 and stands beside the Grand Kremlin Palace. The Annunciation Cathedral in

Vladimir served as the model for the one in the Kremlin. Its floor is a beautiful composite of jasper and agate.

Behind the Annunciation Cathedral stands the Cathedral of the Assumption (Uspensky) built in 1475–79. It is the largest and oldest cathedral inside the Kremlin. Assumption Cathedral was designed by the Italian architect Fioravanti, and contains the carved throne of Ivan the Terrible. This cathedral was modeled after the Uspensky Cathedral in Vladimir. The architectural features of both these cathedrals became models for other cathedrals in Russia. A corridor leading to the Assumption Cathedral contains frescoes of Homer, Plato, and other ancient Greeks of renown. The tsars of Russia were officially crowned in the cathedral, and some metropolitans of the Russian Orthodox Church are buried beneath its floors. The roof is supported by huge gilded columns that are decorated with paintings and sculptures. The cathedral has five domes and displays five golden cupolas. The five domes are said to represent the patriarch or metropolitan of the Russian Church and four deacon assistants. The frescoes and chandeliers inside the cathedral are exquisite. In the 17th century exterior paintings were added to the cathedral.

St. Jonah, the last Moscow bishop to become Metropolitan of Kiev, is entombed inside Assumption Cathedral. He tried to save Moscow from the Tartars. When Napoleon occupied Moscow, he reportedly became frightened after having had St. Jonah's coffin opened.

Nearby is the Archangel Michael Cathedral, which is adorned with four cupolas. It was the first Russian church to incorporate the cornice into its design. This beautiful cathedral was built to celebrate the departure of famine from Russia. It was constructed in 1504–1508 by the Italian Alevisio Novy, and is the burial place of 54 tsars and grand dukes. All Russian tsars prior to the time of Peter the Great were entombed in this cathedral decorated in Italian Renaissance style. Their copper cased tombs bear inscriptions about the tsars and are in chronological order. The cathedral was appropriately named as Saint Michael was the patron saint of the tsars. It is interesting to note that the main altar is located behind a carved wooden iconostasis. On its walls can be seen murals of Ivan the III and IV and other tsars. This church is the burial place of Ivan the Terrible, also known as the Great and the IV. Ivan married seven times and tried to centralize his country. The cathedral is quite exquisite and well-preserved by the state. Russian guides tend to say little about religion in the Soviet Union outside of historical context.

Located to the right of the Assumption and Archangel cathedrals stands the Belltower of Ivan the Great built by order of Boris Godunov. This unusual octagonal-shaped structure is crowned with an onion-shaped gilded dome. Originally it served as a watchtower for Moscow from which observers could see for twenty miles around the city. It stands 240 feet high and was the tallest structure in Moscow in tsarist times. The tsars permitted no buildings higher than their palaces. The belltower was built of bricks and covered with white stone in 1600 by Wilke, a foreign architect. It contains three dozen bells, one of which weighs 128,000 pounds. In tsarist times it was called the Festival Bell and was rung only on certain occasions. Napoleon's troops attempted to destroy the tower, but the explosion only partially damaged it.

In one corner of the Kremlin stands the Oruzheinaya Palata, or the Armory. It is located next to the Grand Kremlin Palace. Built in the sixteenth century, it is said to be the oldest Russian museum. Through the centuries it housed the Armory Hall, Treasure Chamber, Court Museum, and the Museum of Decorative Arts following the 1917 Revolution. Here the gifts, jewelry, art, and regalia of the tsars are stored. Items stored in the museum include medieval armor, royal coaches, firearms, fine porcelain, glassware, antique furniture, ecclesiastical objects, tapestries, rare documents, thrones, chandeliers, robes, gold and jewel objects, ivory and 400-year-old English silverware. Visitors can see the boats of Peter the Great, the throne of Ivan the Terrible, and the impressive crown of Catherine the Great which features over 5,000 diamonds.

The Kremlin is situated adjacent to Red Square where many important government activities take place. Within the walls of the Kremlin are buried some of the more esteemed leaders and people in the Soviet Union. All foreign delegations are officially received in the Kremlin. The Kremlin is closed on Thursday.

Your Intourist guide will be most helpful in touring the Kremlin. Many Intourist guides speak perfect English, but do not always comprehend foreign quips and expressions and sometimes think foreigners are being facetious about their country. Guides are often defensive about questions posed to them, particularly if the questions fall in the realm of politics. But by the time you prepare to leave Russia, your guide will likely feel more relaxed in your company.

Outside the cathedrals in the Kremlin there are two objects that symbolize the pride Russian tsars had in huge objects:

The Tsars' Bell (Tsar Kolokol). It is claimed by the Russians as the largest bell in the world. Cast in 1733–35, it weighs two hundred tons and has never been rung. The Moscow bellmonger, Motorin, cast the huge bell from an older bell. Rastrelli decorated it with bas-reliefs. The bell remains where it was cast; it was never moved. In 1737 the bell cracked when water was thrown on it during a fire which destroyed the shed that housed it. The bell fell from its position and became partially buried in the earth. It was dug out in 1836 and moved to the present pedestal on which it stands. Today tourists contribute to a fund to have the bell polished. Below and underneath the bell are the huge gongs that weigh close to sixteen tons. Next to the crevice in the bell stands a piece of the bell weighing eleven tons that fell out when it originally cracked. The Tsars' Bell seems to be an imitation of our Liberty Bell, including the crack. The aperture in the bell is wide enough to permit an adult to walk inside standing erect. There is enough room inside the bell to accommodate easily thirty to forty standing persons. Standing on a large granite pedestal, the bell is 20 feet high, 22 feet in diameter, and 54 feet in circumference. The bottom of the bell is 22 inches thick.

The Tsars' Cannon. It was another example of tsarist ego. It is reput:d to have the largest bore of any cannon in the world. Its barrel is 3 feet in diameter and 17 feet long. It was cast in bronze in 1586 by Andrei Chokhov and weighs 40 tons. Stacked nearby are its enormous cannonballs weighing about 4,000 pounds each.

Outside the Kremlin wall newlywed couples can be seen placing a traditional wreath of flowers on the Tomb of the Unknown Soldier. The newlyweds will then make a tour of the city seeing the sights, much the same as tourists. Newlyweds are traditionally driven through the streets in a taxi with a doll tied to the front of the taxi with large ribbons.

Around the corner from the Tomb of the Unknown Soldier is Lenin's mausoleum. Western tourists wishing to view the coffin of Lenin are customarily escorted to the front of the line that forms on Red Square. Inform your guide in advance as arrangements are necessary for a visit inside the tomb. The police around the tomb constantly look over visitors and make certain that they stay in line. Everyone is checked to ensure that no packages or cameras enter the mausoleum. Finally, after entering the mausoleum, visitors descend a flight of about three dozen steps before reaching the glass coffin that holds the remains of Lenin.

Russia celebrates May 1 as International Labor Day. On that day, a huge parade displaying tanks, rockets, marching soldiers, and civilians carrying placards is customarily held on Red Square.

On the east side of Red Square is GUM. This store is the closest thing in Russia to an American indoor shopping mall. GUM (Gosudarstvennyi University Megazin) was built in the early nineteenth century. It is covered by a glass arcade roof. It consists of three levels with crossover walkways and passages leading to its various sections and shops. A net is spread over the skylight, presumably for the protection of the customers. It is very warm inside.

Shopping in GUM, Russia's largest department store, can be a chaotic and frustrating experience for Westerners. Payment is required in rubles. To purchase an item, the procedure is the same as that described previously in the case of the Berioska shop. Russian stores, like ours, also have seasonal sales.

One can easily spend several or more hours walking through GUM. A grey stone building, it is an assemblage of shops and stores of many varieties and kinds of goods: fish, clothing, shoes, toys, carpeting, curtains, canned goods, bottled wine, mineral water, vodka, radios, souvenirs, etc. Some of the stores permit the taking of pictures, but others refuse permission. It is always best to ask before taking someone's photograph. A large men's shop in GUM sells suits that are made in Belgium, Finland, Yugoslavia, and Austria. These imported suits are superior in quality to the Russian suits in the store and generally range in price from 180 to 215 rubles. An average Russian would have to work about a month to pay for one of these suits.

Adjacent to GUM is the State Historical Museum, which stands on the north end of Red Square. Its twenty rooms contain numerous maps, documents, paintings, and relics tracing the history of Russia from ancient times. The collection dates from the Stone Age. The museum is a historical and anthropological curiosity. A large collection of archaeological items includes pottery, arrowheads, vases, shields, helmets, tools, beads, utensils, ancient stones with inscriptions, and reins of horses.

Opposite the State Historical Museum, southward across cobblestoned Red Square, is the Cathedral of the Intercession (St. Basil's Cathedral). This is one of the most photographed of all the tourist attractions in Russia. Today it is a museum. Inside the cathedral are staircases, crypts, vaults, and galleries. The cathedral is unsurpassed for its fanciful contours and vivid colors. Each of its eight cupolas is different in design. The cathedral's elaborate profusion of fanciful cupolas and towers range from cylindrical and octagonal to pyramidal. These are arranged at different levels. St. Basil's is an assemblage of churches. Originally it began as a stone church surrounded by seven wooden chapels. These wooden buildings were later torn down and replaced by brick structures. The chapels are all small in size, the largest of which is the chapel in the central church. St. Basil's was built (1555–1560) by order of Ivan the Terrible to commemorate the conquest of the Tartar city of Kazan. Legend says that Ivan was so impressed with St. Basil's that he didn't want another church built like it, so he had the builder's eyes removed. The main altar of the cathedral was built by Posnik Yakovlev, a Russian craftsman. In front of the cathedral stands a monument to Minim and Pozharsky, important leaders in the struggle against the Poles in the seventeenth century. In 1612 they helped to drive the Poles from Moscow. The monument was created by I. Martos in 1818. Moscow's huge onion-domed churches are a significant link that reminds one of Russia's connection to the Byzantine and Christian influence.

Beyond St. Basil's, next to the Moskva River, is located the Hotel Russia. This 14-story hotel can accommodate 6,000 people, and has cinemas and a concert hall. On the grounds of the Hotel Russia is St. Ann's Church. This small white church is the oldest stone church in Moscow.

There are fifteen functioning churches in Moscow. According to Intourist, these include one synagogue, one Catholic church, two Protestant churches, two mosques, and nine Orthodox churches.

A trip to Moscow would be incomplete without a boat ride on the Moskva River. A pleasant ride can be made from the Hotel Russia to Keisby Terminal. Along the river you can see some of the sights that we visited earlier, and others like Gorky Central Recreation Park, boats, bridges, and various parts of the city's skyline. Gorky Park was opened to the public in 1928 and is the largest in Moscow. It contains a huge ferris wheel, restaurants, and various amusements. The river is lined with old and new buildings, granite embankments, and historical and architectural monuments. People swim in the river and use the grassy surface beside the river for sunbathing. The river cruise is cool and refreshing in the summer although the temperature may be in the eighties.

The traffic on Gorky Street seems more dense and heavier each year. There are far fewer cars on Russian streets than in the U.S. and Western Europe. In Russian cities, buses, trolleys, and subway trains are the major means of city passenger transport. For the average Russian, automobiles are hard to come by, even when a person has the rubles to purchase one. Autos are in short supply, and a Russian desiring to buy one has to have state approval beforehand. The government may not contact the would-be buyer for years after his application has been received. Many of Russia's city dwellers now live in high-rise apartments, which are usually on the bus and trolley lines. Thus an automobile is not crucial to moving around in the city. Furthermore, Russians are not permitted to travel around their country without first getting a permit to go from one city to the next.

It is always nice to take a leisurely stroll along Gorky Street. The underground walkways beneath it are very helpful considering the traffic above them. Women often use baby carriages for shopping carts. The carriages are even pushed up and down steps of the underground walkways. In summer few children are seen on the streets. Many are away at summer camps, such as those for the Young Pioneers.

Tourists should feel free to wander about Moscow on their own. If anyone is under surveillance at any time, it is not noticeable and it is doubtful that the KGB or local authorities that keep track of foreigners follow tourists without reason.

A short distance from the National Hotel is located the Bolshoi Opera and Ballet Theatre. The word Bolshoi means big. The theatre seats over 2,300 people. The original theatre was built in 1824. After a fire gutted it, it was rebuilt by the architect Kavos in 1853. It is the most famous theatre in Russia, and is one of only three theatres in the city founded before the October Revolution. It has excellent acoustics. Lenin spoke in it on many occasions. Inside, five-tiered balconies look down on an 85-foot long stage. The interior is done in red and gold colors. A huge gold chandelier hangs from the ceiling. The Bolshoi made its American debut in 1959, accompanied by the prima ballerina Galina Ulanova, who was near age 50 at the time. She continued to be the mainstay of the Soviet ballet into the early 1960s.

Less than two blocks down the street from the Bolshoi is located the Hotel Metropole on Karl Marx Prospekt. The Metropole was one of the first hotels built for tourists. Beyond the Metropole is the statue of Sverdlov, the first president of Russia. His statue faces the Bolshoi in the distance.

For a good evening's entertainment try the Tchaikovsky Concert Hall. If you have not seen the Volga Folk Dancers and Singers, who perform Russian dances and sing Russian folk music, attempt to catch one of their performances. Their costumes are eye-catching and appealing. The talent of the young performers is impressive. They are nothing short of fabulous and seem to better themselves after each number. The dancers, singers, and musicians are all superb. The choreography done by V. Modzolevsky is excellent.

Russian actors and dancers venerate their profession. With them it is a passion, a burning desire, an idealism. The audiences adore their triumphs. For the Russians, acting and dancing is an adoration that is close to being a religion. The performers can mesmerize an audience, and are exalted in the hearts and minds of Russians. Western audiences are more sophisticated than their Russian counterparts but what the Russians lack in sophistication, they more than make up for by the sincerity and emotionalism they exhibit for their performers.

Anyone with an interest in art should not miss strolling through the Tretyakov Art Gallery with its collection of 40,000 works of Russian art. In its vast collection are ancient icons and paintings by contemporary Soviet artists. In addition to the gallery's thousands of paintings, drawings, and engravings, there are about 900 pieces of sculpture. Many of the works are remarkably lifelike and resemble colored photographs depicting religious, historic, and literary portraits and scenes rather than paintings. The Tretyakov collection was amassed in the latter part of 1800s and presented to the city in 1892. The paintings date from the tenth century and fill fifty halls. One of the most revered paintings is that of "Our Lady of Petersburg," done by Petrov-Vodkin in 1920. It portrays the virgin and child standing on a balcony in St. Petersburg. Including masterpieces by Serov, Levitan, and Ruble, the collection is considered to be the largest assemblage of Russian art. Amidst its works is the icon of "Our Lady of Vladimir," dating from the twelfth century. The icon originally came from Byzantium, and legend attributes to it the working of miracles. It is thought that Russian icons were traditionally made from oak, and the artists used vegetable oil to preserve the colors. Some of the icons are bent, because once the wood ages it tends to expand or contract. The Tretyakov Art Gallery is located south of the Moskva River, not far from the Kremlin.

Another exquisite gem of art is the Ostankino Serf Art Museum, which is located near the Exhibition of Economic Achievements. It is a timber palace erected in the eighteenth century, and completely built by serf craftsmen. The palace was part of an estate belonging to Count Sheremetyev. The floors are a masterpiece of parquetry. Ornate crystal chandeliers are suspended from its ceiling. There is great use of marble, malachite, and bronze in the design of the museum. The former palace is a masterpiece of Russian classical architecture. In order to preserve the floors, visitors must wear slippers over their shoes. It is a bit slippery trying to walk on its floors.

The Serf Art Museum has an excellent collection of paintings, sculptures, and porcelain. The painting which stood out in my mind was a black one with a green silhouette of a peasant's house shadowed by a green moon. It was translucent. I had never seen anything quite like it. Many of the paintings were done by Italian, French, Flemish, and other West European painters. Russian art is also well represented.

While in Moscow, don't miss a drive around the circular boulevards forming a ring around the city of Moscow. The central part of the city, to include the Kremlin, is surounded by the Boulevard Ring. Further out is the Sadovoe (Garden) Ring, and beyond that is the ring of the Moscow Circular Motorway. Moscow is very functionally designed and laid out in terms of traffic patterns. It is quite capable of handling a substantial traffic flow, much more than now exists on its streets.

From the Garden Ring you can proceed down Gorky Street to Pushkin Square, *Izvestia* newspaper office, and *Novosti* Press Agency. *Izvestia* is one of the two main nationally read newspapers in the Soviet Union. Founded in 1917, it has been published as an evening paper since 1960. The other major Soviet paper, *Pravda* (Truth) began publication in 1912, and is the officially recognized party paper. In 1961 *Novosti* was established as an unofficial news agency for the circulation of news to both the Soviet and foreign press. *Novosti* is the source of foreign news. *Soyuza* (Tass), founded in 1925, is the official Soviet agency for news inside the Soviet Union. About 98 percent of all information about the Soviet Union comes from Tass. "Moscow News" is published in five languages, one of which is English. It is published weekly by *Izvestia*. Most of its news is about the Soviet Union and the socialist countries. *Izvestia* has a daily circulation of eight million, while that of *Pravda* is nine million daily copies. Moscow has over thirty national newspapers and seventy publishing houses. However, the average Westerner feels lost while in the Soviet Union for lack of news coverage to which he has been accustomed back home.

A large bronze statue of Pushkin erected in 1880 stands at the entrance of Pushkin Square. Also on the square is located the cinema "Rossiya," the largest in the Soviet Union. It was opened in 1961.

Add to your city visit the Moscow Art Theater, located a short distance off Gorky Street, not far from the Hotel National. This theater was founded as a playhouse in 1897. Its intellectual founders wanted to provide aspiring, unknown playwrights the opportunity to present new acting styles and ideas. In 1923 its company visited and performed in the United States.

There are 50 theaters in Moscow. Five are children's theaters, staging plays and opera performances for children. Twenty are drama theaters which present both Russian and foreign classics. Two other well-known theaters are the Gypsy Theater "Romen" and the Central Puppet Theater.

Tourists are commonly ushered to a Round Table Conference, apparently sponsored by the Soviet government. One of these conferences, with many tourists present, went as follows: Seated at a table were three men and one woman whose stated purpose was not to convert us to communism in one day, but to clear up any misconceptions we might have about their form of government and the Soviet Union in general. The Soviet panel consisted of four commentators: Professor Maja Gordjeva, a woman from the Institute of Foreign Languages; Leonid Zoliotarevdav, a Soviet television commentator; Rudolph Zimenko of the United States and Canadian Institute; and a Mr. Litvin from the Institute of World Economy.

At first I thought the question and answer session might be related to our tour, but this impression was soon dismissed. The meeting turned out to be a propaganda session. We were given a two-hour sell on communism. The panel first explained how far communism had brought their country into the twentieth century. As in any sales pitch the best points were emphasized, and then the panel stated that they wanted to correct any false notions or erroneous ideas we might have about communism.

I was of the opinion the panel had done a good job until the question and answer portion began with the audience participating. I was very proud of my college students and the others in attendance; they did not pull any punches. They asked pointed questions regarding education, religious freedom, the military budget, space program, health, welfare, pensions, agricultural and industrial status, Soviet grain purchases, and the home life of the ordinary Soviet citizen. According to the panel, Russia expected to catch up to American living standards in the next ten years. The panel made it clear that the Soviet Union was militarily strong, but desired peace. It became clearer as the discussion continued that the panel often misinterpreted statements by the audience. At length the panel became frustrated with the audience. They ended the session by saying: "We'll let history decide which form of government will survive—communism or capitalism." Later back on the bus, my entire group concurred that the experience had left an unpalatable taste in their mouths.

Some of the information the panel gave us follows: Education in the Soviet Union is compulsory for a period of ten years, and since 1930 the country has been completely literate. English is taught in the third year of school. There are presently over 60 million students in schools, five million of these in colleges and five million in technical schools (1976). Since education is free, the graduate must work for the government for a period of three years to repay his debt. At present the Soviet Union has trained one-fourth of the world's doctors. About 72 percent of all Soviet doctors are women. There is a shortage of manpower in Russia since twenty-two million people were lost during World War II. Women must take over many of the men's jobs, and over one-half of all women are employed. The average employee in the Soviet Union receives about 200 rubles a month, and there is no welfare or unemployment. There is a shortage of teachers in the U.S.S.R., and of the four million high school graduates each year, about one million go on to college and trade schools. Entrance exams for the colleges are very difficult.

There is no commercial television in the Soviet Union; it is financed by the state. Soviet television does not show commercials. Each republic has its own network, and Moscow has four channels. Soviet television is complimentary with the educational establishment, and television programs are broadcast in fifty-seven languages. About thirty U.S. programs are televised each year on Soviet channels. American movies shown on Russian television have included "Tootsie" and "Some Like It Hot."

A good place for lunch is the Aragvi Restaurant on Gorky Street. The Aragvi is a popular eating establishment whose specialty is Georgian cuisine. As always in a Russian restaurant, more food and drink keep coming. The most typical drinks are tea and vodka and the toast in Russian is "na zdorovie." Russian delicacies include black Beluga caviar and chicken Kiev. Caviar is the roe (eggs) of the female sturgeon acquired by pounding the ovaries of the fish and then straining the roe and other membraneous matter through a sieve. The roe is then salted for preservation. Pepper, onions, and other ingredients may be added. In the Soviet Union and other parts of Europe, caviar is a delicacy that is served as an hors d'oeuvre or appetizer. Most Russian caviar is prepared in the city of Astrakhan near the Caspian Sea. A little-known fact is that the word caviar is not of Russian derivation. It most likely stems from the Italian word *caviala*. The Italians were importing thousands of barrels of caviar by the seventeenth century.

Fresh fruit is not plentiful in Moscow and the northern Russian cities, especially in the winter. Only occasionally does one see imported oranges, bananas, and lemons during the winter. Both fruits and vegetables are usually seasonal items. Even their quantities are usually limited. In winter when one does find an item like tomatoes in a state store, the price may be twenty times or more that during the summer. It is not unusual to see lines of one hundred or more people queued up at a store waiting to purchase an item(s) that just became available. Queues are a way of life in the Soviet Union.

The Ararat is another expensive restaurant which has a cover charge. It specializes in Armenian cuisine. The Ararat is in reality a night club. The food and drink are excellent. The floor show is rich in variety; there is usually singing, dancing, a hat tumbler, magician, and a rope performer. After the floor show you will be served an excellent meal. The finest of crystal and linen are used for serving. Typical drinks include vodka, champagne, beer, and mineral water. A meal may consist of caviar, crepe suzettes, and a swiss steak with all the trimmings. The desert is usually ice cream. After dinner many dance to music played by a sixteen-piece Russian orchestra. Some of the music is distinctly American. Ararat seats 2,000 and reservations are required. Wedding receptions are commonly held at the Ararat.

Soviet women like to marry early if possible, usually before the age of twenty. The number of eligible women greatly exceeds the number of available men. This imbalance is due in part to World War II, but more recently the male death rate has been much higher than that of women. The prospects for marriage after age thirty are dim. The national divorce rate is high, about one in every three marriages, but in many of the larger cities, it is closer to fifty percent.

Alcoholism is a major problem in the Soviet Union. It is widespread and attributable to a large proportion of all crimes. Drunk drivers are also a factor. Do not attempt to take a picture of policemen arresting a drunk on the street. The purchase of vodka has been curtailed in recent years to reduce alcoholism. The sale of vodka is restricted generally to the hours between 9 a.m. and 4 p.m. Inebriated individuals can be encountered on the streets. A drunken Muscovite once came in from the rear entrance of our bus with a bottle of vodka. Our driver attempted to escort the old fellow off, but finally opted to take him where he wished to go.

Comparing Moscow with London, Paris, or New York in the way of excitement, entertainment, amusement, fashions, and attractions is ludicrous. One does not visit Moscow for these reasons. For the tourist, Russia is hollow in those sensations compared to their Western counterparts.

Prostitution is not very apparent on the streets of Moscow or other cities in Russia. However, in the hotel bars and bar/restaurants, the trade is practiced and visible. Tourists are often approached by women plying their trade in hotel bars in Moscow, Odessa, and other cities, and it is not uncommon to receive phone calls late at night in your hotel room from English-speaking women offering their services. Many of the women wish to make the acquaintance of foreigners in hope of a proposal of marriage.

Phone calls can be made into and out of the Soviet Union. A pay phone requires two kopecks, but in hotels the calls usually are free. Attempting to reach a Soviet citizen in another city may be difficult and require much patience and waiting on the part of the caller.

One of the standard tours of Moscow includes the Central Lenin Library, Novodevichy Convent, Lenin Stadium, Moscow University, and other sights. The Lenin Library is located just west of the Kremlin. It contains thirty million books, manuscripts, and other items. In the early 1970s the library was computerized to the extent that all new editions coming into it have been recorded on the computer's memory bank. In terms of its holdings, the library is the second largest in the world; only the U.S. Library of Congress exceeds it in size.

On a strip of land shaped like a finger near the central part of the city, and around which the Moskva River meanders, is located the Novodevichy Convent. This very beautiful convent looks like a fortress on approach. It is surrounded by a huge white wall that encloses about eight acres of ground. In the sixteenth and seventeenth centuries it was the southwest outpost of the city. The Novodevichy (New Maiden) Convent was founded in 1524 by Grand Duke Vasilli III to commemorate the liberation of Smolensk. The convent was rebuilt in 1685, but many of its former structures were left intact.

On its grounds stand the beautiful Cathedral of Our Lady of Smolensk in which Peter the Great's half-sister, Princess Sophia, and Peter's first wife are buried. The cathedral is capped with five golden cupolas. Peter had Sophia confined here in 1689 to become a nun. Outside her window the *Streltzi* were hung as she was forced to observe their execution.

The convent served as a political prison in tsarist times. The nuns in the convent came from royal families. Irene, daughter-in-law of Ivan the Terrible, and her brother, Boris Godunov, also spent time in Novodevichy. However, Boris stayed only briefly, leaving it to accept the crown as tsar.

On the ground of Novodevichy is the Bell Tower, a tall, red and white stone structure capped with one golden cupola. It is built in the baroque style. There is also one functioning church on the grounds, in which the metropolitan of Moscow (an archbishop) lives. The gateway to Novodevichy enters through the Transfiguration Church built in the seventeenth century. It has gilded domes that contrast with its red and white exterior decorations. The opening scene of the well-known play "Anna Karenina" depicts a skating scene on the pond beside Novodevichy.

A cemetery on the grounds of Novodevichy contains the graves of many famous artists, poets, writers, and dancers. Anton Chekhov, a famous Russian dramatist and short story writer and Maxim Gorky, another well-known writer, dramatist, and novelist are buried here. Nikita Khrushchev, Soviet premier from 1958–1964, is also buried in the cemetery. My guide explained the reason for his burial here was that he died out of office, and only those figures who died while in office are buried in the Kremlin wall.

In 1812 the French plundered the convent. It was declared a museum by the Soviet government in 1922. Many ancient icons can be seen in the old convent.

The tip of the land finger along the Moskva River is occupied by the Luzhniki Sports Complex and Lenin Central Stadium. This area was the site of the 1980 Olympics. The sports complex area houses over 130 facilities, and is located on about 4,500 acres of land. The Lenin stadium can accommodate 103,000 spectators, and the Luzhniki Sports Palace seats 17,000. An open-air swimming pool complete with grandstands is also located on the grounds of Luzhniki.

The Russians had to raise the level of the ground by five meters to build the Sports Complex. The area was originally a marsh or swamp. The new high-rise building located south of the sports stadium is the Academy of Science. Moscow is the Soviet Union's main scientific, cultural, and industrial center.

Opposite these features and across the Moskva River stand the Lenin Hills and Moscow State University. The Lenin Hills form the high right bank of the Moskva River and stand 655 feet in elevation. They provide a beautiful panorama of Moscow. These hills were formerly known as the Sparrows Hills. Their actual level above the river is only about 200 feet. The Lenin Hills were originally a hunting preserve for the tsars. Stretching from near the river back toward the university are over 100 acres of formal gardens. A huge, long sloping ski jump stands above the river and slopes down to it.

Moscow University was originally founded in 1755 by Mikhail Lomonosov, a noted Russian scientist. The central edifice of the university was a three-story structure built on stone foundations by Matvei Kazakov in 1793. An eight-column portico and a huge dome offset the building. During Napoleon's invasion in 1812 the university was burned. After Napoleon left the city, Kazakov's old building was restored by Gilardi to its present state. The old university building is located on Prospekt Marx near the Kremlin Wall. A newer building was added to the old university in 1836, and stands opposite the old university building. Other buildings were later built around the two original structures. In time, the old university and its site proved inadequate, so in the early 1950s the new university was built on the Lenin Hills by the architects Rudnev and Chernichev. Moscow University is the major university in the Soviet Union. The new university is outlined by its main building, a 32-story high structure, around which a complex of educational facilities are located. The buildings are spread over 700 acres. There are seventeen departments in Moscow University. There are dormitories for both students and faculty. It has the second largest library in Russia. Today, Moscow University has an enrollment of 32,000 students, most of who receive stipends from the state. About 2,000 foreign students attend Moscow university. Students at the university are paid 40 to 100 rubles each month depending on their grades. The students can also obtain grants.

There are 78 institutes of higher learning in Moscow, with a combined enrollment of over 700,000 students. In addition to Moscow University, there is also the well-known Patrice Lumumba University and its medical center. Many Third World students study at this university, which was opened in 1960.

Just beyond Moscow University, where the Lenin Hills run north along the Moskva River, is located the Holy Trinity Church. It was built in 1812 to commemorate victory over Napoleon. Nearby is Moscow Film Company, the largest in the Soviet Union.

A short distance further is located the "Battle of Borodino" Panorama Museum alongside Kutozov Prospekt. The main part of the museum is a huge, circular-shaped annex. The museum opened in 1962 and is dedicated to Russia's struggle with Napoleon during the 1812 invasion. Inside the museum is a huge battle-scene painting measuring 377 feet long and 49 feet high, depicting the intensity of the battle of Borodino. It was painted in 1912 by F. Rubo. The painting is so realistic in its portrayal of the battle that one stands in awe before it and feels like a participant in the carnage that is unfolded. With a bit of imagination, I could almost hear the musical crescendo of Tchaikovsky's *Overture 1812* in the background.

The battle of Borodino was fought September 7, 1812, on a hilly landscape surrounding the village of Borodino, located about eighty miles southwest of Moscow. The legendary Russian general Kutuzov attempted to halt Napoleon's advance on Moscow with a major defensive effort. In the course of the daylong battle there were intense artillery duels, cavalry charges, and assaults by formations of thousands of infantry. The battlefield resounded with the massive fire of hundreds of cannons. Deafening explosions, fires, and clouds of smoke permeated the landscape. When the Russians finally withdrew, the sanguinary battlefield was littered with over 70,000 killed and wounded soldiers. Both sides claimed victory in the savage battle. A large monument now stands on the battlefield, and nearby is a military-historical museum. Tourists can arrange for a visit to Borodino, but this should be done at the earliest opportunity.

Another legendary name in Russia is that of Leo Tolstoy. Tours are commonly made to his estate in Moscow. Separated from it by a few blocks is the Tolstoy Museum. Tolstoy is regarded by many as Russia's greatest novelist.

Count Leo Tolstoy was born of parents of nobility in 1828 at Yasnaya Polyana, the family estate located about 125 miles southwest of Moscow. He spent most of his life on the estate, but before he became celebrated for his literary achievements, he preferred the social life of Moscow. Privately tutored at an early age, he later studied at the University of Kazan. After several years there the studies bored him, so he returned to his estate and attempted unsuccessfully to manage it. In 1852 he joined the army and fought bravely against rebellious tribes in the Caucasus Mountains. The same year he had published in a magazine his first literary work, *Detstvo* (Childhood). From 1854–56 he fought in the Crimean War at the siege of Sevastopol. Between 1857 and 1861 he traveled widely in Western Europe, and in 1862 was married and settled on his estate. His wife bore him nine children while he wrote his two most noted works, *War and Peace* during the 1860s and *Anna Karenina* during the 1870s. His profound sympathy for the lot of the peasants ultimately led him to conversion to Christ. He then adopted a simple life, lived like a peasant, and became a philanthropist. His family deplored his new lifestyle, and finally when he saw no chance of reconciling with them, he fled from his home at age 82 seeking a sanctuary in which to meditate and live a simple existence. Traveling by train he died several days later in Ryazan province. It was November 1910, the Russian air was cold and windy, and at the small, secluded railway town of Astapovo he succumbed to pneumonia. He was later buried on his former estate at Yasnaya Polyana. The estate is now a museum, located amidst 860 acres of woods, gardens, and fields. The Germans occupied it in 1941 and burnt Tolstoy's bedroom and many of the furnishings of his house. The large two-story house has since been restored. Some of its original furnishings can still be seen, including the two pianos that Tolstoy often played.

Don't miss a journey into the environs of Moscow to visit the museum-estate of Arkhangelskoye, located about fourteen miles northwest of Moscow. The palace was designed by a French architect on the estate of Prince Yusupov (1751–1831), a wealthy landowner in tsarist Russia. He was a politician, traveler, director of crown lands, president of the College of Manufacturers, and governor of the Kremlin. The prince had an eye for beautiful women and lived in extravagance. The exterior of his palace is finished in yellow stucco with a green roof, while its interior is elegantly designed in eighteenth- and nineteenth-century wooden architecture. From the ground level a long tier of steps leads up past stately colonnades that surround the front entrance of the palace. The rooms and gallery inside contain paintings, some by the celebrated Flemish painter Van Dyke, fine porcelain, sculptures, and tapestries. Winding hallways and staircases lead to the gallery. Prince Yusupov kept cages of parrots and exotic birds in the palace. Some of the original glassware and china made on the estate is also on exhibit. Surrounding the palace is a magnificent park complex. A serf theater is found in the park. Skilled serfs were often superb artists and intricate wood-carvers. Their work can be seen in many of the buildings and architecture surrounding Moscow. The park on which the estate is built contains many pavilions and sculptures. It slopes down to the Moskva River.

In the southern suburbs of Moscow is located Kolomenskoye, a former country estate built in the sixteenth and seventeenth centuries. Kolomenskoye, however, dates from the fourteenth century. It is easily reached in less than an hour's ride from downtown Moscow. This estate was used as a summer residence by the tsars. It is now a museum. Located on the estate is the Ascension (Vozneseniya) Church built in 1532. The stone church is topped by a tall, single dome which is shaped in the appearance of a tent, and is an example of the type of old Russian architecture known as the "tent" style. It was the first church in Russia with a stone dome.

Another old church on the former estate is that of St. John the Baptist, built in the sixteenth century. Ruins of an old palace date from the seventeenth century. Other palaces and churches built on the estate have long since disappeared. Still visible, however, is a tower brought to the estate from Bratsky prison, and Peter the Great's log house which once stood in Archangel. Art exhibitions on the estate display ceramics, woodcarvings, metalwork, icons, and Russian tiles.

Fans of the great classical composers should take the time to visit the town of Klin, located fifty miles northwest of Moscow on the Leningrad Highway. It was in Klin that the great Russian composer Peter Ilyich Tchaikovsky lived and composed many of his noted masterpieces. He was the first Russian composer to gain international fame, and is regarded as the most famous of all Russia's composers.

Tchaikovsky (1840–1893) was born in Votkinsk, studied jurisprudence in St. Petersburg until age nineteen, then became a clerk there in a government office. He later entered the St. Petersburg Conservatory to study music, and after graduation accepted the post of professor of music in Moscow Conservatory. For the next twelve years he intensively devoted his talent to composing music. His first great orchestral masterpiece, *Romeo and Juliet* (1869), was finished by age thirty.

Tchaikovsky was a homosexual but in 1877 married a student from the conservatory who greatly admired him. The marriage caused him considerable mental torment and within a few weeks of his wedding he attempted suicide by wading in the icy water of the Moskva River. He was spared from death but left Moscow for St. Petersburg, where he divorced his wife.

In St. Petersburg a rich widow, Madame von Meck, came to adore Tchaikovsky's music and became his benefactor for many years. Meanwhile, Tchaikovsky became famous abroad, and visited the United States in 1891. He gave a series of concerts in New York, Philadelphia, and Baltimore, and visited Washington and other cities. His last monumental work, *Pathetique,* was conducted in 1893. He died the same year from cholera at age fifty-three.

Tchaikovsky adored Russian folk music, but borrowed from French, German, and Italian works for his own musical compositions. He lived and composed at a time known as the Romantic period in music, which lasted from about 1820–1900. Romantic music is known for its great variety, richness, colorful harmony, and expressive tone color. Romantic composers were greatly influenced by nationalism and incorporated its emotionalism into their musical works. Tchaikovsky's *Romeo and Juliet* and *Overture 1812* evoke strong mood, emotion, and fervor. Other musical scores of his include *Swan Lake* (1876), *Sleeping Beauty* (1889), and *The Nutcracker* (1892).

Tchakovsky's house at Klin became a state museum in 1921. He spent considerable time in Klin between 1885 and 1893, and composed his Third Piano Concerto, Sixth Symphony, *Sleeping Beauty,* and *The Nutcracker* while in this town. At his house-museum, one can listen to records of his performances. Each May 7 and November 6 his works are performed in his house-museum by some of Russia's best pianists.

Klin is an ancient town located on the Sestra River and dates back to 1234. In World War II the Germans occupied the town, but the Russians had removed all valuable items from Tchaikovsky's house. These were returned after the Nazis left and the Russians reopened his museum in 1945. Tchaikovsky's house-museum is a two-story wooden frame building with an attic as a third-level. A porch supported by pillars extends outward over the front entrance. The museum contains Tchaikovsky's desk at which he wrote some of his works, his books, paintings, grand piano, death mask, suitcases, trunks, diairies, letters, and other personal belongings.

Other interesting features in Klin include the sixteenth-century Assumption (Uspensky) Monastery and the Church of the Resurrection with a tent-style belfry built in the eighteenth century.

One might wish to choose from several other itineraries that are offered by Intourist to surrounding areas of Moscow. One frequently chosen by tourists is the journey to Vladimir and its neighboring town of Suzdal. Vladimir is located on the Gorky Highway, a little less than half the distance between Moscow and Gorky. Another popular itinerary takes tourists to Zagorsk, the present ecclesiastical center of Russian Orthodoxy, located about forty-five miles northeast of Moscow on the Yaroslavl Highway. Zagorsk and Russian Orthodoxy will be the subject of another chapter.

Vladimir, located about 130 miles east-northeast of Moscow, was founded in 1108 by Prince Vladimir Monomachus. The grand princes who succeeded Vladimir lived in the city until 1328, when Grand Prince Ivan Kalita moved his residence to Moscow. The city lies in the coniferous forest belt stretching from the Gulf of Finland to the Ural Mountains and on across Siberia to the Pacific Ocean. Pine, spruce, and cedar trees surround the city, and lesser numbers of birch, poplar, and alder can be seen. Vladimir is built on a tributary of the Oka River known as the Kliazma. It was this city in which

Prince Vladimir chose to built a fortress to defend the surrounding territory against Tartar raids. The fortress, and later the city, was given the name Vladimir in honor of its founder. Vladimir was founded before Moscow. Today the city is the site of a huge tractor factory and machine-tool plants. The population of Vladimir is over 300,000.

The city became the seat of the Vladimir-Suzdal Principality in 1157. Tartar hordes invaded it in 1238. During the twelfth and thirteenth centuries a number of beautiful churches were built in Vladimir. The period of their building is referred to as the Golden Age of architecture in Vladimir. The Russian metropolitans made it their seat of power in 1299, but by the mid-1300s Moscow had usurped its influence and became the dominant political center of Russia. Near the Klyazma River stand the ceremonial Golden Gates built in 1158–64 and rebuilt in the seventeenth and eighteenth centuries. The outstanding architectural monument of the city is the Cathedral of the Dormition, a white stone, five-domed church built in 1158. The original church was destroyed by fire in 1185, but was rebuilt by Prince Vesvolod III. The cathedral was used as a model in building the Assumption Cathedral in Moscow. It was damaged in the Tartar invasion of 1408 but Andrei Rublyov, the great icon painter, restored its beauty. Today it is a functioning cathedral.

Close to the Uspensky Cathedral is located the Cathedral of St. Dmitri built in 1194–97. About eight miles from Vladimir is the Church of the Intercession on the Nerl built in 1165 for Andrei Bogoliubsky. The ruins of his palace are also seen. It is a small, square-shaped, stone church with one cupola. The Byzantine influence can be seen in the building of these churches; however, their structural styles were modified from the earlier Byzantine designs to incorporate local adaptations. Stone replaced the familiar brick of the Byzantine churches, and changes were made in the domes, windows, and roofs to reflect the climatic conditions of the cold snowy Russian winters. The skills long developed by Russian serfs in wood carving and design also became a part of the character of Russian architecture.

About twenty-five miles north of Vladimir is the town of Suzdal. It is older than Vladimir, and mention of the town dates back to 1024. Suzdal has more than fifty relics of church and secular architecture built between the twelfth and eighteenth centuries. The Tartars burned the city in 1238. A masterpiece of architecture is the Cathedral of the Nativity of the Holy Virgin, built in 1225. It is located inside the Kremlin walls of the city. The cathedral is famous for its Golden Gates with their exquisite ornamental panels. Surrounding the cathedral is a group of buildings known as the Archbishop's Chambers. Nearby is the Church of St. Nicholas from Glotovo (1766), the

Church of the Dormition (1650), the Church of St. Nicholas (1739), and the Church of the Nativity of Christ (1775).

In another part of the Kremlin is the Church of the Resurrection (1732) and the nearby Church of Our Lady of Kazan (1739). Outside the Kremlin walls is the Monastery of the Deposition of the Virgin's Robe (1207), and the Pokrovsky (Intercession) Convent (1364). In the days of Imperial Russia a number of tsarinas were exiled to this convent and later buried there. Nearby this monastery is that of the well-known Spaso-Evfimiyevsky Monastery (fourteenth century) overlooking the Kamenka River. Leaving Suzdal, the road soon crests a hill and the city is gone from sight but not from memory.

Traveling through the streets of Moscow, one's nose detects the inescapable smell of gasoline. The odor seems ubiquitous. Russian vehicles are not stringently regulated by pollution-control devices and spew out a steady stream of smoke and obnoxious fuel odors. Commonly seen Russian-made cars include the Moskovich, Volga, and Zaporozhets. In Moscow it is possible to see perhaps a half dozen American cars on the streets, many of which receive a lot of close scrutiny by Muscovites.

Four ring roads encircle Moscow. More and more tourists visiting the Soviet Union find a motoring holiday a good way to see the country. (See Chapter 1, Introduction, for rules and regulations governing driving in the U.S.S.R.)

EXCURSIONS

General Sightseeing Tour of the City of Moscow (by bus, with a guide/interpreter; duration, 3 hours)

The route of this tour passes through the city's historical center as well as the new residential areas and parks. You will be able to have a close look at the architectural features of Red Square and see the Bolshoi Theatre; meanwhile your guide will tell you about the capital's cultural life. The bus will take you along Gorky Street (Ulitsa Gorkogo) to Garden Ring (Sandovoye Koltso) and then to Kalinin and Kutuzov Prospekts; then you will pass by the old walls of the Novodevichy Nunnery and more in the direction of Lenin Hills from where you will be thrilled by a splendid parorama of Moscow. Your final stop will be at the building of Moscow University on Lenin Hills.

Moscow, a City of Sport
(by bus, with a guide/interpreter; duration, 3 hours).

During this excursion you will learn about the development of sports in the U.S.S.R. and will see palaces of sports, stadiums, major sports complexes, the Olympic Village, and the Lenin Central Stadium in Luzhniki, where the opening and closing ceremonies of the 1980 Olympic Games were held.

Moscow's Architecture
(by bus, with a guide/interpreter; duration, 2.5 hours)

This excursion will give you an opportunity to see some unique monuments of old Russian and modern architecture in the city.

Moscow and Literary Culture
(by bus, with a guide/interpreter; duration, 2.5 hours).

This is a tour of memorable places linked with the lives and work of outstanding Russian and Soviet writers, as well as with the history of Russian and Soviet literature.

A Boat Trip on the Moskva River
(duration, 1 hour 10 minutes).

It begins on the pier near the Kiev Railway Station (Kievskaya Metro Station). Excursion boats start from the pier every thirty minutes. You will have a wonderful opportunity to see the embankments and bridges of the Moskva River and some of the city's architectural sights.

If you are free in the evening and would like to get to know Moscow better, Intourist invites you to a "Moscow in the Evening" tour (by bus with a guide/interpreter; duration, 3 hours).

The Moscow Kremlin
(by foot; duration, 2 hours).

The cathedrals and palaces of the Kremlin contain treasures of old art; its age-old walls have witnessed major events of Russian history. This excursion begins at Cathedral Square with its late fifteenth- and early sixteenth-century buildings, the Annunciation, Assumption, and Archangel Cathedrals, the Faceted Palace, the Bell Tower of Ivan the Great, and the Church of the Deposition of the Robe.

Organically integrated in the old architectural ensemble of the Kremlin is the Palace of Congresses, erected in 1961, where congresses of the Communist Party of the Soviet Union and other important meetings are held.

This excursion includes a tour of the Kremlin grounds, a visit to one of the cathedrals, and a close-up view of two remarkable specimens of Russian foundry work of the sixteenth to eighteenth centuries—the Tsar Cannon and the Tsar Bell.

You may also visit interesting museums of the Moscow Kremlin—the Church of the Deposition of the Robe and the Patriarch's Palace.

Around Red Square
(by foot; duration, 1.5 hours).

Facing the Kremln wall, Red Square is an inseparable component of the architectural ensemble of the Kremlin. Its history dates back to the fifteenth century.

On Red Square is the Lenin Mausoleum. (Foreign tourists may visit the mausoleum (check with Intourist for information about visiting hours).

In the south part of Red Square stands the exquisitely decorated Cathedral of the Intercession (better known as the Cathedral of St. Basil the Blessed, or St. Basil's Cathedral), a unique monument of the sixteenth century; facing it across the square from the north is the History Museum, built over a hundred years ago. Opposite the Kremlin and forming the eastern boundary of Red Square is the country's largest State Department Store (GUM).

Around Moscow Zaryadye
(by foot; duration, 2 hours).

One of the oldest districts of Moscow, Zaryadye (13 hectares in area) boasts a whole collection of architectural monuments of the sixteenth to nineteenth centuries. Together they comprise a unique open-air museum of old Russian architecture.

The U.S.S.R. Economic Achievement Exhibition (VDNKh)
(by bus, with a guide/interpreter; duration, 3 hours).

The numerous pavilions of VDNKh are set amidst greenery, flowers, and fountains. We recommend that you begin your tour of the exhibition grounds with a general sightseeing ride in the minibus taxi, and then visit the pavilions which most interest you, perhaps, "Education in the U.S.S.R.," "Soviet Culture," "Atomic Energy," and "Health." You will certainly want to visit the "Cosmos" pavilion, whose exhibits include mock-ups of the artificial earth satellites, spaceships and Luna-probes.

The Russian Winter Festival is held on the VDNKh grounds between December 25 and January 5, featuring concerts, popular games, and troika sleigh rides.

VDNKh is open daily. The VDNKh Metro Station is near the main entrance to the Exhibition.

A Tour of the Moscow Metro (duration, 1 hour) will acquaint you with one of the world's most beautiful and convenient underground transportation networks. Many stations of the Moscow Metro are decorated with mosaics, sculptures, and stained-glass panels.

Museums

The Central Lenin Museum (2 Ploshchad Revolyutsii). More than 45 million people from 111 countries of the world have visited this museum since its opening in 1936. Carefully preserved in the Museum's 34 halls are Lenin's works and personal belongings, historical party documents, photographs, books.

The museum is open daily, except Mondays: from 11 a.m. to 7 p.m. on Tuesdays, Wednesdays, and Thursdays, and from 10 a.m. to 5 p.m. on Fridays, Saturdays and Sundays. Admission is free.

The Central Museum of the Soviet Armed Forces (2 Ploshchad Kommuny). Exhibits at this museum deal with the history of the Soviet Armed Forces, tell about the courage and heroism the Soviet people displayed in defending the revolutionary gains and in the struggle against the Nazi aggression. Films about the Great Patriotic War (1941–1945) are shown in the museum.

The Museum is open from 10 a.m. to 5 p.m. (on Wednesdays and Thursdays from noon to 7 p.m.). It is closed on Mondays and on the second and last Tuesday of each month.

The Tretyakov Art Gallery (10 Lavrushinsky Pereulok). A depository of works of Russian national art from the eleventh century to the present. The gallery's collection includes 40,000 canvases, drawings, and sculptures by Russian and Soviet artists. The gallery was founded by Pavel Tretyakov (1832–1898), an eminent figure in Russian cultural life.

The gallery is open from 10 a.m. to 7 p.m., daily, except Mondays.

The Pushkin Museum of Fine Arts (12 Ulitsa Volkhonka). The stocks of this museum contain fabulous collections of Babylonian and Egyptian art, of classical Greek and Roman art, and of eighteenth to twentieth century Western European paintings.

The museum is open daily from 10 a.m. to 8 p.m. (on Sundays to 6 p.m.), except Mondays.

The Donskoy Monastery (1 Donskaya Ploshchad). This monastery is a remarkable example of sixteenth to nineteenth century architecture, and a historical monument. You can see some fine specimens of Russian memorial sculpture and works of Russian icon painters in the monastery.

The monastery is open from 10 a.m. to 6 p.m. daily, except Mondays, Fridays, and the last Thursday of each month.

The Karl Marx and Friedrich Engels Museum (5 Ulitsa Marksa i Engelsa). The exhibits include documents, works, photographs, and personal belongings of Karl Marx and Friedrich Engels.

The museum is open on Tuesdays, Wednesdays, and Fridays from noon to 7 p.m., and on Thursdays, Saturdays, and Sundays from 11 a.m. to 6 p.m. It is closed on Mondays and on the last day of each month.

The Museum of the History of the Young Communist League and Youth of Krasnaya Presnya (32 Bolshaya Gruzinskaya Ulitsa).

The museum is open from 11 a.m. to 6 p.m. daily, except Sundays.

The Novodevichy Nunnery Museum (1 Novodevichy Proyezd). This is an architectural ensemble of the sixteenth and seventeenth centuries. Most of its buildings are in the Moscow Baroque style.

The museum is open from 10 a.m. to 5 p.m. daily, except Tuesdays and the first Monday of each month.

The Cathedral of the Intercession (St. Basil's Cathedral) Museum (Red Square).
The museum is open from 9:30 a.m. to 5 p.m. daily, except Tuesdays and the first Monday of each month.

The Zaryadye Chambers of the 16th–17th Centuries (10 Ulitsa Razina).
The museum is open from 10 a.m. to 5 p.m. daily, except Tuesdays and the first Monday of each month.

The Church of the Trinity in Nikitniki, A museum of seventeenth-century architecture and painting. (3 Nikitnikov Pereulok).
The museum is open from 10 a.m. to 5 p.m. daily, except Tuesdays and the first Monday of each month.

The Andrei Rubylov Museum of Early Russian Art (10 Ploshchad Pryamikova). This museum has on display the rarest works of early Russian painting—icons of the fifteenth to seventeenth centuries, including master-pieces by Andrei Rubylov and Dionisius. A special program under the title "Architecture, Painting, Music" is organized at the museum by Intourist in the summer.
The museum is open from 11 a.m. to 6 p.m. daily, on Mondays and Tuesdays from 1 p.m. to 8 p.m., except Wednesdays and the last Friday of each month.

The Museum of Folk Art (7 Ulitsa Stanislavskogo). This museum has a fine collection of handicraft wares and works of peasant folk art beginning with the seventeenth century. The exhibits include works by the famous painters of Palekh, Mserta, and Fedoskino, as well as by Zagorsk carvers and Vologda lacemakers.
The museum is open from 11 a.m. to 5 p.m. daily, except Mondays.

The Museum of Oriental Art (16 Ulitsa Obukha). On display here are outstanding works of art created by the peoples of the Soviet East and Oriental countries. Among the exhibits are one of the world's finest collections of Japanese miniature sculptures, Iranian rugs, and Turkish brocade.
The museum is open from 11 a.m. to 7 p.m daily, except Mondays.

The Ostankino Palace and Museum of Serf Art (5 Pervaya Ostankinskaya Ulitsa). The museum has rich collections of paintings, sculptures, prints, and porcelain (some two thousand exhibits altogether). The central section of the palace is an eighteenth-century theatre.

The museum is open May 15 through September 14 from 10 a.m. to 6 p.m.; September 15 through May 14 from 10 a.m. to 3 p.m. Closed on Tuesdays and Wednesdays.

The Kolomenskoye Estate Museum (Kolomenskaya Metro Station, 31 Proletarsky Prospekt). Kolomenskoye is the site of one of the first tent-shaped stone churches built in Russia, the famous Church of the Ascension of Christ (sixteenth century). Other exhibits include genuine early Russian wooden structures and precious collections of Russian tiles and seventeenth-century icons.

The museum is open from 1 p.m. to 8 p.m. on Wednesdays and Thursdays, and from 11 a.m. to 6 p.m. on Fridays, Saturdays and Sundays. Closed on Mondays and Tuesdays.

The Kuskovo Estate and the Ceramics Museum (2 Ulitsa Yunoski). This magnificant eighteenth-century architectural ensemble is situated in a large park with fanciful rotundas and pavilions. The museum has a fabulous collection of Russian porcelain and antique ceramics, as well as Chinese, Danish, English, and French majolica, pottery, and glass. The museum is open April 1 through September 30 from 11 a.m. to 7 p.m.; on Saturdays and Sundays from 10 a.m. to 6 p.m.; October 1 through March 31 from 10 a.m. to 5 p.m.; on Saturdays and Sundays from 10 a.m. to 4 p.m. Closed on Mondays, Tuesdays, and the last Wednesday of each month.

While in Moscow, you can also visit theatrical and music museums, such as the Bakhrushin Theatrical Museum (31/12 Ulitsa Bakhrushina) and the Glinka Central Museum of Musical Culture (4 Ulitsa Fadeyeva).

Intourist also suggests you visit Moscow's memorial museums. You will have an opportunity to see the homes of celebrated personalities in the fields of art, culture, and science, and learn about their work.

OUT-OF-TOWN EXCURSIONS

Gorki Leninskiye (35 km. from Moscow by bus). The Lenin Memorial Museum is housed in the mansion where from 1918 the leader of the revolution frequently stayed and where he lived from May 1923 until his death in January 1924. Everything at Gorki has been kept as it was during V.I. Lenin's lifetime. The museum is open from 10 a.m. to 5 p.m. daily, except Tuesdays and the last day of each month. Duration of the excursion, 4 hours.

The Arkhangelskoye Estate is an architectural monument of the eighteenth and nineteenth centuries set in picturesque surroundings 16 km. from Moscow. The park, sloping down to the Moskova River, is embellished with decorative stairways, pavilions, and sculptures. Near the museum is a restaurant offering an extensive selection of Russian cuisine.

The museum is open May 3 through September 30 from 10 a.m. to 5 p.m.; October 1 through April 30 from 11 a.m. to 3 p.m. Closed on Mondays, Tuesdays and the last Friday of each month. Duration of the excursion, 4 hours.

The Abramtsevo Estate (62 km. from Moscow) was a meeting place for such prominent figures in Russian cultural life as Sergei Aksakov, Mikolai Gogol, Ivan Turgenev, Viktor Vasnetsov, Valentin Serov, Ilya Repin, and Mikhail Vrubel. Fyodor Chaliapin took part in amateur theatrical performances staged at Abramtsevo.

The museum is open daily from 11 a.m. to 5 p.m. Closed on Mondays and Tuesdays. Duration of the excursion, 5 hours.

The Zagorsk History and Art Museum-Preserve (71 km. from Moscow). The museum contains magnificent relics of Russian culture of the fourteenth to eighteenth centuries. The Troitse-Sergiyeva Lavra (Trinity Monastery of St. Sergius), built in the 1340s, played a major role in the history of Moscow and the Russian state.

The museum is open from 10 a.m. to 5 p.m., except Mondays and Tuesdays. Duration of the excursion to Zagorsk, about 7 hours.

Also at Zagorsk is the Museum of Toys.

On the way to Zagorsk, 43 km. from Moscow, is the Russkaya Skazka (Russian Fairy Tale) restaurant where you can have a delicious lunch.

Pyotr Tchaikovsky Memorial Mansion in Klin (84 km. from Moscow). This was the home of the great Russian composer Pyotr Tchaikovsky.

The museum is open from 10 a.m. to 6 p.m. daily, except Wednesdays and Thursdays. The excursion to Klin takes about 7 hours.

Lev Tolstoy Yasnaya Polyana Estate (200 km. from Moscow). The great Russian writer Lev Tolstoy was born and spent most of his life at Yasnaya Polyana, and is buried there.

The museum is open from 9 a.m. to 5 p.m. daily, except Mondays and Tuesdays. The excursion to Yanaya Polyana takes 12 hours.

Excursions to the Moscow countryside should be booked, preferably well in advance, through the Service Bureau in your hotel.

THEATERS

Moscow has some forty theaters and concert halls. Here are some of them:

The Bolshoi Theatre. (Its opera and ballet productions are famous the world over. Address: 2 Ploshchad Sverdlova (Ploshchad Sverdlova, Ploshchad Revolyuitsli, Prospekt Marksa Metro Stations)

The Kremlin Palace of Congresses. (Gala concerts, performances by the Bolshoi troupe, and concerts by the country's best variety companies are held in the Palace. Address: The Kremlin (entrance through the Trinity Tower gates).

The Stanislovsky and Nemirovich Danchenko Musical Theatre. The second opera house in Moscow. Operas, ballets, and musical comedies by Russian, Soviet, and foreign composers are staged at this theater. Address: 17 Pushkinskaya Ulitsa (Pushkinskaya or Ploshchad Sverdiova Metro Stations).

The Central Puppet Theatre. Directed by Sergei Obraztsov. Children and grown-ups alike love its puppet shows. Here children find themselves in the wonderful world of fairy tales, meet their favorite characters, and enjoy the performances to the utmost. Address: 3 Sandovaya-Samotechnaya Ulitsa (Kolkhoznaya Metro Station).

The Moscow Circus. Performances are held on two arenas: 17 Prospekt Vernadskogo and 13 Tsvetnoi Boulevard.

The Large Hall of the Moscow Conservatoire. (13 Ulitsa Gertsena).

The Tchaikovsky Concert Hall. (20 Ploshchad Mayakovskogo).

Central State Concert Hall. (Hotel Russia, 6 Ulitsa Rzina). A cultural center for foreign tourists has been organized in this concert hall. Lectures, talks and other events are held at the center during the day to acquaint guests with the Soviet way of life; in the evening, choreographic and folk groups as well as famous Soviet actors perform on its stage. In summer the cultural center is open daily, except Fridays; in winter, on Mondays only.

Evening performances in all Moscow theaters begin at 7 p.m.; matinees, at 12 noon. Concert and circus shows begin at 7:30 p.m.

For information concerning the repertoire of Moscow theaters as well as tickets and transportation arrangements, apply to the Service Bureau at your hotel.

HOTELS

Hotel	Address	Rooms	Telephone
Belgrade	5 Smolensk St.	921	248-6692
			248-6843
Berlin	5 Zhdanov St.	90	225-6910
			225-6901
Bucharest	1 Balchug St.	210	233-1005
			23-2436
Intourist	3-5 Gorky St.	466	203-0131
			203-4008
Cosmos	150 Peace Ave.	1,777	217-0892
			217-0785
Leningradskaya	21/40 Kalanchevskaya St.	400	228-3401
			228-1108
Minsk	22 Gorky St.	300	299-1216
			299-1214
Metropole	1 Marx Avenue	344	225-6673
			228-0716
Mozhaiskya	165 Mozhaisk Hwy.	153	447-3435
			447-3434
National	14/1 Marx Ave.	205	203-6539
			203-5566
Ostankino	29 Botanicheskaya St.	968	219-4526
			291-4539
Rossiya	6 Razin St.	1,000	298-5410
			298-1753
Sevastopol	la Bolshaya	726	119-6450
			119-0567

Tsentralnaya	10 Gorky St.	140	229-2887
			229-8957
Ukraine	2/1 Futuzov St.	625	243-3021
			243-3095

RESTAURANTS AND BARS

Menus at Intourist restaurants in the U.S.S.R. are printed in Russian and foreign languages. Prices are quoted in rubles. Travelers may pay for "a la carte" meals at Intourist restaurants in foreign currency.

Some of Moscow's more popular restaurants with their national cuisine are listed below:

Aragvi (6 Gorky St.)—Georgian cuisine
Arbat (Kalinin Prospect and Sandovaya St.)—Russian cuisine, floor show
Arkanselskoje (Arkhangelskoje Estate)—Russian cuisine
Baku (24 Gorky St.)—Azerbaidzhan cuisine
Budapest (2 Petrovskie Linii)—Hungarian cuisine
Centralny (10 Gorky St.)—Russian cuisine
Intourist, "Skazka" Hall (3/5 Gorky St.)—Russian cuisine, floor show, discotheque, Russian folk ensemble
Metropol, "Russkaya Chainaya" Hall (1 Marx Prospekt)—Russian cuisine, Russian folk ensemble
Peking (1 Bolshaya Sandovaya St.)—Chinese cuisine
Praga (2 Arbat St.)—Czech cuisine
Rusj (Saltykovskaya)—Russian cuisine
Russian Hut (Ilyinskoye)—Russian cuisine
Seventh Heaven (Ostankino Tower)—Russian cuisine
Slavyansky Bazaar (Street of October 25)—Russian cuisine
Sofia (32 Gorky St.)—Bulgarian cuisine
Uzebekistan (29 Neglinnaya St.)—Uzbek cuisine
Ukraina (Tarasa Shevchenko Nab.)—Ukrainian cuisine
Vilnius (12 Butlerova St.)—Lithuanian cuisine

PUBLIC TRANSPORT SERVICES

The Metro, or subway system, is open from 6 a.m. to 1 a.m. The fare is five kopecks (about 1.4 cents in U.S. currency—there are 100 kopecks in a ruble). The subway system, or Metro, carries over 7 million passengers daily.

The trolley bus system carries passengers from 6 a.m. to 1 a.m. The fare is five kopecks. This system can carry up to 2.1 million passengers daily.

The bus system operates from 6 a.m. to 1 a.m. and charges a fare of five kopecks. It carries 5.4 million passengers each day.

Streetcars run from 5:30 a.m. until 1 a.m. Fare is 5 kopecks. About 1.4 million passengers ride streetcars daily.

Express minibuses (vans that carry eleven passengers) operate on regular routes from 7 a.m. to 8 p.m. They will stop anywhere along their routes and charge 15 kopecks for a ride. Minibuses carry about 150,00 passengers daily.

Taxis operate around the clock. Their fare is 20 kopecks a kilometer, plus 20 kopecks from time of pickup. About 600,000 passengers ride taxis daily in Moscow.

Chapter II.
ZAGORSK
Orthodoxy and Religion

Any notion of a Lord God,
even any trifling with a Lord God
is an unspeakable abomination.
—Lenin

This chapter on religion in the Soviet Union became part of the narrative of this book for several reasons: (1) to explain to the reader how Zagorsk, the present ecclesiastical center of the Russian Orthodox church, came to possess its present religious importance; (2) to further inform the reader of the importance of religion in helping to shape the historical genesis of the Russian people and their country (this is to some extent discussed in Chapter 6); and (3) to provide the layman with a general knowledge of the status of religion in the Soviet Union today. The author has attempted to accomplish these objectives without writing a scholarly analysis on the subject of religion but, rather, by providing the reader and layman with an insight and appreciation of its background and relevance in order to better know Russia. The tourist does not need to read a dozen or more books on Russia to understand the excitement and exhilaration he feels when looking at the landscape, its churches, and other features. The average tourist is looking for a shortcut, not a dissertation, to explain the phenomena he is observing and photographing for the folks back home. It is with this idea in mind that this chapter is written, and indeed this book.

The city of Zagorsk (Sergiev prior to 1930) is located about 45 miles northeast of Moscow on the Yaroslavl Highway. Zagorsk has a population of about 110,000 people and has long been revered as a site of pilgrimages. It was formed as a town in 1919 when several local villages and settlements were combined. In 1930 its name (Sergiev) was changed to Zagorsk to honor Vladimir Zagorsky, an important Communist party official. At first glance Zagorsk looks like a setting for a Hollywood movie. Russian filmmakers, aware of its aesthetics, have filmed many episodes in the city. The ancient walls and cathedrals of the city stand as solemn reminders of the past. Today Zagorsk is the ecclesiastical center of Russian Orthodoxy and contains significant architectural, historical, and religious works. Lack of attention has cost Zagorsk some of its beauty. Nevertheless, its golden and multicolored onion-shaped domes form an ensemble which is still sufficient to make the city one of the most notable examples of ecclesiastical architecture in the Soviet Union.

Zagorsk was founded in 1337 by the monk Sergius, who built the Trinity Monastery on its site. In 1391 the Tartars invaded the town and destroyed the monastery. In 1422 the abbot Nikon rebuilt the monastery (Troitse-Sergieva Lavra) on the site where Sergius had erected his wooden monastery. The Trinity (Troitsky) Cathedral was built from 1422–42, and the remains of St. Sergius were placed in a silver sarcophagus inside this cathedral. The cathedral and its sarcophagus are a favorite visiting site of tourists and pilgrims to Zagorsk. Sergius helped to rouse the Russians and Grand Prince Dmitri against the Tartars. The monastery played a major role in the economic and political life of the Muscovite region of Russia, while the church helped to forge Russian national unity. The Orthodox church canonized Sergius as a saint for his contributions to the church.

A high stone wall was built around the monastery between 1540 and 1550. Its walls helped the town to withstand a siege lasting 16 months by the Polish army in 1608–09. The monastery covers about 27 acres within its walls.

The Assumption (Uspensky), another well-known cathedral in Zagorsk, was dedicated in 1585 to observe the conquest of the Tartar cities of Astrakhan and Kazan. Ivan the Terrible ordered the building of this cathedral, which has five blue domes and displays golden stars and crosses on its onion-shaped domes. Tsar Boris Godunov and his wife are entombed outside the west door of Assumption Cathedral.

Between the fourteenth and seventeenth centuries the Trinity and St.

Sergius Monastery became significant cultural and artistic centers. Rublyov and Dionysius, two famous icon painters, applied their artistic talents to the vestry and walls of the monastery. During the eighteenth century, paintings by Russian artists were added to the collection of the monastery. Other works of applied art in the monastery include embroidery; bone, wood, and stone carvings; and papier-mâché paintings.

Another celebrated church inside the monastic walls of Zagorsk is the Smolensky Church. Built from 1746–48, this church acquired its name from its famous icon "Our Lady of Smolensk." An older church is the Church of the Descent of the Holy Spirit, built from 1476–77. Other churches on the grounds of Zagorsk include the Gateway and the Church of St. Nikon. One can also see St. Sergius's Well, the Belfry (eighteenth century), and the Refectory (seventeenth century).

Zagorsk is also the residence of the patriarch or head of the Russian Orthodox church. In addition, the monastery houses the Moscow Theological Academy and Seminary which turns out priests, teachers, and prelates for the church. At any one time, as many as several hundred seminarians and 100 academicians may be studying at Zagorsk. Hundreds of other persons annually take correspondence courses in theology from the Zagorsk seminary. Still these numbers are insufficient to offset the shortage of ecclesiastical personnel in Russia. The Russian church does have other monasteries that belong to it and some of these also have seminaries. Church property is no longer taxed by the government, but this is still a far cry from the past when Zagorsk alone counted a million serfs under its control.

By faith most of the people of Russia belong to what was once a part of the Greek church. The Russian branch of the Greek church has been independent of the main Greek body since the sixteenth century. Russian culture owes much of its distinctiveness to Orthodox Christianity. The Orthodox church formulated the early Russian models of artistic expression and the genre of its religious subjects basic to the unity of modern Russian culture. Indeed, it was not the theology of Christianity which drew the early Russians to its fold, but in large measure the beauty and sensation of its liturgy that had a charismatic appeal to the Russians. The sermons of the Orthodox church, the majestic garments worn by its clergy, and the beautiful icons, mosaics, and frescoes were further forms of artistic embellishment which appealed to the Russians.

In 988 Prince Vladimir and the pagan Russians of Kiev were converted to Christianity. With the conversion of Vladimir, Christianity became the state religion of Kiev. The form of Christianity adopted by the Kievans was that of the Byzantine or Orthodox form. Thus, Christianity was imported by the Russians from Constantinople.

The Russian church was the inheritor of Byzantium's legacy. Greek influence was transmitted by the church. Ironically, even when the Kievan state was subordinate to Constantinople, the church represented Russian national unity or at least the foundation of political thought in Russia.

In spite of their adoption of the Greek religion, not all matters went smoothly between the Russians and Greeks. A thorny issue which developed between them stemmed from authority over the Russian church. Since the Russians had adopted their religion from the Byzantine Greeks, it stood to reason that the patriarch of Constantinople was the ecclesiastical authority to direct the affairs of the church in Russia. On the other hand, Prince Vladimir, the ruler of Kievan Russia and a recent convert to Christianity along with his subjects of Kiev, believed that the metropolitan chosen to head the Russian church should be a Russian subject selected for his position by the ruling head of the Russian state. The issue of the nationality of the metropolitan was resolved when Iarosalv, Vladimir's son, conceded in 1037 that the patriarch of Constantinople could select and consecrate the metropolitan head of the Russian church; however, the Russian rulers claimed authority to choose the bishops and lesser ecclesiastical officials which the metropolitan assigned to posts in Russia. The Russians remained under the authority of Constantinople until its fall to the Turks in 1453. More than 130 years later, in 1589, the Russian bishops declared their independence from the Greek patriarchate. After 1589 the Russians selected their own patriarchs; presided over their bishops; built their own churches, monasteries, and convents; chose their angels and saints; and formulated their own adaptations of Byzantine art.

An account of Christianity in Russia must make mention of two "apostles of the Slavs" born in northern Greece in the ninth century. These two apostles and brothers were the Saints Cyril (b. 827) and Methodius (b. 825) from the city of Thessalonica. They spoke many tongues and were renowned scholars and theologians. Both traveled widely and in 860 they preached Christianity to the Khazars in the Black Sea area of southern Russia. In 862 the patriarch of Constantinople sent them on a mission to Moravia to bring Christianity to its Slavic inhabitants. As proficient linguists, the brothers used the Slavic tongue in liturgy, and invented a Slavic alphabet based on Greek letters that enabled them to translate the Holy Scriptures into the Slavic language. This alphabet eventually became known as the Cyrillic alphabet, taking its name from St. Cyril. Both brothers played a prominent role in bringing the Orthodox faith and liturgy to the southern Slavs, and were canonized as saints by the Eastern church. It is through the Cyrillic alphabet that most of the Slavic languages are usually communicated.

Through the efforts of Cyril and Methodius, the Orthodox faith and liturgy spread through the Balkans before making its way into Russia and Kiev. The Cyrillic alphabet helped to mold the thoughts, faith, and language of the southern Slavs and Russians to a degree of unity that they had previously lacked. Byzantine liturgy helped to transform the Russian mind and civilize its pagan tribes. When the Cyrillic alphabet reached Kiev, it enabled the Russians to translate and write Byzantine liturgy, and provided them with a literary *lingua franca.* Great Russian, Ukrainian, and Byelorussian are all written in the Cyrillic alphabet.

Michael (d. 991), the first metropolitan or head of the Russian church, preached Christianity in both the countryside around Kiev and within the city. He visited villages and towns, preached to and baptized their inhabitants, and later journeyed to northern Russia to spread the faith of Christianity to Novgorod and Rostov, cities located northwest and northeast, respectively, of present-day Moscow. Prince Vladimir also did his share of spreading Christianity beyond Kiev. He traveled to Volhynia to bring the faith to its people, and dispatched his sons to Smolensk, Lutsk, Polatsk, Tmutarakan, Pskov and other cities to convert their peoples. For his efforts in spreading Christianity, the Russian Orthodox church canonized Vladimir, making him a saint.

Leontius (d. 1008), the metropolitan successor to Michael, achieved the ecclesiastical organization of the Russian church. He set up the first diocese in Russia and appointed bishops as their heads. The see or seat of authority of the Russian church was first located in Pereyaslav, near Kiev, but was later moved to Kiev, which became the recognized seat of the metropolitans. Most of the early metropolitans of the Russian church were Greeks that were consecrated by the patriarch of Constantinople. The Russian metropolitan was less encumbered by the patriarch than other Greek appointed metropolitans, because Russia was a large self-governing realm not subject to Greek political rule.

The authority of the metropolitan was virtually absolute in all ecclesiastical matters. Only rarely was there an appeal to the patriarch of Constantinople to decide an important case pertaining to ecclesiastical affairs. However, the patriarch was recognized in Russian services, where he was acknowledged in prayers. The Russian church also sent contributions and gifts to the patriarch in Constantinople. The Byzantine heritage left its influence on the Russian church and other Russian institutions.

The Mongol invasion of 1237–40 was a great setback to Christianity in Russia. Many churches and monasteries were destroyed, and the monks were scattered across the land. Most of the devastation was so shocking to southern Russia, that many of its people migrated northward into the forestlands. This forested region became the new geographical, political, and religious focus of Russia. Northern cities like Novgorod, Yaroslavl, Suzdal, Rostov, Vladimir, and Riazan had already been in existence nearly as long as Kiev. These centers of Byzantine-Slavic culture were the recipients of the power formerly held by Kiev, but they were effectively shut off from Constantinople, which itself was declining in power. The newfound power and influence of northern Russia was further enhanced in 1240, when Alexander Nevsky, defeated the Swedes, and again in 1242 when he was victorious over the Teutonic knights.

Kiev's decline was further witnessed in 1300, when the metropolitan Maximus moved to Vladimir, taking with him the authority of the Russian church. Like Maximus, the metropolitan St. Peter (1308–26) also chose Moscow, then a relatively minor city, as his place of residence. Meanwhile, Kiev and southern Russia fell under the rule of Lithuania and the influence of Kiev in ecclesiastical affairs waned even further. Kiev's decline, combined with that of the fall of Constantinople in 1453 to the Turks, led to a schism in the Russian church resulting in its division into the provinces of Kiev and Moscow in the middle of the fifteenth century.

The province of Moscow gradually expanded its boundaries and influence, added to its wealth, consolidated its power, and amassed more of Russia's land and people under its rule. The founding of the Trinity or Troitse-Sergieva Monastery at Zagorsk in the fourteenth century was a significant event in the life of the Russian church and the Muscovite state. This important monastery near Moscow had roughly the same impact on northern Russia as the Perchersk Monastery had on Kiev and southern Russia. The Trinity Monastery aided the rapid rise of Muscovoy, supported its leadership with resources in turning the Tartar tide in 1380, and helped restore monastic revival and Russian civilization. This monastery was only the second to be founded in Russia. Its chronicles helped provide an ideological bond for the consolidation of Muscovite power and the unity of the Russians around Moscow.

In 1472, Ivan III, ruler of Muscovoy, married the niece of the last Byzantine emperor, and took with him the remaining hopes of the Byzantine Orthodox church to Moscow. Even the double-headed eagle, the imperial Byzantine symbol, was later adopted in Moscow as the official emblem of Russia and its tsars. To some, Moscow became known as the "third Rome," signifying that it was the site of a new empire, with status equal to that of Rome and Constantinople in the past. Some monks, clerics, and others saw Moscow as the protector and savior of the Christian faith. In 1547 the title of tsar was bestowed on the Prince of Moscow, which further enhanced both his civil and ecclesiastical authority.

A Lutheran church built in 1575–76 in Moscow, was the first foreign Protestant church erected in Russia. In 1629 Moscow also became the location of the first Calvinist church in Russia. The Orthodox Russians in the sixteenth and seventeen centuries looked with disfavor on these foreign Protestant churches, but despised the Catholic church and forbade its entrance into Russia. Catholicism and Russian Orthodoxy have traditionally resisted and shunned each other. Eventually Catholic churches were permitted in Russia, but their numbers were restricted. The Russians permitted the Protestant churches as a concession to foreigners since the Russians needed their skilled architects, technicians, and other essential professionals.

A major change took place in the administration of the church during the reign of Peter the Great. Peter realized that the church played an important role in the life of the Russian people, but he was also aware that his reforms were not popular with the clergy. To ensure the success of his reforms, Tsar Peter decided that he would subordinate the church to his authority by altering its administrative organization. The Byzantine concept of rulership supported the premise that the tsar's authority was supreme in matters of both church and state. Peter seized upon this concept and used it to his bidding. To check the influence of the patriarch, Peter abolished the patriarchate, and had set up in 1721 a religious college known as the "Most Holy Synod." The synod was largely composed of members of the clergy, but the tsar appointed or dismissed its members whenever it suited his purposes. The head of the synod was a layman known as the chief procurator, who reported directly to the tsar. He watched over the meetings of the synod, and exercised his authority to halt or circumvent decisions unfavorable to the tsar. In effect the church became subordinate to the state from 1721 to 1917, during which time there was no patriarchate in Russia. The patriarchate was perceived by the tsars as a challenge to their authority.

During the time of the Holy Synod, the Russian clergy by and large was little more than a body of bureaucrats subservient to the tsar. They still performed prayers, services, and rituals, but these were mainly ceremonial gestures and did little to convert the hearts and souls of the peasants. There were few attempts by the clergy to raise the peasants out of their squalor, ignorance, and poverty; thus, there passed a golden opportunity to win over the large body of the populace into the bosom of the church at a critical time in its history. This lack of initiative by the clergy was a drastic mistake that would haunt the church in the coming years.

The church further parted itself from the masses when by 1905 it became openly involved in politics. It campaigned for and supported political candidates, and curried favor with those in power. The partisan activities of the church widened further the gulf between it and the masses.

Land ownership by the church was another touchy issue with the peasants. Along with the aristocracy and other large landlords, the church owned significant tracts of land. As many as ten million acres of Russia's best farmlands belonged to the church. In the eyes of millions of landless peasants who coveted a plot of land of their own, the church stood in their way of realizing their dreams.

Before the overthrow of the tsar in 1917, the church was given an annual subsidy by the state of nearly $35 million. The great accumulation of wealth by the church was visible in its magnificent cathedrals, art treasures, resplendent vestments worn by the clergy, and extensive holdings of land and property. The masses of the poor felt trapped in a society in which the one institution they looked to for spiritual salvation had degenerated into a debauched bureaucratric puppet of the state. In addition, prayers and liturgy could not substitute for bread and land.

Not only was the purpose of the church incoherent in a time of its critical need, but its image was further tarnished by the notorious Rasputin, an unordained holy man from Siberia. Between November 1905 and March 1916, this mystic, who seemed to possess hypnotic powers, commanded considerable influence in both governmental and religious affairs. His uninhibited sexual activities and intrigues were widely renowned and further undermined the church and the religious spirit of the masses. His murder was not enough to save either the monarchy or much of the church in the revolution and its aftermath.

In 1917 the monarchy collapsed and the Bolsheviks, having grasped the reins of power, turned their vehemence against the church. The Bolsheviks were atheists and espoused the philosophical ideals set forth by Lenin and Karl Marx. They believed that religion had the same effect on the people as an opiate or drug. The Bolsheviks (members of the Communist party since 1918) philosophized that religion was addictive to the masses and made them forget their pain and sufferings. Lenin viewed religion as an exploitation of the people; he believed it provided the upper classes with a tool or means to serve their own purposes and ends. In the Bolshevist mind, religion was a form of bondage; only there were no physical chains attached to its adherents. Lenin warned against religion and urged the people to throw off its shackles. The Bolsheviks promised tangible objects such as bread and shoes to the people; not the intangible prayers and liturgy of the church. Lenin viewed religion as a form of oppression, seeking salvation in future life rather than one on earth. He believed in economic determinism, not rewards in heaven. Coexistence with the church was not possible; Marxist-Leninist dogma was incompatible with religion.

The church represented a threat to the Communists. They saw the church as a center of opposition to the goals of the Communist party. To the Communists the church was an anachronism whose time had passed. The Communists viewed the church as incongruous with their own system. The Communists perceived their own order as a religion. There should be no other gods before the ones idolized by communism.

In early 1918 the Bolsheviks enjoined a crusade against the church. By a series of maneuvers they were able to reduce the power and prestige of the church. The Bolshevik campaign began by separating church and state, and assuming control of all church schools. Next, the state confiscated all church property and lands, and cut off all subsidies to the church. Some churches were converted into schools, and in others the people were given the right to hold lectures, organize demonstrations, stage concerts, and perform other activities that did not violate Soviet law. Monks, priests, and nuns were stripped of their secular activities and forced to pay taxes. Bolshevik teachers were placed in all schools to instruct the youth in the philosophy of communism and atheism. The clergy was denied the right to educate their children.

During the Stalinist era many of the clergy were imprisoned, exiled to slave labor camps, or executed. Many churches were turned into museums and others became clinics or hospitals. Sermons were censored and a barrage of antireligious propaganda was aimed at wiping out religion.

In spite of all the measures taken against the church, Yaroslavsky, the leader of the "Union of the Godless," was forced to admit in 1933 that religion was alive and would not go away. He compared religion to a nail; the harder and more often it was hit, the deeper it became embedded.

When Germany invaded Russia in 1941 the state made some concessions to the church and achieved a partial reconciliation with it. Seminaries were allowed to be established, the church was permitted to reorganize, new churches were built, the patriarchate was reestablished, the printing of religious literature was permitted, and antireligious propaganda was abolished. The church threw its support behind the state, denounced Hitler, set up stations to care for the wounded, prayed for victory, and supported the leadership of Stalin. Once the war was over, relations between Stalin and the church cooled, but no longer were the church and its personnel excessively persecuted.

Khrushchev, the premier of Russia during 1958–64, followed a less harsh approach toward the church than that displayed during much of the Stalinist era. Still, the League of the Militant Godless was active under Khrushchev; some clerics were imprisoned and some were sent to mental institutions. Many of the gains the church made in World War II were divested from it. Antireligious campaigns were active in the Khrushchev era, and persuasive tactics were employed against the church. Concessions made to the church during World War II were never codified as laws.

Violence against religion subsided in the post-Khrushchev period. The churches have quietly extended their influence while the government appears to use propaganda and education as its main tactics in promoting the spread of atheism. The government's goal seems more one of containment of religion rather than open competition with it.

The Soviet Communists have not abandoned their long-sought goal to eradicate religion. Only their tactics vary. Today, the church survives under conditions that are difficult for Christians in the West to imagine. The fact that the church survives at all under the Soviet system seems illogical. Yet, survive it does, despite decades of repression, hostility, resentment, and confiscation of much of its property and belongings. In spite of all the measures taken against the church and religion in the Soviet Union, their survival persists and is not in fear of extinction. Like the vigorous character of the Russian peasant, the church has a will of its own which supersedes all barriers to its existence. At the height of its glory the mighty Roman Empire could not subdue Christianity any more than the present or past rulers of Soviet communism can do so.

There have been few signs of outright persecution of the church in the Soviet Union in recent years. Perhaps the rulers of the Soviet state have realized that no matter the extent of the harshness of their tactics in dealing with the church, its resolve to exist remains indomitable. More than half a century has passed since Lenin denounced the church and attempted to wrest its roots from Russian soil; however, the church remains as deeply embedded in the conscience of its Russian believers as ever. Surveillance of the church and its congregation has not ceased, but no longer are its clergy shipped off to slave labor camps and its monasteries converted to museums.

The position of the church in the Soviet Union is akin to that of walking a tightrope. As long as the church refrains from criticism of the Soviet state and its policies, the state in return allows the church to exist at a level of "peaceful coexistence." There are those critics of the church, both inside and outside the Soviet Union, who advocate a more vocal and active position on the part of the church for greater freedom of religion from the Soviet authorities. Yet, many church supporters accept the present accommodation maintained by the church and state, and believe that open dissension or demonstrations might trigger new repressive measures against the church.

Ironically, freedom of religion is guaranteed by the Soviet constitution, though in actual practice the state places many roadblocks in the path of religious believers. In order to preach in the Soviet Union, one must first obtain a license from the government. Furthermore, all churches and places of worship must be officially sanctioned by the state. By law the state forbids religious instruction to children in their home, contending this violates their rights as Soviet citizens.

Many of the churches in the Soviet Union have been designated as historical landmarks. A number of these have been described in this book. Not all Soviet Communists agree or share the view that these edifices of religion should be allowed to stand. Some of the hardline Soviet Communists decry the restoration and preservation of churches by the state. Churches made into historic landmarks are, in the opinion of some, favorable propaganda for the church because they are emblematic of religion.

Estimates place the number of practicing Christians in the Soviet Union at between fifty to sixty million. Another thirty to forty million people profess allegiance to some religion. Combined, these figures represent more than one-third of the total Soviet population, and between four to five times the membership of the Soviet Communist party.

Christianity is by far the largest religion in numbers in the Soviet Union. The Orthodox church is by far the largest religious group in the country. Its membership is estimated at between thirty and forty million. Roman Catholics, which number about four to five million people, comprise the second largest Christian order. Most of its followers live in the Ukrainian and Lithuanian Republics. The third largest Christian denomination is Baptist, which numbers approximately four million advocates. In an NBC television program in March 1985, Dr. Billy Graham stated that 125 new Baptist churches had been built in the Soviet Union since 1979. The Baptists are probably the fastest growing denomination in the Soviet Union. The Pentecostal church is another that has grown rapidly in the last several decades. However, it, along with the Reform Baptists and Jehovah's Witnesses, does not enjoy the same status and harmony with Communist authorities as that permitted the Orthodox and Baptist churches.

There are approximately two million Jews in the Soviet Union. The Soviet government views them as a nationality or ethnic group, and not a religious group. There are less than sixty synagogues in the Soviet Union.

The Protestant and Catholic churches are usually look-alikes to those in the West. At Christmas nearly all the churches are full of worshipers, even though there is no Christmas holiday in the Soviet Union.

The Islamic religion numbers about 18 million followers in the Soviet Union. Only the Russian Orthodox church has more adherents than Islam in the U.S.S.R. Muslim believers are found predominantly in the republics located east of the Caspian Sea.

What is there about the church that attracts the attention of even some members of the Communist Youth League known as Komsomol? The civil ceremonies in which marriages are performed are routinely drab and evoke little of the interest or appeal generated by religious ceremonies. The pageantry of the religious ceremonies with their procession, pomp, color, and social festivities consummate a spectacle of variety and enrichment which attract even some young Communists to wed in the church. Children of some Communist parents also participate in baptismal ceremonies, with their parents supporting and often requesting the baptisms.

The state often attempts to draw attention away from religious ceremonies and functions by staging concerts, performances, and other activities at the same time the churches are observing their celebrations and festivities. The party feels hostility toward the church which, like the party, is engaged in a form of indoctrination to shape basic beliefs.

Religion appears to frighten the Communists. Persuasion, threats, persecution, and repression have not silenced it. The vitality of religion and its endurance in the Soviet Union continue to be a thorn in the side of the Russian bear. At any rate, religion is staging a small revival in the Soviet Union today.

Chapter III.
LENINGRAD
Venice of the North

I love you, Peter's great creation,
Your stately aspect, perfect ranks,
The Neva River's undulation,
The granite vestments of its banks.
                    —Pushkin

In the high latitude of Leningrad (60° N.) there exists a phenomenon of early summer called the "White Nights." On June 21 the sun reaches its northernmost latitude, and those lands in the high latitudes surrounding the Arctic Circle have diurnal hours of sunlight which greatly exceed the nocturnal hours of darkness. Approaching Leningrad, someone may say in Russian, "Bialy Noch," which means "White Nights." At 10 p.m. it is still very light in summer, with a semidarkness or dusk appearing about 10:30. Even then one can read the large print of a newspaper on the street. The white nights arrive about two weeks before the vernal equinox and last into July. At their peak the days are as long as nineteen hours. During the apex of winter the days are as short as six and one-quarter hours. Darkness, rather than cold, is more characteristic of the Leningrad winter.

On arrival at the Leningrad airport there is a distinct impression of having entered into a different country than the Soviet Union. The facial features and expressions of the natives seem different. Many look Scandinavian rather than Russian. The people seem carefree and relaxed.

During the period of the summer sun the sky is still light at 11 p.m. Basking in the rays of Leningrad's white nights one stands in awe and admires nature. From the airport it is a delightful drive along the Neva River to the Leningrad Hotel, a modern-looking high-rise structure. During the evenings a pale mist often arises from the Gulf of Finland and hangs over the city and its islands. The never-ending twilight of midsummer pierces the mist and gently touches the shores of the Neva River. Across the placid Neva from the hotel, above the ramparts of the Peter and Paul Fortress, soars the slim spire of the Peter and Paul Cathedral, a symbol of the city's grace. In front of the hotel, on the Neva, is anchored the old cruiser "Aurora." It was from this ship that the first shot was fired that started the October Revolution in 1917 and signaled the attack on the Winter Palace. The curtain at last had been drawn on the rule of the Romanoffs. The imperial dynasty of Russia was no more; when the Winter Palace fell a new epoch in Russian history was begun. For Holy Russia little would remain of the way it had been. Since then Leningrad has been known as the "Cradle of the Revolution."

It is difficult to restrain one's enthusiasm to begin exploring the "Venice of the North," another title by which Leningrad is well known. The city is built on 101 islands connected by more than 600 bridges. The Neva River, together with its many branches, flows around the city's many islands. Several smaller rivers and numerous canals add to the waterways of the city. When Peter the Great decided to build his city on this site, much work had to be done. Canals had to be dug for drainage, marshes drained and filled in, and the Neva lined with stone embankments. In order to lay the foundations of the city's buildings and palaces, huge quantities of boulders and rock were required to fill the marshlands. To accomplish this task Tsar Peter mandated that all boats, barges, and carts entering the city had to bring in boulders and rocks to be deposited in the marshes. Nearly 100,000 workers perished the first year of building St. Petersburg. Their bones went into the marshes, and 30,000 houses were built over them. Huge piles had to be driven into the marshes to support the weight of the buildings. Beautiful St. Isaac's Cathedral required 24,000 piles to support its massive weight.

The piles that Peter the Great drove into the Neva marshes were the surest foundation of the Russian empire. St. Petersburg was the pulse of imperial Russia. Tsar Peter was determined to move Holy Russia out of its feudal past, and give it the status, strength, and prestige of a state equal to its European neighbors. He decided to make St. Petersburg his "window" to Europe, and the national consciousness of Russia. The city became the imperial residence in 1712 and his reign marked a significant step forward for Russia. Tsar Peter was 6'7" tall and reigned from 1682–1725. He fostered the growth of both

Russian industry and trade by employing western ideas and skills. Peter coveted western technology and was particularly interested in military and naval affairs. Ambitious to learn these arts from the western powers, he formed a delegation of 250 men, including himself, and set out in pursuit of the knowledge of shipbuilding, gunnery, navigation, engineering, and printing in the European lands. Peter traveled incognito, visiting Berlin and later Holland, where he studied commerce and worked as an ordinary shipbuilder. From Holland he journeyed to England, where he was employed as a mechanic. Peter was an indefatigable worker. Upon his return to Russia he set about to modernize Russia into a strong power using the West as a model. Peter's skills in diplomacy and generalship, together with his reforms of the army, enabled him to defeat Sweden in the Northern War (1700–21), push Russian expansion to the Baltic Sea, and acquire the ground on which he built the city of St. Petersburg.

Leningrad huddles in the eastern niche of the Gulf of Finland around the mouth of the Neva River. It is the major Baltic seaport of the Soviet Union. The delta of the Neva contains forty-two islands, the largest of which is Vasilyevsky. Located on this island are the Academy of Science, Leningrad State University, and the Central Navy Museum. From the eastern apex of the island, where the Neva divides into two branches, one can stand in front of the Central Navy Museum and look ahead about one-half mile to the left and see the Peter and Paul Cathedral and Fortress. Looking immediately to the right across the Neva, the Hermitage Museum comes into view.

The port of Leningrad is a major shipbuilding and ship-repair center. At the Admiralty Shipyard was launched the "Lenin," the world's first atomic-powered icebreaker. The Neva freezes over during the winter, but the port itself can continue to operate through the use of icebreakers, except for a period of two to three months. Timber from nearby forests is exported through the port, as are huge hydrogenerators from the city's large "Elektrosila" plant. Leningrad also lies on good rail and inland waterway communications.

Early St. Petersburg had a history of flooding by the Neva. After a disastrous flood in 1824 buildings on every street were marked to show the height of inundation. In that flood horses drowned in the streets, and the trees of the city were filled with more human beings than birds. More than 800 people drowned, and 1,300 houses were destroyed. The high-water marks of past inundations can still be seen on the sides of many of Leningrad's buildings. The Neva is a short river. From its source at the southwest corner of Lake Ladoga, a huge lake lying mostly northeast of Leningrad, the river runs a total of about 45 miles until it reaches the Gulf of Finland. In flowing through Leningrad it reaches a maximum width of about 700 yards. The Neva is usually frozen over from November to April.

In the time of Imperial Russia the approach of winter and the freezing of the Neva signaled the return of the Imperial Court from Moscow. Social invitations, balls, and dinners were the order of the season.

The Emperor's Ball held in the Hermitage Palace was the highlight of the social season. The windows of the Winter Palace afforded a view of the observance of the festival of Epiphany. In this celebration many holes were cut in the ice of the Neva, the waters of the river were blessed, and people by the thousands were immersed and baptized in the icy waters. Skating, sledding, and troika races were annual events on the icy surface of the Neva.

Facing the Bolshaya Neva is the equestrian statue of Peter the Great, poised on the edge of a huge 1,600-ton block of granite hewn from a quarry in Finland. The statue of Peter is 11 feet high, mounted on his horse, which stands 17 feet high. The bronze statue of Peter I and his horse atop the granite block was unveiled in 1782. This familiar monument to Peter, known as the "Bronze Horseman," inspired Pushkin to write a poem of the same title to commemorate the statue. On both sides of the monument is an inscription, one in Russian and one in Latin, which translates to read: "To Peter I from Catherine II, 1782." It took Etienne Falconet, its sculptor, nearly twelve years to complete the statue. The monument to Peter I stands in the center of Decembrists' Square (Ploshchad Dekabristov), which is named for the month in which the Imperial Guard rose up against the tsar on this spot in 1825. As one stands beside the statue and listens to guides recite its history, it is somewhat amusing to hear the contradictions in their statements. At one moment guides extoll the feats of Tsar Peter, and a minute later denigrate the memory of the tsars by pointing out their faults in terms of Marxist-Leninist ideology.

A short distance to the east of Peter's statue, the left or west wing of the Admiralty building abuts one corner of Decembrists' Square. To the rear of the Admiralty is Maxim Gorky Garden. From afar, the golden spire of the Admiralty is often confused with that of the neighboring spire of the Peter and Paul Cathedral on the opposite side of the Neva. A weather vane in the replica of a small ship can be seen atop the 230-foot spire of the impressive Admiralty. The beautiful Admiralty was designed by Andrei Zakharov and Ivan Korobov, and was built from 1806–23. A former Admiralty built in 1704 had a shipyard surrounding it. Beneath the graceful spire of the Admiralty can be seen a level of white columns that blend perfectly with the yellow stone of the building.

From the Admiralty a short walk through Decembrists' Square in a southwest direction away from the Neva will bring you to St. Isaac's Cathedral, which is now a museum. The magnificent cathedral is located on St. Isaac's (Isaakiyevskaya) Square. Most churches in Russia that were not destroyed after Lenin came to power were turned into museums. St. Isaac's is one of the world's largest cathedrals. Built of forty-three varieties of marble, it is a truly impressive structure. This grand cathedral took nearly forty years (1819–1858) to build. Its exterior is adorned with 112 enormous red granite columns.Like many of Leningrad's noted structures and monuments, it was designed by an imported European architect, Auguste Montferrand of France, whose bust stands inside the doors of the cathedral. St. Isaac's covers two and one-half acres and is Leningrad's largest cathedral. As you look at its two main entrances, you are struck by the similarity of its columned portico to the one that forms the entranceway to the Pantheon in Rome. Massive columns of red granite sixty feet high and seven feet in diameter support each portico of St. Isaac's. The polished granite columns shine like mirrors; and few columns in the world can match their magnificence. Inside St. Isaac's more beautiful stones (marble, jasper, malachite, alabaster, and porphyry) are found in its floor, walls, railings, and columns. St. Isaac's is 330 feet high, 364 feet long, and 315 feet wide.

St. Isaac's is a classic example of Greek architecture, built in the shape of a Greek cross. It has an enormous gilt dome, the third largest, after St. Peter's in Rome and St. Paul's in London. The huge dome is overlaid with a veneer of gold, and supported by thirty huge pillars. The dome can be reached by climbing 262 steps. From the dome a magnificent view of the city is afforded the viewer.

The number of domes featured on Russian churches have symbolic meaning, stemming from Christian doctrine. By their number the domes are symbolical accordingly:

2 domes—the two natures of Jesus
3 domes—the Trinity
5 domes—Jesus and the four evangelists
7 domes—the sacraments
9 domes—the celestial hierarchies
13 domes—Jesus and the 12 disciples

St. Isaac's is entered through colossal oak and bronze doors that weigh more than twenty tons each. The cathedral's beautiful iconostasis measures more than 220 feet in length. Most of the floor is built of jasper. St. Isaac's is remarkable inside and out.

This imposing cathedral is a monument to the labor of the tens of thousands of Russian peasants who for nearly forty years toiled and died constructing the huge edifice. It was said that mercury and gold were mixed to paint the dome of the cathedral. Since the fumes from the mixture were toxic, many of the workers died but they were immediately replaced by others and the work continued. Within the church are thirty-three tombs of tsars and their wives. The center of the building also contains a huge Foucault pendulum that is 325 feet long, descending from the cupola of the cathedral. The pendulum constantly swings and each passage it makes alters the angle of its movement, so that the pendulum marks the exact rotation of the earth about its axis. It was used by the architects to determine the proper location for the painting of each of the twelve apostles which decorate the upper dome. There are many captivating scenes on the walls and ceiling, such as the Resurrection, Assumption, Ascension, Sermon on the Mount, Judas and Jesus, Adam and Eve, and others. The cornices or corners of the ceiling and walls are inlaid with beautiful braids of gold, paintings, and marble. Much of St. Isaac's is neo-classic in style.

The very essence of beauty is the only way to describe its interior; huge gold chandeliers descend from the ceiling, and the painted murals depicting biblical Old and New Testament themes bring the walls to life. Many of the paintings are being replaced by mosaic replicas because the originals are deteriorating.

St. Isaac's Cathedral was named after St. Isaac, a Byzantine monk and minor saint of the Russian Orthodox church. The cathedral is the fourth St. Isaac's; the first was a very small structure, and two others burned down. The cathedral was opened as a museum in 1934 by the state, since (according to my guide) the Russian Orthodox church could not support it. During World War II the cathedral suffered great damage. Five years after the war ended it was restored magnificently. St. Isaac's is now the headquarters of the Working People's Deputies of the city.

On the outside of the cathedral an equestrian statue of Nicholas I faces it from across the street. Nicholas reigned from 1825–55, and was forced to put down a revolt of his troops on the day he was crowned. Riding up to the mutinous troops on his horse, he sternly ordered them to return to their ranks, which they did. Even the conspirator who planned to assassinate Nicholas withdrew in the face of such courage. To the rear of the statue is Mariinsky Palace, a wedding gift of Nicholas to his daughter Maria.

A short walk to the rear of St. Isaac's will bring you to the prison that was used during the Revolution of 1917. Many of the aristocracy, men and women, were imprisoned in it during the October revolution. The prisoners were chained to their cots and forced to lie motionless. The slightest noise brought the guards with straight jackets. Death might have been easier.

On St. Isaac's Square is located the Hotel Astoria, one of the older but better hotels of Leningrad. Built in 1912, it was a majestic hotel in its heyday. Guides relate the story that Hitler had planned to hold a victory celebration in the hotel as soon as the German army captured Leningrad. Supposedly, Hitler issued orders that engraved invitations be printed and ready for distribution to Nazi party officials the moment the city fell. Since the Germans failed to capture the city, Hitler had to forego his planned celebration at the Astoria.

On the northeast side of the city is Piskaryevskoye Memorial Cemetery. Soon after the Germans invaded Russia on June 22, 1941, they marched on Leningrad, which became the victim of one of the most horrible chapters in world history, a 900-day siege by the Nazis during which an appalling 1.5 million Russians perished. The Russians lost more people in the siege of Leningrad than the U.S. lost in all of World War II. In 1941 Hitler's forces closed in on the city; he ordered it razed to the ground if necessary. The winter of that year, combined with the German siege and blockade, brought about quite severe circumstances for the people to endure. But frozen Lake Lagoda to the northeast made it possible to bring in food, supplies, clothing, and ammunition, and at the same time evacuate the old and sick, women and children. Food and water were scarce, but the morale and courage of the people remained high. Leningrad withstood a longer siege than Stalingrad. The people were determined not to yield their city, and they accomplished this feat. Neither bombs, shells, nor famine could induce the city into surrender. For the Russians there is always the reminder of Naziism and its cruelty. Movies depicting the drama, courage, and fortitude of Russia during World War II are popular on Soviet television.

Throngs of people visit Piskaryevskoye Cemetery to pay their respects to those who died in defense of their city. A long walkway, much the same as an avenue, leads past common, mass graves on either side of it. At times during the conflagration so many people were dying in such a short time span that it was utterly impossible to bury the dead in individual graves. Massive holes were dug, and bodies by the thousands were dumped into them. When the holes were full, huge mounds of earth placed over them identified each massive gravesite. For those lying buried in each mound, the only epitaph is a small marker inscribed with the numerals of the year, which identifies when that particular earthen mound was created. An eternal flame in the center of the square burns as a beacon to the memory of those departed. A twenty-foot high statue of a woman cast in bronze stands at the end of the walkway leading past the gravesites. She symbolizes the sorrow for those who perished. A memorial, etched in Russian, is translated to read: "No one here is forgotten, and nothing is forgotten." The honorary title of "Hero City" was bestowed on Leningrad for its stamina and courage in the face of the Nazi armies.

According to an Intourist guide, Leningrad has nineteen functional churches: fifteen Russian Orthodox, one Catholic, one Mosque, one Baptist, and one synagogue. Compared with any major American or West European city these numbers would simply be inadequate vis-a-vis the population.

In July Leningrad has an average high temperature of 71°F. and a low average of 57°F. January has an average high of 23°F. and a low average of 12°F. July averages nine days with rain while January averages eight rainy days. The city is located at approximately the same latitude as Seward, Alaska; Nanortalik, Greenland; and Oslo, Norway.

Leningrad is a rapidly growing city set amidst many gardens and parks. The tallest building is twenty-two stories high and none can go higher because of the marshy conditions of the land. Only those buildings over five stories high have elevators, and the rent for an apartment is ten rubles per month. A telephone plus utilties costs an additional four to five rubles. Many of the buildings had been destroyed during World War II but rebuilt during the latter 1940s and in the 1950s. During the war many buildings were camouflaged, like the Winter Palace, in an attempt to avoid damage to them.

Despite immense damage, all traces of the war have been removed. The entire city has been rebuilt, with whole squares repaved with many of the original cobblestones. The fountains in the parks once more gush with vigor, and many of the same statues that lined the walkways in the parks before the war adorn them again with their beauty and elegance.

Leningrad is one of those great cities of the world whose name alone beckons the avid traveler and tourist. The city has a genuine charm about it; poets and artists have perpetuated its image and mystique. The city has little of the frantic rushing that one sees in London, Rome, or New York. Traffic jams are unknown; such things do not happen in Leningrad, though at certain times during the day one may experience such an event in parts of Moscow. Life in Russia moves along at a much slower pace than in the West. Leningrad has a gentle touch about it; it is a cultural center of students, writers, and artists.

By comparison to many of Europe's cities, Leningrad is a young city. Since its founding by Peter the Great, the city has not yet reached its 300th birthday. Indeed some American cities are older than Leningrad. The city has had its name changed twice since it was originally founded as St. Petersburg by Peter I in 1703. In 1914 at the beginning of the First World War, its Germanic sounding name was offensive to many Russians, so the city was renamed Petrograd. In 1924 following the death of Lenin, the city changed its name to Leningrad to honor the man who founded the present Soviet state.

Today, Leningrad is the home of about 4,500,000 people. A number of vast, new housing districts surround the city. Known as micro-regions, each of these housing developments have located near their center a school, laundry, and civic center. Many of the units consist of three rooms, plus the kitchen and bath. There are approximately fourteen such districts within the city.

In spite of its low-lying, marshy conditions and other physical restraints, Leningrad is admirably laid out and designed in terms of modern urban planning. When Peter the Great decided to found his city on this site, he sought the most prominent foreign and Russian architects of his age to design the city that he chose to be the new capital of Russia. These architects laid out broad streets, ruler-straight avenues, beautiful parks, monumental squares, and other architectual ensembles.

The city's main artery is the broad avenue known as the Nevsky Prospekt, which runs a distance of three miles. When built in 1710 it was designed as the main road to Novgorod, a city located southeast of present-day Leningrad. The Nevsky Prospekt begins at the Admiralty and runs generally east-southeast to the Moscow Railway Station, and then veers southeasterly to the Alexander Nevsky Monastery. Other features along its course include the Museum of the History of Religion and Atheism (Kazansky Cathedral), the Comedy Theater, M.I. Glinka (Philharmonic) Hall, Pushkin Drama Theater, Pioneers' Palace (former Anichkov Palace), and the Anichkov Bridge over the Fontanka River. Built from 1839–41, the bridge is noted for its statues of the "Taming of the Horses," by Pyotr Klodt. Montferrand, the architect of St. Isaac's Cathedral, designed the railings of the bridge.

The wide, spacious Nevsky Prospekt is often compared to the boulevard Champs Elysees in Paris. Many of Leningrad's best shops, cafes, restaurants, cinemas, and theatres are found along its thoroughfare. Also on the Nevsky Prospekt are several major hotels, bars, book shops, and the large Saltykov-Shchedrin Public Library, said to contain fifteen million books. It was founded in 1814 and contains many valuable manuscripts, maps, portraits, periodicals, and old newspapers. Some of the oldest religious documents in existence are preserved in its collections. During the day the street is filled with shoppers, tourists, and those strolling along peering into the store windows; by night, theater- and concertgoers move to and from their destinations along the Nevsky Prospekt. The underground or subway that provides access to much of the city has several major stations on this busy street. The metro was built in 1955, but extension of it to new areas of the city has continued. The subway has many beautiful stations, some of which resemble palaces.

A short distance down Nevsky Prospekt from the Admiralty is the beautiful colonnade of Kazansky Cathedral, supported by 136 massive columns of stone. Designed by the Russian architect Andrei Voronikhin, who used St. Peter's Cathedral in Rome as its model, Kazansky Cathedral was built to honor Russia's victory over Napoleon in 1812. The former cathedral was named after an icon it once housed, known as "Our Lady of Kazan," which is said to have been responsible for a number of miracles. Today, the cathedral houses the Museum of the History of Religion and Atheism, also a synonym by which it is known. Beautiful icons set amidst devices of torture form a startling contrast to the exhibits on display. In front of the 264-foot high cathedral stand the statues of the Russian field marshals Barclay de Tolly and Kutuzov, the respective commanders of the Russian army in its struggle with Napoleon. Kutuzov's tomb is also located near the entrance to the cathedral. Many trophies of Russian war victories were kept in the cathedral.

From Kazansky Cathedral a walk of about twenty minutes down Plekhanova Street in a southwesterly direction will bring one to Teatralnaya Square, on which stands the Kirov Opera and Ballet Theater (formerly the Mariisky Theater). The theater is immediately recognized by its bluish-green color. The green is similar to that of an olive, but the bluish tint in it gives the composite of the colors a less than purity that approaches a pale green. In 1983 the theater celebrated its 200th season of giving performances. Tickets can be purchased for as little as one ruble.

The theater is named in honor of Sergei M. Kirov (1886–1934), a communist leader who served as secretary of the Leningrad organization of the party. In tsarist times the theater was open only to the imperial court and the nobility. Tourists and visitors now flock to its performances. Our group attended an evening performance, occupying seats that were covered in velvet. Many of the top ballet dancers in the Soviet Union can be seen performing on the Kirov stage. Here the divine Pavlova and Nijinsky danced in the past; more recently Nureyev and Makarova have dazzled the theater's audiences. One feels almost privileged to sit in this theater. Amidst its oppulence the mind is tempted to drift back to the days of the tsars, and wonder who were the rich and powerful individuals that once occupied the space that one may sit in now. No less impressive are the lavish and ornate fixtures decorating the interior of the theater of this day. Beautiful, extravagant crystal chandeliers help to provide the lighting that sparkles on the hundreds of pounds of gold used to embellish the grandiose features of the balconies and stage. The natives of Leningrad proudly proclaim that their city has the best ballet dancers in the country, although Moscow's Bolshoi Theater and dancers are perhaps better known, particularly outside the Soviet Union. It is not uncommon to hear Leningraders quip that Moscow often lures or snares some of their best performers. There are more than twenty theaters and concert halls in Leningrad.

Not far from the Kirov theater is located the Academic Choreography School alongside the Fontanka River embankment. This school trains many of Russia's outstanding ballet dancers. Training for and study of ballet is an extensive and rigorous routine that demands high standards of excellence in versatility and proficiency of movement. Grace, speed, agility, control, and lightness of the body are mainstays of successful ballet executions. At this school youth often begin serious ballet study by age nine or ten. Of the more than one thousand applications to the school each year, only about seventy to eighty will be chosen for entrance to ballet training.

Historically, the ballet was firmly implanted and widely recognized in Russia by the time of the reign of Catherine the Great (1762–96). Around 1900 the ballet had stagnated in much of Europe and America, but in Russia a long line of brilliant dancers were being turned out in the Imperial Academy of Dancing. Marius Peptipa, a French dancer who came to St. Petersburg in 1847, soon established himself as an accomplished choreographer and largely dictated the style of the Russian ballet after 1862. Following Peptipa's death in 1910, the great Russian choreographer Sergi Diaghilev exerted a tremendous influence on the Russian ballet into the late 1920s. The renowned composer Igor Stravinsky provided many of his original ballet scores for Diaghilev. In the early 1900s the contemporary classic ballet was made popular.

So many sights in Leningrad; their profusion seems endless. Eastward along the Neva is a large horn of land around which the river forms a loop. At this location is the Smolny Institute, in front of which is a statue of Lenin. During the October Revolution of 1917, this building served as Lenin's headquarters. Both Lenin and Trotsky lived in it. Before the 1917 revolution the nobility sent their daughters to a school in this building. Today it serves the local Communist party of the city as its headquarters. The area around the Smolny was originally a tar yard, *smolny dvor,* hence the derivation of the present name of the building on its site. Built by Giaccomo Quarenghi, the Smolny is a three-story lemon-yellow structure with a row of huge white columns supporting a portico over the center of the two upper levels.

Nearby is the beautiful Smolny Cathedral, built from 1748–55 by Rastrelli. Designed in a bluish rococo architecture, the church, now a museum, displays the decorative sculpture and painting characteristic of rococo style.

Its altars are made of yellow marble from the Ural Mountains. On its top are five onion-shaped cupolas, each capped by a cross. Fifty-six columns made of jasper support the structure.

The architect of the Smolny Cathedral, Bartolomeo Rastrelli (1700–1771), deserves further mention. His name is linked with many of the city's buildings and palaces. During the reign of Empress Elizabeth, daughter of Peter the Great, the Italian Rastrelli became her chief architect. The Smolny Cathedral and the Winter Palace, both done in rococo style, were among his most noted works. The Vorontsov and Stroganov palaces were also his works. The Stroganov Palace, on the Moika embankment, not far from the Hermitage Museum, is an excellent example of Russian baroque style. Built from 1752–54, it displays splendid white columns that are characteristic features of many of Leningrad's buildings. The Stroganovs were descended from a wealthy commercial and trading family from Novgorod. Peter I conferred the rank of nobility on the family.

From the Stroganov Palace it is a relatively short distance to the Hermitage Museum, which also includes the Winter Palace. The majestic Winter Palace was built in Russian baroque style from 1754–62 by Rastrelli. This sumptuous palace stands on the left bank of the Neva River. Its beautiful ceilings, murals, and multispecied wood floors are imposing features of this former residence of Russia's tsars. Consisting of nearly 1,100 rooms, 353 hallways, and 117 staircases, the Winter Palace is indeed an impressive sight. Many of its remarkable hallways are decorated with marble and several other carved stones hewn from the Ural Mountains. The palace measures 657 feet long, over 200 feet wide, and 72 feet high.

Empress Anne began its construction in 1754, and Catherine the Great completed it in 1764. The former palace contains rooms decorated in red, green, silver, purple, yellow, pink, gold, and orange colors. The tsars lived in extravagant luxury. After Tsar Nicholas II abdicated, Kerensky and some of his ministers lived in part of the palace. Some of the fixtures and paintings of the palace were destroyed on October 25, 1917, when the revolutionary mob stormed into it. After the Bolsheviks took over the palace, they sold some of its treasures, part of which ended up abroad.

In all, the palace consists of five buildings: the Winter Palace, the Small Hermitage, the Old Hermitage, the Hermitage Theatre, and the New Hermitage. One is usually not permitted to visit and see more than about forty rooms in the former palace. A person would have to walk 15½ miles to make a complete round of the halls in the palace. This baroque fantasy displaying much gold, and often called the Buckingham Palace of the tsars, now houses the incomparable Hermitage art collection.

The sizable West European art collection that fills 120 rooms of the Hermitage is represented by many of the old Italian, Dutch, and Flemish masters. The Spanish and French schools are also well represented. Their illustrious names include Leonardo DaVinci, Raphael, Michelangelo, Cezanne, Renoir, Velasquez, El Greco, Rembrandt, Van Gogh, Goya, Picasso, and others. A veritable who's who in the field of art. The collection is so enormous that anyone spending just thirty seconds viewing each "object d'art" would spend nine years here. In all more than three million art objects are housed in the Hermitage. Some of the noted works here include Leonardo DaVinci's "Madonna Litta," acquired from the collection of the Duke di Litta of Milan (hence its name); Michelangelo's sculpture of the "Crouching Boy"; and Fra Filippo Lippi's "Blessed Trinity." There are twenty-five Rembrandts, a large collection of Reubens, and twelve of Rodin's sculptures. The Impressionist painters are represented in the Hermitage by the works of Claude Monet, the "Father of Impressionism," Renoir, Cezanne, Van Gogh, Gauguin, and others. The Impressionists made use of light, space, and sky in their paintings. Not to be left unmentioned is Pablo Picasso, whose works here display the familiar blue, pink, and cubism styles for which he is well known. Swords, clocks, brooches, plaques, jewelry, and other rare objects abound in the Hermitage collections. Gold, diamonds, precious stone, and crown jewels belonging to the tsars are also on display. Elegant frescoes and silken tapestries cover the walls of the Hermitage.

Also kept in the Hermitage Museum is the spectacular Orloff diamond, which weighs more than 194 carats. The diamond was presented to Catherine the Great by Count Gregory Orloff (1734–83), a central figure in the dethroning of Peter III, and one of Catherine the Great's lovers. Count Orloff bought the diamond for 90,000 pounds in Amsterdam. Before the diamond came into the hands of Orloff in that city, it was first stolen from a Brahmin idol in India by a French soldier, who in turn had it stolen from him by a ship's captain. Catherine the Great gave Count Orloff command of Russia's armies for his affections. While on a foreign visit he became insane, and later married his niece.

In the Winter Palace dining room where the Provisional Government was arrested, stands a clock with its hands fixed on 2:19, marking the exact time at which this event occurred. A tour of the palace includes throne rooms and the ambassadors' staircase. The Hermitage rivals and ranks with the Louvre as two of the worlds' outstanding museums.

To the southwest rear of the Hermitage Museum is located Palace Square (Dvortsovaya Ploshchad), in the center of which stands the Alexander Column. The column was ordered erected by Nicholas I to commemorate Tsar Alexander I, the Russian tsar when Napoleon invaded Russia. The huge block of granite on which it rests stands 26 feet high. Nearly 150 feet high and 14 feet in diameter, this enormous column is one of the tallest in the world. Ironically, it was designed by the celebrated French architect, Montferrand, as a Russian monument to celebrate the defeat of Napoleon. Carved out of red granite from Finland, the 600-ton column was elevated on its site it 1834 by 2,000 soldiers using ropes and pulleys to lift and erect it in place. On January 9, 1905, the tsar's troops massacred scores of workers and peasants on Palace Square until its stones were reddened by blood. Thereafter, the square was bloodied again in October 1917 when revolutionary forces charged across it in the attack on the Winter Palace.

On the south side of the square is a horseshoe-shaped building that once housed the headquarters of the General Staff of Imperial Russia. Over a soaring 92-foot high archway in the center of the building is a Chariot of Victory commemorating Russia's victory over Napoleon. Built by Carlo Rossi, the facade of the General Staff Building measures over 1,900 feet in length.

Leningrad is a city of many cultural attractions, events, and festivities. Many dance and singing troupes from other Soviet cities perform on its stages and in its auditoriums. The costumes of many of these performers are works of art, such as those of the Armenian Folk Dance Troupe or that of the Volga Chorus. This troupe has won first prize in the Leningrad Festival. Their performance and talent is excellent.

A good place to start a tour of the city is by visiting the St. Peter and Paul Cathedral and Fortress (Petropavlovskaya Krepost). The fortress and church stand on a small island in the Neva River along its northern shore. It was on this site in 1703 that Peter the Great had earthenworks erected as a fort to defend his newly won land from Sweden. In 1706 brick walls forty feet high replaced the earthenworks; later granite slabs were used to cover over the bricks. Peter not only started its construction but also supervised the building of the fortress.

The small Zayachy Island on which the fortress was built is today connected by bridges to the larger surrounding islands. From the fortress the Hermitage Museum can be seen diagonally to the right across the Neva. Just beyond the fortress the Neva forks into two branches to flow around Vasilyevsky Island.

The Peter and Paul Fortress was built by 20,000 troops and laborers working and struggling in the harsh environment of the Neva marshes. The fortress with its 65-foot thick walls was eventually turned into a political prison. It became a prison when its military significance was lost. In time it became the Bastille of Russia. Peter's son Alexei, by his first wife, became one of the first inmates of the fortress prison. Alexei was a cruel, cowardly, treasonable person who was critical of his father. He drank heavily and maltreated his wife before her death. Later, his mistress confessed to Peter that Alexei planned to claim the throne, desert St. Petersburg, and undo his father's innovations. Peter then had Alexei tried for treason before a court. Tortured in the fortress prison, Alexei died while awaiting his court-ordered execution. Peter, the master-builder of St. Petersburg, was not without violent passions and sensual excesses of his own. He participated in orgies, could consume large amounts of liquor, and would torture and kill when it suited his whims. A man of impulses, Peter once said, "I wish to reform my empire, but I cannot reform myself."

Inside the fortress one can see the area where the new prisoners were initially processed, received their prison garb, and then went on to their cells. It was mainly a political prison, so when a man or woman was confined there it usually meant their whereabouts were kept a secret. The person simply disappeared and was perhaps never heard from again. Inside the dark, lonely cells the prisoners had little in the way of furniture: a small table, a chair, and hard iron bed on which to sleep. The only comforts consisted of a small straw cushion and small ragged blanket to keep warm. Food was a meager diet of bread, water, and potatoes.

The prisoner was not permitted to move around or make any sounds. The prisoners customarily wore heavy shoes that would make much noise in movement, thus attracting the attention of the guard outside who, walking on a carpet to muffle his footsteps, could sneak up and observe the movements of the prisoner. Should the prisoner take off his shoes, walking barefoot he might catch pneumonia in the damp, cold prison and die. The cells were first lit by candles, but later kerosene was used, and if the strain was unbearable the prisoner could douse his body with the kerosene and burn himself to death. The prisoners learned to communicate by using a tapping code developed by an early inmate.

Alexander Ulyanov, Lenin's brother, was a resident of the prison before his execution. His death probably was an added motive to Lenin to commence the 1917 revolution. Many revolutionaries languished in the morbid cells of the prison.

The names of a few of the others imprisoned in these cells include Fyodor Dostoevski, Maxim Gorky, and Nikolai Chernysheveski. Dostoevski (1821–1881), a renowned international novelist, is known for such works as *The Brothers Karamazov, Crime and Punishment,* and *A Little Hero,* the latter written while he was imprisoned in the Peter and Paul fortress.

Nikolai Chernyshevski (1828–1889), the son of a poor priest, wrote about the social and economic misery in tsarist Russia. He was endeared by the Russian intelligentsia of his time. His noted novel *Shto Delat'?,* written in prison, was translated into English with the title *What Is to Be Done?* in 1866. Maxim Gorky (1868–1936) was the pen name used by Aleksei Peshkov as the author of the triology *Childhood, In the World,* and *My Universities.* His early life was one of bitterness, hard physical work, and poverty. When he began to have his writings published, Peshkov chose the Russian word *gorki,* meaning "bitter," for the pseudonym in his pen name because it reminded him of the harsh conditions under which he grew up.

In the center of the fortress grounds stands the St. Peter and Paul Cathedral. Designed and built by the Italian architect Domenica Trazzini in 1712–33, it was later rebuilt by Trezzini with the assistance of Chevakinsky after a fire gutted it. Its 407-foot spire is the dominant edifice of the fortress, and stands out above the skyline of the city. This cathedral was the first baroque building in Leningrad. A thin sheathing of gold covers its needlelike spire. The cathedral is now a museum (since 1922) adjacent to nearby barracks and the prison.

The cathedral is beautifully decorated, but has no seats except for the one which remains that was set aside for the tsar. This gives the inside of the cathedral the appearance of a large reception hall. The masterpiece in this large space is the multitiered wooden iconostasis carved in 1722–26 by craftsmen from Yaroslavl. Its carvings are very expressive, and incorporate gold leaf into the design. Peter the Great, according to our guide, stood during the religious services. This cathedral became the mausoleum of the imperial family (Romanoff). There are a total of thirty-two coffins of the tsars and their relatives in the cathedral. One can distinguish a tsar's coffin from the rest by the emblem of Imperial Russia on each of its four corners. In addition to the gilded eagles on the corners, each coffin of a tsar bears a cross. Thirty coffins are made of white marble and two of precious stone, jasper, and rodonite. These two belong to Alexander II and his German-born wife, Maria. Known as the "Tsar Liberator," Alexander introduced a number of liberal reforms, including the abolition of serfdom in 1861. He is also remembered for his sale of Alaska to the United States in 1867. There are no bodies in the coffins, but the cathedral was the burial site of all the tsars of Russia from the time of Peter I to Alexander III, with the exception of Peter II.

An old mint built in 1724 and used to make metal coins stands near the church. Other structures nearby include the boat house of Peter the Great and the burial vault of the Grand Dukes.

At the rear of the cathedral guides point to a stairway that leads to the belfry of the church, and state that the body of Alexei, Peter the Great's son, was buried beneath the steps of the stairway after his torture and death in the fortress prison. Supposedly Peter chose this spot because the bell ringer in making his rounds each day up and down the stairway would disturb the spirit or ghost of Alexei and not permit him any peace in the hereafter.

At the tip of Vasilyevsky Island, around which flow the two arms of the Neva, stand the Rostral Columns decorated with the prows of ships. Built in 1806, the two stone columns each stand 105 feet high, and were once used as beacons for shipping on the Neva. The area around the columns was once part of the port of the city, which today lies closer to the Gulf of Finland. At the top of each column is a huge copper cup into which oil was once poured and then lighted at night to guide ships into the port. Near the base of the columns are white marble statues that were erected as tributes to Russia's great river waterways. Each column has protruding from it the prows of ships, which gives the illusion that ships are sailing through the column of stone. This concept supposedly originated with the Romans, who took bows off defeated ships and placed them on towers in an arrangement similar to that seen on the Rostral Columns.

Behind the Rostral Columns stands the former Stock Exchange building, which now houses the Central Navy Museum. Surrounding the large square building on all sides are huge Doric columns, which total forty-four in number. The eastern facade facing the Rostral Columns displays a relief of Neptune driving a chariot. A number of sculptures decorate the eastern and western facades of the building, which was erected in 1810–16.

To the west of the Central Navy Museum and immediately behind it, across Mendeleyevskaya Prospekt, is located Leningrad State University. The building that houses the university was established by Peter the Great to hold the ministries of government, then known as the Twelve Boards. In the early nineteenth century, the already familiar row of twelve adjoining, three-story pavilions officially became the new university. Today American students enrolled at the university blend in with Russian students in the hallways and classrooms.

Another area of interest in Leningrad centers on Ploschad Iskusstv or Arts Square. This square is located in the central part of the city between the Moika River on the north and Nevsky Prospekt on the south. Major sights of interest around Arts Square include Maly Opera and Ballet Theater, Russian Museum, Leningrad Philharmonic, Musical Comedy Theater, Museum of Ethnography of the Peoples of the U.S.S.R., and the monument to Pushkin.

The name Pushkin is a legend in Leningrad and indeed in the Soviet Union. Of Leningrad he said: "How fair thou art, O city of Peter." Alexander Pushkin (1799–1837) lived at a time when the arts were flourishing in Russia. He is revered as Russia's greatest poet and is considered the father of modern Russian literature. Pushkin was born into an aristocratic family, learned to speak and read French, and was early exposed to literary friends of his father, who stimulated him to write. At age twelve he went to Tsarskoe Selo near St. Petersburg to enter the Imperial Lyceum. There he launched his career in literature, and after leaving the Lyceum went to St. Petersburg to work in the foreign office, whereupon he became active in literary and theater circles and began publishing. In 1820 he was exiled to Moldavia; his poems were too politically objectionable to the government. Pushkin had many friends among the Decembrists and voiced their ideas and aspirations against autocracy. While banished to southern Russia he made his reputation as a poet and literary author. In 1826 he was allowed by Nicholas I to live in Moscow, and in 1831 once more moved to St. Petersburg upon his marriage. He returned to service with the government, continued to write, and moved in court circles. In 1837 some of his enemies forced him into a duel to defend the honor of his wife. Gravely wounded in the duel, he died several days later. A few of his prolific literary works include the poem *Ruslan and Ludmila, The Negro of Peter the Great,* and *The Bronze Horseman.* Other works include the tragedy *Boris Gudunov,* and the historical novel *The Captain's Daughter.* Pushkin was recognized as a literary genius even in his own lifetime. His statue stands in front of the Russian Museum on the north side of Arts Square.

The Russian Museum (formerly the Mikhailovsky Palace) contains over one-hundred rooms filled with such items as exquisite tenth-century icons, beautiful paintings, secular art, and revolutionary propaganda posters. The former palace that houses the museum was built by Carlo Rossi, and is now the second largest museum in the city next to that of the Hermitage. Prominent artworks by such Russian artists of the past as V. Serov, I. Repin, V. Surikov, M. Vrubel, Andrei Rublyov, and others fill many rooms of the museum, dating back to 1898. Works by more recent Soviet artists, including M. Grekov, I. Brodsky, S. Konenkov, and V. Mukhina can also be seen. One of the museum's better-known paintings is that of "The Volga Boatsmen," done by the artist Elijah Repin (1844–1930).

After the Russian Revolution all private art schools and academies were abolished. Many Russian artists emigrated to the West. The Communist party decreed the style and taste of socialist art. Russian art by the 1930s had become drab and tasteless, stylized by revolutionary ideology.

A short distance north of the Russian Museum on a tract of land running along the west side of the Fontanka River and facing the Neva River is the Summer Garden (Letny Sad) and Summer Palace (Letny Dvorets) of Peter I. The Summer Palace is set amidst dense trees through which are cut spacious walkways lined with ornately sculptured statues. The two-story Summer Palace is a modest structure when compared to the other spacious and magnificent palaces of the city. Designed in 1710–14 by Trezzini for use by Peter the Great, it had a decoratively tiled kitchen and stoves, and paintings on the ceilings. Bordering the Summer Garden on the northside along the Neva is a long, high iron fence with huge, twin iron gates in the middle opening into the Summer Garden.

Opposite the Summer Garden, across Sadovaya Street, is located the spacious Marsovo Polye (The Field of Mars). This twenty-five acre square is dedicated to those whom the Communist government refers to as the "Heroes of the Revolution and the Civil War." Large, wide ruler-straight walkways lead from all corners of the square toward its center, where a monument to the 1917 revolution is located.

Once more we turn our attention to the great thoroughfare, the Nevsky Prospekt. Heading easterly along it one soon passes Gostiny Dvor (Merchant's Yard), a vast department store whose wings enclose a square. It was built in the latter 1700s by the Frenchman Vallin de la Mothe and contains a variety of hundreds of shops. Gostiny Dvor is comparable in size and selection of merchandise to the huge GUM Department Store in Moscow. It is also one of the stops on the metro. Continuing along the Nevsky Prospekt, we visited the Pushkin Drama Theater, in front of which stands Catherine II's monument. She was such a fascinating and colorful figure in Russian history, that more must be said of her at this point.

Catherine was a German import brought to Russia by the Empress Elizabeth, youngest daughter of Peter the Great, to marry her nephew, Charles Peter of Holstein, another German import. They were Elizabeth's designated successors to the throne. Charles was weak, disliked Catherine, and took a mistress. Catherine liked dancing, riding, and men; not necessarily in that order. She took a number of lovers, and gave birth to a son of dubious paternity. Intelligent, ambitious, and cunning, Catherine plotted to seize the throne. When Elizabeth died, Catherine's husband took the throne as Peter III, but in 1762 Catherine staged a coup d'etat using regiments of the guards with whom she was popular. Peter was forced to abdicate and died mysteriously, while Catherine declared herself the Empress and reigned as Catherine II from 1762–96. She had an enormous appetite for sex and once confessed that she could not go for an hour without it. Next to her bedchamber she kept an apartment for her lovers. Several of these she richly rewarded; Gregory Potemkin was made Prince of Taurida and given a palace; and Stanislaus Poniatowski was put on the throne of Poland. Catherine once said, "I have never fancied myself extremely beautiful; but I have the art of pleasing which, I think, is my greatest asset." She chose wisely those to run her government, nurtured cultural and scientific developments, expanded the frontiers of Russia, and initiated some internal reforms. An enlightened despot to the end, she died at age 67 allegedly following a night of sexual indulgence.

Along the eastern end of the Nevsky Prospekt is the approach to the Alexander Nevsky Monastery, which stands near the Neva River. Legend and history both are interwoven with the fabric of time on the site on which this church stands. In 1240 Prince Alexander of Novgorod won a battle with the Swedes, which legend says was fought on the grounds where this monastery is located. After his victory on the Neva he became known as Alexander Nevsky, and the Russian Orthodox church proclaimed him a saint. Many years after his death his remains were brought to a church built by Peter the Great on the former battlefield. His silver tomb is now on display in the Hermitage.

The monastery, now the Museum of Urban Sculpture, is one of the largest in Russia. The monastery contains a library with a large collection of valuable books and manuscripts. Designed by Trezzini in 1710–16, the monastery includes eleven churches, a seminary, an academy for religious studies, and four cemeteries. Standing on the grounds of the monastery is the Troitsky or Cathedral of the Holy Trinity, which formerly held the remains of Alexander Nevsky. The cathedral was built in 1778–90 by Ivan Starov upon the request of Peter the Great. In front of the cathedral are buried such celebrities as Rubinstein, a famous composer, and Rosenhein, a well-known poet. In another graveyard are buried Tchaikovsky, Mussorgsky, Glinka, Arensky, Brodin, Serov, and Rimsky-Korsakov (all composers). Carlo Rossi and Andrei Voronikhin, two well-known architects, are also buried on the grounds of the monastery. Other graves contain known writers, actors, and actresses.

From the monastery a drive back toward the Hotel Leningrad, recrossing the Neva, brings one to the Lenin monument in front of the present Finland Railway Station built in 1960. It was at the old station on this site on April 16, 1917, that Lenin arrived after a journey that began in Switzerland and took him through Germany and into Finland. From Helsinki he boarded the train which soon arrived in Petrograd. Lenin first arrived in the city in 1893 with a law degree in his hand, which had been granted to him *in absentia* from St. Petersburg University for completion of external studies. Already a Marxist, Lenin stayed in St. Petersburg until May 1895, then went to Switzerland to make contact with Russian revolutionaries, and returned to St. Petersburg in September. He was arrested in December, sent to prison, and in 1897 exiled to Siberia where he was married the following year. Lenin did not arrive back in St. Petersburg until 1905, after having spent over five years in Western Europe following the end of his exile. He stayed in St. Petersburg less than a year, then emigrated around from Finland to Switzerland, until his return in 1917 to lead his revolutionary party. When the Kerensky government was overthrown on the night of November 6, 1917, Lenin became the head of the new Soviet government. Lenin died in Gorky in 1924 following a stroke. That same year Petrograd, formerly St. Petersburg, changed its name once more to that of Leningrad to honor the man who had altered the course of Russian history. In Leningrad many wept for the death of their leader; some remembered and wept for the days of tsarist Russia, but it was gone forever.

Shoppers in Leningrad are out early along its streets. For the tourist, shopping usually means a trip to a Beriozka store, but local department stores offer a few good buys, such as Russian worker's hats. A good one can be purchased for eight or nine rubbles.

For a memorable boatride and trip, go to the dock along the Neva and board a hydrofoil for a ride down the Neva into the Gulf of Finland, and thence to the Summer Palace of Petrodvorets built by Peter the Great. Peter himself is credited with having chopped down some of the trees that went into the building of the palace. The palace sits facing the south shore of the Gulf of Finland about nineteen miles from Leningrad. Built in 1725 the palace sits on 300 acres of landscape and is often referred to as the "Versailles" of Peter the Great. Work on the estate was begun in 1709. Petrodvorets is an ostentatious showcase. Sitting on the hillside overlooking verdant gardens and parks and the blue waters of the Gulf of Finland, it is a splendid sight to behold. In front of the Grand Palace is a canal-like waterway known as the Great Grotto, which stretches to the Gulf of Finland. The grotto is lined by a total of 64 fountains and 255 sculptures, and is spanned by bridges. In front, and on a level below the palace, a number of gold-covered statues stand amidst sprouting fountains, the largest of which is the Samson Fountain. The statue of Samson is seen tearing or pulling apart the jaws of a lion. The statue symbolizes Russia's (Samson) defeat of Sweden (the lion). From the mouth of the gold-covered statue of the lion a jet of water spews 69 feet into the air. There are 129 fountains on the estate, all of which operate from water supplied by springs that are over thirteen miles away. During World War II the Germans occupied the palace and later destroyed much of it. The Russians had removed most of the treasures of the palace but left "Samson" behind. The Germans had the statue cut in half and shipped back to Germany but after the war a duplicate was made and has stood in its place since 1955.

Other fountains at Petrodvorets include the one of Adam from the creation story in the Bible, the Magic Fountain of Peter the Great, the Pyramid Fountain, and the Checkerboard Cascade. One must not miss the Magic Fountain, also known as "choutikhi" or joke fountain. It is a big treat to Russian children, who think that if they touch a certain stone in the walkway next to it, water will gush out and spray them. What actually happens is that an inconspicuous person hiding in the bushes works a lever controlling the flow of water. Peter the Great had a fetish for collecting fountains.

Petrodvorets, formerly Peterhof, was designed and built by J. A. Leblond. In 1752 Rastrelli, one of the master architects of St. Petersburg, enlarged and added further features to the palace. The glass panes alone that went into its design cover 900 symmetrical feet. The palace is a three-storied structure finished in cream and greenish colors. Largely destroyed by the Germans, less than half of its 63 rooms have been fully restored.

Also of interest is Peter's small palace nearby, which he came to like better than the Summer Palace. He preferred the small palace because he loved to walk through its surrounding gardens and relax in its homey atmosphere. The small palace contained a gallery of paintings. Also a victim of World War II, it was later restored to its original state.

Peter's youngest daughter, Elizabeth, born in 1709, inherited from him his gifted and talented architect, Rastrelli. It was she who commissioned Rastrelli to use his genius in redesigning Petrodvorets in 1752. Elizabeth was a beautiful and seductive woman. She often dressed as a transvestite, took lovers, but never married, except perhaps secretly to the Ukrainian peasant singer Rasumovsky. Elizabeth ruled from 1741–62 while encouraging the arts, supporting the theater, and adopting the French language and fashions. She was extravagant in her tastes and had the sumptuous Winter Palace built and left as her legacy. When she died, she left behind a wardrobe of 15,000 dresses in her closets, and 5,000 pairs of shoes.

Elizabeth, like Catherine the Great, had many lovers and enjoyed amusing herself. She was an unintelligent person who, according to many accounts, never read a book. Elizabeth was malicious, spiteful, and vengeful. She had thousands of her subjects imprisoned. Others simply disappeared. Those who flattered Elizabeth and gained her recognition could easily secure an order to dispose of an enemy or have a despised person imprisoned. In spite of Elizabeth's fallibilities, Russia managed to progress during her reign.

To keep track of the Russian monarchy in their proper perspective, a chronology of the House of Romanov follows:

Michael Romanov	1613–1645
Alexis Romanov	1645–1676
Feodor Romanov	1676–1682
Peter I (the Great)	1682–1725
Catherine I	1725-1727
Peter II	1727–1730
Anna of Courland	1730–1740
Ivan VI	1740–1741
Elizabeth	1741–1762
Peter III	1762
Catherine II (the Great)	1762-1796
Paul	1796–1801
Alexander I	1801–1825
Nicholas I	1825-1855
Alexander II	1855-1881
Alexander III	1881–1894
Nicholas II	1894–1917

Another abode of monarchy was the town of Pushkin (formerly Tsarskoye Selo or "Tsar's Village") located about fifteen miles south of Leningrad. The town's name suggests, correctly, an association with Alexander Pushkin, the famous Russian poet. As noted previously, Pushkin went there to study at the Imperial Lyceum in 1811. His first poems were composed at the Lyceum, where he stayed until 1817 when he left for St. Petersburg. There are two Pushkin museums and a life-size statue of him in the town.

After the 1917 revolution, Tsarskoye Selo was renamed Dyetskoye Selo (Children's Village), because of the number of schools, hospitals, and clinics it contained to provide for the needs of children. The first railroad built in Russia ran from St. Petersburg to Tsarskoye Selo in 1837.

At Pushkin the Russian aristocracy reached the zenith of its fairy-tale existence. The superb architectural masterpiece in Pushkin is the eighteenth-century Yekaterinisky Palace built for Catherine the Great. Its more than 200 rooms are magnificently decorated. This lavish piece of architecture is the work of Kvasov and Rastrelli. Its three-story edifice is done in Russian baroque style; the blue and white facade is breathtaking. The palace is decorated with lacy balcony grilles, artistic stucco moldings, and huge stone columns. The interior of the palace is exquisite. It has rooms displaying Chinese teakwood, Japanese bamboo, amber, lapis lazuli, jasper, wood mosaics, pearl, and other exotic decorations. The palace even has its own cathedral, capped with golden onion-shaped domes.

Catherine the Great adored this palace and frequently entertained her lovers in it. One of Catherine's lovers, Count Rotari, an artist, was dispatched to travel her empire and paint the portraits of its beautiful females. Rotari sent more than 800 of his paintings back to the palace.

Catherine kept an army of about 600 gardeners busy trimming, arranging, and caring for the 2,000 acres of land on which the palace was built. On its grounds were constructed lakes, fountains, statues, boathouses, and other fanciful decorations. White marble statues set amidst verdant gardens embellish the grounds of the palace.

Peter the Great's daughter, Elizabeth, detested the rough carriage rides to Tsarskoye Selo, and ordered the building of a canal to the village from St. Petersburg so that she might ride there on the comfort of a boat. The canal was unfinished at the time of Elizabeth's death, but the residents and visitors to Tsarskoye Selo used parts of it for swimming.

The design of the palace is similar to that of the Winter Palace, however, Yekaterinisky appears much more warm, serene, and pleasing to the eye. For these reasons many favor it over the Winter Palace. The palace was largely destroyed by the Germans during the war, but has since been restored to its original elegance. Catherine II would be proud of it even today.

To the rear of the Catherine Palace, and offset from it at an angle, is the Alexander Palace and Alexander Park. Designed by the Italian architect Giaccomo Quarenghi, the Alexander Palace was built in the 1790s in Russian classical style. It is a large, two-story palace with two wings attached to a center, and contains over one hundred rooms. Quarenghi was commissioned by Catherine the Great to build this palace for her grandson, who later became Alexander I in 1801. In 1895 Nicholas II, the last Russian tsar, brought his young bride, Alexandra Fedorovna, born Princess Alix of Hesse-Darmstadt, to live in the Alexander Palace. They lived in it for twenty-two years, before departing it forcefully in 1917 on their way to their massacre in Ekaterinburg. It is a palace in every sense of the word. Inside are exquisite chandeliers; rooms decorated in gold, marble, and polished hardwoods; floors of parquet design covered with Oriental rugs; silk curtains; gleaming crystal; Chinese vases; etc. A beautiful tree-lined boulevard leads from the palace gates to the railway station beyond. Here Nicholas and Alexandra raised their four daughters—Olga, Tatrina, Marie, and Anastasia—and only son, Alexis. One of the bodyguards to Nicholas II was Jim Hercules, an American Negro. Hercules visited the United States on his vacations and returned to the Alexander Palace with jars of jelly which the tsar's children enjoyed.

Alexis, son of Tsar Nicholas, had hemophilia, and once suffered a nosebleed which nearly led to his death. He was tortured by one hemorrhage after another, and when Alexandra heard that a mysterious Siberian peasant, Gregory Rasputin, supposedly had healing powers that were proclaimed miraculous, he was invited to the Alexander Palace in 1905. Rasputin's success in stopping Alexis's hemorrhages endeared him to Alexandra.

Alexandra believed that Rasputin was indispensable to the health of her son and the well-being of the royal family, but in the end it was he who was mainly responsible for their execution. Rasputin, however, did not live to see the overthrow of the monarchy as he was poisoned, shot, and thown in the icy waters of the Neva in December 1916. Rasputin was buried in the grounds of the Imperial Park in a small chapel, and Nicholas and Alexandra attended his funeral. In 1917 soldiers entered the chapel, removed Rasputin's coffin, doused the corpse with gasoline, and burned it atop a pile of logs. In July 1918 the royal family met their doom at Ekaterinburg, later renamed Sverdlovsk. Over this same city in 1960, Francis Gary Powers, the American U-2 pilot was shot down.

From Pushkin it is a drive of about two miles to the southeast to Pavlovsk, at which is located the beautiful Pavlovsky Palace, built in the eighteenth century. This remarkable palace was designed by the great Scottish architect Charles Cameron in 1782. Catherine the Great commissioned him to build it, later presenting it as a gift to her son Paul, thus the origin of the name of the palace and the town.

Paul I (1754–1801), son of Peter III and Catherine II, was mentally deficient and during his reign few persons felt secure or immune from his cruelty. He imprisoned many of the nobility or sent them into exile; made the free classes of Russians subject to torture and execution by repealing a law that forbade such acts; and on the belief that the French Revolution had been caused by the wearing of waistcoats, banned them from wear in Russia. In 1801, officers of the imperial guards strangled Paul as he slept one night in St. Petersburg.

Rossi and other architects later enlarged the palace. A total of sixty-four huge columns support its dome. The palace is built of a blend of baroque and classical features. Built on a high bluff overlooking the Slavyanka River, the palace affords a lovely view of its park laid out in geometric designs. Inside the park Alexander I held a victory celebration in 1814 at the Rose Pavilion and toasted his defeat of Napoleon. The palace was badly damaged by the Germans but restored after World War II.

About twenty-one miles west of Leningrad along the northern shore of the Gulf of Finland, lies the town of Repino. Here is located the country home of the great Russian painter Ilya Repin, which is now a memorial museum. Repin (1844–1930) created many of his masterpieces here between 1900 and 1930. The Repin estate is known as Penates, and Repin's grave is located on the grounds of the estate.

Repin was a painter of Russian history and won a gold medal from the St. Petersburg Academy of Fine Arts. Among his better known works are "Ivan the Terrible's Murder of His Son," "The Reply of the Zaporozhic Cossacks," "The Arrest of the Propagandist," "The Religious Procession in Kursk Province," and the renown "Volga Boatsmen," done in 1873, which can be seen in the Russian State Museum in Leningrad.

A realist artist, Repin tried to capture on canvas the national consciousness of Russia. He was less concerned with the aesthetics of art than with its social and moral ideals. A tour of Repino may be arranged at a local Intourist Service Bureau in Leningrad.

Most foreign tourists and visitors to Leningrad find it more to their liking than any other Russian city. Visitors depart Leningrad with many memories and with a certain feeling of reverence for the city.

EXCURSIONS

Sightseeing Tour of the City.

Tourists are taken on a tour of the center of the city and its historical and revolutionary monuments: the Peter-and-Paul Fortress, the cruiser "Aurora," the Smolny—the headquarters of the Revolution, the ensemble of Nevsky Prospekt, new residential districts, the Piskaryovskoye Memorial Cemetery, or the monument to the Heroic Defenders of Leningrad.

Architecture in Leningrad.

Acquaintance with the most interesting architectural ensembles of the eighteenth to twentieth centuries and the history of the construction of the city.

St. Petersburg in the Days of Peter the Great.

Introduction to the history of construction of the city, a tour of the Summer Palace and the Lodge of Peter the Great (Peter the Great was the founder of the city).

MUSEUMS

V. I. Lenin Museum.

Assembly Hall and V. I. Lenin's Room in the Smolny.

Museum of the Cruiser "Aurora." The cruiser "Aurora" fired the first signal shot which heralded the beginning of the October Revolution of 1917.

Museum of the Great October Socialist Revolution.

Museum of the History of Leningrad.

Peter-and-Paul Fortress. The first stone edifice in the city, a former political jail of czarist Russia. The Cathedral of Sts. Peter and Paul is an architectural monument of the eighteenth century, the burial place of the Russian czars.

Museum Lodge of Peter the Great. The only wooden structure that has lasted from the days of the city's foundation to the present day.

Summer Palace of Peter the Great in the Summer Garden. An architectural monument of the eighteenth century. Displayed in the palace's halls are works of fine and applied arts, articles of domestic use of the eighteenth century, and clothes of Peter the Great.

Piskaryovskoye Cemetery.

Monument to the Heroic Defenders of Leningrad. The memorial is dedicated to the hundreds of thousands of Leningraders and defenders of the city who fell during the siege of Leningrad in the years of the past war.

Central Museum of the Navy. The history of the development of the Russian navy from the days of Peter the Great.

Russian Museum. The biggest repository of masterpieces of Russian painting, sculpture, graphic and applied art from old Russian art to the present day.

Hermitage. The biggest art museum in the U.S.S.R. It houses more than three million works of art and monuments of culture.

St. Isaac's Cathedral. An outstanding monument of Russian architecture and construction engineering of the nineteenth century.

Museum of the U.S.S.R. Acadmey of Arts. Works of painting and sculpture and architectural drawings.

Museum of Urban Sculpture. Located on the territory of the Alexandro-

Nevskaya Lavra (Monastery) where prominent figures of Russian culture are buried.

Museum of Anthropology and Ethnography.

Museum of the Ethnography of the Peoples of the U.S.S.R.

Zoological Museum.

Literary Museum, "Pushkin House." The exhibits are devoted to the lives and activities of Russian authors.

Museum of the Theater. Devoted to the history of the theater in Russia and its present day significance.

Museum-Flat of F. M. Dostoyevsky. Exhibits are devoted to the famous Russian author of the nineteenth century.

Museum-Flat of F. I. Challapin. Narrative about the life of the celebrated Russian singer.

OUT-OF-TOWN EXCURSIONS

Petrodvorets. A palace-and-park ensemble of the early eighteenth century. Distance from Leningrad: 34 km. Tour duration: 4 hours.

Town of Pushkin (former Tsarskoye Selo). A tour of the Catharine Palace and a garden-and-park ensemble of the eighteenth century. Distance from Leningrad: 27 km. Tour duration: 4 hours.

Town of Pavlovsk. A tour of the park and the czars' palace of the late eighteenth century. Distance from Leningrad: 35 km. Tour duration: 4 hours.

Sarai and Shalash Museum-Monuments. Dedicated to the life and activities of V. I. Lenin. Distance from Leningrad: 35 km. Tour duration: 4 hours.

"Penaty"—Museum Estate of I. Repin. The prominent Russian painter Ilya Repin lived here. Distance from Leningrad: 44 km. Tour duration: 3½ hours.

THEATERS

Quite popular among Leningrad's theaters and concert halls are: Kirov Opera and Ballet Theater, Maly Theater of Opera and Ballet, Shostakovich Philharmonic, Lensoviet Palace of Culture, Oktyabrsky Concert Hall, and Leningrad State Circus. Intourist has its Cultural Centres functioning at the Palace of Youth and the Nevsky Palace of Culture.

HOTELS

Hotel	Address	Rooms	Telephone
Astoria	39 Herzen St.	380	219-1100
			219-1160
Europeiskaya	1/7 Brodsky St.	250	211-9149
Leningrad	5/2 Pirogovskaya Embankment	746	542-9411
Moscow	2 Alexander Nevsky St.	777	274-2051
			274-9515
Oktyabrskaya	10 Lisdvsky Ave.	738	211-5362
Pribaltiskaya	14 Ulitsa Korablestroitelei	1,200	356-0158
			356-0176
Pulkovskaya	1 Pobeda Sq.	540	264-5122
			264-5121
Rossiya	11 Chernyshevsky Sq.	414	298-7349
			298-7659
Sovetskaya	43 Lermontov Ave.	1,120	216-0032

RESTAURANTS

Some of Leningrad's more popular restaurants, with their national cuisine are listed below:

Europejskaya, "Sadko" Hall, (1/7 Brodsky St.). Russian cuisine, folklore floor show.

Pribaltijskaya (14 Korablestroiteley St.). Russian cuisine, floor show.

Pulkovskaya (1 Pobeda Sq.). Russian and Finnish cuisine, floor show.

Chapter IV.
NOVGOROD
Father of Russian Cities

O swarming city, city full of dreams,
Where in full day the specter walks and speaks.
—Baudelaire

Novgorod, meaning "New Town," lies nearly due south of Leningrad. My journey to this city was made by car from Leningrad. Leningrad is huge and vibrant by contrast to Novgorod.

Novgorod lies approximately 121 miles by road from Leningrad. Only a few small villages and towns are found between the two cities. These include Tosno, about 37 miles south of Leningrad; Lyuben, about 20 miles beyond Tosno; then Chudnovo; and finally Podberezye near Novgorod. Novgorod is located on the Moscow-Leningrad Highway.

The city is surrounded by the Great European Plain, and the area around it is relatively flat, although extensive tracts of land to the south and east are covered by swamps and marshy lowlands. The soils have been glaciated and are relatively infertile. Agriculture is insignificant in the area compared to the Ukraine or Black Earth Belt, but from the highway can be seen fields of rye, barley, and oats. Along the roadside are fields of potatoes, a chief food crop in the area and in Russia; and fields of flax, a plant grown for its seed and for manufacture into linen. Meadows and pastures abound in the Novgorod region, and dairying is a major farming enterprise in the area. Many orchards can also be seen from the highway.

The weather is usually cool during the summertime, with rain falling about ten days per month in that season. Temperatures for the area average in the low twenties during January and in the low sixties during July. The climate of the area is classified as continental, but proximity to the Baltic Sea and the Atlantic helps to ameliorate temperatures. Novgorod is located at 58° 30′ north latitude, almost identical to that of Juneau, Alaska.

When Novgorod appears to the eye, first the cupolas from its old churches and monasteries come into view, then the newer portions of the city, and finally there is the Volkhov River in the center of the city. The Volkhov divides the city into two parts, the Sofiyskaya Storona (Sophia Side) and the Torgovaya Storona (Market Side).

The Volkhov has its source in the Lake Ilmen, about three miles south of the city. It then flows through Novgorod before continuing its 141-mile journey to Lake Ladoga, northeast of Leningrad. The river is navigable in the vicinity of Novgorod, but farther north it contains rapids.

The ghosts of past civilizations keep tryst with ancient Novgorod. The mist of years hangs over the city. Here amidst ruins of the past flourished a great commercial civilization. Among its shadowy arches and behind its facade of modernity lies a heritage endowed by the centuries of the city's existence. Legend and mystery are part of the written record of Novgorod. Vikings, Russians, Germans, and others have left their imprint on the city.

Present day Novgorod has a population of about 218,000 people. The city has grown rapidly since World War II but it is not the modern Novgorod that the tourist comes to see. One's mind and thoughts are soon transported back more than a thousand years in time. Novgorod is old; it had streets paved with cleaved wooden logs five hundred years before the muddy streets of London were covered over. Major excavation work done at Novgorod in 1951–62 revealed 28 different layers of log streets in parts of the city. Novgorod is a blend of old and new.

Some zealous chroniclers of medieval Novgorod wrote that the city was founded by Noah's third son, Japheth, while others maintain that the apostle Andrew personally brought Christianity to Novgorod. According to tradition, St. Anthony journeyed to Novgorod from Rome and arrived in the city via the Volkhov River. The saint then settled in the city, built a church there, and after his death was buried in Novgorod. Medieval travelers to the city were told his body reposed in the Monastery of St. Anthony, but the Russians forbade foreigners to enter the monastery to view his supposed remains.

Some of Novgorod's chroniclers also denied the existence of most connections between Novgorod and Byzantium, charging the latter with wickedness
and sin, and alleged that God had bestowed upon Novgorod his good graces.
The Mongol rape of Kiev was regarded as a sign by many Novgorodians that
their city was smiled upon by God. More accurately speaking, historians
record that the Ilmen Slavs founded the city in the ninth century, and that its
name first appeared in chronicles in 862 A.D. Finns and Baltic peoples were
the forerunners of the Slavs in the Novgorod region. The Slavs, it is believed,
migrated there during the sixth and seventh centuries A.D. By any account
Novgorod is over 1,100 years old. However, excavations have not yet confirmed the existence of a settlement on the site of Novgorod by the year 862.
The origins of the city are not as clearly determined as some historians
believe.

Early Novgorod became a stronghold of the Varangians (Vikings). The
Vikings knew Novgorod as Holmgard, meaning "island town." The *Russian
Chronicle,* a traditional version of early Russian history, contains the account
that the Varangians were invited to Novgorod by the Slavs to restore order
among their feuding factions and tribes. According to legend, the Varangian
Rurik, two of his brothers, and a host of warriors arrived and took control of
the town. Rurik then became prince of the city in 862. Later the Norse
warriors Askold and Dir departed Novgorod, captured Kiev, and established
there the foundations of the Russian state. The two Varangian city-states of
Novgorod and Kiev were united in 879 when Oleg, upon arrival from
Novgorod, treacherously slew Askold and Dir and imposed himself as ruler
of both cities. In 989 Prince Vladimir I, ruler of Kiev (979–1015), forced the
inhabitants of Novgorod to be Christianized. This occurred one year after he
had had Kiev's populace baptized. When the people of Novgorod became
Christians they flung an idol of their god called Perun into the Volkhov River
in a scene reminiscent of that in Kiev when its population accepted Christianity. Later a church called Perun Monastery was built on the site where the
idol formerly stood.

The history of the founding of the Russian state and that of Novgorod is
closely intertwined. In 1019 Yaroslav became grand duke of Kiev, which he
ruled till 1054. He was the last of Kiev's rulers to administer joint control over
both that city and Novgorod. He had previously ruled Novgorod as the
representative of his father, Prince Vladimir I.

The historic site of Yaroslav's court is located on the Market side (east
bank) of Novgorod along the Volkhov River. The Market side once had a
wooden wall around it and was the site of a pagan cemetery. Yaroslav's court-
residence was used by his descendants in ruling Novgorod until the early
twelfth century. His court in the mid-twelfth century became the seat of the
veche, or people's assembly, which was the chief legislative authority of the

city.

From the time of Yaroslav the *veche* chose the ruling prince of Novgorod. The prince was accountable for his actions to the *veche,* who could strip him of his power if that body so wished. In reality, the role of the prince was little more than commander of the army of Novgorod.

Novgorod was ruled by a prince as its supreme sovereign until 1136, after which time monarchical rule ceased an an independent republic was established. According to Thompson in *Novgorod the Great,* the city "was not a mercantile republic, as has sometimes been represented, but a feudal state ruled by a few score aristocratic families."[2] Forced out of the Novgorod kremlin during the twelfth century, the prince of that city took up residence in Gorodishche, a nearby hill-estate located about one-half mile south of Novgorod. Later when the Russian tsars or members of the royal family visited Novgorod, they customarily stayed in Gorodishche. The hill became the property of Alexander Menshikov during the reign of Peter the Great. Until 1270 a prince remained the titular head of authority over Novgorod, but without power to rule. No prince ruled Novgorod after that date, from which time a burgomaster or mayor was chosen by the *veche* as the main administrator of the city. The *veche* preserved its power in Novgorod until the end of the fifteenth century. In the fourteenth century a grand duke replaced the prince as overlord of the city. Indeed, before Ivan III (the Great), grand duke of Muscovy (1462–1505), created the title of prince in Russia, no such rank existed there.

The birth of modern Russia sprang from the unification of the principalities of Kiev and Novgorod. From the time of its founding in the nineteenth century, Novgorod lay on an important trade route stretching from the Baltic Sea to Novgorod and Kiev and thence to Constantinople, the old capital of the Byzantine empire now known as Istanbul. The trade route between Novgorod and Constantinople was known as the route "from the Varangians to the Greeks."

Novgorodians tell the story, related in their ancient chronicles, that at one time the men of the city marched southward to attack Greece, and fought there in a siege lasting seven years. Not knowing if the men of Novgorod would return, the women of the city married the serfs who were bound in servitude to local families. When the men of Novgorod returned from their war in Greece, the serfs attacked them and defeated them in an engagement. Later the defeated masters of the serfs rallied and employed psychological warfare to defeat their vassals in a second encounter. The masters cast aside their swords and other weapons and attacked their serfs with whips and large sticks, instruments customarily used to discipline and punish the serfs. So surprised were the serfs that they fled before their masters. Subsequently the hostile serfs were rounded up and put to painful deaths. The sorrowful wives of the serfs then hung themselves for their shame and guilt.

Novgorod decided to distance itself from the influence of Kiev in 1125 when Vladimir II died. Thereafter, Novgorod cast off the economic, political and military grasp of Kiev. During its heyday as a medieval principality in the eleventh to fifteenth centuries, Novgorod's rule extended over a large part of northern Russia from Lithuania and the Baltic Sea on the West to the Ural Mountains on the east, and northward to Lake Peipus.

Between 1125 and 1270, Novgorod continued to prosper in trade with Constantinople. In addition to its Black Sea trade route, the city also lay along an active merchant route from the Baltic to the Volga River and the Caspian Sea. From there an active trade flourished with India and parts of the Arab world. It was in the fur trade that Novgorod excelled, but the city's markets contained diversified goods such as honey, cloth, textiles, jewelry, copper and silver objects, slaves, leather goods, silk, pottery, jade, amber, wax, grain, and birch bark.

Merchants from the Hansa League of northern Europe were also frequent traders in Novgorod's markets and streets by the mid-twelfth century. Furs and wax were the main items that the Russians traded to the Germans. Novgorod's clergy, landed classes, and wealthy merchants were literate. Records kept by means of writing on birch bark recorded trade, commercial, and monetary arrangements.

Novgorod escaped invasion by the Tartars in the 1230s but was forced to pay tribute to them. However, another threat to the city was more serious than that posed by the Tartars. To the west and southwest of Novgorod the Teutonic knights and Swedish forces were preparing to attack Russia. In 1240 the Novgorodians led by Prince Alexander Yaroslav met the Swedish army on the Neva River and defeated it. The people of Novgorod gave the prince the surname of "Nevsky" in appreciation of his victory. They were even more jubilant when in 1242 he routed the Teutonic knights at the battle of Lake Peipus. After Prince Nevsky's victories, Novgorod recognized the leadership of the city of Vladimir and its princes.

Next to Kiev, the Novgorod-Pskov area was a rich center of religious art and architecture. Novgorod was at first influenced by the artistic styles of Kiev and her Byzantine inheritance, but in the thirteenth and fourteenth centuries produced its own native artists and sources of inspiration, and was the leader in the field of artistic endeavor in Russia.

The end of Kiev's control of Novgorod did not bring a halt to the city's quest for independence and freedom. By the twelfeth century, the city of Suzdal which lay northeast of Moscow had grown sufficient in strength to challenge the power of Novgorod. Suzdal provided Novgorod with the majority of its grain supply, and in the latter twelfth and early thirteenth century the two cities fought each other, with Suzdal the loser.

Novgorod was to have no peace, however. Its next adversary, Moscow, had steadily been gaining in power, and in 1332 Novgorod was forced to fight this newcomer in the first of many battles. The local history of Novgorod records much violence. During the fourteenth century, while Novgorod contended with Moscow, it was hard hit by major fires and a plague.

Novgorod held out until the fifteenth century against the supremacy of Moscow for control of Russia's trade routes and markets. But once Moscow threw off the Mongol yoke its authority and influence established it as the dominant force in Russian affairs.

Also in the fifteenth century a united Lithuania and Poland vied with Moscow for Novgorod. Lithuania attempted to attach Novgorod to its rule, and later Poland courted the city to join it. However, Novgorod's wealth and power could do little to spare the city from further attacks. In 1427 a Polish army advanced on the city with such force that Novgorod's populace was forced to approach the Poles, offer them gifts, and barter for peace.

In 1456 Moscow attacked the city again and forced it to relinquish its foreign diplomatic ties. Again in 1471, Moscow defeated the city after its flirtations with Lithuania and took territorial possessions from it. Resistance to Moscow continued, and a long struggle ensued that culminated with the entrance of Ivan III into Novgorod in 1477. Ivan III heaped his vengeance on the city. His soldiers filled over 300 wagons full of gold, silver, and other valuables and took these to Moscow. The city was then required to pay heavy taxes yearly to Moscow.

Shortly after the city fell to Ivan III, its archbishop extended an invitation to the tsar to dine with him, hoping to establish himself in the favor or good graces of the ruler of Moscow. At the very time the tsar and the archbishop were dining, Ivan III's soldiers entered Novgorod's beautiful cathedral of St. Sophia and stripped it of all valuables, religious vestments, and ornaments. Ivan III later had all the monks and abbots in attendance at the dinner ruthlessly executed. The archbishop was forced to ride through the streets of Novgorod tied to a mare in foal. Another citizen of Novgorod was placed in a large kettle of boiling water covering his legs to induce him to reveal the whereabouts of his fortune. When his brother delivered the rich man's treasure to Ivan III, the tsar promptly had both men dismembered and their pieces thrown into the Volkhov River.

After Ivan the Great pillaged Novgorod and forced it to submit to his rule, the city's citadel came under the rule of a military governor and was rebuilt as a strong fortress defended by many cannons. In addition, many of the city's people were removed to other areas of Russia.

Again in 1569–70, Moscow under Tsar Ivan IV (the Terrible), suspecting a plot against it by the Novgorodians, attacked the city and mercilessly slaughtered thousands of its populace, throwing many of their corpses into the waters of the Vokhov River, with the result that the river's flow was obstructed, causing it to overflow its banks. Ivan IV then proceeded to wreak further havoc on the lands of Novgorod by burning more than 150 of its monasteries.

Following the cruelties of Moscow upon Novgorod, the city next fell to Swedish forces who occupied it from 1611 to 1617, when Russia regained control of it. After these hardships, the city fell in population from about 400,000 people in the fourteenth century to less than 8,000 in the mid-seventeenth century. At the beginning of the eighteenth century Novgorod became a fortress under Peter the Great, but the heyday of the city had long since passed. The rise of St. Petersburg eclipsed whatever hopes Novgorod had of regaining its lost power and influence, and the city lapsed into minor importance as a provincial capital.

When the city was redesigned in 1778 during the reign of Catherine the Great, two distinct street patterns emerged: a grid system identified the Market side of Novgorod, while a radial pattern identified much of the St. Sophia side of the city. All wooden structures in the city were ordered destroyed at the time, leaving only the structures made of stone, including the city's stone walls.

Local forests around the city contain pine, birch, elm, spruce, oak, and other varieties of trees. Birch from these forests around medieval Novgorod were felled for their bark for writing materials. Scratching or engraving was done on the soft surface, and birch bark once formed an important part of the trade of Novgorod. By the seventeenth century pens and ink were used to write on the bark. Birch-bark writing resembled a printed script form rather than that of a cursive type. Birch-bark documents and writings have helped to shed much light on old Novgorod. Nearby forests and lakes also provided large quantities of fish, meat, honey, and game that found their way into Novgorod markets.

The Market side of Novgorod flourished as an ancient crafts center. There carpenters, silver and coppersmiths, shoemakers, bakers, brewers, leather-workers, and others practiced their trades. The city also made hemp cording and linen. The crafts industries on the Market side were most prominent and active in the eleventh and fifteenth centuries. Trade between Novgorod and Kiev reached its apex in the eleventh century, but still by the fifteenth century Novgorod continued to enjoy a healthy trade climate. The city's wealth and influence from its prosperous trade earned it the title of "Lord Novgorod the Great." Novgorod even minted its own coinage.

Russian merchants from Novgorod actively traded with the Baltic lands of northern Europe until the end of the fifteenth century. Novgorod was one of only a handful of Russian cities that, before the time of Peter the Great, permitted foreign merchants to trade actively within it. Kiev, Archangel, and a few other cities were also exceptions to the ban on foreign merchants inside Russian cities.

On the west bank of the Volkhov, opposite the old Market side or trading section of the city, is located the Novgorod kremlin surrounded by an old wall. The term kremlin is commonly applied by the Russians to anything that is walled or fortified. A wall existed around the kremlin in the eleventh century, but the present wall dates from the fifteenth century. The kremlin, or *detinets* as it is also known, was originally built in 1044. It was rebuilt through the centuries, while the late fifteenth-century version of it is one that stands today. The Novgorod kremlin is an oval-shaped citadel enclosed by a massive stone wall reinforced with large stone towers. A deep ditch and sloping banks circle the kremlin away from the river.

The Novgorod kremlin originally contained only wooden buildings and walls, but in 1044 stone was used to replace the old wooden wall. A portion of the old earthen wall can still be seen. The kremlin has been rebuilt numerous times since it first appeared. In the fifteenth century its stone wall had eleven towers, but only nine of these exist today. The present wall is 4,500 feet in circumference, and measures about 12 feet in thickness. Its height ranges between 28 to 35 feet.

Inside the kremlin stands St. Sophia Cathedral, built during 1045–50, which is one of the most inspiring architectural monuments of Russia. Its six onion-domed cupolas rise to a height of 131 feet. The remains of its ancient frescoes date from the eleventh century, as does its large double door, the "Sigtuma," which is made of bronze molded by Magdeburg craftsmen. Some historians contend one or both of the Sigtuma doors came from Constantinople.

Located on the west side of St. Sophia, the ornate, bronze Sigtuma doors are embellished with a variety of figures representing subjects in mythology and the Old and New Testaments. The oaken doors to which the bronze plates are attached stand nearly twelve feet high. The Church of St. Sophia (Holy Wisdom) was built by Vladimir, son of Prince Yaroslav the Wise. It was constructed on the model of St. Sophia in Kiev. The Germans ravaged it in World War II. They destroyed all but about forty-five historic buildings in the city.

During the 1830s St. Sophia was redecorated and the original frescoes on the walls were covered over. The first St. Sophia was erected in 989 out of wood.

St. Sophia was built by Greek architects from Kiev. Its large central dome, according to local guides, is said to resemble the helmet worn by ancient warriors in the area. Indeed, the resemblance can be noted. The other domes of St. Sophia display the usual shape of inverted onions. Each dome is topped by a cross, and on the cross of the helmet-shaped dome is a metal dove that, according to local legend, will fly away when the city's existence is near its end.

Adjacent to St. Sophia Cathedral is the old Vladychny Dvor (Archbishop's Court), the former reception site of dignitaries and diplomatic representatives. There court was held in the ancient Hall of Facets, dating from 1433. This structure now houses an art exhibition center displaying centuries-old art, some of which dates to the eleventh century. The courtyard also contains St. Sergius Rodonezsky Church, built in the fifteenth century, and a clock tower built in 1673.

Standing against the kremlin wall next to the Volkhov River is St. Sophia Bell Tower built during the fifteenth to seventeenth centuries. Four huge bronze bells that formerly hung in the bell tower now reside near it on stone pedestals. Each bell is of different size and weight, with the largest (cast in 1659) weighing in excess of forty tons.

Next to St. Sophia cathedral and its bell tower is the Church of the Entrance into Jerusalem, a modest, unappealing structure. The nearby church of Andrei Stratilatis (built in 1360–61) is another small, unobtrusive structure. Novgorod is full of ecclesiastical objects. The city contained 350 churches by 1413.

In the center of the kremlin stands the Monument to the Millenium of Russia, erected in 1862. It was designed by the sculptor Mikoshin to celebrate Russia's 1,000th anniversary. The monument is decorated with 129 sculptured figures, and its summit displays a large angel standing next to a towering cross. The angel represents a watchful eye, looking over Russia to keep it sacred. Below the angel are six statues, each of which represent a period in the history of Russia prior to Peter the Great becoming tsar. The bottom row of statues on the monument depict well-known writers, scientists, state and public officials. The statue weighs over eleven tons and is nearly 51 feet in height. During the German occupation of Novgorod in 1941–44, they disassembled the Millinery monument for shipping to Germany, but the Russians retook the city before the Germans had time to remove the monument.

The highest of the nine towers on the kremlin wall is the Kokui Tower, standing 136 feet in height. Built in the seventeenth century, its base is covered with brick over a stone lining of limestone. The Kokui Tower is located on the west wall of the kremlin opposite the portion of the wall facing the Volkhov River.

Adjacent to the Kokui Tower is the Pokrovskaya (Intercession) Tower, behind which is the Church of the Intercession built in 1389. The Intercession Tower has holes for guns in its upper level, indicating its more recent origin, probably in the late fifteenth or early sixteenth century. In the past it served as a gate tower, and took its name from the Church of the Intercession. The Intercession Tower now contains a restaurant.

Beyond the Intercession Tower is located the Zlato-Ustovskaya Tower, which took its present name in the seventeenth century from the adjacent Church of John Zlatonst. Most tourists know it as Chortova (Devil's) Tower, due to the fact that in the sixteenth century it was used as a torture chamber and prison.

North of Devil's Tower a bridge spans the deep ditch around three sides of the kremlin, and enters its wall just below where a long staggered series of connected buildings abut the wall and extend the distance between it and St. Sophia Cathedral. These buildings were the metropolitan's chambers. Continuing north along the kremlin wall, the next tower on it is known as the Metropolitan Tower. It is a circular tower of fifteenth-century origin. Next to this tower is the Archbishop's Palace, a huge belfry built in 1443, and the Granovitaya Palace built in 1433. The Germans converted this palace into an officers' club during World War II.

The northern portion of the kremlin wall contains the Tower of Theodorus (fifteenth-century origin) and the Tower of Vladimir (built in 1311). Excavations have revealed the existence of Vladimir's Gate Church next to the tower with his name.

Other churches located on the St. Sophia side, but outside the kremlin, are those of the Church of the Twelve Apostles, Trinity Church, Church of St. Blaise, Church of St. Peter and St. Paul in Kozhevniki, and the Dukhov (Holy Spirit) Monastery.

Also outside the kremlin wall, on its western side, is located Victory Square in which stands a monument to V.I. Lenin. Beyond Victory Square the Volkhov Hotel faces Desyatinnaya Street.

Standing near the Volkhov River on the southern side of Novgorod across from Lake Myachino is the Yuriev (St. George) Monastery. The monastery contains two churches, those of the Cathedral of St. George (built in the twelfth century) and the Exaltation of the Cross Church (dating from the nineteenth century). This monastery was built as an outpost on the southern edge of the city to help protect if from attack in that direction. St. George Church is a splendid example of old Russian architecture. Nearby the monastery is located the Yurievo Museum of Russian Wooden Architecture, beside Lake Myachino.

Another old monastery, the Zverin, or Antoniev, is located along the Volkhov River in the northern part of the city. Built in the twelfth century, it helped to guard the northern approaches to Novgorod. On the grounds of the monastery is the Cathedral of the Nativity of the Virgin (Our Lady).

Across the Volkhov the Market side of Novgorod had a stone wall surrounding it earlier than the St. Sophia side. Since the citadel of the city once stood on the Market side, and was later transferred to the St. Sophia side of the Volkhov, the likelihood exists that its transfer gave rise to the current name of the city, Novgorod, or "new city."

Also on the Market side of Novgorod is the old church of St. John the Baptist (built in 1127), the Yaroslav Dvorishche (Yaroslav's ninth-century Court) and its Church of St. Nicholas with beautiful exterior frescoes dating from 1113. It is the second oldest church in the city, with only St. Sophia predating it. The churches and monasteries of Novgorod, with one exception, are museums today. A monument to Alexander Nevsky stands on the Market side of Novgorod near the Volkhov River. The Sadko Hotel is also located on the Market Side.

Today the city is loacted in the *oblast* (an administrative division equivalent to an autonomous province) of Novgorod and functions as its seat of government. The *oblast* is part of the Russian Federated Republic.

Novgorod was the birthplace in 1861 of the celebrated composer Anton Arensky. Arensky's parents were also talented musicians and encouraged him to pursue a musical career. He attended St. Petersburg Conservatory, where he studied with the renown Rimsky-Korsakov and was an honor student. After graduation he accepted the position of professor of music at Moscow Conservatory, where he taught harmony and counterpoint from 1882–94. Arensky also conducted the Passion Choral Society there, and later moved to St. Petersburg to conduct in the Imperial Chapel. In 1906 he died in a sanatorium in Finland.

Arensky's compositions reflect the influence of both Tchaikovsky and Rimsky-Korsakov. His principal works include operas, cantatas, vocal and instrumental music. His noted operas include *A Dream on the Volga* (1890) and *Raphael* (1894). Also of note are his orchestra and piano works, respectively, of *Variations on a Theme by Tchaikovsky* and *Fantasia on Russian Folksongs.*

The great poet Gavrila Derzhavin (1743–1816) also came from the region of Novgorod and is buried in its kremlin. Derzhavin was noted for his superb neoclassical odes, particularly that of *Felitsa,* which extolled Catherine the Great.

Aside from its present administrative functions, Novgorod has important industrial and commercial activities including those of clothing and textiles, handicrafts, fish-canning, lumbering, matchmaking, chemicals, furniture manufacture, chinaware, brickmaking, foodstuffs, and leather goods. Small boats and river craft are also built and repaired in the city.

In the way of cultural features, Novgorod contains a drama theatre, a philharmonic orchestra, three colleges, and a stadium. Time has bypassed Novgorod. This once proud, wealthy city and artistic center is but a symbol of its past glory.

EXCURSIONS

Sightseeing Tour of the City. A visit to the Novgorod Kremlin (1044) and the architectural complex of Yaroslavovo Dvorische (Yaroslav's Palace, 12th–17th centuries).

Museum of History and Fine Arts. Located on the grounds of the Kremlin. The display includes specimens of old Russian painting, icon painting of the 12th–19th centuries, and works by contemporary Novgorod artists. The history section is devoted to the ancient times and the present day of the city.

Granovitaya Palata (Palace of Facets). Located in the Kremlin. Displayed are specimens of Russian decorative and applied art of the 11th–19th centuries.

St. Sophia's Cathedral (11th century). Located on the grounds of the Kremlin. The cathedral played an important role in the history of ancient Novgorod.

OUT-OF-TOWN EXCURSIONS

Museum of Wooden Architecture and St. George's Cathedral of the Yuriev Monastery (12th century). A complex of wooden buildings that are of great historical and artistic value. Distance from Novgorod: 5 kilometers. Tour duration: 2½ hours.

Town of Staraya Russia (known from the 11th century). A motor-launch trip across the picturesque Lake Limen, a city sightseeing tour, a visit to a local health resort, the picture gallery, and the house-museum of the Russian writer Fyodor Dostoyevsky (1821–1881). Tour duration: 9 hours.

Spas-Nereditsa Church in the village of Seltso. Fragments of frescoes of the 12th century. Distance from Novgorod: 5 kilometers. Tour duration: 3 hours.

HOTELS

Hotel	Address	Rooms	Telephone
Intourist	16 Dmitrievskaya St.	122	7-5089 9-4290

Sadko	16 Gagarin Ave.	124	9-5170
			9-5174
Volkhov	24 Nekrasov St.	112	9-2498
			9-2479

CAMP SITE

Located 10 km from Novgorod. Total capacity, 250 beds. Parking lot for 150 cars. Telephone: 7-2448.

Chapter V.
KIEV
Heart of the Ukraine

Dear to me always was this lonely hill,
And this hedge that excludes so large a part
Of the ultimate horizon from my view,
But as I sit and gaze, my thought conceives
Interminable vastnesses of space
Beyond it, and unearthly silences. . . .
—Leopardi

Borispol Airport near Kiev is a busy air traffic center. It is a large airport with direct flights abroad and many flights to other Soviet cities. Borispol's modern air terminal is clean and odorless. The walls of the airport building are lined with aluminum and ceramics that appear spotless and shine lustrously when light reflects from their surfaces. Huge glass windows in the concrete building let in brilliant gleams of sunlight that illuminate the large lobby of its interior. The huge, high dome forming the ceiling of the building has rows of cell-like structures which remind one of a honeycomb shaped by bees. From Borispol it is a forty-five minute ride into downtown Kiev.

Borispol is located on the eastern or left bank of the Dnieper River. On approaching the Dnieper, a look directly ahead will reveal the Paton Bridge spanning the river. The east bank of the Dnieper at Kiev is low-lying and flat. Across the Dnieper a steep embankment rises from the western shoreline. The Dnieper, like many of the Soviet Union's major rivers, runs basically in a north-south direction; and like its cousin, the Volga, is generally higher in elevation on its western bank. The same phenomenon is characteristic of many rivers of the western part of the Soviet Union.

This topographic factor figured prominently in the military campaigns and battles in that region during World War II. As the German panzer divisions advanced, the Russian armies were at a disadvantage vis-a-vis their defensive posture and the terrain along their rivers. The high western banks of the rivers favored the Germans who could race up to them and then fire down on the Russians on the opposite side. This advantage still sided with the Germans when in retreat; fighting from the high western banks they were able to inflict enormous losses on the Russians advancing from the east.

The Dnieper carries with it a certain sense of power, one that is steady, on going, and undiminished by time. Great rivers always seem to exhibit this characteristic. The impression they make upon the mind may depend on the scenery through which they flow, the mysteries surrounding their veil of secrecy and origin, or the profound and reverent journeys of the ships which come and go upon their waters.

After the Volga and the Danube, the Dnieper is the third longest river in Europe. It runs 1,400 miles from its source in the Valdai Hills, west of Moscow, to the Black Sea on the south. A chain of dams and power stations harness the energy of the Dnieper along its course, creating huge reservoirs of water from north of Kiev to Kakhovka on the south.

The bluff on the west bank at Kiev rises 300 feet above the river. Opposite Kiev on the east or left bank of the Dnieper the land is low-lying and flat. The floodplain of the river once stretched for a distance of ten to twelve miles across this flat terrain. Flat fields succeed one another in a monotonous succession around Kiev.

After crossing the Paton Bridge over the Dnieper, the road meets the spacious Naberzhnoye Highway paralleling the right bank of the river. Across the highway is the Narodov Boulevard leading toward the central part of Kiev. The streets of Kiev are lined with beautiful chestnut trees that form part of the picturesque landscape of the city. Lovely parks and gardens make up over half of the area of the city. In summer the many gardens, trees, and flowers afford a verdant picture everywhere one looks.

Kiev is the capital of the Ukraine and the third largest city in the Soviet Union. It is located at 50° 30′ north latitude, approximately the same latitude as Lille, France, and Calgary, Canada. Its population of nearly two and one-half million inhabitants is comparable to that of Chicago or Philadelphia. Historians and chroniclers have referred to Kiev as the "Mother of Russian

Cities.'' In the ninth century the city became the capital of the Eastern Slavs, the Kievan Rus, and flourished as the birthplace and cradle of Russian civilization. Before Moscow was born, Kiev abounded in the culture of its glorious past. Age-old relics of art and architectural treasures are found throughout the city. Russian history and Kiev are closely intertwined.

The remote beginnings of Kiev date back to the Stone Age. Savages once sat upon the hills shaping the present site of the city, and overlooked the steppes surrounding it. Archaeological excavations have proved the site of an ancient city called Kij, which existed at the end of the sixth century. Three major hills comprise the site of Kiev. Legendary Kij was built on the site of Mount Staro-Kievskaya.

Kievan history is closely linked to the geography of its nearby forests and the steppes and rivers that abound in the surrounding area. The Dnieper River connects the southern steppes of Russia with the Baltic lands of the north. Trading posts were early established along its course and at portages connecting it with rivers and streams which flowed toward the Baltic. Along these routes early traders and explorers found their way to Kiev and later to the Black Sea. This was before political unity was achieved in the area, and prior to the establishment of the state known as the Kievan Russia.

The prosperous trade routes linking the Baltic Sea with Kiev soon attracted the attention of the Varangians (Norsemen) from Sweden. The Varangians moving southward over these routes found their way to the Slavic city of Kiev, and in time they came to monopolize the commerce and trade of the city. Successful in their trading and commercial endeavors, the prosperous Varangians then achieved political control over Kiev. During the ninth century a Varangian tribe known as the Rus made Kiev their capital, thereby establishing the state which became known as Kievan Russia. The word Rus is of uncertain origin, but may stem from the Finnish name for Sweden in that bygone era when the Finns called that land Ruosti, in reference to the mighty warriors who rowed their boats across the waters of northern Europe. It is from the word Rus that the name Russia is derived.

Kiev relied on trade and it became a major commercial center for the East Slavs. Under the Varangian princes the city became a principality from which they ruled the surrounding countryside and sought to protect its trade routes. Chronicles relate that Askold and Dir, two Varangian princes, founded the principality of Kiev.

In 856, when Askold and Dir arrived in Kiev, the city was in the hands of the Magyars who controlled the hills overlooking the Dnieper River. An Eastern Slavic tribe known as the Poliane lived in the hills, but were subject to the Magyars. It is recorded by a chronicler that among the Poliane there lived three brothers known as Kii, Shchek, and Khoriv and their sister, Lybed. This family is said to have founded a town on the site of the hills above the Dnieper, and called it Kiev, after Kii, the oldest brother. The other two brothers each had a hill named after them, and the river was named for their sister, Lybed.

After their arrival in Kiev, Askold and Dir, together with the Varangians who accompanied them, sought the support of the Magyars and local tribes for an attack on Constantinople, capital of the Byzantine Empire. Constantinople was a wealthy, thriving commercial center. The attack was launched in 860, but was only partially successful, and the Norsemen and their Russian allies returned to Kiev. Nevertheless, relations between the Russians and the Byzantine Greeks were soon established. The prosperous trade of the Byzantine Empire was too great a magnet for the Russians and the Varangians to resist.

Askold and Dir had failed to defeat the Greeks, but other Varangian princes that ascended to rule Kiev renewed the rivalry with Byzantium. In 879, Oleg, the new Varangian Prince of Novgorod, led a band of warriors southward, finally reaching Kiev. By deceit Oleg lured Askold and Dir to their capture and death, then seized Kiev for himself in 882, proclaiming it "the mother of Russian cities." Oleg soon commanded all the major cities and the Russian tribes in the vicinity of the Dnieper. Then in 907 he led a raid on Constantinople, besieged the city, and forced it to pay tribute to him. A peace treaty was concluded in 911 and Byzantium and Kievan Russia became formal trading partners. Under Oleg, powerful Kievan Russia dispatched the yoke of Khazar influence and rule, and established the foundation of Russo-Slavic authority and independence.

Oleg died in 913 and was succeeded in power by his companion Igor, whose rule was less successful than that of his predecessor. The Greeks defeated him in a naval battle in 941 in which they used an incendiary material hurled through copper tubes, setting the Russian ships on fire. In 945 Igor was slain by the Drevliane in attempting to exact tribute from them.

Olga, the widow of Igor, then took possession of the Kievan principality. She was a wise leader and gifted in the art of statecraft. She visited cities and towns throughout her realm, founded others, promoted trade and commerce, and maintained law and order. She decided to visit Byzantium to learn of the Christian religion, and further promote trade with that empire. The emperor Constantine Porphyrogenetos welcomed her and is reported to have been so overwhelmed by her wit, beauty, and charm that he proposed marriage to her. During her stay in the Greek city, its patriarch set about to instruct her in Christianity. It is uncertain if Olga was baptized in Byzantium at that time or later in Kiev. The Russian chronicler records that her baptism took place in 955 in St. Sophia's Cathedral in Byzantium. Either then or later Olga took the Christian name of Helena, and urged the Russians to accept Christianity. She had churches built in her realm and was later canonized by the Russian church. Olga ruled Kiev from 945–962 and died in 969.

Olga's son, Sviatoslav, became ruler of Kiev in 962 and proceeded to make war on the enemies of the Kievan principality. First he defeated the Viatichi, an eastern Slavic tribe, and then marched down the Volga subduing the Volga Bulgars and destroying the Khazars in their lower Don and Volga strongholds. His successes unified the Eastern Slavs with Kiev. He next campaigned at the urging of the Greeks against the Bulgarians along the Danube River. Defeating the Bulgarians he then took up residence in their country, finding it to his liking. Once he had defeated the Bulgarians the Greeks no longer needed his services, and requested that he return to Kiev. The Russians refused to leave and were compelled to fight the Greeks. The Greeks forced Sviatoslav from Bulgaria, and on his return to Kiev he was attacked and killed by the Pechneiegs along the Dnieper.

With Sviatoslav dead, his three sons vied for the rule and power of the Kievan principality. Sviatoslav had earlier dispatched his youngest son, Vladimir, to rule the northern city of Novgorod. His second son, Oleg, governed the Slavic tribe known as the Drevliane; and Iaropolk, the eldest son, exercised authority in Kiev. In the civil war that ensued Oleg was killed and Vladimir was forced to flee Russia. After two years abroad he returned at the head of a mercenary army that defeated Iaropolk, who perished in battle. Vladimir assumed control of Kiev in 980 and ruled until 1015.

The reign of Vladimir marked a significant step forward in the history of Russia. Until his reign Russia was largely a barbaric land unrecognized by the nations of Europe. At first the Greeks were also reluctant to trade with the Russians; they were contemptuous of the Russian barbarians, and in addition the Greeks were not in need of the Russian trade. However, trade brought Greek culture and Greek religion to the Russians. The die was now cast for the conversion of pagan Russia to Christianity.

The early life of Prince Vladimir Sviatoslavich showed little inclination toward Christianity. Vladimir was in fact a pagan; he had seven wives prior to accepting Christianity, and worshiped pagan gods. Paganism was highly venerated in Russia prior to its conversion to Christianity. Even human sacrifices were offered to pagan gods.

There are many different accounts and traditions regarding the baptism of Vladimir. By some accounts he was baptized in Kiev; according to others he accepted Christianity in Korsun, a town in Crimea. In the account of one chronicler Vladimir received four missionaries of different religious faiths in 986; a Mohammedan, then a Catholic, next a Jew, and finally a Greek Orthodox philosopher. The Greek philosopher is said to have impressed him the most, so he sent emissaries to Constantinople to witness and observe firsthand the Greek Orthodox religion. The emissaries were, by account, greatly impressed with the Byzantine liturgy and the magnificence of the service. Following their return to Kiev, they urged Vladimir to accept Greek Orthodox faith. The same narrative continues and relates that Vladimir in

988 attacked Korsun, capturing it, and then demanded the sister of the two emperors in Constantinople for his bride. The emperors refused Vladimir's demand because he was a pagan, whereupon he agreed to be baptized in their faith if Anna, their sister, would marry him. Accordingly, he was baptized, married, freed the Greek city, and returned to Kiev to baptize its inhabitants. A Greek Orthodox priest was taken along to Kiev to perform the baptisms.

The baptismal ceremony in which the people of Kiev were converted to Christianity took place in 988 along the Dnieper below the hills rising from its shoreline. The entire city was converted to Christianity, while the statue of the pagan god Perun (god of thunder and lightning) stood motionless on the hillside looking down on the ceremony below. The new converts to Christianity then took horses and ropes and pulled Perun down, dragging him into the river and "drowning" the pagan god.

Standing on the site Perun once occupied is now a statue of Prince Vladimir that was erected during the 1800s. Vladimir's statue faces the river and grasps in its right arm a huge cross. From the east bank of the Dnieper the statue is quite visible to the observer even though it is surrounded by shrubs.

During the reign of Prince Vladimir, Christianity became the dominant religion in Russia. Not only was it preached and observed in worship services, but it was woven into the fabric of Russian institutions and laws. Secular schools were opened and clergymen were trained as teachers and translators of religious literature. Monasteries were built and the church was permitted to own land. The church opposed slavery, polygamy, and the purchase of brides.

Russian churches, particularly their interiors, were modeled after those of Byzantium. In the early years of Christianity in Russia no national Russian art existed, so the Russians copied Greek art until their own ecclesiastical style emerged, but even then the Greek influence left its impression on the fabricated Russian model. Thus, the Russo-Byzantine style of art that developed in Russia was a counterpart of its Byzantine progeny.

The Byzantine period of Russian art dates from 988 to 1530. From Kiev the Byzantine art heritage spread northward to the principalities of Novgorod and Suzdal. Ecclesiastical architecture during this period centered on the magnificent edifices of the churches. The Byzantine model dictated the design, decorations, and structural elements of Russia's new churches. The Greek Byzantine prototype of church architecture had as its scheme a rectangle with a cross fitted into it; the roof or dome of the church was modeled on pendentives in the shape of spherical triangles. The number of cupolas on the dome of a church varied. In time, cupolas became the recognizable feature of Russian churches on the landscape. When approaching a Russian town or city the silhouette of one or more cupolas is an unmistakable landmark to the observer.

The Byzantine period also introduced icon painting to Kievan Russia. This art form of picture or image representation depicted the likeness of sacred personages such as Christ and the Virgin Mary or saints and angels on wooden panels or enameled metal. Other icons took the shape or form of mosaics. Few of the icons of the Kievan period have survived to the present. The fall of Kiev during the Mongol invasion in 1240 shattered and corroded the brilliant stage of Byzantine art in southern Russia. In northern Russia Greek artists and monks continued their role in preserving the Byzantine art traditions, but local changes in icon painting gradually took root and the genesis of a Russian national art was born. The Moscow or National period of Russian art evolved by 1530, lasting until 1703 when European influences ushered in the Petersburgian or European period of art.

Once the Russians had adopted Christianity and accepted the Byzantine faith, an ecclesiastical hierarchy had to be determined in Russia and defined in connection to the Patriarch of Constantinople. The Greeks were invited to assist in the organization of the church in Russia, but Vladimir was concerned about the nationality of the ecclesiastical official, known as the metropolitan, chosen to head the church in Kievan Russia. Vladimir, understandably, preferred a Russian national as metropolitan; he did not want Kievan Russia to be subordinate to Constantinople. This issue was resolved in 1037 when Vladimir's son, Iaroslav, recognized the authority of the Patriarch of Constantinople in selecting the metropolitan of Kiev, but retained the right to select the bishops and clergy from which the metropolitan had to choose to fill ecclesiastical positions. Accordingly, the early metropolitans were mostly Greeks dispatched to Kiev from Constantinople. Theopemptus reached Kiev in 1039 and became the first metropolitan head of that city. The metropolitan of Kiev was the official head of the Russian church until 1448. The sack of Kiev in 1240 by the Tartars, and the subsequent growth of power and prestige by the principality of Moscow, led the metropolitans of Kiev to take up residence in Moscow after 1328. In 1589 the rank of patriarch was bestowed on the metropolitan of Moscow, and the Russian Orthodox church became independent of Constantinople.

Kiev is rich in churches. St. Sophia's Cathedral, which stands near the north-central part of the metropolis, is an architectural masterpiece. The name "Sophia" was borrowed from the Greeks. Its literal translation means "the Wisdom of God." The holy name was adopted for St. Sophia's Cathedral (Sofiiskii sobory), but correctly translated the name of the church would appropriately be the Cathedral of Holy Wisdom (Sofiiskii sobor). St. Sophia's foundation was laid in 1037 during the reign of Yaroslav. It required forty years to build, although the finishing touches and alterations to it spanned another two hundred years. The summit of the cathedral displays a total of thirteen cupolas with the one in the center representing Christ, and the other twelve surrounding the highest central cupola portraying the apostles. The inside of the cathedral is richly decorated with lively frescoes and mosaics. Most of the frescoes in St. Sophia date from the eleventh to the eighteenth centuries. Fresco painting was done on wet plaster and required great skill. The walls, ceilings, pillars, and arches of St. Sophia's abound in frescoes. The frescoes depict secular subjects. Frescoes of Yaroslav and members of his family can be seen on the walls of the cathedral. It is on the western wall that the portrait of Yaroslav, his elder son and daughter, and the Grand Princess Irina is depicted. Other frescoes inside the church portray birds and animals, hunting scenes, dancers, musicians, and games.

Numerous mosaic works add to the magnificence of the cathedral. In the central apse is a beautiful mosaic image of the Praying Virgin (Mary) dating to the eleventh century. Just beneath the Praying Virgin a mosaic depicts the twelve apostles. Near the top of the main cupola is a mosaic of the four apostle saints. Inside the entranceway of the church the four daughters of Yaroslav are depicted on the right wall. The mosaic works were produced by setting pieces of smalt into wet plaster. The various shades of the smalt and the angles at which it was introduced into the plaster radiate rays of light that illuminate the cathedral's beautiful mosaics.

St. Sophia's frescoes and mosaics are lively, vibrant, and vigorous. They are inspiring in their beauty. It is easy to see why the grandeur of St. Sophia's appealed to and influenced the soul of its congregation.

During the thirteenth century much damage was done to the cathedral during the Tartar invasion. Its reconstruction was not undertaken until the seventeenth century. Between 1699–1707 St. Sophia's belfry was added to the cathedral. In the 1850s a fourth story and a huge cupola were built onto the belfry.

Yaroslav is buried in a marble sarcophagus inside the cathedral. In 1955 Yaroslav's coffin was opened. It contained two skeletons, that of Yaroslav and his wife. His marble sarcophagus was made in Greece and weighs six tons. Yaroslav could speak four languages. A bust of him can be seen in one of the galleries of the cathedral. According to legend, St. Sophia's Cathedral is built on the site where Yaroslav defeated the nomadic Pechenegs in 1036 during their invasion of Kiev.

Two metropolitans are buried in the galleries of St. Sophia. On the grounds of the church can be seen the old home of the metropolitans and the residence of the monks.

The cathedral was more than a symbol of Christianity in ancient Kiev. It was also a cultural center and housed the first Russian library. Manuscripts and books were collected, written and cataloged in the church. Many of its ancient books were brought from the Greek lands, while others found their way into the library from all parts of Europe. The cathedral further served in the organization of cultural events, the crowning of princes, reception of ambassadors, and the investing of episcopal authority. The Cyrillic alphabet was introduced into the cathedral, and was used for the first time in writing and translation into Slavic works. The original use of the alphabet was for writing Old Church Slavonic.

The murals executed on the walls of St. Sophia's are distinctively Greek in their source and composition. The churches of Russia were greatly influenced by Greek art and embodied the Byzantine embellishments of frescoes, mosaics, and icon painting. St. Sophia's Cathedral in Kiev was built in the shape of a Greek cross, and retains this original form to some extent. The dome of the cathedral portrays mosaic figures of Christ, the archangel Gabriel, the apostle Paul, and displays medallions of more than three dozen martyrs.

Another historic old church in Kiev is that of the Church of St. Andrew, located a short distance north of St. Sophia's Cathedral. St. Andrew's sits high on the heights above Kiev at the end of Vladimirskaya Street. Legend says that St. Andrew visited the site where the church stands and planted a cross there. It was built in 1747–1753 by the eminent Italian architect Bartolomeo Rastrelli, but work was continued on it until 1867. His role in designing some of the notable edifices of Leningrad has already been noted. The church is located in the oldest part of Kiev.

The high central dome of St. Andrew's Church is capped with a large cupola. Surrounding the central dome are four towers, each peaked with a cupola about one-half the size of the dominant central cupola. A two-story high flight of steps leads up to the level supporting the large, imposing edifice of St. Andrew's. The height of the church above its surroundings lends to it a majestic outline overlooking much of Kiev. Its five blue and white domes are easily visible in the surrounding area. The church was built without any bells, prompting the people of Kiev to reply that the magnificence of the church dispelled any need for it to announce its presence for worshipers. The church was closed in 1961 (due to drainage problems beneath it, according to my guide). It is now a concert hall.

Located along the banks of the Dnieper, southeast of the main center of Kiev, is the Kiev-Perchersk Monastery. This seventy-five acre religious preserve is also known as the Lavra. The preserve is an assemblage of churches, towers, walls, museums, monastic cells, a printing works, and a labyrinth of subterranean caves within which are found burial places, chapels, and ecclesiastical objects. This religious preserve was founded by the monks Anthony and Theodosius in 1051. It was the site of the first monastery established in Russia.

The Perchersk Monastery Preserve has a thick smell of history about it. It still retains many of its ancient characteristics. It is rich in architectural and historical objects. In walking on its ancient grounds one can sense the breath of some bygone warrior or venerable monk on your cheek. This monastery was very wealthy and powerful before the Tartar hordes ravaged it in 1240. It never recovered from this shock and not until the fifteenth century was it reconstructed and restored.

The monastery is spread over two large hills and a valley lying between them. Numerous caves exist beneath the grounds of the monastery preserve. The so-called Near Caves are found in the valley between its two hills. Within the valley is the Belfry of the Near Caves and the passage into their entrances. The Far Caves are a different group of cave-like cells, and are found on the smaller hill of the preserve. The Russian word for cave or catacomb is *peshchere,* hence the derivation of the name of the monastery.

After the conversion of ancient Kiev to Christianity, the monastery became the base of ecclesiastical power in Russia. As the stronghold of Russian Christianity, the monastery became both powerful and wealthy. In order to maintain the feudal system in Kievan Russia, the princes of Kiev sought the support of the church and in turn lavished on it lands and expensive gifts.

The monastery became a center for the development of trades and arts. A factory was built on its grounds for the production of smalt used in mosaic artwork. Books and manuscripts were also produced by the monastery's scholars and writers.

The earliest church constructed on the grounds of the monastery was the Church of the Assumption of the Holy Virgin, built in the eleventh century. Accounts differ as to whether it was originally constructed of stone or wood. In 1614 Bracci, a well-known Italian architect, restored the church from its decaying ruins. Built in Byzantine style, the church has a rustic baroque appearance to it. It is an enormous church capped with golden cupolas. Recessed tympanums on the exterior of the church display pictures of various saints.

A number of stone buildings were added to the monastery in the latter part of the eleventh century. In that same period the Dormition Cathedral was constructed (1073–1089) of brick and mortar, and embellished with paintings and mosaics. It was built on the plan of a cross. This cathedral was used as a model for the construction of other churches in the Dnieper region during the twelfth and thirteenth centuries. Destroyed in World War II, its ruins can be seen in the middle of the cluster of structures located on the high hill of the monastery.

The entrance to the preserve is guarded by the Church of the Trinity, which faces Yanvarkogo Vosstaniya Street. It once served as a lookout post for the monastery. Nearly four hundred steps lead to its top. Its Russian architecture is well preserved. Built in 1108, the church is small by comparison to some of its neighbors on the preserve. During the eighteenth century it was redecorated with frescoes and a beautifully carved iconostasis. A single huge cupola with a cross crowns this church.

On the north side of the preserve, situated outside its main complex, is the Church of the Savior at the village of Berestovo. The palace of Prince Vladimir once stood nearby. He ordered the building of the church before his death in 1015. Vladimir's son Yuri Dolgorusky, the founder of Moscow, is buried in the church. In 1947 a granite tomb was erected over Yuri's grave. The church suffered much damage from the Tartars but was rebuilt and decorated by Greek artisans in the seventeenth century. Inside the church are two large slabs of red slate that have mythological figures shown in reliefs carved into them. The beautiful interior of the church represents some of the last works of Byzantine art in Russia. The Church of the Savior has five large cupolas built over it.

Located down the hill a short distance from the Church of the Savior is the All Saints Church over the Economic Gates. Built in 1696–98, its ornamentation and interior are extravagantly designed. Its lavish pediments, pilasters, semi-columns, and ornate windows display profuse detail in their construction. A huge cupola surrounded by four smaller ones projects the roof of the church toward the sky.

Between the Church of the Trinity and the ruins of the Church of the Dormition stands the huge Belfry of the Higher Monastery. This four-story high structure is capped with a small cupola and a cross. Built in 1731–45, it measures almost 315 feet high. In its era it was the tallest structure in Russia. The ground floor plan is octahedral in design. A total of 46 stone columns of Ionic, Roman-Doric, and Corinthian design surround its upper three tiers. Constructed by a serf-architect named Kovnir, its dome is capped with gilded copper. Kovnir's gifted talents can be seen in a number of other structures on the grounds of the monastery. Just beyond the ruins of the Church of the Dormition stands the white-colored Kovnir building, constructed in the same century as the belfry. It was partially used as a bakery. A printing works adjacent to the Kovnir building was also built by him, as was the Belfry of the Lower Monastery.

The caves that are found beneath the monastery preserve form two distinct systems of passageways. The "Far Caves" lie beneath the Upper Monastery, while the "Near Caves" lie below the Lower Monastery. The underground passages through these caves are about six and one-half feet high. The "Near Caves" are approximately 709 feet long, while the "Far Caves" are about 872 feet long. Doors are spaced at intervals throughout the labyrinth in which are located cells where the monks ate, prayed, and died. Several chapels are located in the catacombs.

The subterranean catacombs are very winding and cool inside. Many ancient monks are buried there. Their bones can be seen in piles in places and individually in others. Many of the monks spent a considerable part of their lives in the underground catacombs, and following their death, the cells in which they lived became their tombs. In front of their cells some of the monks built earthen and stone walls, leaving only small openings through which food and water could be passed to the occupant inside. When an immured monk died in his cell, he was customarily entombed in it by having the small opening into the cell sealed. Other monks were buried in coffins constructed of wood or glass. Some of the monks were buried in tree trunks hewn out until hollow, with the corpses then pushed inside the logs. The twelve Greek brothers who built St. Sophia's Cathedral are buried in the catacombs.

The catacombs are a literal maze of tunnels. They are lighted by electric lights. Some icons are located in the catacombs. At the end of the catacombs is the Exaltation of the Cross Church.

On the grounds of the Upper Monastery there is also the small church of St. Nicholas enclosed by monastic cells; the metropolitan's residence, which is now the Museum of Ukrainian Decorative Folk Art; the Church and Tower of St. Onuphri, built in 1698–1701; the Chasovaya Tower; and the Church and Tower of Kushchnik, built in 1698–1701. On the site of the "Near Caves" is the Church of the Holy Cross, a multi-cupolated church built in 1700.

The Ukrainian Museum is noted for its exhibits of embroidered national costumes from all parts of the Ukraine. Excellent specimens of Ukrainian decorative folk art can be seen on the hundreds of Easter eggs in the museum. Other notable exhibits in the museum include porcelain, glassware, china, wood carvings, and ceramics. In all, the museum contains 60,000 items on display.

The monastery once owned 80,000 peasants. It also owned more than a dozen other monasteries, numerous villages, glass works, and other enterprises. After 1927 it was closed. The last active church on its grounds was closed in 1961.

Located near the Kiev-Perchersk Monastery and the Paton Bridge is the huge statue of "Motherland" built in 1981. It forms a spectacular sight to the observer when crossing the Paton Bridge from the east bank of the Dnieper. The statue resembles to some extent a similar statue in Volgograd. It is part of a memorial complex known as the Ukrainian State Museum of the History of the Great Patriotic War. The statue of "Motherland" stands 334 feet high above a towering bluff and hilltop facing the Dnieper. The statue depicts a woman with a sword held aloft over her head and pointing skyward. It symbolizes Russia's courage, fortitude, and the enormous sacrifice the country paid for its struggle with Nazi Germany in World War II. Beneath the statue are a number of memorials and monuments dedicated to the heroic struggle with the Nazis. One such memorial is titled the "Crossing of the Dnieper," and depicts Russian soldiers crossing that river to attack German troops. A few hundred yards away from the "Motherland" is an open-air museum of Russian military hardware on display. Items in the display include tanks, planes, and guns of World War II vintage, and more recent military paraphernalia as Soviet jet fighters, guided missiles, monstrous tanks, and artillery pieces.

Kiev was the scene of early fighting between the Germans and Russians in World War II. On June 22, 1941, the Germans invaded Russia with 145 divisions of troops. The Russians were ill prepared to resist the German advance. German armored columns drove through and around Russian armies, capturing hundreds of thousands of prisoners. Many Ukrainians assisted or fought with the Germans during World War II. Their loyalties were often divided.

Kiev held out against the Germans from August 7 to September 21, 1941. The Germans captured the city in bitter fighting in its streets. The city lay largely in ruins upon its fall. When the Germans captured Kiev, 30,000 Jews were rounded up in a single day, herded to a large ravine at Bari Yar within the city, lined up at its edge and shot, with their bodies toppling into the ravine. Nearly 200,000 of Kiev's people were killed during the Nazi occupation. There were several concentration camps around the city in World War II. The Russians liberated Kiev on November 6, 1943.

A large but more recently built cathedral than those mentioned previously is that of St. Vladimir's, located on Taras Shevehenko Boulevard not far from the Kiev Opera. Work on this cathedral began in 1862 but defects in its construction delayed its completion until 1896. St. Vladimir's was built to commemorate the conversion of the people of Kiev to Christianity 900 years previously. The cathedral is built in a combination of architectural styles to include Byzantine, Russian, and Romanesque. It is capped with seven cupolas with a cross on top of each. The artistic decorations of the cathedral include frescoes, icons, and murals. Gilding, marble, bronze, and other artistic materials are used in profusion, adding to the magnificence and splendor of St. Vladimir Cathedral. The interior has a huge figure of the Madonna cradling the child Jesus in her arms. Other venerable portraits in the cathedral represent the "Crucifixion," "Last Supper," and those of Princess Olga and Saints Boris and Gleb.

Immediately opposite or to the west of the Kiev-Pechersk Monastery stands the obelisk beside the Tomb of the Unknown Soldier. These landmarks are located in the Park of Eternal Glory, dedicated to the soldiers who perished in battle in World War II. The dark gray obelisk made from polished granite rises 81 feet above the heights of the Dnieper. An eternal flame burns over the Grave of the Unknown Soldier lying at the foot of the obelisk.

Chestnut, poplar, and maple trees surround the park. Soldiers and citizens of Kiev regularly visit the gravesite to lay flowers on it.

It is common to begin a tour of Kiev by visiting a small house on Ul-yanovikh Street. In this three-story house on a quiet street, Vladimir Lenin's relatives lived during 1903 and 1904. Lenin, at that time, was living abroad.

Near the heart of downtown Kiev and offset to the west of Vladimirskya Street are located the remains of the Golden Gate. During the eleventh century a high defensive wall was erected around the city. The Lvov, Lyadski, and Golden Gates led through the wall into ancient Kiev. Today, only the Golden Gate remains. Once covered with earth, it was excavated in the 1830s. The Golden Gate was built during the reign of Yaroslav.

Facing Vladimirskaya Street on the opposite side from St. Sophia's Cathedral are the Bogdan Khmelnitsky Monument and Square. The statue depicts Khmelnitsky on horseback with his right arm outstretched, pointing his staff in the direction of Moscow. The bronze equestrian statue was cast by the sculptor Mikhail Mikeshin in 1888 in St. Petersburg. Khmelnitsky is revered as a hero in local Ukrainian folklore. He was a seventeenth-century Ukrainian statesman and military leader. During that century he headed Cossack uprisings against the Polish rule of the Ukraine. In several major battles in 1648 Ukrainian forces defeated the Poles. Khmelnitsky then sought to unify the Ukraine with the Russian State, an act that was formalized in 1654. Many Ukrainian and Russian writers have written poetic works in honor and memory of Khmelnitsky.

Kiev University, also known as Shevchenko State University, is located on a tract of land between Taras Shevchenko Boulevard on the north and Tolstoy Street on the south. The university was founded in 1834 and today has over 20,000 students. Among its faculties are those of physics, chemistry, economics, journalism, geography, history, philosophy, law, foreign languages, biology, and mathematics. The university has twenty departments in all. Many African and Asian students study at the university. The university has many laboratories, experimental research centers, botanical gardens, and museums on its grounds.

The front of the main building faces Tolstoy Street. It consists of three levels, in the center of which is a portico with eight Ionic columns. The building is painted a light red color to symbolize an act of the tsarist government in 1901 in which it conscripted students from the university to serve in the army. The students revolted against the conscription order and a demonstration ensued. The local authorities had the university painted its characteristic color so that it might blush with shame for the students.

In a park adjoining the university stands the monument of the Ukrainian poet Taras Shevchenko, after whom the university is named. The monument was unveiled in 1939. Shevchenko (1814–1861) was a talented poet, writer, and artist. He was the son of serfs and during his life he fought against serfdom and its hardships. The Shevchenko State Academic Theater of Opera and Ballet located in the heart of downtown Kiev is also named in honor of the poet. The five-tier opera house was built in 1898–1901 and faces Vladimirskaya Street.

Running through the heart of downtown Kiev is Kreshchatik Street— Kiev's main thoroughfare. The word *Kreshchatik* means crisscrossed. Many streets cross it. This street is to Kiev what the Nevsky Prospekt is to Leningrad. Kreshchatik is short by comparison to its cousin in Leningrad. It is only slightly more than a mile in length. Along it are important hotels, businesses, restaurants, and administrative offices. The large Kreshchatik Metro Station is located at the southwest end of the street. The Kiev Metro was opened in 1960 and links areas on both sides of the Dnieper. The metro system has twenty-six miles of lines. The Metro is fast and efficient, and its Kreshchatik station has an adjoining restaurant. The street was literally destroyed during World War II, but after the Germans retreated it was rebuilt, doubled in width, and lined with strips of green lanes and trees. It reminds one of the Champs Elysses in Paris. The Kreshchatik is wide and spacious and fronts the large Kalinin and Leo Tolstoy Squares along its course. The stately looking Moskva and Dnipro hotels are located near its juncture with Kirov Street. Theaters, cinemas, and several huge markets add their distinctiveness to Kreshchatik.

Modern Kiev is a significant industrial center of the Ukraine. Before the 1917 revolution there were few large factories in the city and food processing enterprises were the main industrial employers. Today, large industries in the city include those of metal-working, instruments, automatic lathes, river boats, chemicals, textiles, shoes, cameras, motorcycles, furniture and woodworking, wine making, electric measuring devices, earth-moving machinery, printing and publishing, and an assortment of food industries. Kiev is also an important filmmaking center. The oldest film studio in the U.S.S.R. is in Kiev. It was founded in 1906, built in 1919, and was the studio that produced the filming of *Battleship Potemkin*.

Atop Kiev Mountain along the Dnieper River stands the recently constructed (early 1980s) Arch of Friendship. The site of the arch overlooks the Dnieper River and much of Kiev. Beneath the arch is located the Memorial to Russian and Ukrainian Workers. A long flight of steps leads to the top of the mountain, which provides a good view of the surroundings. In winter the wind blows over it with ferocity. Kiev has an average high of 27°F. in January, and an average low of 16°F. However, the winter winds often produce a chill factor below zero. The high in July averages 73°F. In winter Kiev is covered with a blanket of snow.

South of the Arch of Friendship and on the east side of Kiev is the large, palatial palace known in tsarist times as the Mariinsky. It was named after Maria, daughter of Tsar Paul I. Designed by Rastrelli and built in 1750–55, it was destroyed by fire in 1819 but was rebuilt in 1868–1870 in an imposing baroque style by K. Mayevsky. The palace was again destroyed in World War II, and rebuilt in the latter 1940s. The Ukrainian parliament now uses it as a reception hall. The palace was built for Peter the Great's daughter, the Empress Elizabeth, who lived in it during the latter years of her life. It is a two-story structure designed in pale blue. In front of the palace is a wooded park with walkways through it.

On the heights overlooking the Dnieper River and along the southern fringe of Sovietsky Park stands the memorial built over the grave of Prince Askold. Prince Askold, along with Prince Dir, was treacherously murdered in 882 by Prince Oleg who then seized control of Kiev. According to legend, Askold was buried on the heights above the Dnieper and a wooden church was later built over his grave. A rotunda was built on the gravesite in 1810 and in 1938 a colonnade was constructed above the rotunda with an entablement atop the columns. The Metro Bridge over the Dnieper lies but a short distance south of Askold's memorial.

For sports enthusiasts Kiev has several large sports stadiums. The largest of these, Kiev Central Stadium, seats 100,000 persons. Construction started on the stadium in 1937 but World War II held up its completion until 1946. Expansion of the stadium took place in the 1970s and 1980s. The stadium includes gymnasiums, a ski jump, skating rink, indoor swimming pool, assembly hall, and other facilities. It is located on Fizkultury Street, south of the heart of the city.

Another sports arena is the Palace of Sports built in 1958–60 out of aluminum, glass, and concrete. It can accommodate 12,000 individuals. The building measures 452 feet long and stands 60 feet high. The Sports Palace is located just north of Central Stadium. Skating competitions, concerts, and various sporting events are held in the palace.

Kiev is a culinary delight. *Borscht,* a palatable soup dish consisting of cabbage, beet root, and other vegetables fried in lard and seasoned with onions, is very popular. This dish makes a plentiful meal in itself. A thick sour cream is customarily served with it. Chicken Kiev is another local dish that is tasty. It is rolled in breadcrumbs and served with hors d'oeuvres. Cherry dumplings or *vareniki* is an old Ukrainian dish that is very delicious. If one understands little of the Ukrainian except his food and music, then the time spent there has been worthwhile. Kiev, a vibrant city with relics of a departed grandeur, is no less credible than its food and music.

EXCURSIONS

Sightseeing Tour, "Kiev, the Capital of the Ukrainian S.S.R."
(Duration: 3 hours).

You will learn a great deal about Kiev's past and present, see the main sights of the city.

The tour starts from the park on Vladimirskaya Hill that commands a splendid panorama of the city; it then goes on to Bogdan Khmelnitsky Square with a monument to Bogdan Khmelnitsky, an outstanding Ukrainian statesman, and St. Sophia Cathedral, a world famous monument of eleventh-century architecture. A short distance from the cathedral is the reconstructed Golden Gate, the "front door" of ancient Kiev.

Tourists will see the T.G. Shevchenko Opera and Ballet Theater, the history of which is inseparably connected with the rise and development of Ukrainian musical culture; Kiev University, the largest of the city's eighteen higher educational establishments; the Republican Stadium; and, of course, the magnificent Kreshchatik, the city's main avenue.

Over the last two decades large new housing developments of original architecture, with wide green streets, have been built on the left bank of the Dnieper.

A Tour of the Ukrainian S.S.R. Exhibition of Economic Achievements
(Duration: 3 hours).

More than 25,000 exhibits on display here demonstrate the economic, scientific, and cultural progress of the Ukrainian people. The pavilions are located in a picturesque park area.

A Ride on the Kiev Metro
(Duration: 1.5 hours).

The Kiev Metro was opened in 1960. The number of its spacious, light, and beautifully decorated stations keeps growing from year to year.

A Motor Ship or Launch Trip Along the Dnieper (Duration: 1 hour).

You will see Kiev's recreation zone, the city's splendid embankments and beaches, and enjoy a breathtaking view of this ancient city in its second youth. A most exhilarating outing.

KIEV'S MUSEUMS

The Kiev Branch of the Central V.I. Lenin Museum. Numerous exhibits of the museum recreate important periods of V.I. Lenin's life, tell of his contacts with Ukrainian revolutionaries, show the role of the leader of the Great October Socialist Revolution in the formation and strengthening of Soviet Ukraine, demonstrate the successes the Republic has achieved to date in communist construction.
Open daily, except Mondays,
from 10 a.m. to 6 p.m.
Address: Leninskogo Komsomola Square

The Memorial Complex "The Ukrainian State Museum of the History of the Great Patriotic War, 1941–1945." This museum was opened on May Day, 1981, Victory Day, a national holiday of the Soviet people. The exposition depicts the great battles of the past war. There are many interesting exhibits: weapons of those years, rare war documents, etc.
Open daily, except Mondays and the last Tuesday of each
month, from 10 a.m. to 5 p.m.
Address: 33 Yanvarskogo Vosstaniya St.

The State History Museum of the Ukrainian S.S.R. There are more than 500,000 exhibits on display, including various archaeological finds, jewelry, coins, weapons, documents, numerous works of art. The exposition traces the history of the Ukraine and its culture from antiquity to the present. It tells visitors about the early settlements on the territory of the present-day Ukraine, about Kiev Rus, the Ukrainian people's struggle for independence, their voluntary reunification with the fraternal Russian people in 1654, the Ukraine's joining the U.S.S.R. in 1922, the Ukraine's revolutionary, combat, and labor glory.
Open daily, except Wednesdays, from 10 a.m. to 6 p.m.
On Mondays, from noon to 8 p.m.
Address: 2 Vladimirskaya St.

The State Architectural and Historical Preserve "St. Sophia Museum." St. Sophia Cathedral, founded in 1037 by Prince Yaroslav the Wise of Kiev, was the main Christian church of Kiev Rus, its political and cultural center. The cathedral is world famous not only for its outstanding architecture, but also for its magnificent mosaics and frescoes that have come down to us from the eleventh century.

Open daily, except Thursdays, from 10 a.m. to 5:30 p.m.

On Fridays, from noon to 8 p.m.

Address: 24 Vladimirskaya St.

The State Kievo-Pechersky Historical-Cultural Preserve. (More than eighty structures were built on the territory of the former Kievo-Pecherskaya Lavra (Monastery) over the 900 years of its existence. Most of these structures, which are of great historical and artistic value, have survived. The monastery played a prominent role in the development of Russian culture in the early Middle Ages.

The Museum of Ukrainian Folk Decorative Art, the Museum of Books and Printing, the Ukrainian S.S.R. Museum of Historical Jewelry, the Museum of Music, the Theater, and the Cinema are all located on the territory of the preserve. The exhibitions "Science and Religion," "The Structure of the Universe," "Peshchery (caves) and Mummification," "Decorative Fabrics and Embroideries of the 16th-19th Centuries" also function here.

Open daily, except Tuesdays, from 9:30 a.m. to 6 p.m.

Address: 21 Yanvarskogo Vosstaniya St.

The Monument-Museum "St. Andrew's Church." St. Andrew's Church was designed by Bartolomeo Rastrelli, an outstanding eighteenth-century architect. Although it was the simplest in design of all his structures, it is perhaps superior to them in the exquisite gracefulness of its proportions, and in the way it harmonizes with the surrounding landscape. The church's interior and iconostasis were decorated by the Russian artist Alexi Antropov and the Ukrainian master Grigori Levitsky.

Open daily, except Thursdays, from 10 a.m. to 5:30 p.m.

Address: 23 Andreyevsky Spusk St.

The Museum of "St. Cyril's Church." St. Cyril's Church is a historic and architectural monument of the twelfth century. In it one can see ancient frescoes, as well as paintings excecuted by well-known Russian artist Mikhail Vrubel at the end of the nineteenth century.

Open daily, except Fridays, from 10 a.m. to 5 p.m.

Address: 103 Frunze St.

The State Museum of Ukrainian Fine Arts. Established in the 1890s, this museum possesses a fabulous collection of Ukrainian paintings, sculptures, and drawings. The exhibitions include icons of the fourteenth and fifteenth centuries, ancient wooden sculptures, works by outstanding portraitists of the eighteenth and nineteenth centuries, etc.

Open daily, except Fridays, from 10 a.m. to 5 p.m.

On Mondays and Wednesdays, from noon to 8 p.m.

Address: 6 Kirov St.

The State Museum of Russian Art. An exposition of Russian art covering the period from the twelfth century to the present. There are icons of the Novgorod, Moscow, and Stroganov schools; works by Dmitri Levitsky, Vladimir Borovikovsky, Ilya Repin, Ivan Shishkin, Alexander Deineka, Arkadi Plastov, and other Russian and Soviet masters.

Open daily, except Thursdays, from 10 a.m. to 6 p.m.

On Tuesdays, from noon to 7 p.m.

Address: 9 Repin St.

The State Museum of Ukrainian Folk Decorative Art (a visit to this museum is included in the tour of the Kievo-Pechersky Preserve). The museum's exposition traces the development of Ukrainian weaving, carpet-making, embroidery, wood-carving and pottery from the 16th century to the present.

Open daily, except Tuesdays, from 10 a.m. to 5:45 p.m.

OUT-OF-TOWN EXCURSIONS

Kanev. A picturesque city on the Dnieper, one of the Ukraine's oldest towns, known since the twelfth century. Taras Shevchenko, the great Ukrainian poet, lived and was buried here. An imposing monument stands on his grave. The T.G. Shevchenko Memorial Museum will acquaint you with the life and work of the poet.

Chernigov. This very old town was the center of the powerful principality of Chernigov Seversky in the eleventh to thirteenth centuries. Its historical and architectural monuments—the Spazo-Preobrazhensky and Borisoglebsky Cathedrals, the Pyatnitskaya Church, the Trotsky and Yeletsky Monasteries—date back to that period.

THEATERS, CONCERT HALLS

T.G. Shevchenko Opera and Ballet Theater—50 Valdimirskaya St.

Ivan Franko Ukrainian Drama Theater—3 Ivan Franko Square
Lesya Ukrainka Russian Drama Theater—5 Lenin St.
Operetta Theater—53/3 Krasnoarmeiskaya St.
Young Spectator's Theater (names after the Leninist Komsomal)—15 Rosa Luxemburg St.
Republican Puppet Theater—13 Shota Rustaveli St.
Philharmonic Concert Hall—2 Vladimirsky Spusk St.
Republican House of Organ and Chamber Music—79 Krasnoarmeiskaya St.
Circus—1 Pobedy Square
"Ukraina" Palace of Culture—85 Krasnoarmeiskaya St.
Intourist Cultural Center—The best folk ensembles of the city and of the Republic perform here.

There is a lecture hall for foreign tourists in Kiev.

The "Kiev Spring" (end of May–early June) and "Golden Autumn" (second half of September) art festivals are held in the capital of the Soviet Ukraine every year. Well-known theatrical companies, orchestras, and dance groups take part in them.

SHOPS

The following shops are recommended:

Podarki (Souvenir Shop)—9 Karl Marx St. and 5 Lesya Ukrainka Blvd.
Perlyna (jewelry)—22 Kreshchatik
Drezhba (books in foreign languages)—30 Kreshchatik
Mistetstvo (books on art)—26 Kreshchatik
Art Salon—27 Lenin St.
Ukrainsky Souvenir (Ukrainian souvenirs) Store—23 Krasnoarmeiskaya St.
Kashtan (jewelry)—26 Lesya Ukrainka Blvd.

TRANSPORT

Public transportation operates from 6:00 a.m. to 1:00 a.m. Cabs are available around the clock. Tram fare is 3 kopecks; trolleybus fare, 4 kopecks; bus and Metro fare, 5 kopecks, irrespective of distance. Cab rate is 20 kopecks per kilometer (plus a 20-kopeck meter charge). Tram and trolleybus tickets can be bought from vending machines and kiosks in the Metro as well as from "Sojuzpechat" kiosks. All trains, buses, and trolley-buses are fitted with fare boxes.

COMMUNICATIONS

There is a post office in every Intourist hotel. The Central Post Office at 22 Kreshchatik, is open from 8 a.m. to 12 p.m. The Central Telegraph Office at 10 Vladimirskaya St. functions around the clock. Through the reception desk of your hotel you can place a telephone call to Soviet or foreign cities.

HOTELS

Hotel	Address	Rooms	Telephone
Desna	46 Milyutenko St.	151	58-40-90
Dniepro	1/2 Kreshchatik St.	200	91-48-61
Leningradskaya	4 Taras Schevchenko Blvd.	80	25-71-01
Lybid	Pobedy Sq.	280	74-00-63 74-20-66
Moscow	4 October Revolution Sq.	370	29-28-04
Prolisok Motel	1 Brest-Litovsky Ave.	102	44-00-93
Slavutich	1 Enthusiasts' St.	250	55-09-11 55-79-26
Teatralovaya	17 Lenin St.	200	25-50-35 24-50-45
Ukraina	5 Taras Shevchenko Blvd.	207	21-73-33

RESTAURANTS

There is a restaurant in every Intourist hotel. Ukrainian dishes are also served in the following restaurants:

Verkhovina, 223 Brest-Litovsky Prospekt
Vitryak, 135 Prospekt Sorokaletia Oktyabrya
Dubki, 1 Stetsenko St.
Kureni, Petrovskaya Alleya),
Mlyn, Gidropark
Myslyvets, Gidropark
Natalka, 18 Borispolskoye Highway
Khata Karasya Svyatoshino, Chetvertaya Proseka, Motel "Prolisok"

Chapter VI.
AGRICULTURE
State Farms and
Collectives

Though this be madness, yet there is method in 't.
—Shakespeare

Agriculture in the Soviet Union is collectivized, with the exception of a small number of plots cultivated by peasant farners. Since initiation of the first Five-Year Plan in 1928 to regulate the Soviet economy, agriculture has been subject to planning and control by the state. The state asserts monopolistic control over this enterprise, prescribing production goals and the types and quantities of agricultural goods to be produced.

There are two main types of farm units in the Soviet Union: the collective farm *(kolkhoz)* and the state farm *(sovkhoz)*. Both types are large in terms of area, labor force, and the amount of acreage allotted specific types of crops. In terms of numbers collective farms greatly outnumber the state farms, but the former are decreasing in number due to the conversion of some collectives into state farms and the merger of collective units to form larger farms.

Following the chaos of the First World War and the civil war that bled its land and people, the new Soviet government moved rapidly to change gears from tsarism and capitalism to socialism. Governmental changes were revolutionary and visualized Utopian goals. Utopian planning soon became a characteristic feature of Soviet socialism. To achieve the goals of its plans, the state justified their attainment by any means possible. The wants and needs of individuals mattered little in Soviet totalitarian philosophy.

The first and second Five-Year Plans placed heavy emphasis on industry, coal and steel production, railway and transportation facilities, chemicals, oil, and electricity. Military defense took precedence in planning. Not until 1938 did food and agricultural production receive some emphasis, when the Third Five-Year Plan was introduced.

In 1928 about 8 percent of the Soviet Union was considered arable land. Pastures, grasslands, and meadows accounted for an additional 5 percent of the land, raising the amount of total agricultural area to 13 percent of Soviet soil. By 1940 over 100,000 acres of new-sown land had been brought into production, with most of this increase carved from virgin lands in the steppes of Siberia or the area east of the Volga-Caspian line. Most of the best agricultural lands lay west of the Urals. In 1939 the Soviet Union had about 2.2 acres of land in cultivation per person, compared to 2.8 acres per person in the United States.

Prerevolutionary Russia was an agrarian society. At the time of the revolution in 1917, 82 percent of Russia's people lived in rural areas. The land was distributed and owned accordingly: large landowners, the aristocracy, and church claimed 41 percent of the land; peasants held and farmed communal plots amounting to 37 percent of Russia's farmland; and well-to-do independent farmers held 22 percent of the agricultural land. Millions of peasants were without land.

During 1905–07 there were over 1,000 violent incidents of agrarian unrest in Russia. Serfdom had been abolished by royal decree in 1861, but the lot of the serfs improved only marginally following their emancipation. The serf was made a free citizen and allotted land that once belonged to his master but he found himself bound to a system known as the commune, which was collectively controlled by his local village. The commune collected local taxes and dues from the peasants and distributed lands under its control. In most cases the serf had only exchanged one master for another, and usually found himself worse off financially than before his emancipation. Under the communal system the peasant discovered that he was often allotted less land than the acreage he tilled prior to 1861, and that the rents and taxes he paid after emancipation often were higher than before. Thus, the situation of the peasant remained essentially unchanged after emancipation.

By 1900 the conditions described above led substantial numbers of peasants to seek employment in the towns. A rural to urban movement of peasants seeking industrial jobs in the cities was widespread. Nevertheless, most of the new migrants retained their ties with the communes, and channeled money back to the villages to help support relatives or pay for land allotments.

Despite the unfavorable situation of the peasants in pre-revolutionary Russia, the harvests in many years yielded surpluses of foodstuffs. The harvests were at the mercy of the unpredictable Russian weather and droughts, but some abundant harvests were reaped. Foodstuffs were an important component of the Russian foreign trade; conversely, any foreign trade surplus was dependent upon food exports. This is illustrated by the fact that in 1913 Russia had exports of grain totaling twelve million tons. Most of this exported grain, however, came not from peasant holdings, but from the estates of large, independent landowners and the more prosperous farmers.

Before the Bolsheviks seized the reigns of power the peasants had succeeded in forcibly taking possession of the large estates in Russia. The days of the wealthy landlords and aristocracy were numbered. The peasants in fact had already decided the agrarian issue on land ownership by the time Lenin ascended to power. Lenin recognized their exploits and de facto takeover of the former estates the day after he became the head of the new government and issued an edict nationalizing all land, thus making it the property of the state.

Following the October Revolution the peasants controlled and farmed most of Russia's arable land. There were no powerful landlords subjugating the peasants, yet their livelihood fared little better. The new government imposed food requisitions upon them, leading the peasants to believe the Bolsheviks had betrayed their cause. The ensuing civil war further destroyed many of the farmlands and dispersed or killed countless numbers of peasant farmers. Agricultural production in 1920 amounted to only one-half of that prior to 1914. Thus, entering the third decade of the twentieth century, Russia found itself with no long history of an independent class of farmers, and an agricultural base substantially chaotic and in ruin. Little in the way of mechanization had crept into the agrarian picture. Rural Russia in 1920 was not unlike the Middle Ages when compared to farms in the United States or Western Europe. Its neglect of the social and economic ills of the peasant farmers cost Russia dearly in the following decades, and continues to haunt its Communist rulers today.

After 1921 the agricultural situation improved briefly when Lenin, recognizing the urgency to structurally change its organization, halted surplus grain requisitions, and permitted a free market to operate in which produce could be bought, sold, and traded in the open. Farmers still had to satisfy state-mandated quotas of foodstuffs, but all produce in excess of the government quotas could enter the open market system. The free-marketing system flourished and independent farmers grew in prosperity. The farmers reaped surpluses of food and became a vigorous part of the Russian economy.

With the rise of Stalin to power, the agricultural sector of the economy once more underwent a drastic permutation. The growing prosperity of the independent farmers together with a weakly structured Communist Party apparatus in the rural countryside, prompted Stalin to initiate and enforce a system of socialized land tenure in 1929. The prosperous independent farmers and peasants alike had their lands and livestock seized, and collectivization was vigorously carried out. Enforced collectivization centered on a framework of collective and state farms.

At the time Stalin forced collectivization on the farmlands of Soviet Russia, about 75 percent of the country's population were engaged in agriculture. The first Five-Year Plan had just been initiated, and its major emphasis on expansion of heavy industry required enormous numbers of new laborers to build and work in the factories. These laborers had to come from the farm since there was no large, skilled middle class from which to draw to fulfill the necessary labor requirements. Time was of the essence. Old industries had to be modernized and entire new factories built where none existed. Accordingly, this is where the system of collectivization devised by Stalin fit into the scheme of socialist planning. Large, mechanized farms centered on machine-tractor stations would furnish the harvesting and plowing services, thus reduce farm labor requirements and release farm workers to flow into the industrial sector. In theory, collectivization of agriculture was a logical innovation to Stalin and the Communist leadership. In practice, collectivization proved elusive in its goals of raising production and output of farm commodities.

Collectivization was an agricultural experiment on an unprecedented scale. The changes that it envisaged would help reshape the economy of the largest country on earth. Collectivization was designed as a corollary to an equally large revolution planned in the Soviet industrial sector. Millions of people were uprooted and resettled. The more prosperous independent farmers and peasants had their land and property confiscated. The Soviet Union was, for all purposes, a classless society. There were no longer the very rich and very poor; neither was there a middle class. The party supervised every phase of life; planning was the key-note of socialism.

Collectivization was widely unpopular and resistance to it mounted. The peasants countered confiscation with destruction; they burned their crops and slaughtered their livestock rather than hand them over to the collectives.

Stalin responded with liquidation. During the 1930s as many as five to eight million people became victims of Stalinist repression.

Enforced collectivization functioned badly and the collective farm system was largely inefficient. Party members, often inexperienced, guided and controlled every operation of the collective farms. The farm work teams were often poorly organized, and planning frequently lacked coordination. A further handicap was lack of experience; many of the best farmers had been killed or had disappeared. The crops often suffered from extreme weather, shortages of food occurred, and famine was severe. Not until the mid-1950s did Soviet grain and meat production match the levels achieved before the First World War.

Farm organization under Communist leadership centered on two types of farms—collectives and the state-operated farms. A collective farm is run by a chairman who plans and directs its activities. The chairman is a member of the Communist party, and is chosen by the party for assignment to his post as farm director. State planning boards determine what crops and commodities are to be produced on the collective farms. It is up to the farm chairman to see that the production quotas set by the state are met. Collective farms are self-financed; they depend upon their own financial resources for their operation. Thus, the collective farm is theoretically independent of state control; in reality the state sets the prices for its goods as well as its production quotas. Workers on collective farms receive a share of the income made from the sale of the farm's harvests. The worker's income is derived by the accumulation of workday credits. The worker does not punch a clock and earn an hourly wage, rather he accumulates credits based on the task he performs and his skills. For purpose of illustration, suppose a tractor driver plows a five hectare (12.35 acres) field in eight hours. For this task and his skills as a tractor driver, he is awarded two workday credits. In a different situation a farm milkmaid may have milked cows for eight hours while the tractor driver was plowing, but she may have earned only one workday credit in her less skilled job. Collective farm workers receive cash and other forms of compensation periodically. At the end of the year their workday credits are tabulated, and the workers are remunerated for any balance of their credits.

State farms, by contrast, are both financed and directed by the state. Their workers are paid wages. Prices for state farm goods and production quotas are both set by the state, as in the case of the collective farms. The manager or director of a state farm is also a party member. The first state farms were organized in 1918, and by 1938 there were 3,961 in existence, compared to 242,000 collective farms. By 1967 the number of state farms had grown to 12,700 while the number of collective farms stood at 36,800. Thus, there was a substantial decline in the number of collective farms between 1938 and 1967. By the late 1960s the number of hectares of land under the control of state farms was about 312 million; at the same time collective farms totaled 228 million hectares of land. In 1967 the sown area of a collective farm averaged about 2,800 hectares (6,916 acres), compared to the average sown area of 6,900 hectares (16,063 acres) for a state farm.

Agricultural production has remained a persistent problem in the Soviet economy in spite of various measures to shore it up. The Five-Year Plans consistently stressed increasing output by obtaining higher yields per hectare or expansion of sown areas. In addition, the agricultural ministry urged greater use of fertilizers, moisture conservation procedures, irrigation, and crop rotation. In 1954–56 the government made a concerted effort to push back the frontiers of production into areas uncultivated. This cultivation expansion effort was known as the Virgin and Idle Lands Program. Much of its attention was directed at northern Kazakhstan, but other areas it focused on included the Volga Region, the Urals, and Western Siberia. Between 1953 and 1960 roughly 115 million acres of new arable land were added to Soviet agriculture, and hundreds of new state farms were created on these lands. Most of these were grain farms concentrating on producing spring wheat. Railroads were constructed into the new lands to haul their produce. Substantial areas of the new lands were carved from lands of marginal rainfall and other climactic limitations, therefore they were inferior in yields compared to older farmlands located mainly west of the Volga.

The agricultural heartland of the Soviet Union is known as the Fertile Triangle. The corners of this triangle are defined by three important cities. Beginning at Leningrad on the Gulf of Finland, the northern arm of the triangle runs southeast across the Urals and Western Siberia to the city of Irkutsk on Lake Baikal; the southern arm of this triangle stretches from Irkutsk back across Western Siberia and the Urals to Odessa on the Black Sea; while the triangle's western arm runs north from Odessa to Leningrad. The lands lying within this triangle form the agricultural core of the Soviet Union. The triangle is the leading producer of nearly all the major crops in the Soviet Union, with the exception of cotton and subtropical fruits. It is also the leading producer of all major types of livestock. The triangle is customarily divided into two major crop zones. In its southern part is the Black Soil Zone of the steppes, which derives its name from the extensive *chernozem* or "black earth" soils located in that region, although chestnut and other soil types are common there as well. The Black Soil Zone is an immense wheat growing area, with winter wheat grown mainly in the western part and spring wheat concentrated in the east. Within the Black Soil Zone are produced the bulk of the corn, sugar beets, barley, hemp, and sunflowers grown in the Soviet Union.

The northern part of the agricultural triangle consists of the Nonblack Soil Zone, whose soils are poorer than those in the Black Soil Zone. Its more northern location places it in a cooler climate, but one which is more humid. The Nonblack Soil Zone is the principal rye-growing area in the Soviet Union, and produces over half of all Soviet rye. The area also leads in the production of potatoes, flax, and oats. Some wheat is also grown, and herds of dairy cows can be seen grazing on meadows of the Nonblack Soil Zone. North of the Fertile Triangle is the taiga, an immense forested region which stretches from the Gulf of Finland to the Pacific coast.

Large-scale agricultural activities in the Soviet Union are relatively mechanized, especially the large wheat farms. Tractors and machinery are utilized in most plowing and harvesting activities. The Soviet Union is a large tractor producer, and even exports some to other countries. However, some areas of agriculture are notably lacking in mechanization, particularly the livestock industry. Most dairy cattle are still milked by hand, and there are few conveyor belts and machinery used in their feeding operations. Maintenance problems with machinery and frequent lack of spare parts often idle important farming operations.

The Soviet Union is the world's leading producer of potatoes, beet sugar, wheat, barley, rye, sunflower seeds, and flax. This high ranking, however, is not achieved by high yields per acre or low labor input. The U.S.S.R. has about four times as many people in agriculture as the United States, and approximately one and one-half times the amount of acreage devoted to crop production.

The status of Soviet agriculture has lagged behind that of other sectors of the U.S.S.R. economy. For example, Soviet industry has expanded much faster than agriculture, and when agriculture is compared to industrial growth, the picture is one of stagnation for most areas of farm output. Soviet agriculture, in contrast to that in the United States or Western Europe, is relatively inefficient. Both the five- and seven-year agricultural plans implemented in the past achieved few successes. Actual net increases in production, even in the successful sectors of farming, have been diminished by failures in other areas of agricultural output. In short, agricultural production has not kept pace with the rising demands of population growth and the avowed goal of Marxist-Leninist dogma to bring it up to or surpass the production levels of the capitalist countries. The agricultural picture remains a nightmare for the Soviets. Agricultural ministers have come and gone, but the dilemma in Soviet agriculture remains essentially unchanged.

An indication of the extent of the problem in Soviet agriculture has been the increasing amount of grain imports by Russia since 1978–79. In that period the Soviets imported 15 million metric tons of grain, but by 1984–85 this figure had grown to 55 million metric tons.

The Soviet Union must feed nearly forty million more people than the United States. Soviet agricultural production and efficiency continue to be hampered by lack of incentives. Farm incomes have increased in the Soviet Union in recent decades, but when compared to the incomes of farmers in the United States, the Russian farmer still lives a meager existence.

TREBUCHOVSKY—A Model State Farm in the Ukraine

The following presents a brief description and evaluation of Trebuchovsky state farm as a case study in Soviet agriculture. The information presented herein is a narrative of a visit by the author to this farm, and an interview with its director. The reader should be cautioned in attempting to relate comparisons between this farm and those in other parts of the Soviet Union, due to rapid changes in Soviet agricultural policy and land use, and the pecularities of the operation of the different types of farms. Moreover, the author cannot vouch for the validity of the statistics presented in the case study of this farm, inasmuch as the Soviet data may be exaggerated.

The *sovkhoz* (state farm) is a distinctive feature of Soviet agriculture. Changes in its land uses have occurred frequently in response to the objectives of Soviet policy. Trebuchovsky state farm, located about 20 miles east of the city of Kiev in the Ukraine, reflects the characteristic features of a Soviet state farm. Its existing agricultural patterns provide an insight to understanding the impact of government policies on Soviet agriculture.

The Ukraine is a beautiful republic with highly developed industries, and boundless fields yielding bumper crops of wheat, potatoes, sugar beets, fruits, vegetables, and grapes. This republic has long been known as "the bread-basket" of the Soviet Union. About one-fourth of all grain grown in the Soviet Union comes from its fields. The Ukraine accounts for about one-fifth of all Soviet agricultural production. Over one-half of the granulated sugar and one-fourth of the U.S.S.R.'s tractors are produced in the Ukrainian Republic. Located amidst this rich agricultural land is the ancient city of Kiev, capital of the Ukrainian S.S.R., and a leading center in the Soviet Union for the processing of meat and dairy products. Also included among Kiev's large enterprises are wine-making industries, utilizing locally grown grapes.

It was from this city, located along the beautiful banks of the Dnieper River, that I set out with a small group of travelers, including a handful of students and a Russian guide, to visit Trebuchovsky state farm. From the Hotel Lybid in the center of the city, the small bus carrying my group soon crossed Kreshchatik—Kiev's main thoroughfare—reaching the gigantic arch of the relatively new Metro Bridge over the Dnieper about ten minutes later. Crossing to the left bank the bus continued through Darnitsa, a rapidly growing industrial district of Kiev with blocks of new high-rise apartment buildings. Passing Darnitsa the road cut through beautiful forests of maples, poplars, and pines.

Turning southward on a secondary road, the bus traveled about six miles before halting in front of a two-story dwelling, to either side and in front of which large bulletin boards displayed posters showing workers marching forward to achievements under the banners of communism. On the front of the building, identified as the headquarters of the Trebuchovsky state farm, a large portrait of Lenin overlooked the entrance.

Inside the building the director of the state farm cordially welcomed our group and then led us to a small room in which were several tables and chairs. Behind one of the tables hung a portrait of Lenin on the wall. Standing in front of the portrait, the farm director proceeded to speak in Russian, pausing at intervals to allow our Russian guide to make translation into English. Speaking at length, the director facilitated his talk with the assistance of notes typed on sheets of paper, some of these containing tables of production statistics for Trebuchovsky state farm, and Soviet agriculture in general. According to the guide, the director stated that "Trebuchovsky state farm was founded in 1963 when a number of small collective farms combined to form a single operation." Continuing to translate, the guide said: "Trebuchovsky state farm is one of the 1,015 state farms found in the Ukrainian S.S.R. The first collective farms appeared around Kiev in the early 1930s, and approximately 8,800 of these are presently in operation in the Ukraine."

Other statistics revealed by the director disclosed that Trebuchovsky state farm comprises 5,500 hectares (1 hectare = 2.471 acres) of arable land, specializing in growing vegetables and producing milk for Kiev, the third largest city in the Soviet Union. Crops growing on the farm included 1,000 hectares of grain, 650 hectares of potatoes, and 200 hectares of vegetables (10 hectares of which were growing in hothouses). The farm produces on an annual basis about 3,000 tons of grain, 8,000 tons of potatoes, 3,000 tons of vegetables, 2,000 tons of fruit, and 3,500 tons of milk. Pastured on the farm are 2,500 livestock, of which 1,600 are dairy cows. The director added, "Milk cows now make up over half of all the livestock of many Ukrainian farms." Other crops grown on the Trebuchovsky farm include corn, sugar beets, and grapes.

The director continued by observing that corn is widely grown in the Ukraine and is used extensively as a fodder crop for livestock. "On some farms," he said, "it has replaced fields formerly reserved for wheat." As a result of the increase in corn production, livestock numbers have increased on Ukrainian farms. There is a substantial dairy and poultry industry in the Ukraine. (One indication of the latter was the large basket of boiled eggs placed on my breakfast table in the hotel each morning.)

Irrigation and mechanization play important roles on Trebuchovsky farm. Irrigation is supplied from sewage waters of nearby towns, and distributed to 1,200 hectares of the farm. Many farms in the Ukraine are now using irrigation. The director claimed that 95 percent of the operations on Trebuchovsky farm were mechanized. "Cattle breeding," he stated, "was 80 percent mechanized, while the lowest branch of farming using mechanization was that of vegetable production, with 60 percent." He added, "30 percent of our labor force is unskilled."

Trebuchovsky state farm operates under five-year state farm plans. The state plan designates the kinds and acreage of crops to be grown. State farm directors are appointed by the state, whereas directors of collective farms are selected by the members of each particular farm. Both the state and collective farms permit their workers to have small private plots of land on which to grow whatever they wish. The director explained: "state farms permit private plots in the size of .06 to .20 hectares." On these private plots are cultivated potatoes, fruits, vegetables, and other selected crops. Private ownership may also be extended to possession of a cow, a pig or two, poultry, and even goats and sheep. Workers on a state farm who do not own a cow or pigs may buy meat and other products from the state farm at reduced prices. In spite of the smallness of their size, private plots produce a significant share of the overall Soviet food supply, aside from wheat and other grains. "As much as one-half or more of the total production of meat, milk, eggs, and vegetables in the Soviet Union," said the director, "is grown on private plots."

Both state and collective farms are assigned quotas by the state of goods to be produced and sold at fixed prices. However, goods produced in excess of quotas are purchased by the state at a higher level of prices. State farms pay their workers in cash wages according to the quality and amount of work performed. When a work team exceeds its set quotas, the team members receive about 20 percent of the excess income from the goods sold as a bonus. The director of Trebuchovsky state farm stated that "under the system of socialist competition, workers are paid bonuses from a special fund set aside for over-production, and medals are given the outstanding production members of each team exceeding its quotas." Bonuses paid workers on the state farms are allocated by the planning commission of each farm. In addition to paying bonuses, the income derived by the farm goes toward repairing and maintaining machinery, and paying laborers.

Assisting each state farm director are specialists who direct specific areas of production. Each branch of production is organized around one of the specialists who heads a work team or main unit of work. A work unit, for example, may have as its responsibility the maintenance of the tractors, machines, and equipment used on the farm. The average salary of a machine operator or tractor driver is 175 rubles a month. Cattle caretakers earn about 108 rubles per month. All workers have a working day of seven hours and receive paid leaves. Workers on sick leave receive grants and aid in the amount of their salary, providing they are members of a trade union; if not, their compensation is reduced to 50 percent of their salary.

The farm director stated that approximately 6,000 people live on Tre-buchovsky state farm, but only 1,200 of them work regularly on the farm. About 900 of the farm inhabitants work in nearby industry. But, he declared, "One member from each farm family is employed on the farm." During the peak of the harvest season labor shortages sometimes occur, and workers must be recruited from outside the farm. During the harvest season the farm director can increase the customary seven-hour work quota to ten hours a day.

Trebuchovsky state farm has a school for 1,100 pupils, a nursery, and a kindergarten. Also located on the farm is a hospital that can accommodate 50 patients.

When the director had finished speaking and answering questions, he led our group back to the bus, whereupon he directed us on a guided tour of the farm. Debarking from the bus at several stops, the group walked through fields of tomatoes, potatoes, cucumbers, and sugar beets. In some of these fields men and women were gathering the harvest. Commenting further, the director said, "The area around Kiev is in the heart of the major sugar beet producing area in the Soviet Union," and that "over half of all sugar beets grown in the U.S.S.R. come from the Ukraine."

Trebuchovsky farm displays the quite familiar concentrated rural settle-ment pattern characteristic of Soviet state farms. The farm headquarters and major buildings are centrally located with respect to access to the fields. The principal farm buildings are clustered near the farm headquarters. Corru-gated sheet metal covers most of the roofs of the farm buildings. The gal-vanized metal sparkles in the sun. Thatched roofs, once a ubiquitous feature of the rural landscape, can still be seen on a few of the older farm buildings. Most of the farm's inhabitants live along the main road in front of the farm's headquarters or in its vicinity. The majority of the houses and buildings on the farm form a compact village around the headquarters building. The visit to Trebuchovsky state farm was concluded with a tour of a cucumber-canning factory, adjacent to which was a winery. Stacked in neat rows outside the cucumber cannery were thousands of fruit jars used to hold the cucum-bers. Inside the cannery stainless steel vats with temperature controls were utilized in processing the cucumbers. Several dozen workers, mostly middle-aged women wearing white aprons and uniforms, oversaw the operation. As compensation they received about 120 rubles per month. As some of the women lined up for photographs outside the cannery, the farm director commented that only 12 percent of all workers are members of the Commu-nist party. In a field near the cannery ducks, chickens, and geese wandered about.

Trebuchovsky is a typical state farm in the Ukraine. In terms of size it is smaller than some of the large wheat farms. In the Ukraine the merger of smaller farms into larger units continues, thus reducing the total number of farms. Perhaps the most significant feature of Trebuchovsky and other Soviet farms is the small private plot, and the significant role which it plays in the total food picture of the U.S.S.R. Undoubtedly any Soviet decree or policy affecting its status would register an impact on the whole agricultural system of the Soviet Union.

Chapter VII.
VOLGOGRAD
City of Fallen Heroes

On that too long afflicted shore,
Up to the sky like rockets go,
All that mingled there below:
Many a tall and goodly man,
Scorch'd and shrivell'd to a span,
When he fell to earth again,
Like a cinder strew'd the plain.
                    —Lord Byron

Volgograd is located at 48°40′ north latitude, on approximately the same parallel as that of Seattle, Washington, and St. John's, Newfoundland. The city is situated on the high west bank of the Volga River, the main waterway of Russia. Present-day Volgograd is a city of about 1,100,000 population, and stretches for nearly forty miles along the Volga.

Volgograd is a city of fate. On more than one occasion the future course of Russian history depended on the outcome of events focused at its location. Some of the more dramatic pages of Russian history have been written about this city. Devastation has heaped its toll on Volgograd, but each time the city has managed to survive.

Volgograd is about 400 years old. The city was founded in 1589 and given the name Tsaritsyn, borrowed from that of "tsarina," meaning wife of the tsar. Its original purpose for founding was twofold: (1) it was built as a fortress to protect the Volga and Don trade routes (the city is situated at the narrowest point between the two waterways), and (2) it served to guard Russia's southern frontier against invasion by nomadic tribes. During the last half of the eighteenth century, however, the strategic significance of Tsaritsyn greatly diminished, and the city became a transshipping point and a minor trade center. Then, during the nineteenth century, rail transport reached Tsaritsyn, shipping again increased in volume, and industry grew, leading to a rebirth of the city. During the Russian Civil War of 1918–20, Tsaritsyn was the scene of one of its most decisive battles. The Red Army won an important victory when Joseph Stalin organized the city's defenses and prevented a linkup of the White armies. In 1925 Tsaritsyn was renamed Stalingrad to honor Stalin.

By 1940 the city had developed into a large industrial center, with 126 factories turning out items such as iron and steel, tractors, machinery, wood products, rivercraft, tile, building materials, shoes, foodstuffs, and clothing.

During World War II Stalingrad was the scene of a decisive battle that largely turned the tide of the war in Russia against the Germans. The battle of Stalingrad was actually fought in a series of stages, several of which occurred before the Germans reached the outskirts of the city. Between the middle of July and the first week of August 1942 the fighting centered near the large bend of the Don River, west of Stalingrad. During the second and third weeks of August the Germans crossed the Don and captured a number of towns west and southwest of Stalingrad. In the third stage of fighting (August 19–September 3), the Germans pushed the Russians into and around Stalingrad, and reached the Volga north of the city. The next stage of action (between September 3 and 13) saw the Germans reach the suburbs of Stalingrad and the Volga south of the city. After September 13 the Germans entered the city and proceeded to capture most of it.

Hitler could have bypassed Stalingrad but chose instead to capture the city that was named after the man who headed the struggle against him in Russia. Both Hitler and Stalin were determined that Stalingrad would be a major victory for the winner.

The city was the scene of some of the fiercest fighting in World War II. The intensity of the fighting equaled that around Leningrad and Sevastopol, and only these Russian cities suffered longer sieges than that of Stalingrad. Stalingrad narrowly escaped capture by the Germans in five months of sanguinary fighting in its streets.

General Friedrich Paulus had his German 6th Army in and around Stalingrad on the north and west of the city. General Hoth's 4th Panzer Army was concentrated just south of Stalingrad. Two Romanian armies and an Italian army, allies of the Germans, were assigned to cover the flanks of the two German armies. The 4th Romanian Army stood south of Hoth's army in positions west of the Volga, while the 3rd Romanian Army covered the northern flank of Paulus's along the west bank of the Don River. The 8th Italian Army was located north of the 3rd Romanian Army, and also along the west bank of the Don. The undermanned and weak German 48th Panzer Corps, consisting of one German Panzer division and one Romanian armored division, was deployed about two hundred miles west of Stalingrad. The Germans had two other armies in the Caucasus area about 350 miles further south, but Hitler refused to bring these north to Stalingrad. Had he done so, the outcome of the battle of Stalingrad would probably have been in favor of the Germans.

The Romanian armies by comparison to those of the Germans were poorly equipped and were no match for a major Russian thrust into their positions. The Romanians had no armor-piercing shells and few antitank guns to combat the Russian tanks and armor.

By October 4, 1942 most of the southern and western sides of Stalingrad were in German hands. On that date General Paulus attempted to capture the city in a major offensive that thrust over a quarter of a million Germans at the city's defenses. The German troops poured into the maelstrom of the fighting were among the best in Hitler's armies at the time. Many were crack divisions, battle-tested in other bloody encounters with the Russian armies. The Germans had previously in September tightened their grip on the city by forcing the Russians inside it into a narrow corridor along the Volga River. The Russians held a strip about five miles long, with their backs against the river. They could have made their way across the river to comparative safety on the eastern bank, but their orders were to hold their positions. These positions were only about 2,000 yards wide, or less than four-tenths of a mile. The city was a pile of rubble, with most of its buildings in ruins or standing as skeletons of their former structures. Chunks and slabs of concrete lay amidst the ruins, some held together only by strands of steel used in their architectural design. Fighting in these conditions was difficult and trying. Attacks and counterattacks measured successes in a few yards. Fighting was often hand-to-hand or in close range of the two adversaries. Capturing a building or even a single room in it was often a major achievement. The battle for Stalingrad was a gruesome and costly struggle for both sides.

As October 1942 wore on, the Germans wanted to capture the city before the frigid Russian winter was upon them. They had already experienced one winter previously in the bitter cold and icy winds of Russia, and did not relish having to fight both the Russians and their winter at the same time. The Russians, however, were counting on the onset of winter to slow down the

German war machine and launch their own counteroffensive against the Germans. The Germans were better prepared for the winter of 1942 than they had been during that of 1941, but their lines were stretched thinly in places, and in others were nonexistent.

The strongholds of the Russian 62nd Army were three factory buildings in the northern part of the city. These factory buildings were lined in a row from north to south, with the tractor factory on the north, the Barrikaddy factory in the middle, and the Red October factory in the south. After four successive attempts on the tractor factory, the Germans broke through around it, finally captured it, and then attacked the Barrikady factory and Russian headquarters near it. However, Russian reinforcements crossed the river and arrived in the nick of time to ward off the German drive. The Germans mounted another big attack and actually reached the Volga briefly only to be thrown back again. Their attacks persisted through October and mid-November 1942, but they were weaker, and the Germans' chances of successfully capturing the city diminished as their losses mounted.

Back in Moscow, Stalin and his top generals had developed a counteroffensive plan to throw a net around Stalingrad, trapping the 6th Army in it. The Rusians mustered three army groups consisting of over a million men to mount the counteroffensive. On November 19, 1942 the Russians sprang their trap. After an enormous artillery barrage the Russian infantry and tanks advanced, driving through the 3rd Romanian Army, headed for the Don River in the rear of Stalingrad. Next, the Russian armies south of Stalingrad attacked the 4th Romanian Army defending the southern flank of Paulus, driving through it in the direction of the Don to meet the Russian Army headed south. On November 22 a weak encirclement of Stalingrad was accomplished. Paulus proposed to Hitler that he be allowed to leave Stalingrad and break through the Russian lines to the Don River before the Russians tightened their ring around him. Hitler refused Paulus's request and told him to stand firm and await relief forces.

The German relief force (57th Panzer Corps) left Kotelnikovo, about ninety-three miles southwest of Stalingrad, on December 12. It had been scraped together from existing units and some recently arrived forces, but was still weak compared to the Russian forces it had to dislodge in order to reach Stalingrad. The German plan was to have the relief force drive within twelve to fifteen miles of Stalingrad, and then have the Germans there push out in its direction to join the two forces.

The 57th Panzer Corps got within thirty miles of Stalingrad but was halted at that point. Hitler refused to allow Paulus to attempt a breakout and possibly effect a juncture with the relief force, and this opportunity soon passed because the 57th Panzer Corps had to retreat in the face of attack by huge Russian forces. By the end of December 1942 the 57th Panzer Corps was back in Kotelnikovo, and Paulus was still in Stalingrad. The 6th Army in Stalingrad fought on, but just for survival. On January 31, 1943 the 6th Army, now hungry, hotly contested, and short of ammunition, surrendered. Some of its units fought on for two more days in the northern part of the city, but the long nightmare of Stalingrad was over. With the surrender, 91,000 Germans inside the city became prisoners. The city was a pile of rubble, but it would be rebuilt.

Such a historic and noted city should not go unvisited, particularly if one is interested in the history and culture of the Soviet Union and has planned a visit to that country. After reading this brief introduction to the city, perhaps you will decide to add Volgograd (the name given the city in 1961 to replace that of Stalingrad) to your itinerary for the Soviet Union. From Moscow it is a short plane ride to see this "Hero City" of the Soviets.

About one and one-half hours from Moscow your plane will set down at Volgograd airport. For a city the size of Volgograd, the airport is small and unimpressive. An airport at any American city half the size of Volgograd would be more impressive and have better facilities. Its waiting room is drab and boring by Western standards. If you arrive late at night, you will likely have to wait some time for transportation into the city. This writer had to hitch a ride in a busload of Bulgarian tourists headed toward hotels in the center of the city.

The Intourist Hotel in Volgograd is by far the best in the city. This hotel is old by comparison to some of the newer hotels in other Russian cities, nevertheless, it is clean and its dining facilities are very good. The hotel does not receive many Americans, and when several visit it, a small American flag is placed on the table at which Americans dine. Flags of other nations can also be seen on the various tables in the dining area. The service is courteous and the food is reasonably good. The hotel has a good Intourist Service Bureau. It is centrally located with regard to the city and many of its sights. The Intourist Hotel is a large, yellow stone building with five floors facing Ulitsa Mira.

Volgograd has a regional drama theatre named after Gorky, a theatre of musical comedy, a philharmonic society, young people's theatre, puppet theatre, circus, planetarium, a television center, fifteen cinemas, an art school, children's music schools, and a sports stadium. Also the city has three museums, including the Volgograd Museum of Fine Arts.

Adjacent to the hotel is the Square of Fallen Heroes, in the center of which stands a high granite obelisk surrounded by a public garden with many trees and flowers. The obelisk stands near a common grave holding the remains of those reportedly massacred on that spot by White Guards in 1919. The Square of Fallen Heroes is crossed by a relatively new thoroughfare, Peace Street, which stretches as far as the Planetarium, a gift to the city by East

Germany. Behind the obelisk, granite slabs cover the gravesite, which is crowned with an eternal flame. The gravesite is replenished with fresh flowers and wreaths laid upon it daily. Leading from the square is a long, twin walkway known as the Alley of Heroes which stretches down to the Volga River. Its walkways are lined with trees. A short distance from the gravesite is an old tree imbedded with bullets and fragments of shells from the fierce fighting around it in World War II. Across the square and behind the Intourist Hotel is located the Central Department Store of the city. In its basement General Paulus had his headquarters and surrendered his army.

The Alley of Heroes leads down to the Volga embankment, the favorite promenade of the city. The embankment is planted in roses and many flowers, trees, and shrubs, and has a huge granite stairway leading down it to the Volga River. The stairway consists of more than one hundred steps. It reminds one of the Potemkin stairway in Odessa leading down to the Black Sea. At the top of the spacious Volga stairway stand two monumental colonnades, one on either side of the stairs. Each colonnade consists of eight marble columns supporting an entablature on their top. Above the entablatures are bas-reliefs crowned with the hammer and sickle. At the foot of the stairway along the river's edge is located the River Terminal, which is linked with shipping.

Near the river's embankment and north of the central business district are located the ruins of an old flour mill. This five-story brick structure is a derelict which stands as a reminder of the terrible siege of the city in World War II. The mill stands alone surrounded by a grassy field and picket fence. Its roof is missing and it is pock-marked by many bullet and shell holes.

Adjacent to the old mill is a large building that houses the Panorama of the Battle for Mamayev Hill or "Height 102." The actual Hill is located in the northern part of Volgograd and was the scene of fierce battles for control of the city. The panorama measures 393.7 feet in circumference and is 52.5 feet high. It surrounds a large circular platform reached by a high, winding flight of steps. The distance between the platform and the point of observation of the panorama measures 98.4 feet in all directions. Around the top portion of the panorama warplanes can be seen diving and firing on the Mamayev battlefield. Mamayev Hill is illustrated with many trenches, bunkers, and tanks. Soldiers around these are seen in combat. Old water tanks set in holes on the hill before the war were captured by the Germans who used these for strongpoints during the fighting. In the panorama the Russians are seen capturing one of these and marching its occupants off to captivity. The panorama depicts battle scenes that actually occurred during the fierce fighting for the hill. The scenes in the panorama appear so realistic and lifelike that one feels transported back into time, and actually standing amidst the carnage that occurred. In one portion of the battleground a Russian soldier is shown clutching a severed communications cable in his teeth in order that the two pieces of it will make contact in his mouth and restore the current flowing through the cable. Another Russian soldier is seen aflame as he charges a German tank with gasoline containers in order to destroy the vehicle. The panorama reveals a great tragedy as it unfolded.

Mamayev Hill, the subject of the panorama, lies between the business and central part of Volgograd on the south and the industrial sector on its north. It was the scene of intensive fighting due to its strategic importance. In 135 days of combat it was hit by enormous numbers of bombs and shells and covered with shrapnel. The last fighting at Stalingrad took place at Mamayev Hill. In the spring of 1943 grass could not grow on the hill due to the thick blanket of metal fragments and shells (500–1,250 per square yard) that were strewn over its surface. The hill stands 334 feet (102 meters) high and is the highest point of elevation in Volgograd. It was named for a Tartar chieftan.

On the summit of the hill stands a grandiose statue of "Motherland," commemorating those who fought and died in defense of the city in World War II. The "Motherland" monument is the tallest statue in the world of a complete figure. The statue represents a woman's figure with a huge sword held aloft in her right hand. The massive statue is made of prestressed concrete and measures 290 feet from its base to the tip of the raised sword.

Several flights of long steps lead up to the vicinity of "Motherland," in front of which is an avenue of sculptural pieces depicting soldiers who fought in the battle for the hill. Nostalgic and eerie musical compositions are played on loudspeakers located around the hill. The music reminds one of a funeral march.

Also atop the hill is a large, circular pantheon, which is open to the sky from a hole in its rooftop. An eternal flame burns in a huge stone torch held aloft by a stone hand and arm emerging from the floor of the pantheon. An honor guard stands inside the pantheon, which displays many wreaths and flowers. The names of Soviet heroes who fought in the battle of Stalingrad are inscribed in gold on numerous plaques. A huge sculpture, 39 feet high, known as "Mother in Grief," stands near the pantheon. The combination of all the statues, monuments, and memorials found on Mamayev Hill leave a profound impression on the visitor. The Soviets seem to revel in memory of their sorrows and losses in World War II. But, perhaps any nation would if it suffered such grievous losses as the Soviets did in that war. Tens of thousands of Russians and foreign visitors climb Mamayev Hill each year to see its sights. The hill affords a good view of the city and the Volga River.

The Volga River on which Volgograd is located is the longest river in Europe, running 2,300 miles from its source in the Valdai Hills northwest of Moscow to the Caspian sea southeast of Volgograd. The river flows north of Moscow, but is connected with that city by the Moscow Canal and by several of its tributaries on the southern side of Moscow. Along the course of the Volga more than a half-dozen dams back up huge reservoirs of water. More than one-fourth of Russia's people live in the drainage basin of the Volga. Between one-half and two-thirds of all river traffic in the Soviet union is carried on its waters. From Gorky to Volgograd the right bank of the Volga is generally higher than the left bank. The dams across the Volga are bypassed by locks. In the past the Volga was subject to flooding, particularly the floodplains along the left bank of the river. In the spring when the snows melt, tributaries feeding the Volga deliver to it large quantities of water. Autumn rains also help fill the river. The large dams along the river now help to control its flow and water level so that the seasonal variations in maximum and minimum flow are more regulated and controlled.

Large quantities of water from the Volga are used for irrigation purposes. The southern portions of the Volga are drier than the northern parts, and irrigation waters are more needed the further south the Volga flows. At Volgograd the river generally freezes over by mid-December. By mid-November large ice floes can be seen in the river. The temperature high for December averages 25°F., while the low averages 13°F. In July, the warmest month in the city, the average high reaches 66°F, while the average low is 55°F.

About ten miles north of the city is located a long dam across the Volga River that was completed in 1960. It is one of the larger dams in the Soviet Union, and has a capacity exceeding 2.5 million kilowatts. The dam holds back the long Volgograd reservoir stretching northward from Volgograd toward Saratov. The reservoir is nearly 375 miles long, and covers an area of more than 1,200 square miles. Much of its power is utilized locally, particularly in the smelting of aluminum ores, but more than one-third of the dam's power is delivered to Moscow by high-voltage transmission lines. The dam was named after the 22nd Congress of the Communist party of the Soviet Union. In the vicinity of Volgograd the dam is the only means of crossing the Volga River, except by boat. A new bridge is planned to span the Volga in the area of the city in the future.

Power from the dam is heavily used by the city and its industries. Its usage by the aluminum industry has been noted. The northern area of Volgograd nearest the dam is the location of the Red October Steel Mill originally built in 1897, and rebuilt on its former site after the war. It is one of the largest steel mills in the Soviet Union. In the same area is the Caterpillar tractor plant, the largest producer of tractors in Russia. The plant was founded in 1930 and during the war produced T-34 tanks, many of which were made while fighting raged in the city. Rebuilt after cessation of the fighting, the factory currently produces 300 tractors every twenty-four hours. Both the steel mill and the tractor factory, Volgograd's two leading industries, are built on a thin stretch of floodplain along the Volga.

Present-day Volgograd has more than 150 industrial enterprises, and is one of Russia's main industrial centers. Goods made in the city include aluminum, chemicals, iron and steel, tractors, medical equipment, river boats, steel cables, building materials, petroleum products, wood products, foodstuffs, shoes, and textiles.

South of the city the Volga-Don (V.I. Lenin) Canal enters the Volga. The canal connects the Volga and Don rivers close to the narrowest point between these two important waterways. It was opened in 1952. Work on the canal began in 1950, with thousands of German prisoners helping to dig and construct it. The canal enters the Volga at the town of Krasnoarmeysk, a short distance south of Volgograd. West of Krasnoarmeysk the canal enters the huge Tsimlyansk Reservoir, which stretches 112 miles along the course of the Don River. The actual canal itself is about 63 miles long, stretching from the Volga to Tsimlyansk Reservoir. Locks in the canal move ships from one water level to the next. At Krasnoarmeysk the entrance to the canal is marked by a 131-foot high arch spanning the waterway. Cut timber from the forests of the upper Volga and its tributaries are floated down the river and shipped west through the canal, while coal from the Donetz Basin is the main cargo carried by ships moving east through the canal into the Volga. Peter the Great planned to build a canal to connect the Volga and Don in 1697, but little work was accomplished on it and the project was abandoned.

Between the Volga embankment and Prospekt Lenina is located the city's large sports stadium. The stadium seats 42,000 spectators. From the stadium one can look across Prospekt Lenina and see the outline of Mamayev Hill, which is but a short distance away.

Prospekt Lenina is the city's longest thoroughfare, running the entire length of the city from north to south. It is 256 feet wide, and in its middle are located gardens that contain maples, elms, poplars, acacias, and flowers. Approximately every 1,000 feet, fountains are built along the street.

Volgograd is a city of monuments that bear testimony to the conflagration that ensued there. Many of its streets and squares are named in memory of military units or other wartime symbols of heroism; for example, 13th Guards' Street, the Alley of Heroes, the Square of Fallen Heroes, and the embankment named after the 62nd Army. Other memorials related to the war include the House of Sergeant Pavlov (site of a two-month siege where Pavlov and his small unit held off German attacks), and the Monument to Reuben Ilbarruri and other soldiers killed during the war.

For history buffs the Volgograd State Museum of Defense, located in the center of the city near the hotel "Intourist," is another place of interest. This red stone building contains many displays related to the Russian Civil War and World War II. Five of its halls hold many interesting documents, photographs, drawings, and portraits from those war years. A sixth hall contains a sword from King George the Sixth of Britain given to the city for its victory over the Germans; a message from President Franklin D. Roosevelt commending the Stalingrad soldiers and citizens for their impressive defense of the city, and turning the tide of the war against Hitler; a flag from Cuba; a "victory" statue from Czechoslovakia; weapons; and other exhibits.

Throughout the city there are many secondary and higher educational institutions, vocational and technical schools. In 1980 the city opened its new university. More than 2,000 foreign students study at these facilities. Nearly 4,000 students are preparing to become physicians at the Volgograd State Medical Institute. The majority of its students are women, who comprise more than three-fourths of the Soviet Union's doctors.

To feed all the students and the large population of the city, farms around Volgograd produce a variety of agricultural commodities. Wheat is the main crop grown in the region of Volgograd. The nearby area also grows 65 percent of Russia's mustard plants, and surrounding farms produce large quantities of watermelons, tomatoes, fruits, and vegetables. Between Volgograd and the Caspian Sea, large herds of cattle and sheep graze on the steppes. Volgograd lies about 285 miles from the Caspian Sea.

Volgograd is not an exciting city by comparison to Leningrad, Moscow, or Kiev. The war left a traumatic scar on the city, one which has not yet healed in the minds of its people. Before leaving Volgograd, I sat in the private office of the director of the city's largest bookstore and talked with her for more than an hour. "Peace," she said, "is the most important thing I want for my children." While we spoke, President Reagan and Premier Gorbachev were on their way to Geneva for disarmament talks. "America and the Soviet Union," she said, "should be friends; there must never be another war." We both wished the two leaders success in the disarmament negotiations, but somehow the stoic face of Lenin in a picture on the wall behind the bookstore director did little to assure me that Soviet and American positions on the subject of disarmament would ever be significantly harmonized. Maybe if the citizens of Volgograd, whose city was destroyed by war, were empowered to negotiate the SALT talks for Russia, the outcome of these talks would be more fruitful.

EXCURSIONS

Sightseeing Tour of the City. A visit to the memorial on the Mamayev Hill erected in honor of the heroes of the crucial battle of the Great Patriotic War of the Soviet Union (1941–45) and the Battle of Stalingrad (1942–43).

Museum of the Defense. The exhibits depict the heroic past of the city.

Museum of Fine Arts. Displayed are canvasses by prominent Russian and Soviet painters.

Planetarium.

Volzhskaya Hydro (named after the 22nd congress of the Cpsu). The Town of Volzhsky.

V.I. Lenin Volga-Don Canal.

Hotels

Hotel	Address	Rooms	Telephone
Intourist	14 Mira Street	98	36-4553

Chapter VIII.
ROSTOV-ON-DON
Home of the Don
Cossacks

Nor with the plough is our dear glorious earth furrowed,
Our earth is furrowed with the hoofs of horses,
And our dear glorious earth is sown with the heads of Cossacks;
Our gentle Don is adorned with youthful widows;
Our gentle Father Don is blossomed with orphans;
The waves of the gentle Don are rich with fathers' and mothers' tears.
                              Old Cossack song from
                              And Quiet Flows the Don
                              —Mikhail Sholokhov

Rostov-on-Don is an important industrial city on the lower course of the Don River, about thirty miles from its mouth with the Gulf of Taganrog, an arm of the Sea of Azov. The city's name is sometimes confused with that of the town of Rostov, located northeast of Moscow. Rostov-on-Don is located at 47° north latitude, on approximately the same parallel as Olympia, Washington; Fargo, North Dakota; and Lucerne, Switzerland. The city has a population of one million people, and can be reached by air from Moscow in about one hour and twenty-five minutes. Its air terminal is modern-looking, larger and more impressive than that of Volgograd. Rostov-on-Don has important air, rail, and water communications with the Caucasus region to the south and southeast, and is known as the "Gateway to the Caucasus." The city is also connected by oil and natural gas pipelines running northward from the Caucasus area.

Rostov-on-Don is a comparatively young city. In 1749 a customs port known as Temernitsky was officially established at the site of the present city along the banks of the Don River. A fort named St. Dimitri, after the metropolitan Dimitry Rostovsky, was built in the settlement in 1761, and in 1797 the town was given official status, and renamed Rostov-on-Don. After the Turkish threat was removed from the Sea of Azov, the city became the main trade center for southern Russia.

Turkey and Russia were enemies before Peter the Great was born. In 1569 the Turks attacked the city of Astrakhan at the mouth of the Volga, and in 1672 the Sultan invaded the Ukraine and claimed to be the ruler of all Cossacks. Further Turkish attacks destroyed the Cossack capital of Chigirin (near the Dnieper south of Kiev) in 1677–78. The Turks and Russians then agreed to a twenty-year truce in 1681, but fighting was renewed in 1687, and again in 1695 when Peter the Great attacked the Turkish fort of Azov at the mouth of the Don. Peter was unsuccessful in his first attack because he lacked ships to prevent the Turks from supplying their fortress by sea. He then retired to Voronezh, a Don town north of present-day Rostov-on-Don, to build a fleet for another attack on Azov. In 1696 Peter the Great brought his fleet of ships down the Don, anchored them alongside its banks at the present site of Rostov, and from there he sailed to the mouth of the river to attack Azov a second time. With his fleet blockading Azov, he attacked and forced the city to surrender. But that was not the end of Turkish rule over that city; it exchanged hands several times between Turkey and Russia in the early 1700s. Under Catherine the Great, both Azov and nearby Taganrog were retaken by Russia in 1770, and in 1774 Catherine won Kerch declared the Crimea free of Turkish rule, and extended Russian control of Black Sea lands westward to the Bug River. Further battles with Turkey resulted in Russia claiming possession of Crimea and extending her boundary to the Dneister River in 1791. The northern lands of the Black Sea were now in Russian control. By 1800 the port of Rostov was filled with corn-laden barges from the steppes, and a pig-iron factory was operating in the city by 1860. Once the railroad between Rostov and central Russia was completed, the city grew very quickly. By the end of the nineteenth century there were 120,000 residents and 140 industries.

The area of the Don has long been renowned as the home of the Don

Cossacks. The river and the Don Cossacks share an association that has become an inseparable identity. Those living in the area of the Don affectionately refer to it as "Father Don."

The term Cossack, as generally used by most Americans and many others, refers to those people living in the grassy steppes of southern Russia north of the Black Sea, who are descendants of tribes of fierce warriors noted for their skills in horsemanship. This concept, however, is a bit limited or narrow by definition. Actually, there are many tribes of Cossacks in Russia, the largest of which are the Don Cossacks, whose ancestral home was centered near the lower portion of the Don River in settlements surrounding present-day Rostov-on-Don. It is this group of Cossacks that is best known to most Western tourists and foreigners familiar with the Soviet Union. The Cossack peoples are scattered over vast areas of Russia.

During the Middle Ages the Turks, who were quite familiar with the Cossacks, used the word *kazak* from their language, which means "independent or free person," or a "free warrior," to refer to these nomadic peoples who valued their freedom of movement to that of being serfs on the land. Originally many of the Cossacks were of Turkish blood. The Poles later chose a word in their language, *kozacy,* similar in spelling and meaning to the Turkish *kazak,*to refer to those peasants who preferred to live beyond Polish rule in what is now the general area of the eastern Ukraine. The Russian word for Cossacks is *kazaki.*

About two hundred years had passed from the sacking of Kiev by the Tartars before the Cossacks appeared on the steppes of southern Russia. The Cossacks along the Don built their first settlements along the lower course of that river around the 1540s. Their small communities included Cherkassk, Akasaiskaya, and Razdorskaya, all in the nearby vicinity of present-day Rostov-on-Don. Rostov actually sits on the former site of Akasaiskaya, which in 1570 was the headquarters of the *ataman* (Tartar, meaning chief) who governed over six Cossack villages in the area. Starocherkasski, a Cossack town located about thirty miles northeast of today's Rostov-on-Don, was often flooded by the river, and later moved its inhabitants to the nearby high ground now occupied by the city of Novocherkassk.

When the first railroad reached the Don near Novocherkassk, the Cossacks caused it to bypass their city because it interfered with the pasturing of their cattle in the area, and restricted their approach to the Aksai River. The consequence of this action was the spurring of the growth of nearby Rostov-on-Don at the expense of Novocherkassk.

Today, Novocherkassk has a population of about 185,000. The city is located on the more elevated areas around the small rivers of the Aksai and Tuzla. Its large locomotive factory produces high-speed electric engines for Russia's railroads. The local Museum of the History of the Don Cossacks has a fine collection of exhibits on the history and culture of the Don Cossacks.

Both the Russians and the Poles hired the fierce Cossacks as mercenaries to help defend their frontiers. But when either tried to restrict the privileges and freedoms of the Cossacks, they would rebel and often attack those who were attempting to repress them. For two hundred years (1600–1800) the Cossacks were the leaders of most of the revolts against the Russian regime. One such rebellion was led by the Cossack leader Emelyan Pugachev who was born on the Don River and became a veteran of many battles. In the 1770s he led the largest Cossack revolt ever, burning and destroying many towns and cities before his final defeat near Tsaritsyn and subsequent capture and execution. Although the Cossacks attacked the Russian state, they on occasions supported it when it was in crisis. Longworth states in his book *The Cossacks* that one can find "striking parallels between him (the Cossack) and the American frontiersman; indeed, both of them sprang from similar roots."[3] The Cossacks today are more of a legend than a symbol of force.

Most Cossacks lived in villages, with fish from the Don and its tributaries providing their main source of food and livelihood. By the second half of the seventeenth century more than fifty Cossack villages and ten thousand Cossack warriors lived along the Don. Still by the end of the nineteenth century only fourteen Russian cities had Cossack populations in excess of five thousand of their numbers, and three of these were located in the area of the Don.

For a good insight into the lives of the Don Cossacks, one should read the historical novels by Mikhail Sholokhov. He wrote some of the most inspiring literary fiction dealing with the period prior to, during, and after the revolution in Russia. Sholokhov was born in the lower Don area in the small village of Veshevskaya in 1905. In 1925 he completed his first book, *Tales of the Don,* consisting of a series of short stories, and began work on *Tikhi Don (The Quiet Don),* published in four volumes from 1928–40. *Tikhi Don* was later translated into English by Stephen Garry, who divided the novel and published it under the titles *And Quiet Flows the Don* (1934) and *The Don Flows Home to the Sea* (1941).

The Quiet Don is a fictional work that describes the activities of the Don Cossacks during the period between 1912 and 1922, the Russian Revolution, and the Civil War. The Don Cossacks are described in terms of their traditions and culture, day-to-day living, at love and in war. The Cossacks traditionally served in the employ of the tsar and his army. A Cossack detachment guarded the Winter Palace and the tsar in St. Petersburg. In return for their loyalty, the tsar granted the Cossacks special privileges and a high degree of social and economic independence in their Don Valley homeland. The world of the Don Cossacks suffered a severe setback with the over-throw of the tsar and the revolution. During the Civil War the Cossacks were divided in their loyalties between the Reds and Whites, and lost many of their freedoms and possessions. In 1919 the Cossacks staged a revolt to recover their losses but to no avail. Both the Cossacks and their hero in the novel *The Quiet Don* suffered torment and grievous losses. *The Quiet Don* has been translated into more than fifty languages, and over five million copies of it have been printed.

Sholokhov continued his saga of the Don Cossacks in his next fictional novel, *Virgin Soil Upturned*. The first installments of it appeared in 1931. This work describes the compulsory collectivization of agriculture in the Don area during the Stalin era. The novel describes the hard physical labor on the farms (plowing, communal harvesting, cutting timber, etc.), and the uprooting of the former way of life of the Cossacks. The communes stripped the Cossacks of their independent ways, and in the process robbed them of much of their pride and self-respect. The Cossacks were mainly a provincial people, proud of their customs and traditions. The Cossack legend has been preserved in their dances, songs, and ballads.

Virgin Soil Upturned was later translated into two volumes in English under the titles *Seeds of Tomorrow* and *Harvest on the Don. Seeds of Tomorrow,* the first part of *Virgin Soil Upturned,* describes the liquidation of a Cossack village, while *Harvest on the Don,* the second part of the novel, ends with an unsuccessful counterrevolutionary plot against the regime in Moscow. For his works, Sholokhov won a Nobel Prize in Literature in 1965.

During the Civil War period both the Cossacks and Rostov suffered considerable losses in lives and property. Under Soviet rule after the war, Rostov became an important industrial center, and the Soviets made it the administrative center of both the Northern Caucasus area and the Rostov region. The city reached 308,000 in population in 1926 and 510,000 in 1939. The period of the city's rapid urban growth in the 1930s occurred at a time when rural-urban migration had reached its apex in Russia.

The Soviets built the huge "Rostelmash" agricultural machinery works in Rostov-on-Don in 1932. Another large machinery factory, the Drasny Aksai Plant, was updated and expanded, and the city became the largest producer of agricultural machinery in Russia prior to World War II.

Today, "Rostelmash" produces 320 combines daily, and the city has over fifty plants engaged in the making of machinery. The largest branch of industry in the city is that of engineering, which comprises over 40 percent of all industrial activity in Rostov. Presently the city is still the Soviet Union's leading agricultural machinery manufacturer.

In World War II Rostov saw much fighting. The Germans captured it twice and lost it twice. Near the end of 1941 the Germans had successfully moved through much of the Ukraine, capturing Taganrog (October 17), Kharkov (November 2), and other large cities. Beyond Artemovsk the Germans held the line of the Donetz slightly to the east of that river.

The German attack on Rostov began on November 16, with the temperature at $-4°F$. The ground was frozen and it was difficult to dig for defensive positions or to bury the dead. After heavy fighting and large losses the Germans took Rostov on November 20. The city fell to General von Kleist's 1st Panzer Army. Still, the Russians counterattacked and the Germans had to ward off swarming attacks on the city. Finally the Germans had to relinquish the city in heavy fighting on November 28.

At the end of November 1941 the German line around Rostov stood at half the distance between the Mius River and the Donetz River. By the end of December 1941 the Germans had withdrawn west of the River Mius, which remained the German line until the summer of 1942.

For the Russians, the German withdrawal from Rostov was an important event because it was the first time the German army had suffered a significant setback since Hitler began World War II. At the time of their reversal the Germans were overextended, the winter weather was a problem, and the troops were in a weakened condition from long drives and hard fighting. Credit was due the Russians, however, because their counteroffensive plan had been well formulated and executed.

In June 1942 the Germans began their summer offensive by overrunning the Crimean Peninsula, after which they drove eastward to the Don and in the direction of Stalingrad. Rostov fell again on July 23 to the Germans who advanced into it from the north and northeast. With or without orders, the Russian defenders of the city practically abandoned it, although it is doubtful if the city could have been held in any event against the strong German offensive.

During the city's on again, off again occupation in the war it sustained enormous damage. Before their final withdrawal from Rostov, the Germans destroyed most of it and left little but rubble behind. After the Russians recaptured Rostov in February 1943 a rapid rebuilding of the city and its industries commenced. The population of the city greatly declined during the war.

Rostov grew rapidly as a port and industrial center after 1952 due to the building of the Tsimlyansky Hydroelectric Complex and the Volga-Don Canal. Rostov is a major shipping center. Its docks handle large quantities of grain, coal, timber, and petroleum. Many large passenger-carrying vessels tie up at its river docks. On the docks of the city large cargoes of timber that have floated down the Volga and then through the Volga-Don Canal are unloaded. Some of the timber is used in woodworking enterprises in the city, while much of it is reloaded on boats to continue its journey to the Black Sea area and other ports. The city's excellent transport facilities have helped make it an important communications, trade, and distribution center.

The Don River runs nearly 1,220 miles through southern Russia. The river has its source in the central Russian Upland near the city of Tula, about 110 miles south of Moscow. From Tula the Don flows southeast to its big bend west of Volgograd, thence to the Gulf of Taganrog. The Don drains part of the rich *chernozem* or Black Soil Zone. The banks of the river are dotted with fishing villages and the river is an important source of herring, salmon, and caviar. Rostov, Liski, and Voronezh are the major cities along the banks of the river. The Don joins the huge Tsimlyansk Reservoir near its great bend opposite the Volga. From the reservoir southward, past Rostov to the Gulf of Taganrog, the Don flows across the broad expanse of the steppes in an indolent, lazy motion. The city sits on the high right bank of the Don at a point where two of it tributaries, the Termernik and Moyechny, empty into the river. The lower Don, especially south of its great bend, has historically had a problem with silting in its channel. Emptying into the Gulf of Taganrog, the silt-laden Don has for many centuries been filling up that shallow-water body. Today a dredged channel is kept open from Rostov to the Sea of Azov.

Irrigation waters from the Don are important in agricultural production, particularly in the drier southern area of the steppes. The Rostov region, which is about 40,000 square miles in area, is a rich agricultural land on which are found about 250 each of collective and state farms. These farms grow wheat, rice, sunflowers, barley, cattle, hogs, corns, melons, poultry, fruit, and grapes. Horses are also raised and bred on the nearby steppes. Local studs and racers are sold at international auctions.

Rostov's climate is continental: hot and dry in the summer, and cold in the winter. The steppelands around the city receive less than twenty inches of rainfall a year. The July temperatures average 68°F. for the high and 58°F. for the low, while January averages 23°F. for the high and 10°F. for the low.

Surrounded by farms of the steppes, the city relies heavily on its output of agricultural machinery. Other important industrial products made in Rostov include ball bearings, glass, electrical machinery, textiles and clothing, flour, chemicals, shoes, boats and barges, earthmoving machinery, heating units, wire and cables, vodka, and foodstuffs. Additionally, the city repairs railway equipment and ships, and processes wine and tobacco.

The city's educational institutions include eighteen research and thirty-eight design institutes, eight music schools and a musical training college, and Rostov University, which was founded when the Russian revolution was beginning. The city's medical research institute has over 6,000 students enrolled.

Along the low left bank of the Don in the heart of the city is a workers' complex consisting of many summer cottages, restaurants, and recreation facilities. This complex was built by local industries, Intourist Hotel, and the government for use by their employees and workers.

Adjacent to the riverbank and the workers' complex is "Peter's Mooring," at which may be seen a replica of the ship in which Tsar Peter sailed down the Don to attack the Turkish fortress of Azov. It is a wooden ship with three masts, and portholes for guns in its sides. It was at this site that Tsar Peter moored his ships in 1696 prior to sailing to Azov. Crossing the Don in the vicinity of "Peter's Mooring" is a long concrete bridge spanning the river. From the dockside of the high right bank of the river a good view is afforded of the large number of ships tied up at the city's docks. Along the docks are cruise ships, hydrofoils, barges, and seagoing vessels. Huge cranes on the dock stand ready to load or unload any ship. As late as mid-November the waters of the Don remain unfrozen. At Rostov the Don freezes over only about one month out of the year.

A statue of Maxim Gorky faces the Don in the area of its dockside. Gorky once worked in the port of Rostov. On Engels Street is located the Gorky Drama Theatre, named after the celebrated writer in 1936.

Rostov has a large old Armenian quarter comprising part of the city. In the latter part of the eighteenth century thousands of Armenians and Greeks migrated to the Rostov area to escape Turkish rule. They were encouraged to resettle in southern Russia by Catherine the Great who gave them land and property. Catherine wanted to weaken the power of Turkey around the Black Sea, and the Armenians and Greeks that settled there were skilled artisans, merchants, traders, and scientists useful to Russia. Formerly located on the outskirts of Rostov, the old Armenian section of the city is now enclosed by modern suburbs.

The city and the area around it include more than 10,000 acres of parks and public gardens, of which there are forty within the city. Rostov has many wide and spacious boulevards, some of which have large underground walkways beneath them connecting opposite sides of the streets. The large Intourist Hotel (built in 1973 on the former site of Fort St. Dimitry) faces Frederick Engels Street, the promenade and main street of the city. Engels Street is a wide boulevard that runs parallel to the Don River. Along it are parks, gardens, memorials, book shops, restaurants, a huge children's toy store, and a variety of other shops. The street is busy both during the day and in the evening. Walking its promenade I observed the facial features of the local inhabitants who are a mixture of many nationalities—Russian, Greek, Armenian, Turkish, Ukrainian, and others. The centuries-old combination of the genes of these ethnic groups has produced in Rostov some of Russia's most beautiful women, a trademark by which the city is well known. Almost as if to demonstrate this claim, along Engels Street smartly dressed young women can be seen peering in shop windows; enjoying tea or some other drink in local restaurants; strolling by themselves; or walking with friends. In Russia, women frequently walk together with arms interlocked.

Rostov enjoys a variety of local cultural and historical establishments.

There are four theatres, a philharmonic society, a well-known circus, fine arts museum, local history museum, and a civic center.

On Soviet Street is located a memorial mass gravesite and an eternal flame burning in memory of those fallen in combat for the Communist state. Young schoolchildren in uniforms march daily with rifles to and from the memorial in an honor-guard changing ceremony. In Russia it is difficult to escape the many monuments in memory of the war dead and those that sacrificed for the Soviet system.

About eight miles from the city lies a huge ravine in which is built the Zmiyevskaya Memorial. In this ravine 27,000 civilians of Rostov were murdered by the Nazis. A nearby museum contains exhibits and photographs portraying the atrocities committed against the people of the city. Altogether 48,000 of Rostov's inhabitants were killed during the German occupation.

Rostov-on-Don is considerably more interesting, charming and exciting than Volgograd and has more in the way of cultural activities to offer the tourist. Its opera house and circus are packed when performances are given. But a Leningrad, Kiev, or Moscow, it is not.

EXCURSIONS

Sightseeing Tour of the City. The tour's itinerary passes through the main thoroughfare of the city, Engels Street, and the central squares—Theatrical Square, K. Marx Square, Square of the Soviets, Lenin Square. Acquaintance with the main attractions of the city is afforded.

An Excursion to the Zapadny (West) Residential District. Includes a visit to a memorial complex in the Zmiyevskaya Ravine. Acquaintance with the extent of housing construction in the city and with the memorial complex erected in memory of the prisoners of war and civilians of Rostov-on-Don slaughtered by the Hitlerites in the Zmiyevskaya Ravine during the Great Patriotic War of the Soviet Union (1941–45).

Museum of Regional Studies. Exhibits are devoted to the history of the Don Cossacks, as well as the history of the development of the region after the Great October Socialist Revolution of 1917.

Museum of Fine Arts. Displays works by Russian artists of the sixteenth to twentieth centuries. In three of the museum's halls temporary exhibits are arranged.

OUT-OF-TOWN EXCURSIONS

Novocherkassk. City sightseeing tour. A visit to the museum of the history of the Don Cossacks. Distance from Rostov-on-Don: 40 km. Tour duration: 4 hours.

Taganrog. City sightseeing tour, including the sights associated with the life and activities of the celebrated Russian writer Anton Chekhov. Taganrog has a picture gallery in which works of Russian and Soviet fine arts are represented. Distance from Rostov-on-Don: 75 km. Tour duration: 8 hours.

HOTELS

Hotel	Address	Rooms	Telephone
Intourist	115 Engels St.	273	65-9066
			65-9082
			65-9065

Intourist also rents part of space at the following hotels:
Rostov—telephone: 39-1818
Moskovskaya—telephone: 38-8700
Tourist—telephone: 32-4309

CAMP SITE

Located 12 km. from the city center. Intourist rents 150 beds. Parking lot capacity: 110 cars. Telephone: 57-0586, 57-0404.

Moscow University is the major university in the Soviet Union.

The Bolshoi Theater seats more than 2,300 people.

Hotel Intourist is a marked contrast to ornate Moscow buildings.

Honor guard goes through paces in front of Lenin Mausoleum on Red Square.

Doll tied to front of taxi indicates passengers are newlyweds.

House in the rural area around Zagorsk

Young Pioneers march in Zagorsk.

Massive St. Isaac's Cathedral was built over a marsh.

Peter the Great selected the site for the city of Leningrad.

Petrodvorets is the Summer Palace built by Peter the Great.

The Winter Palace no longer shows World War II damage.

The Lybid is one of the larger hotels in Kiev, capital of the Ukraine.

The Kiev-Perchersk Monastery is an assemblage of churches.

*St. Andrew's Cathedral was
designed by Italian architect
Bartolomeo Rastrelli.*

*The Arch of Friendship stands
atop Kiev Mountain along the
Dnieper River.*

State farm workers have seven-hour days and receive paid leaves.

A portrait of Lenin overlooks the entrance to the headquarters of the Trebuchovsky State Farm.

Motherland Statue is on Mamayev Hill.

Old mill in Volgograd still shows war damage.

Zmiyovskaya Gorge near Rostov-on-Don was the site of Nazi atrocities.

A replica of the wooden ship of Peter the Great is tied up on the Don at Rostov.

The Taganrog dock area is not large, but is busy with shipping.

Taganrog was the birthplace of Anton Chekhov.

Potemkin Mutineers Monument commemorates the event in which hundreds lost their lives.

The Potemkin Stairway was originally greenish gray sandstone, but is now rose red granite.

A monument near the Black Sea honors sailors.

The largest seaport of southern Russia, Odessa is on the Black Sea.

Odessa is a young city, founded in the latter part of the eighteenth century.

Filatov Institute is the largest eye hospital in Russia.

Chapter IX.
TAGANROG
Birthplace of Chekhov

*the steppes . . . a boundless plain, a harsh climate, a dreary, harsh people
with its heavy, cold history, Tartar yoke, officialdom, poverty, ignorance,
damp capital cities, etc. . . . . In Western Europe people perish because life is
too crowded and close, here they perish because it is too spacious.*

—*Anton Chekhov*

From Rostov-on-Don, the city of Taganrog can be reached in less than two
hours in a sedan with driver, rented in Rostov for about seventy dollars.
Taganrog is located at the northern tip of the Gulf of Taganrog, an arm of the
Sea of Azov. By road the distance from downtown Rostov to Taganrog is
about seventy-five kilometers. The blacktop or asphalt two-lane road to
Taganrog winds through low rolling hills and undulating relief. The road is
busy with traffic in the vicinity of Rostov and Taganrog, and often foggy in the
late fall and winter. The landscape along the road amidst the plowed fields
discloses the dark, rich, black soil of the grassy steppe of southern Russia.
About seven miles from Rostov the road passes through a small city known as
Chaltyr. Chaltyr is an old Armenian town. Its inhabitants work mostly in
agricultural enterprises in the vicinity and in a large brick factory in the city.
The Armenians arrived in Chaltyr from the Crimea in 1779 under the protection of Catherine II who encouraged their migration to weaken the Crimea.

Anton Chekhov visited the village of Chaltyr while still a student in Taganrog, and became enchanted with the daughter of an Armenian farmer. Anton fell in love at first sight with the fifteen-year-old girl. The two met at a well, and Chekhov was so spellbound with her beauty that he embraced the young girl and kissed her. The account of this incident in Chekhov's life is told in his story *The Beauties,* published in 1888.

The roadway to Taganrog is lined with poplar trees. Acacia is also commonly seen. From the highway there can be seen many orchards of apples, pears, and cherries. Vineyards are also common in the area, and wine-making is one of the local enterprises. Many large black ravens can be seen along the roadside.

The drive to Taganrog takes about one and one-half hours by car. On arrival in Taganrog one passes through some newer areas of the city that have grown up as suburbs around the city. Next, the road passes through an old district of the city containing large numbers of wooden houses which look as though they were built around the turn of the century. They are typical of the older houses seen in many parts of Russia, especially in the rural areas. For the most part the only distinguishing features to these houses are their predominantly blue and green shutters. From the highway, dirt roads lead off to the right and left through rows of these drab houses. Most of the dirt roads are tree lined and show little evidence of vehicular traffic.

Passing the older section of Taganrog, the road enters an area with many new high-rise apartment buildings, stores, and businesses. The city numbers 300,000 in population. Beautiful acacia trees line many of its streets. Taganrog is a large industrial center. The main enterprises are the huge combine-machinery plant and the boiler factory.

Taganrog was founded in 1696 by Peter the Great. Peter had the Trinity Fortress built on its site. Taganrog is a Turkish word meaning "Fire on the Cape." On the cape or bluff above the Sea of Azov fires were built in the past to guide ships into the harbor. The city was a competitor at one time in the mind of Peter the Great for his new capital of Russia. However, Peter abandoned Taganrog in favor of St. Petersburg, otherwise Taganrog might have played a significant role in Russian history.

Taganrog is mostly flat except in places along the seacoast, which is hilly and steep. On the bluff where once stood the Trinity Fortress a huge statue of Peter I overlooks the harbor of the city. The statue was built by the sculptor Antokol'sky, commissioned by Anton Chekhov.

From a high bluff overlooking the city and the Sea of Azov a good view is afforded of shipping and the dock area of Taganrog. As one approaches the dock area, a statue of Garibaldi, the Italian patriot, stands near the roadway. Garabaldi spent some time in Taganrog.

The dock area is confined and not large by most standards but is often busy with shipping. Sailors move about the decks of ships, some painting and others loading and tending cargo. Some of the sailors speak reasonably good English and will engage in a conversation if asked to do so. Many of the ships are fishing vessels. From Taganrog ships sail frequently to fish in the waters off Africa and Spain, especially for mackerel. Along the shoreline you can walk among people fishing in the harbor from behind a small wall overlooking the sea. The sea is foggy and visibility is often limited in the winter.

The Sea of Azov accounts for about 20 percent of all fish caught in Russia's waters. It is a shallow sea and consequently warms up quickly. The salt content of the water is very low. Pike, sturgeon, and herring are the principal fish caught in the sea. There are sixty kilos of fish caught in the sea for each hectare of its water surface.

Anton Chekhov loved to swim by the seashore and fish in the waters of the Sea of Azov. He sustained a cut in a diving accident which left a permanent scar on his forehead. Chekhov frequently waded by the seashore and bathed in its waters. Some of his writings describe scenes from the seashore and the sound of waves reverberating against beaches. His boyhood in Taganrog left him with memories that would be etched into his prose.

From the dock area it is a short drive to the central business district of the city. The city is uninspiring except for its many markets, some of which are located outdoors, and help to add a touch of human quality to an otherwise drab and colorless locality. Most of the buildings are plain, old, and featureless in their architecture. They are lined monotonously along the streets, uniform in appearance and lacking any variety. Occasional wagons mixed with trucks haul produce to the markets.

Taganrog is cold in the winter, but hot in the summertime. A heavy overcoat feels good in the cold winter air. The fog along the seashore is only scant in the downtown area. The statue of Anton Chekhov in a downtown park hunches over, as if trying to avoid the cold air of winter as Chekhov sits reposed on a large block of stone.

Taganrog was a relatively unknown city in Russia prior to the time of Chekhov. Before Anton Chekhov was born in the city about the only notoriety it achieved was when Tsar Alexander I died there mysteriously in 1825. In 1855 the city was shelled by the Anglo-French fleet during the Crimean War. Tchaikovsky, the famous Russian composer, later visited his brother in Taganrog and wrote a number of his musical scores in the city.

A short distance from the central business district is located an adjacent residential area where on a quiet tree-lined street with rustic old houses is the birthplace and home of Anton Chekhov during the early years of his boyhood in Taganrog. The house is presently the Chekhov Museum in the city. It is a simple frame building painted white, consisting of four rooms and a small foyer or entrance room at the front. On approach the house appears unsophisticated, artless, and simple. It sits back, recessed about 180 feet from the street. A brick walkway about five feet wide leads from the street to the house, which sits on a wooded lot about five acres in size. Leaving the street and walking toward the house one approaches the statue of Chekhov off the left side of the walkway. It is partially surrounded by trees with numerous bushes to the rear. The statue depicts Chekhov with a beard and mustache and facial features resembling a fortyish-year old man. His bust rests on a block of gray stone chiseled into which are the dates 1860–1904, the years in which he was born and died. He lived only forty-four and one-half years but left behind a decided imprint on Russian and world literature.

Approaching his house, one senses the simplistic lifestyle into which Chekhov was born. The house is virtually featureless and appears to have been built for the caretaker of an estate. Only the green shutters against the white of the house give any distinctiveness to its appearance. In the middle of the house a brick chimney rises above the slanted roofling. Trees surround the house, which has only three windows facing the front, one of which looks out from the foyer.

The four rooms comprising the house are relatively small. The foyer at the front is a small square room attached to the middle of the front of the house. The house is simply furnished. The living room contains a dining table, chairs, and a large tea kettle mounted atop a copper urn in which oil was burned to heat the tea above. Some candles, dishes, and vases may also be seen. The tablecloth and window curtains are both plain white pieces of cotton fabric without any design on them.

Chekhov's parents were devout Orthodox believers. Several icons could be seen in one corner of the room. One hung suspended from a wooden peg on the wall. The Holy Scriptures, a large book, lay on the table. A copper candlestick with a large candle stood nearby. When the Scriptures were read, the candle was lit to provide light for reading. Incense was burned frequently in the room, where the children used to pray each morning. Chekhov's father, Pavel, preferred this room and spent most of his time in it when at home.

To the rear of the living room was the bedroom of Anton's parents. It too is very simple, with the bed taking up much of the space in the room. Chekhov occasionally slept with his parents, particularly on nights when he became frightened of storms. His room was the third room in the house and opened to his parents' room on one side and the kitchen on the other. The kitchen, the fourth room of the house, contains a large stone and clay oven near the doorway. Bread was baked in it, and around the kitchen various utensils, ladles, and containers could be seen. Several cabinets display jars containing spices, seeds, and grains.

Taganrog was a trading city and gathering place of merchants even before Anton Chekhov's time. Wheat from the steppes was its main item of trade.

Wine and corn were other commodities widely traded. The port was still quite active when Chekhov lived in Taganrog but gradually as its harbor silted-up, the city lost most of its trade and became just another provincial outpost. Much of the city was drab, mud-splattered, and dusty. Although the city has grown much larger since Chekhov lived there, Taganrog, today, appears to have changed little in many respects from its past.

Around 30,000 people, mainly of Russian and European background, lived in Taganrog at the time of Chekhov's birth. Foreigners largely dominated the trade and economic life of the city. Wealthy Greek, Italian, and German merchants determined the principal cultural activities and social life of Taganrog. The city supported a symphony orchestra, theatre, and clubs for wealthy patrons. Prominent Italian opera performers were invited to sing on local stages.

Other features of the city at the time Chekhov lived there included a hospital, prison, two secondary schools, a cathedral, customs house, public library, brickworks, brewery, slaughterhouse, approximately one dozen churches, and several banks. Paved and tree-lined streets could be found in the center of the city. Young girls were abducted off its streets at night to be sold to harems in Turkey. In a large square near the Chekhov home prisoners were flogged on a scaffold. Chekhov probably observed the floggings from the windows of his parent's home. As a young boy in Taganrog, Chekhov frequently took walks around the city and into the countryside, and became well acquainted with all the features of Taganrog.

Greek merchants controlled much of the trade of Taganrog. In 1867 Anton was sent by his father to a parish school operated by the Greek Church of St. Augustine. His father reasoned that if Anton studied under the Greeks and learned their language and business methods, he might also in time become a wealthy merchant. Anton learned to speak some Greek but discarded it upon his departure from Taganrog. Following a year in the Greek school his father became disenchanted with his progress and in 1868 enrolled him in the Taganrog School for Boys, a provincial *gymnasium*. He spent eleven years in the *gymnasium*.

Anton's father was a rigid, ill-tempered man who was pious in his belief of the church and God. Anton spent a lot of time churchgoing and singing in the choir. Chekhov was baptized in church. His father whipped him and his brothers frequently. Life in Taganrog in Chekhov's time was cruel, harsh, and often melancholy.

Chekhov escaped being born a serf because his grandfather had purchased the freedom of his family from a wealthy landowner. Chekhov had four brothers and a sister. A seventh child died about three years after birth. Two brothers were older than Chekhov.

Chekhov's father, Pavel, owned and operated a grocery store that he opened in 1857 in the downtown business district of Taganrog. In the store he sold coffee, tea, sugar, olive oil, spices, grain, dried fruit, nuts, sausage, dried currants, and soap. The store today is a historical site. Tours are conducted through it. Two Russian women tend to the upkeep, caretaking, and guided services for visitors to the store. In the summertime tourists and visitors are frequent, but in the winter no American may visit there for months. Apparently few Americans visit Taganrog in any season. One of the two caretakers speaks relatively good English and is very knowledgeable about the store and the history of the Chekhov family. The store is located on the ground floor of an old two-story building. Entrance is through a side door about fifteen feet away from the one that served as the entrance to the grocery in Chekhov's time. Inside a hallway adjacent to the grocery, bags of grain and nuts in burlap bags stand against the walls in facsimile of the time when the grocery was operating. The hallway has an entrance to the one-room grocery, which is small by American standards. Inside the grocery are counters, shelves, some bags of nuts and grain, a balancing scale for weighing commodities, and glass jars, some of which contain seeds and spices. The store looks much as one would imagine it did in Chekhov's time. Anton worked in the store while a student in Taganrog.

Above the store were the living quarters for the Chekhov family. A large living room was directly above the grocery. It was in this room that the Chekhovs received and entertained guests. A piano was among the pieces of furniture. At home Anton took music and French lessons from tutors hired by his father. To the rear of the living room were two bedrooms, the first of which contained an old Singer sewing machine of early vintage. Anton's bedroom was to the rear of the building. His room connected to an adjacent cloakroom and steps to the ground level hallway below. Anton lived above the store for a period of five years.

At age thirteen Anton attended the theatre in Taganrog for the first time. He was obsessed with the theatre and began to write tragedies, give performances, and act in them. He also started a humor magazine and became its editor.

When he was fifteen years old, he developed peritonitis. Close to death, he was treated by a doctor from the *gymnasium* he attended and upon recovery decided that he would study medicine as a career when he finished the *gynmasium*. Provincial life in Taganrog was beginning to bore him.

Anton's father borrowed money to build a new house in 1874, whereupon the Chekhov family moved into it. But Pavel had gone deeply into debt and was unable to repay the bank. By April 1876, Pavel had gone bankrupt and decided to flee Taganrog lest he be arrested and imprisoned. He secretly boarded a railway car and made his way to Moscow to join two of his sons who had gone there previously. Anton was sixteen at the time. Shortly the

Chekhov home was auctioned and the family evicted. In July 1876 the rest of the family departed for Moscow, except Anton and Ivan, who were abandoned in Taganrog.

The new owner of the former Chekhov home needed a tutor for his nephew, and Anton agreed to provide lessons in exchange for room and board. Anton lived three years in Taganrog after his family departed. He continued to edit his magazine, write plays, read literary works, and perform well in school. He even made a trip to Moscow to visit his family. Anton was visibly impressed with Moscow, its many theatres, concerts, broad streets, writers, scholars, and Moscow University. His family, however, had a difficult time in the city making ends meet and frequently had to move. They moved eleven times between 1876 and 1878. Anton sent them money each month, but their fortunes never seemed to improve.

In June 1879 Chekhov passed his final exams at the Taganrog School for Boys. He left Taganrog at age nineteen with a scholarship to study medicine at Moscow University. This reunited him with his family, but he soon became their main source of livelihood. He assumed leadership role of the household of his family and gradually their economic conditions improved. The income for his family was derived from writing that he sold to publishers, and rent from several of his friends who stayed at the Chekhov home.

Many of Chekhov's stories were written and published under a pseudonym. He had 9 stories published in 1880, 13 the next year, and 129 in 1885. In Moscow he met by chance in 1882 with Nicholas Leykin, publisher of the paper *Oskolki* (Fragments) in St. Petersburg. Chekhov and Leykin became friends and Leykin had total control of Chekhov's publications until 1885, when his stories began appearing in *Petersburg Newspaper*. Chekhov was a prolific humorous story writer; he had a talent for devising stories in a brief span of time. He usually took only a day to write a story, and once wrote one while he took a bath. By the end of 1882 his stories were appearing weekly in *Oskolki,* and he began contributing to journals in Moscow. By 1887 he had become a well-known writer in Russia, and counted among his friends Tchaikovksy and Grigorovich. Once his works became serialized in the newspapers of St. Petersburg, he also became well known in the West.

Chekhov began the practice of medicine in December 1884 in the town of Voskresensk, located about forty miles west of Moscow. Voskresensk is now the present city of Istra. Chekhov had previously wanted Leykin to secure a position in medicine for him in St. Petersburg. He was a capable doctor of medicine.

Chekhov first coughed blood in 1884. He suffered from tuberculosis of the lungs for nearly twenty years. As he grew older the tuberculosis became worse.

He returned to Taganrog in the spring of 1887. Springtime was his favorite season in Russia. Altogether he returned to Taganrog a total of five times after he left in 1879 for Moscow. Chekhov wrote a number of his stories in Taganrog while visiting there. He was in Taganrog when *The Steppe* was written.

The Steppe (1888) appears to be an unrelated series of short stories, yet the subject is uncomplicated due to lack of a plot. It is written in eight episodes, and relates a journey by carriage from Taganrog to Kiev. Leaving Taganrog, Chekhov mentions the prison, the cemetery, and the brickworks in the succession they appeared on the road during the 1880s when the story was written. The principal character of *The Steppe*, Egorushka, a small boy reminds the reader of Anton when he was a young lad growing up in Taganrog. There are many similarities between the character Egorushka and Anton Chekhov in his childhood. Like Egorushka, Anton knew and traveled the steppe, and lived in a seaport. Chekhov describes Egorushka as a sad, unhappy child with a degraded existence. He appears to draw upon his childhood experiences to shape the character of Egorushka.

In 1889 his tuberculosis became severe enough to hinder his writing. In the following year, 1890, Chekhov made a long and perilous journey to Sakhalin, an island in the Pacific Ocean off the east coast of Russia. The trip was made through thousands of miles of snow, bitter cold, seas of mud, icy rivers, and dust. On Sakhalin he visited penal settlements, interviewed convicts, and wrote stories about the fretful conditions under which the inhabitants lived. Several of his stories that evolved from the trip to Sakhalin and his return journey to Moscow were *The Island Sakhalin, In Exile,* and *Gusev.* In these and other stories such as *The Gossips, The Mission, The Student,* and *The Necklace,* Chekhov has an introspect for piercing the shell of his characters and permitting the reader to view their faults, morals, and idiosyncrasies. The reader may recognize and identify something of Chekhov himself in the characters he creates. Many of his characters are simple people who lead average lives and eke out an existence. They are mostly anonymous individuals with simple backgrounds, not intellectuals or philosophers. Chekhov is at his best describing the peasant and the rigors of his life. Chekhov has a feeling for the melancholy. He was a pessimist. The reader feels the suffering of the characters in his stories. In spite of his fame, Chekhov was a lonely person. Even to his friends he was often a puzzle.

Chekhov's style of writing and composition give a penetrating view of the *mouzhik* (peasant), who is described in great detail. Chekhov wrote with an instinct for illuminating the peasants' poverty, illnesses, drunkenness, savagery, and miserable existence. Chekhov tried to improve the lot of the peasants. He treated them medicinally, built schools for their education, established a relief organization for their assistance, and helped to improve communications and roads.

Chekhov left Odessa in 1894 on a tour to Vienna, Nice, and Paris. The same year he returned to Taganrog to comfort his uncle who was near death. Chekhov always remembered Taganrog, but its provincialism and cold ruled out any desire to live in that city. He was, however, very benevolent to his hometown, collecting money for its museum and charities, and filling its library with books.

By 1897 he was hemorrhaging from the lungs and spitting up blood. His doctors suggested he try a different climate. Thereupon he journeyed to France, stayed briefly in Biarritz, and then moved to Nice on the Riviera, where he spent the winter. In 1898 he returned to Russia, sold his estate at Melikhovo, and took up residence in Yalta on the Black Sea.

Women admired and were attracted to Chekhov. Mostly, however, their affection for him centered on his intelligence, wit, and charming humor. Chekhov lost his virginity during his boyhood in Taganrog. While he shared intimate relationships with women, marriage was seldom considered. There was a certain sorrow in Chekhov's life; happiness seemed to elude him.

Chekhov and Olga Knipper, an actress, were married in Moscow in 1901 in a simple church ceremony. His health failing, the two entered a sanatorium on the Volga River. Later they journeyed to Yalta, but Olga left shortly for Moscow. They met and parted many times after that, yet their marriage was far from happy. In 1904 his doctors finally relented and let Chekhov leave Yalta for Moscow. His last drama, *The Cherry Orchard,* was at the time being performed at the Moscow Arts Theatre. The play, like the man who wrote it, exemplified gloom and death. That summer he and his wife departed for Badenweiler, Germany, a health resort in the Black Forest. There in July 1904 his heart beat its last beat on a warm night. Chekhov's body was returned to Russia in a zinc coffin. It was transported in a wagon bearing the letters "Fresh Oysters." Had Chekhov been alive and witnessed the scene, he probably would have written another short story with the title identical to that of the lettering borne by the wagon that transported his body. In 1904 Chekhov was buried in Moscow in the cemetery at Novodevichy Monastery. Tuberculosis had ended his life.

Chekhov rejected hate, violence, and hypocrisy. He did not rise from the intelligentsia, and often ridiculed it as being unconcerned, apathetic, and stupid. The Russia about which Chekhov wrote was decadent, largely illiterate, mostly poor, and in decline. Time had already marked its society for revolutionary change.

Chekhov was a literary artist, and an innovator. He was a genuine *belletrist.* His stories combined modesty with the gift of humor. His style of writing was uniquely impressionistic. Chekhov was a brilliant writer and left his mark not just on Russian but on world literature in general. He contributed the short story to Russian literature. However, the short stories of his youth did not have the perfection and perspicuity that his later writings revealed.

Chekhov abhorred death, destruction, and human misery. His view of life was that of a struggle between the strong and the weak. He had a talent for exposing the consciousness of the characters in his stories. The stories of Chekhov are filled with much melancholy. The reader feels their sadness after reading only a short time.

The road back to Rostov from Taganrog is often foggy during winter, even in mid-afternoon. The Intourist guide from Rostov who accompanies you on the tour will state that she likes best Chekhov's early literary works, but acknowledges that *The Seagull* and *Three Sisters* are among his more known dramatic works. The steppe between Taganrog and Rostov looks empty and melancholy for the most part. Chekhov, however, admired the black, rich beauty of its soil.

Chapter X.
ODESSA
Pearl of the Black Sea

I had not felt so much at home for a long time as I did when I "raised the hill" and stood in Odessa for the first time. It looked just like an American city. . . .

—*Mark Twain*
The Innocents Abroad

Odessa is a seaport in the southwest part of the Ukraine on the Black Sea. Stretching from the coast of the Black Sea northward are the steppes of southern Russia. Odessa's potpourri of nationalities includes Ukrainians, Bulgarians, Moldavians, Turks, Armenians, Jews, Greeks, Byelorussians, and others. Russian and Ukrainian are the two most widely spoken languages in the city. Odessa (46° 30′N.) lies in approximately the same latitude as Montreal, Canada; Duluth, Minnesota; and Butte, Montana. It is the largest seaport of southern Russia. The city lies 438 miles from Kiev and 1,072 miles from Moscow by rail. Odessa is the largest Russian city on the Black Sea, and is located along the northernmost extremity of that sea. The city has more monuments than functioning churches, of which there are nine: five are Russian Orthodox, one Greek Orthodox, one Catholic, one synagogue, and one Baptist. Odessa is the third largest city in the Ukraine and has a population of 1,150,000.

A flight from Moscow to Odessa lasts about two hours. At the airport an Intourist official ushers tourists to the taxi area in front of the airport. Although perhaps only a half-dozen foreign tourists may arrive on any flight, they are customarily placed two to a cab. Whereas one or two cabs would suffice for the numbers, the Russians may use three or four. The Intourist official apparently seems to believe that all drivers should be working, meaning everyone should do his share of the work. The cabs hastily make their way into the city, and halt in front of their hotel destinations. Many foreigners stay at the Krasnaya, a four-story, 72-room hotel. It has a splendid dining room with a multicolored tile ceiling. Marble columns adorned with reliefs support the ceiling. A large stairway with nineteen marble steps leads from the lobby to the landing of the second floor. Its 1900 decor is a nostalgic reminder of yesteryear. The tsar himself might have dined in its elegance at one time. The years have left their unkind mark on the hotel, but it is easy for one's mind to drift back fifty or more years and visualize the magnificence of its splendor in the heyday of a bygone era. It is a hotel of nostalgia and vanished faces. Still, it is not without its original creative inspiration, and one should not miss an opportunity to share its uniqueness.

The Krasnaya was built in 1898–99 and combines both baroque and Renaissance styles. The hotel will accommodate 140 guests. It stands on the corner of Pushkin and Rosa Luxemburg Streets. The Krasnaya was designed by Alexander Bernardacci, whose family emigrated from Switzerland and settled in Russia. Bernardacci was born in Russia and moved to Odessa in 1878. The hotel takes its name from the light red color of the sandstone from which it is built. White marble columns and baroque figures lend their fantasies to the facade of the hotel.

Behind the reception desk of the Krasnaya some members of the hotel staff are usually seen watching a black and white television. The television is visible to viewers in the lobby and occasionally a foreigner can recognize a show that is familiar. One of the old film classics that is popular in Odessa is Mark Twain's *The Prince and the Pauper*. Mark Twain is well known in Odessa and is widely read in Russia. He visited Odessa once on sea voyage, as is related in his book *The Innocents Abroad*, which is an account of his excursion to Europe and the Holy Land.

However, Odessa was not originally scheduled on Mark Twain's itinerary for visiting the Black Sea coast of Russia in 1867. As Twain notes in *The Innocents Abroad*, his ship came to Odessa primarily to load coal for its boilers. He was only in Odessa for a few days, but noted with delight his sampling of Russian ice cream in that city.

Present-day Odessa is a comparatively young city. It was founded in the latter part of the eighteenth century. However, the steppelands surrounding Odessa were inhabited or occupied by various peoples and invaders dating back into the first millenium B.C., when tribes such as the Cimmerians, Scythians, and Sammatians occupied the area. The Greeks colonized the lands around Odessa in the sixth century B.C. Later Roman legions marched into the area along the northwest coast of the Black Sea during the first to third centuries B.C. The Romans were followed by the Goths in the third century A.D. and the ferocious Huns in the fourth century. In the third to sixth centuries A.D., Slavic tribes also settled in the area, and Alani-Bulgarian tribes moved in during the eighth century. The Slavs gradually assimilated the latter. The Slavic and Greek role in the area was discussed previously in connection with ancient Kiev. In the thirteenth century Mongol-Tartar hordes overran the steppes and devastated the region. Some Slavic settlements remained in the area, but during the fourteenth and fifteenth centuries they were divided generally into Ukrainians, Russians, or Bylorussians. When Odessa was originally founded is uncertain, but in 1415 a large settlement by the name of Kachibey was mentioned as existing on its present site by the Polish chronicler Dlugosz. During the last half of the fourteenth and in the early fiftteenth century, Odessa's territory was governed by Lithuania. The Crimean Tartars shed the Mongol yoke in the middle of the fifteenth century and proclaimed rule over the northern lands of the Black Sea. In 1475 the Ottoman Turks captured Crimea and lands along the western end of the Black Sea. The Turks both strengthened existing fortifications in these lands and built new ones, including that of Yeni-Duni on the heights of present-day Odessa overlooking its bay. The Turks then closed off the Black Sea to Russia, propagating several wars with Russia, which wanted an outlet to the sea.

During the Russo-Turkish War of 1768–1774 the Russian fleet overwhelmed the Turkish fleet in the battle of Chesman Bay (1770). Crimea was returned to Russia, but in 1787–1791 Turkey again attempted to recapture the northern Black Sea lands and suffered another defeat. Kachibey, the present site of Odessa, fell to the Russians, and in 1791 Turkey was forced to cede the entire northern Black Sea coast to Russia.

In 1783 the Russians built a new fort near the ruins of the one built by the Turks. The remains of this Russian fort can be viewed in Shevchenko Park in the southern part of Kiev. Following construction of their fort, the Russians drew up plans for a town and port facilities and submitted these to Catherine the Great. On her order, plans proceeded to build the new city, and in 1794 it was officially given the name Odessa. Odessa derives its name from the former Greek city of Odessos that once stood in the vicinity of modern-day Odessa during the fourth century A.D. According to legend, Catherine the Great decided on the name Odessa because it was in the feminine gender. In Russia female names always end in "a" or "r," for example, Lena, Natasha, Volga, etc. Thus, Odessa is in the feminine gender since it ends in the letter "a."

In modern times Odessa developed rapidly as a port due to several advantageous geographical factors: (1) its close proximity to the mouths of the Bug, Dniester, Danube, and Dnieper rivers; (2) its location on the relatively ice-free waters of the Bay of Odessa; and (3) sufficiently deep water for shipping.

The city and its port grew further when the railroads reached it in the 1860s. The combination of its water and rail transport facilities played a key role in developing Odessa as a communications center.

Due to its multinational character, Odessa developed a reputation as a center of revolutionary movements during the 1800s and early 1900s. Bulgarian, Greek, Albanian, Russian, and other revolutionaries formed secret societies in the city that became the seeds of political and ideological movements. By the 1870s Russian revolutionaries were launching worker's strikes, and printing revolutionary literature in the city. Lenin was a delegate from the Odessa area in 1905 to the Communist congress meeting held in London.

Odessa was the scene of the revolutionary event known as the Potemkin mutiny that occurred in 1905. The battleship *Potemkin* arrived in the port of Odessa on June 14, 1905. A squadron of naval vessels was sent by the tsarist government to suppress the mutiny on the *Potemkin*. The *Potemkin* was flying the Red flag, and the naval squadron dispatched against it refused to fire upon it.

While the *Potemkin* was in the harbor, strikes occurred in the city and barricades were erected. Many workers and people of Odessa sympathized with the mutiny on board the *Potemkin*. Dock workers furnished the vessel with food and supplies. Meanwhile, local police and troops were dispatched to scatter the crowds assembled in the port area. The crowds were dispersed, only to gather again. When the body of one of the leaders of the mutiny killed on the *Potemkin* was brought ashore, a crowd surrounded it and when the warehouses on the dock were set afire, the troops opened fire on the mob. This June 15, 1905 encounter cost the lives of hundreds of people. Blood flowed on the docks and in the streets. The *Potemkin* then departed for Constanta, a Roumanian seaport. A great stairway of steps leading from the city above it down to the sea was later named the Potemkin stairs in memory of the mutineers on the battleship. The stone for building the stairs in 1837–41 originally came from Trieste and was a greenish gray sandstone. The soft sandstone quickly wore down and was replaced in 1933 with a rose-red granite. The stairway was designed by F. Boffo in 1825. It leads from Ulitsa (meaning street in Russian) Suvorova at the bottom of its steps to Primorsky Boulevard (the popular promenade of Odessa) at the top of the bluff overlooking the harbor. The stairs are 88 feet high from bottom to top, and 465 feet long. The 192 steps are 41 feet wide at the top and 70 feet wide at the bottom. A stone parapet lines both sides of the steps. The staircase is narrower at the top and wider at the bottom to create an optical illusion of greater length. From the bottom only the steps are visible, and from the top only the landings can be seen. Mark Twain described the steps as a "noble staircase." At the bottom of the stairs the murmur of the sea can be heard.

Prince Grigori Potemkin (1739–1791), in whose honor the battleship was named, rose from a lowly rank in the Russian army to that of field marshal through his amorous relationship with Catherine the Great. He was her lover for only a brief period, then became content with assisting Catherine by arranging her amorous affairs and conducting state matters. Potemkin patronized the arts while accumulating great wealth. He died at age fifty-two of apoplexy and is buried in the Catherine Cathedral in Kherson, near the mouth of the Dnieper River.

After the Bolsheviks came to power in 1917 the city saw bitter fighting between revolutionary and counterrevolutionary forces. Then in 1918 Austro-German troops occupied the city, only to withdraw shortly before forces of the Allied powers (British, French, Italian, etc.) landed in late November of that year. These forces left the city in April 1919. Hostilities continued in Odessa as Red and White Russian army units vied for control of Odessa into February 1920.

In World War II the Germans invaded Russia in June 1941, and entered Odessa on October 16, 1941. The Russians, nevertheless, were determined to fight the Nazis from an underground movement in the city. Beneath the city stretch approximately 1,340 miles of catacombs, a virtual underground maze of tunnels. The catacombs are man-made, created by quarrying sandstone. They are about two hundred years old and all but one entrance is now closed. Using the catacombs as headquarters, partisans emerged almost at will to attack the Germans and destroy their trains, supplies, and equipment. The Russian army, with the assistance of the partisans, liberated the city on April 10, 1944. The Germans burnt and blew up much of the city before they withdrew and during their occupation they killed 11,000 of the city's Jews. Odessa earned the title of Hero City for its sixty-nine-day stand against the Germans before they captured the city in 1941.

Before arrival in Odessa, one may have the preconceived idea that the city is mild in climate and relatively warm throughout the year because of its Black Sea location and southern latitude in terms of the Soviet Union. In winter, however, Odessa is cold, requiring overcoat, gloves, and earmuffs to keep suitably warm. Even then it seems difficult to shake the chill that pervades the atmosphere and the city streets. Tourists are not alone in this respect; the native inhabitants of the city bundle up similarly and seem presumably as cold as their foreign visitors. The chilly winds that blow off the Black Sea in winter produce a chill factor that is very discomforting. Odessa

has an average high of 36°F. and an average low of 17°F. in December. When the wind is blowing it seems much colder than the temperature reading on the thermometer. July, the warmest month, has an average high of 81°F. and an average low of 66°F.

Many streets in Odessa are identified by the type(s) of trees growing along them. Pushkin Street, which the Krasnaya Hotel faces, is a broad, straight boulevard lined on both sides with aged but graceful sycamore trees. Primorsky Boulevard, the first built in the city, is a beautiful promenade. It runs in a general northwest to southeast direction, keeping to the higher contours of the plateau-like surface of the city. This promenade, laid out in 1820, is planted with chestnut and linden trees. Another well-known thoroughfare of Odessa, Ulitsa Karl Marx, is lined with catalpa and chestnut trees. White acacia is the most popular tree in Odessa. In spite of all the beautiful, verdant trees lining the streets of Odessa, there are no forests in the vicinity of the city. Many houses in Odessa have grapevines climbing their walls and clinging to balconies as high as the fourth floor. Once the clusters of grapes are ripe, the residents of the buildings covered by their vines gather the grapes and convert them into wine or juice.

Near the intersection of Primorsky Boulevard and Pushkin Street is the Archaeological Museum. A beautiful white marble sculptured group known as the "Laocoon" stands in front of the museum. Laocoon was a priest in ancient Troy who warned that the wooden horse left at the gates of the city by the Greeks was a ruseful device to trick the Trojans. The Greek goddess Athena then dispatched serpents to slay Laocoon and his sons. The sculpture of Laocoon is a replica of the one located in the Vatican in Rome, created by Polydorus and other artists in the first century B.C.

Four huge Corinthian columns support a portico over the entranceway to the museum, which is built in the classical style of architecture. The museum is the oldest in Odessa and contains eleven rooms of exhibits. Founded in 1825, it has displays of artifacts reflecting the history of the northwestern coast of the Black Sea, the Scythians, and Kievan Rus. It also has a superb collection of antiquities dating from Egyptian, Greek, and Roman times. The collections of the museum include jewelry, coins, statues, glassware, pottery, and metals.

From the Archaelogical Museum it is a short walk to the Odessa City Soviet of People's Deputies building at the southern end of Primorsky Boulevard. This long two-story building is immediately recognized by its lemon-yellow color and its immense colonnade of twelve white Corinthian columns separating two wings of the structure at its front entrance. On either side of the colonnade an alcove is recessed into each wing of the building. In each alcove stands a white marble statue: the alcove of the right wing contains a statue of Mercury, while that of the left wing contains a statue of the goddess

Ceres.

Built in 1829–34 by F. Boffo, the building once housed the Odessa stock exchange. In 1899, however, it became the office of the Odessa City Council, and in 1918 Bolshevik revolutionaries took control of it.

In front of the left wing of the building, an old cannon mounted on its carriage sits atop a granite pedestal that has a plaque imbedded into each of its four sides. The antiquated cannon was placed atop the pedestal in 1904 to commemorate the fiftieth anniversary of the battle that occurred in its vicinity during the Crimean War (1853–56). In 1854 the city was shelled by an Anglo-French fleet, with the defenders of Odessa responding with barrages from their guns. After the bombardment the English frigate *Tiger* ran aground in a fog and the Russians captured its crew. The cannon atop the pedestal was a prize taken from the *Tiger*.

Further along on the promenade, near the seacoast, is a monument with a huge bust of Pushkin standing atop it. The monument faces northward up the wide walkway through the center of the promenade. On one side of the reddish-grey monument is inscribed the date 1888, the year the monument was erected, and the opposite side bears the dates 1820–24, the period of Pushkin's exile in southwest Russia. Iron basins, one at each of the four corners of monument, catch water spewed into them by bronze dolphins forming part of the relief of the monument. There are more than 100 Pushkin monuments in Russia.

Pushkin came to Odessa in July 1823, after having been exiled to nearby Moldavia in 1820 by the tsar. He spent the next thirteen months in Odessa, working as an archivist in the office of Count Mikhail Vorontsov, the governor general of Odessa.

It was in Odessa that Pushkin wrote the beginning chapters of his novel *Eugene Onegin*. He also wrote more than thirty of his poems in the city, including "To the Fountain of Bakhchisaray," "Night," "Farewell to the Sea," and part of "The Gypsies."

Relations between Pushkin and Count Vorontsov were uncordial in the beginning and thereafter deteriorated. Pushkin fell in love with the count's wife and she had a daughter by him. Finally, on August 1, 1824 the count compelled Pushkin to leave Odessa.

The former palace of Count Vorontsov stands at the northern end of Primorsky Boulevard. Today it is known as the Palace of Pioneers. It was built in 1826–27, shortly after Pushkin left the city. It is built of white marble and has a covered colonnade on two sides of it. In front of the palace is a separate colonnade, arranged in two rows and supporting a roof. This beautiful colonnade is built on the cliffs overlooking the Black Sea.

Mikhail S. Vorontsov (1782–1856) was the governor general of Odessa from 1823–44. His monument, erected in 1862, stands in Ploschad Sovetskoy

Armii (Soviet Army Square) only a few blocks from Odessa University. The Vorontsov family name was prominent in Russia by the 1740s. His father served as Russian ambassador to London. Mikhail became a distinguished figure in the tsarist army. He fought in several campaigns against the French in the early 1800s, was wounded at Borodino in 1812, waged war against the Turks inbetween struggles with the French, and served in France as a corps commander of Russian occupation forces in the Allied army stationed there after Napoleon's demise. Returning to Russia, he was appointed governor general of Odessa and southern Russia in 1823. He married the daughter of Count Branicki, grandniece of Prince Potemkin in 1819. Vorontsov was vitally interested in the Black Sea and was the first to promote steamship navigation on its waters. He later captured Varna, campaigned in the Caucasus and became a field marshal before his death. Nicholas I made him a prince. He was a benefactor of Odessa and popular with the people.

Another former governor and colorful leader of Odessa during the early 1800s was the Duke of Richelieu. The duke, Armand Emmanuel Richelieu, was born in Paris into an aristocratic family in 1776. He was a grandnephew of Cardinal Richelieu and served both France and Russia in positions of administrative importance. The duke left France during the French Revolution and emigrated to Russia. In 1790 he joined the Russian army and participated in action against the Turks. Tsar Alexander I appointed him governor of Odessa in 1803, and subsequently, made him governor general of the Novorossiisk area, to include Odessa and nearby lands along the Black Sea coast in 1805. The duke proved a capable leader and expanded trade and agriculture during his administration. He lavished most of his fortune on the city he ruled and loved. The duke was discerning and reverent of Odessa, and guarded its interests as though they were his private affairs. When Napoleon was exiled to Elba, he returned to France in 1814, then reentered the tsar's services when Napoleon escaped Elba and later marched on Waterloo. After Napoleon's demise the duke on two separate occasions served as prime minister of France before his death in 1822.

The story is told by Odessa residents that the duke returned to his beloved city of Odessa after having bid France farewell for the last time, and then lived most of his remaining days in the city and spent the last of his wealth there on worthy projects. With his wealth gone, penniless, the duke, with only the clothes he wore and aged in years, slowly descended the great staircase to the sea without acknowledgement or assistance of the local citizens and left his beloved city for that of Sevastopol on the Crimean peninsula. There, as the story goes, he died in poverty, and when the people of Odessa discovered what had transpired, they were filled with great sorrow and mournful of their neglect of their beloved governor, and as a measure of their remembrance of him, they generously contributed funds which they used to build and erect his monument overlooking the splendid stairway to the sea. This is a touching fable, and one that I regard as a beautiful story and moral in itself.

The duke's statue stands on the promenade of Primorsky Boulevard overlooking the Potemkin stairway. The monument was designed by I. Martos in 1826, constructed in bronze by Yefimov, and unveiled in 1829. During the Anglo-French bombardment of Odessa in 1854, a shell hit the monument and became imbedded in its pedestal. Later it was removed and a similar shell was implanted in the pedestal.

To the rear of the duke's statue and a short distance down the promenade stands the Odessa Hotel, built in 1893. The three-story hotel is built in early Renassiance style and is olive green in color. In November 1985 the hotel was being refurbished, and was due to reopen as the Intourist Hotel.

Next door to the old Odessa Hotel is the Seamen's Club, originally a private residence. It was rebuilt after World War II and is used by both seamen and their families. Movies, live entertainment, and dining are available. Its interior is finished in a red decor amidst high, arched ceilings.

Many of Odessa's buildings are constructed of white stone consisting of calcareous materials imbedded with sea shells. This gives many of the city's buildings a whitewashed appearance.

Odessa has a reputation as a city renowned for its poets, writers, and artists. Pushkin's connection with the city has already been noted. Another well-known name in Russian literature connected with the city is that of Nikolai Gogal.

Nikolai Gogal (1809–52), Ukrainian by birth and a great Russian novelist, humorist, and short-story writer, visited Odessa on two occasions, once in 1848 and again in 1851. He was already famous and well known in Russia before his first visit to Odessa. In his youth, while working in the civil service in St. Petersburg, Gogol wrote two volumes of Ukrainian tales, titled *Evenings on a Farm Near Dikanka*. Volume I was published in 1831 and Volume II in 1832. The tales in the two volumes combined realism with imagination to present a meaningful, but not factual, account of the lives of Ukrainian peasants. Gogol attempted in the *Evenings* stories to reproduce the traditions and folklore of the Ukrainian peasants.

While in Odessa on his visits, Gogol stayed at different locations, but on the same street. Once known as Nadezhdinskaya, the street was later renamed Gogolya to honor Gogol. Ulitza Gogolya runs east-west through northern Odessa, connecting on its east side with Komsomolsky Boulevard. The Odessa Scientist's Club is located near the middle of Ultiza Gogolya.

Gogol wrote the second part of his novel *Dead Souls* while residing in Odessa. The first part was written mostly while he lived periodically in Rome during the latter 1830s and early 1840s. Part two was written between 1842–52, but while Gogol was on a visit to Jerusalem in 1848 he was persuaded by a religious figure there that he should destroy the manuscript, which he did in 1852, shortly before his death. Gogal had planned, but never wrote, a third part to *Dead Souls.*

Gogol's *Dead Souls* is a tragicomic novel that mocks the stupidity, ignorance, and inefficiency of the tsarist government and its army of civil servants. Gogol abhorred the ruthless, cruel power of the police. Yet, he never intended that the autocracy of the tsar be abolished. Nevertheless, *Dead Souls* left its stigma on the tsarist regime and aristocracy. Its revolutionary ideas helped to fan the growing criticism of tsarist rule.

Gogol met Pushkin in 1831 and the famous poet gave Gogol the idea for his comedy *Revizor (The Inspector General),* which he finished in 1835. The play was published in 1836, and Gogol helped to produce it for the theatre, where it was performed on stage with Tsar Nicholas I in attendance. The drama-play mocked the wrongs of government officials, but strong criticism of it by his critics compelled Gogol to defend his play by claiming that even misguided bureaucratic officials were capable of altering their behavior and actions. Nevertheless, the criticism leveled against him caused Gogol to leave Russia and reside abroad for more than ten years.

Other works by Gogol include the historical novel *Taras Bulba;* the stories of *The Overcoat, The Portrait,* and *The Carriage;* the plays *The Gambler, A Lawsuit,* and *A Fragment;* and the book *Selected Passages.*

At one time, after Gogol was unsuccessful in finding a job as an actor in St. Petersburg and when one of his poems had been sharply criticized, he considered emigrating to the United States. He actually reached Sweden on his way to America before deciding to return to Russia.

Another writer who once resided in Odessa was Saul Chernikhovski, a well-known Hebrew poet who lived in the city between 1890 and 1899. He was born in nearby Crimea in 1875. After leaving Odessa, he studied medicine in Germany and Switzerland, and later became a surgeon in the Russian army in World War I. He was a prolific writer, producing translations of the *Iliad,* the *Odyssey,* and other works, and writing many short stories, poems, and sonnets before his death in Jerusalem in 1943.

Many other prominent writers, artists, and musicians spent time in Odessa. Anton Rubenstein (1829–1894), a celebrated Russian composer and pianist, performed on the stage of the Odessa Opera. He wrote piano concertos, symphonies, operas, chamber works, and other musical pieces. His well-known operas include "The Merchant of Kalashikov" and "The Siberian Huntsmen." A familiar symphony of his is "The Tower of Babel."

Rimsky-Korsakov (1844–1908) also visited Odessa and provided his musical talents to fans of its opera house. He is remembered as one of the world's outstanding masters of orchestral music, noted for such celebrated works as "Scherazade," "Spanish Capriccio," and "Flight of the Bumblebee." He also composed many well-known operas, including "Snow Maiden" and "The Tsar's Bride."

Vladimir Mayakovski, born 1893, was an early twentieth-century Russian poet who visited Odessa on four occasions. Mayakovski became a prominent poet in Russia shortly before the revolution. During the revolution he supported the Bolsheviks, and his poems during that period reflect the ideological aspirations of the Communist movement and its propaganda. Mayakovski wrote for the masses, and his poetry was bold and exuberant with social impulse and meaning. This theme is projected in his poems "Ode to Revolution" in 1918, "Left March" in 1919, and the play "Mystery Buffo" in 1918. He served the Communist cause faithfully during Lenin's era, and eulogized the Communist leader in his poem "Vladimir Ilyich Lenin" in 1920. He ended his life by suicide in 1930, perhaps due to refusal by a girl he met in Paris to marry him and the poor reception of his play "The Bathhouse" shortly before his death.

Across the street from the Krasnaya Hotel is the Odessa Philharmonic Society. It was designed by the architect Bernadacci in 1894 to house the stock exchange of the city but instead became the home of the Philharmonic Society. This explains why many of the panels decorating its interior depict scenes of commerce and industry. The building is built in a Renaissance style of architecture incorporating Carrara marble and terra cotta tiles, and resembles many of the Renaissance palaces of northern Italy. The concert hall of the building will hold 1,000 persons. An archway from Ulitsa Rosa Luxemburg leads to an enclosed courtyard behind the building.

One of Odessa's natives, Lea Luboshutz (b. 1887), made her concert debut in the Philharmonic Society after having studied at the Odessa School of Music and the Moscow Conservatory. She followed her Odessa debut with others in Europe and then the United States, where she appeared with the Russian Symphony in 1907. An accomplished violinist, she accepted teaching positions in Europe and the United States. Before retirement in 1953 she performed with her musically talented sister, son, and brother Pierre.

Pierre Luboshutz, also born in Odessa (1894), graduated from the Moscow Conservatory, studied piano in Paris, and teamed with his wife to form a prominent piano duo. He, too, gave recitals in many countries and performed with distinguished musicians of his day.

Other Odessa natives who achieved international fame as musicians were the violinists Paul Kochanski (b. 1887) and Nathan Milstein (b. 1904). Kochanski held positions with the Warsaw Philharmonic and the New York Symphony and was a distinguished faculty member of the Julliard School from 1924 until his death in 1934. Milstein gave performances throughout Russia, later performed in Paris and the United States, then went on world tours where he received many awards and honors.

The names of many distinguished persons are associated with the Odessa Opera and Ballet. Local inhabitants claim it to be the second best opera in the world, next to the Stadt Opera in Vienna. A previous opera house built in 1810 stood on the same site but was destroyed by fire in 1873. During its existence it was frequented by Pushkin when he lived in Odessa, while other visitors to it included Gogol; the outstanding Hungarian pianist Franz Liszt; and the Polish poet Adam Mickiewicz.

After destruction of the old opera, the city commissioned the Viennese architects Helmer and Fellner, noted for their design of the Vienna Opera House and the Milan's La Scala, to design the Odessa Opera House. Built in 1884–87, its architectural style is that of Viennese baroque. The acoustics inside are excellent; the slightest voice can be heard throughout the theatre. Painted on its ceiling are Shakespearean scenes from "A Midsummer Night's Dream," "Hamlet," "Twelfth Night," and "A Winter's Tale." There are four tiers of balconies built over a lower row of stalls, and the seats are furnished in red velvet. The balconies are also velvet-draped. A large two-ton chandelier is suspended from the ceiling.

Two sculptures stand at the main entrance of the opera: on the left side is "Hippolytus," a mythological figure tragically killed by Poseidon after his stepmother falsely accused him of raping her; and on the right side stands "The Birds," depicted in a comedy scene by Aristophanes.

Built over the arched entranceway is a portico, on the facade of which are located mythological sculptural groups. On top of the portico Melpomene, the muse of tragedy, stands in a chariot drawn by four panthers.

The opera house seats over 1,600 people and is air conditioned. The main staircase in the foyer is elegantly decorated, ornately designed, and has beautiful gold-color figurines supporting its lighting fixtures. While in Odessa, I attended an evening performance that cost three dollars for a box seat with a good elevated view of the stage.

Many famous composers, singers, actors, actresses, and others have performed or acted on its stage. Among the list of prominent persons appearing on the opera's stage include those of Anna Pavlova, Galina Ulanova, Rimsky-Korsakov, Rubinstein, Tchaikovsky, Caruso, and Chaliapin.

In the 1950s settling of its foundation caused cracks to appear in the walls. Odessa, as previously noted, is underlain by a system of catacombs, and the opera's foundation was threatened by the possibility of subsiding into these subterranean tunnels. To save the opera, more than 2,000 holes were drilled into the ground around it, and 1,584,000 gallons of liquid glass were pumped down the holes to harden and stabilize the foundation. In the 1960s the damaged opera house was restored to its original condition. The opera stands at the eastern end of Ulitza Lenina.

For sailors and those interested in the sea, there is the U.S.S.R. Naval

Museum located adjacent to the opera house. Originally it was built as the English Club in 1842. Its 100,000 exhibits are dedicated to the history of the shipbuilding and navigation. Two massive anchors stand at the entrance of the museum.

Russian seamen are also familiar with the monument to the Potemkin sailors, which stands in Ploschad Potemkinsev (Square of the Potemkin Sailors) near the intersection of Ulitsa Karl Marx and Komsomolsky Boulevard in the vicinity of the Potemkin stairway. The memorial depicts the bronze figures of sailors without their hats, standing on a granite pedestal. By removing their hats before being shot, the sailors were symbolically casting aside the reigns of tsarist power. The monument was unveiled in 1965.

In the southern part of Odessa along its popular beach shoreline stands the Tomb of the Unknown Sailor with Glory Alley leading up to the tomb. The alley descends by way of terraces toward the seacoast until it reaches the 69-foot high red granite obelisk carved with the inscription "To the Unknown Sailor." The monument was unveiled in 1960 to commemorate the defeat of Nazi Germany. On the lower portion of the obelisk are four bas-reliefs depicting historic events in Odessa's history. One bas-relief depicts the Potemkin uprising in 1905. An eternal flame burns in front of the obelisk. Two short flights of stone steps lead from the alley to the flame and the pedestal on which the obelisk is erected. Every day of the year honor guards, who are members of the Young Pioneer Organization, take guard positions around the obelisk. The alley leading to the monument is lined with a long row of stone blocks containing red granite inscriptions bearing memory to those who served the party and the country faithfully in the eyes of the Communists. At this site young members of Communist youth groups receive their membership cards.

Odessa is the main Russian seaport on the Black Sea. Commercial ships from many countries call at its port. Odessa, together with the nearby ports of Ilichyovsk and Yuzhny, handles about one-half of Russia's ship-passenger traffic and 30 percent of the country's cargo traffic. The huge Black Sea Shipping Line has most of its fleet of cargo and passenger ships registered at Odessa and its sister ports.

By the early 1950s the port of Odessa had become too restricted in its ability to expand operations. Accordingly, the new port of Ilichyovsk was built on Sukhovy Liman located about eighteen miles south of Odessa. This new sister port of Odessa was completed in 1958 and has since surpassed its predecessor in tonnage and cargo flow. Nearly half of the Black Sea Shipping Line's fleet is now registered at Ilichyovsk. This port currently has one of the world's largest floating docks. Ilichyovsk became a large handler of container traffic after 1976 when a large container plant was built there. Soviet and Bulgarian ferries began operating between Ilichyovsk and Varna in 1978. The

Sukhovy Liman also accommodates a large portion of the Black Sea fishing fleet of the Soviets, and its port is the home base for the Ukrainian whaling fleet, numerous refrigerated fishing trawlers, and several floating fish factories.

Yuzhny, another new port largely built between 1973 and 1980, is located on Grigoryev Liman about twenty miles northeast of Odessa. This port is the site of a large chemical complex and much of its cargo is of such nature. Yuzhny was expanded in the 1980s to additionally handle lumber, coal, and mineral ores. Shipbuilding and ship repair are other important functions of the Odessa ports.

The Black Sea, on which Odessa is located, has an area of about 175,000 square miles. The sea is approximately 680 miles wide from east to west, and about 375 miles across from north to south. It is darker in color than the waters of the Mediterranean.

The Black Sea connects with the small Sea of Azov on the northeast through the Kerch Straits. The Sea of Azov is a small sea with a depth of less than sixty feet. The shallow parts of the Black Sea lie in its northern waters, with the deeper parts lying further south approaching Turkey. Between the Crimean Peninsula and Turkey depths range between 5,000 feet and 7,500 feet. The northern shoreline of the Black Sea and the Sea of Azov have a number of rivers emptying into their waters, including the Don, Dnieper, Bug, Danube, and Dniester. The northern shoreline of the Black and Azov seas is generally low-lying, especially where the rivers meet the sea, and drowned estuaries and marshes are common. Around Odessa many of the salt-water lagoons and marshes were formerly part of the sea, but in time became enclosed by sandbars and coastal barriers. The Russians call these features *limans*. Mud extracted from the limans is used for medicinal purposes. Many health resorts have grown up around the limans.

The shallow Sea of Azov tends to freeze during the winter months, and portions of the northern coastline of the Black Sea usually develop ice. The Black Sea is open to navigation year-round and is a vital trade route for Russia.

The Black Sea is tideless, and in depths over 5,900 feet only anaerobic bacteria exist due to the presence of hydrogen sulfide. In the upper layers of the seawater and on the shallow seabed hundreds of species of flora and fauna are found. At least 160 species of fish and 640 species of crab live in the Black Sea. Dolphins, sharks, and seals also live in the waters of the sea. Dolphins may be seen following ships and their catch is limited to preserve their numbers. Principal types of commercial fish harvested in the sea include mackerel, sturgeon, beluga, gogy, anchovy, and sevruga.

The Black Sea coast was formerly a retreat for Russia's grand dukes and the tsar. The coastline has long been known as the "Riviera" of Russia.

Splendid palaces, fashionable hotels, beautiful villas, spacious gardens, and large parks dot the former playground of the tsars. Many of the former palaces of Russian aristocrats are now proletarian hotels, museums, hospitals and clinics, and vacation sites for workers.

Odessa is one of Russia's main health-resort centers on the Black Sea. The city is often called the "Western Gate of the Soviet Riviera," and the "Pearl of the Black Sea." The Odessa area consists of nine health resorts in which there are numerous sanitoria and resorts. More than 400,000 people annually visit these facilities that are being expanded and improved each year. Several new health centers are currently being built or nearing completion.

The curative facilities are generally of three types: (1) balneologic (employing the therapeutic effects of baths and bathing), (2) mud treatment, and (3) climatologic. The climate of Odessa is very healthy. It is a mixture of sea and steppe air, which is clean and dry.

The coast of the Black Sea has excellent facilities for bathing and swimming. The waves are small and the water is relatively clean. Measures are employed to divert all sewage waters away from the beaches and in the port area of the harbor, ships are forbidden to discharge wastes into the harbor, while special ships cruise its waters collecting oil and sludge deposits.

The sanitoria use mud collected from the *limans* for medicinal and curative purposes. The mud looks and smells obnoxious, but is noted for its healthful properties. Beneficial effects attributed to the medicinal use of *liman* mud include those of restoring the movement of limbs; producing salutary effects on disorders of the peripheral nervous system; having positive effects on particular gynecological and gastrointestinal disorders; and alleviating the after-effects of damage to the brain.

The oldest of the health-resort districts in Odessa is that of Arkadiya (Arcadia), located along the southwest coast of the city. About twenty sanitoria in Arkadiya treat diseases related to the respiratory, cardiovascular, and nervous systems, as well as metabolic disorders. Multistory hotels in the resort districts can usually accommodate 200 to 400 visitors each. Many of the sanitoria resemble high-rise hotels, while others such as the Moldava Sanitorium look like palatial palaces complete with gardens, tiers of steps, and fountains. The sanitoria often specialize in treating particular diseases, for example, the Rossiya and Ukraina sanatoria treat cardiovascular disorders, while the Stroygidravlika, which belongs to a factory by the same name, has an adjacent clinic where workers from the factory may receive physical therapy, massages, hydropathy (internal and external use of water to cure disease), and exercise therapy. This sanatorium also has a swimming pool filled with mineral water.

Located in the vicinity of the city's main beaches, sanatoria, and health resorts is the Filatov Institute at 49/51 Ploletarsky Boulevard in the southern part of Odessa. The institute is headquartered in a three-story red sandstone building. In front of the institute is a bust of Dr. Vladimir Filatov (1875–1956) chiseled into a twelve-foot high, white marble piece of stone. He was an honorary member of various worldwide academies of science.

The Filatov Scientific Research Institute is named after Dr. Filatov. The institute was founded in 1936 and is the largest eye hospital in Russia. Dr. Filatov was the first ophthalmologist to perform transplantation of the cornea in leukemia patients. He was a very talented eye surgeon and medical engineer. According to my guide, Dr. Filatov also pioneered the technique of autotransplantation of skin tissue. He loved to paint and could speak thirteen languages. Dr. Filatov is buried in Odessa.

In the area of concentration of the sanatoria is located the Sports Palace, separated into two parts, one for children and the other for adults. The large adult palace will accommodate 6,500 people, and includes figure skating, basketball, gymnastics, and other facilities. It was built in 1975.

Located on Proletarsky Boulevard in the vicinity of the Filatov Scientific Research Institute is the Odessa Champagne Factory. Its output of wine and champagne totals about nine million bottles a year. Champagne production began in Russia at the end of the last century. In 1900 Russian champagne was served in Paris and won first prize in a contest.

Odessa is a major industrial center. In addition to wine and champagne, its industrial output includes generators, hoists and wenches, hydraulic presses, farm machinery and tractors, drilling and mining equipment, trucks and trailers, cranes and earth-moving machinery, refrigerators, electric cables, machine tools, chemicals, fertilizers, refined sugar, leather commodities, cameras, foodstuffs, and clothing.

Not only is Odessa a major industrial, health, and medical center in the Soviet Union, but it is also an important educational and scientific research center. The city is one of the centers of the Ukrainian Academy of Sciences. In the health resort district is located the Odessa Polytechnical Institute, which has nearly 11,000 students studying in all areas of engineering. Its large library contains approximately two million books on engineering, scientific, and technical subjects.

In the northern part of Odessa, along the intersection of Ulitsa Petra Velikogo (Peter the Great Street) and Ulitsa Korolenko, is located Odessa State University. The main administrative building was constructed in 1852–57 as a lyceum, which later became Novorossiik University and then was renamed Odessa University following the revolution. Presently in its nine departments more than 12,000 students study subjects ranging from geography and marine geology to chemistry and biology. The university is also known as Menchikov University, named in honor of the Russian bacteriologist who won a Nobel Prize in 1908. Menchikov helped found in

Odessa the first center for the study of rabies in Russia. The oldest meteorological center on the Black Sea was founded at the university in 1882.

Another prominent scientist who taught in Odessa was Dmitri Mendeleyev (1834–1907), a Russian chemist born in Siberia. Mendeleyev received his chemistry degree in St. Petersburg and did most of his research and teaching there until his death. For a period during 1855–56, Mendeleyev taught at a lyceum in Odessa. He is known to scientists the world over for his arrangement of the chemical elements into the Periodic Table of Elements, based on their atomic weights. Mendeleyev predicted the existence of some elements before scientists discovered them. He also studied the properties of liquids, gases, and petroleum.

Research institutes and technical schools abound in Odessa. The Institute of Plant Selection and Genetics has its own artificial climate station, which is one of the largest in the world. It has developed many varieties and kinds of plants, especially agricultural hybrids. There is also the Institute of Physical Chemistry which researches new materials, drugs, and catalytic agents. Another well-known research center is the Institute of Biology of the Black Sea. It studies the structure of the Black Sea, its marine life and ecological environment. In the harbor of Odessa one can often see the large research ship "Cosmonaut Yuri Gagarin." Also visible in the harbor is the eighty-nine foot high Vorontsov Lighthouse connected by a long stone causeway with the port's shoreline.

An excellent view of the harbor is afforded from the top of the Potemkin Stairway, which stretches from the edge of the plateau-like surface on which the city is built down to the harbor. There are no hills in the vicinity of the city, but the plateau around it is dissected in places by ravines, requiring bridges to span some of these in order to connect parts of the city.

Set against the background of the dark blue waters of the Black Sea, Odessa will beckon anyone to return who has seen its charms and graceful features. Its spacious tree-lined boulevards and many monuments give Odessa a dignified beauty that reminds one of Paris or Vienna. The people of Odessa are warm and friendly and the tourist will probably feel more at ease and at home there than in any other Russian city, with the possible exception of Leningrad.

SIGHTSEEING

Tour of the City

Odessa is a major port and a renowned health resort on the Black Sea, an industrial, cultural, and scientific center of the Soviet Ukraine, a hero-city that has covered itself with everlasting glory during the Great Patriotic War of the Soviet Union (1941–45). The sightseeing tour will acquaint you with the historic architectural monuments of the city, and also with its present-day life. You will see the famous Potemkin Stairway, the Primorsky (Seaside) Boulevard, the edifice of the Opera and Ballet Theater, the city's parks, palaces, new residential districts.

Trip by Motor Boat "Sevastopol"

During the period from April till November, travelers may go for a breathtaking trip "Odessa Seen from the Sea" on board the motor boat "Sevastopol." Guide-interpreters will acquaint the guests with the city's seaport and the health-resort zones located along the Odessa coast. While on board, the tourists may use the services of the boat's bar, which offers soft drinks. The boat takes thirty passengers at a time. The duration of the trip is two hours.

MUSEUMS

Museum of Archaeology

Founded in 1825, this museum exhibits a unique collection of archaeological finds vividly demonstrating the daily life and culture of the tribes and peoples that populated the regions adjacent to the Black Sea's northern coast in the Scythian-Sarmatian and Antique periods. Also open in the museum is the permanent exposition "Golden Depository," where ancient jewelry, coins, and medals are displayed. The museum is open daily from 10:00 a.m. till 5:30 p.m.

Fine Arts Museum

The museum is located in an old sea-fronting palace built at the beginning of the nineteenth century. The exposition is arranged in twenty halls. Represented here are ancient Russian icon-painting, numerous pictures by Russian and Ukrainian artists from the eighteenth century to the present. One may see works by Ivan Aivazovsky, Ivan Kramskoy, Ivan Shiskin, Nikolai Rerikh, Alexander Gerasimov, Mikhail Bozhly, and other masters. The museum is open daily except Tuesday from 10:30 a.m. till 4:30 p.m.

Museum of Western and Oriental arts

The museum is located in a building that is an archaeological monument. The exposition is divided into three sections: Antique, Western, Oriental arts. The West-European section is represented by the works of Buanarotti Michelangelo, Merisi de Caravaggo, Frans Hals. In the Oriental Art section more than 2,000 artistic works from Iran, India, Japan, and China are exhibited. The museum is open daily except Wednesday, from 10:00 a.m. till 5:30 p.m.

A. Pushkin and Literary Museum

During the "Literary Odessa" sightseeing tour, tourists will learn about the life and creative works of outstanding Russian, Ukrainian, Soviet, and foreign writers who lived in Odessa or ever visited it. These are Alexander Pushkin, Leo Tolstoy, Anton Chekhov, Ivan Bunin, Lesya Ukrainka, Mark Twain, Theodore Dreiser, George Simenon, Henri Barbuss.

Museum of Partisan Glory

The heroic struggle of the Odessa partisans during the Great Patriotic War of the Soviet Union (1941–1945) is reflected in the exhibits of the museum, located in the catacombs of the steppe village Nerubaiskoye. Here a subteranean camp of one of the partisan detachments was located. Among the exhibits one may see the weapons and the partisans' personal things.

LOCAL TOURS

Odessa Film Studio

During the excursion tourists will learn about the history of the Odessa Film studio, which is one of the country's oldest; they will visit the sound-recording and assembly shops. After a cup of coffee and a talk, visitors will be invited to see a film produced by the studio's workers.

Viticulture and Wine-making Scientific and Research Institute

The institute, named after V. Tairov, is the Soviet Union's oldest establishment engaged in the problems of viticulture and wine-making. The chateau wines of this scientific and research institute have been honored with sixteen gold and silver medals at international competitions. Tourists will learn about the development of viticulture and wine-making in the Odessa region; they will visit laboratories and vineyards, and taste the wines on which the institute is working.

CULTURAL PROGRAM

Theaters, Circus, Philharmonic Society. In Odessa there are several theaters: the Odessa State Academic Opera and Ballet Theater (one of the world's most handsome buildings) two (Russian and Ukrainian) drama theaters, the Musical Comedy Theater, a circus, and a philharmonic society. Tickets may be bought at Service Bureaus of hotels.

FOOD AND DRINK

Wines. The "Neptune" bar invites you to taste the best Ukrainian wines. You may taste the natural wines: Soviet champagne made at the Odessa plant of champagne wines and the famous Crimean wines that received two Grand-Prix cups at international competitions and 207 gold and silver medals.

Vodka with Russian Pancakes (Blyny). Vodka is an old Russian drink known since the fifteenth century. You may estimate it at its true worth in the "Neptune" bar, which will offer you a good choice of vodkas and nastoykas (types of liqueur) as well as Russian pancakes with caviar.

Blyny (pancakes). Blyny are a traditional Russian dish. They were usually made for the Shrovetide—a joyous popular merrymaking, a festival of seeing off winter and meeting spring. The guests are treated to blyny and hot tea at restaurants.

Vareniky (Dumplings). The Ukrainian cuisine offers vareniky with mushrooms, potatoes, curds, cabbage, cherries, apples, plums. The menu for tasting vareniky includes vodka and dry wine.

OUT-OF-TOWN TOURS

Kishinev

The capital of the Moldavian S.S.R. is over 500 years old. Kishinev is one of the Soviet Union's major cities, the capital of a land of innumerable orchards and vineyards, of a land that carefully preserves and keeps up popular traditions.

After a sightseeing tour of the city, tourists may dine at one of the national restaurants, visit a state farm, get acquainted with the rural economy, and take part in the tasting of Moldavian wines.

Kishinev is 180 kilometers from Odessa. Tour duration: 16 hours.

Belgorod-Dnestrovsky

One of the oldest Ukrainian cities (it was founded in the sixth century B.C.) is spread over a wide estuary at a distance of 100 kilometers from Odessa.

During the trip, tourists will get acquainted with the historic past of the city and its present-day life, see the ruins of the antique settlement Tyr, the medieval fortress—an architectural monument of the fifteenth century, and visit the museum of history and local lore. Trip duration: 8 hours.

Kherson (with a visit to a collective farm, or with wine-tasting).

The city is located on the right bank of the Dniester River. It is over 200 years old. Tourists arrive in Kherson by hydrofoils. The program includes a trip by "Raketa" hydrofoil on the Dnieper River up to the town of Novaya Kakhovka, an excursion to a hydroelectric power station, acquaintance with the monument "Legendarnaya Tachanka" (legendary machine gun cart), a visit to a collective farm where tourists will be invited to taste dishes of Ukrainian cuisine, or a visit to the Ukrainian wine-tasting salon. Trip duration: 2 days.

HOTELS

Hotel	Address	Rooms	Telephone
Arkadia	24 Shevchenko Ave.	151	29-6001 29-6099
Chernoye More (Black Sea)	59 Lenin St.	195	24-2031 25-2022
Krasnaya	15 Pushkin St.	72	22-7220
Odessa	15 Primorsky Blvd.	71	22-5019

CAMPSITE

Delfin—15 km. from city center, 15 km. from airport, 176 rooms, parking lot for 186 cars. Telephone: 55-0066, 55-5052.

Chapter XI.
CRIMEA
Riviera of the
U.S.S.R.

Yalta (was) the watershed between wartime co-operation and the opening sorties of the postwar era—"the Cold War."
                                    —Diane S. Clemens

The Crimean Peninsula is situated in the south of the European part of the U.S.S.R., in the steppe and subtropical zones. Found here are cities and towns such as Yalta, Simferopol, Bakhchisarai, Sevastopol, Balaklava, and Alupka. Crimea is an exciting and mysterious place. Roses, myrtles, cypresses, acacia trees, and lilacs lend an effervescence to the atmosphere. Sweet-smelling magnolias and graceful palms are also part of the vegetation. The peninsula juts southward into the Black Sea and has an area of 10,425 square miles. On the northeast the small Sea of Azov is connected to the Black Sea by the narrow Strait of Kerch.

About three-fourths of the peninsula is a dry plain, comprising most of the northern and central areas. Little water is found on the surface and the vegetation is steppe. The eastern part of the Crimea is the Kerch Peninsula, a hilly area which is also dry steppe. Southern Crimea is largely mountainous. These mountains, known collectively as the Crimean Mountains, consist of three chains running parallel to the coast. The southern chain along the Black

Sea rises to heights of more than 5,000 feet with very steep slopes. Limestone is the major rock of the Crimean Mountains. Covered in many places by forests, the mountains block cold, northern winds from the southern coast with the effect that the greater Yalta area has a subtropical or Mediterranean climate. Along the seacoast is a narrow plain, often broken by bluffs and hills. The southern coast of the Crimea, known as "the Soviet Riviera," is extremely popular with the Russians for vacations and health treatments. Thousands of East Germans, Czechs, Poles and other Eastern Europeans journey annually to the Crimea. Many other nationalities, including Americans, find the Crimea a pleasant and enjoyable place to visit. Yalta is the highlight of the Crimea, but the recently opened Crimean War battlefield of Balaklava is drawing large numbers of tourists. These and other historic sites are the subject of this chapter.

Most foreign tourists reach the Crimea by air from either Moscow or Kiev. The flight time from Moscow is about two-and-one-fourth hours, and from Kiev about two hours. Simferopol is the gateway airport for visiting the Crimea. Its air terminal is neat and clean and has a service bar for food and drink. Directly in front of the terminal is a nice restaurant serving a varied menu. Yalta has no airport, so tourists must take a bus or taxi to that city.

SIMFEROPOL

The city of Simferopol is the administrative center of the Crimean region of the Ukrainian S.S.R. It is also the principal industrial and cultural center of the Crimea. The city has over 300,000 people. It is situated in almost the middle of the peninsula, in the steppe zone, in the valley of the Salgir River, about 53 miles from Yalta. Most tourists bypass it and head directly for Yalta, but if your itinerary can spare an extra day, Simferopol has some interesting features worth seeing. Its climate is moderately continental. Its average temperature is 19°F. in February (the coldest month), and 69°F. in July.

Between the 3rd century B.C., and 4th century A.D., a city called Neapolis, which was the capital of ancient Scythia, stood on the site of Simferopol. In the 15th century, a Tartar settlement called Ak-Mechet (White Mosque) occupied the site. The area became independent of Turkey in 1774, and Catherine the Great annexed the Crimea as part of Russia in 1783.

The present city of Simferopol was founded in 1784. Pushkin lived here in 1820. The city was damaged, but not as much as many other Soviet cities in World War II. The Germans had little time to destroy much of it before the Red Army offensive rolled into it.

Simferopol contains over 100 factories, several theaters and research institutes. Among its higher educational institutions is Simferopol University with more than 7,000 students. The Crimean Medical Institute is a beautiful structure whose facade is finished in a Greek style of architecture with supporting white columns. The Musical College is a new, modernistic building with tall panes of glass comprising most of its huge second-story rectangular structure. The Ukrainian Theatre of Drama and Musical Comedy is another large modern-looking building with a primarily glass exterior. The white-facaded Builders' Palace of Culture is yet another attractive building in the city. The Central Post Office on Rosa Luxemburg Street is a huge, white concrete structure. The Simferopol Cinema, also white, is eye-catching with its twin circular towers and huge Greco-Roman columns. Along the Salgir River are several parks which are lush with greenery and flowers.

Notable monuments in Simferopol are those of A.S. Pushkin, A. V. Suvorov, and K. A. Trenev. An eternal flame burns at the Unknown Soldier's Tomb. Wide Kirov Avenue cuts through the city and then becomes the Feodosia Highway. Rows of new high-rise buildings stand along and around Mate Zalka Street. Tourists are usually accommodated in the large eight-story Moskva Hotel.

The road from Simferopol to Yalta is a relatively good one, but it winds and twists through the mountains, in and out of villages, around sharp curves, and through posted speed zones, so that it takes two-and-one-half to three hours to reach downtown Yalta. A trolleybus line built in 1960 connects Simferopol with Yalta. Many poplar trees line the road as it winds through part of the Salgir valley. Large rose plantations along the route grow roses for the production of rose oil. (Over 40 percent of the U.S.S.R.'s rose oil comes from the Crimea.)

Continuing, the road passes through a mountain pass, skirting the Chatyr-Dag cliffs and high peaks. The scenery is spectacular. In the winter the mountains are covered with snow. Chatyr-Dag means "Attic of Heaven" in the Tartar language, which is an appropriate name for the towering peaks. Mt. Eklizi-Burun (5,003 feet) is the highest peak in its range. Closer to Yalta is Roman Kosh which rises to 5,062 feet. After winding through the Angarsky Pass (3,000 feet above sea level) the highway suddenly descends toward the Black Sea and a bas-relief portrait of Mikhail Kutuzov in a fountain constructed in 1824–26 to honor his service in the Russo-Turkish War. (Kutuzov later drove Napoleon from Russia in 1812.) The road now approaches the resort town of Alushta on the Black Sea coast, after passing through many vineyards.

ALUSHTA

Alushta is both a holiday resort and health treatment center. The Black Sea coast of the Crimea is lined with dozens of sanatoria (preventative-medicine establishments), polyclinics, and therapeutic institutes. Many have their own private beaches. The slopes of the mountains overlooking the sea as well are dotted with health treatment centers and trade union hotels. Russian workers generally have their vacations and health treatments subsidized in whole or in part by their trade unions. The picturesque town of Alushta soon passes, and the highway turns westward for about 25 miles before reaching Yalta. At Alushta the highway forks, with one road following the coast into Yalta, while the other route is a new road that follows the relief of the mountain slope away from the seacoast and avoids the towns along it. The first route, although slower going, is preferred. The coastal road now passes large Mt. Medved (Bear) off to the left. Just beyond begins the Artek Pioneer Camp.

ARTEK

Along this stretch of the coast leading to Gurzuf lies a Young Pioneer establishment which compares several camps with hundreds of buildings. Artek is the Soviet Union's largest children's resort, where 4,500 boys and girls from all the Soviet republics and from foreign countries spend their holidays in a single shift. A small camp on the site began functioning as a children's sanatorium as early as 1902, and then in 1925 the area was founded as a full-fledged children's resort. Now more than 10,000 children attend the camp annually. It is also visited by many writers, artists, and politicians.

GURZUF

Leaving behind Artek, the road enters Gurzuf, another coastal resort. Several sanatoria and rest homes are set amidst the large, green parks and trees of the town. Gurzuf is home to the huge Melos Sanatorium of the U.S.S.R. Defense Ministry, and the Korovin Artists' Rest Home. Alexander Pushkin recalled Gurzuf with delight, and it was there that he wrote his poem "The Prisoner of the Caucasus." The house where the poet lived has been preserved, and one can still see the olive grove where he liked to walk. A cliff and grotto have been given the poet's name. The Sputnik International Youth Camp is also located at Gurzuf.

Several miles past Gurzuf the road passes the entrance to the beautiful Nikitsky Botanical Gardens, founded in 1912. The entrance to the gardens is marked by a large rotunda. This unique open-air museum contains 28,000 species and varieties of plants from all over the world, which thrive amidst 1,250 acres of greenery. More than 600,000 people trek through these gardens, where plant research is conducted, each year.

Beyond the Nikitsky Gardens the road approaches the suburbs of Yalta.

Massandra, a coastal resort with a large park, is on the left of the road. A relatively new large Intourist Hotel has been built here. From here one can see and feel the presence of Yalta.

YALTA

Yalta is a veritable paradise washed by the warm waters of the Black Sea, soundly protected by the mountains from the cold northern winds, as if nature itself had selected the spot for resting and holiday vacationing. Yalta is a gem, and it would require a poet to accurately describe its beauty. My impression of it was that if I had to pick a place in the Soviet Union to live, this is the spot I would likely choose. If you are planning a visit to the Soviet Union, be sure to place it on your itinerary.

Yalta is frequently called the "pearl of the Crimea." Mark Twain spoke affectionately of it on his visit there, and described it as beautiful and charming. The city is full of gardens and green parks. The city receives 2,200 to 2,300 hours of sunshine annually. It is one of the best known climatic resorts in the Soviet Union. The city's population is over 80,000.

The salubrious dry air, fine beaches washed by the white foam of the surf, the picturesque mountains with their gorges and waterfalls, orchards and vineyards running right down to the edge of the sea, festive hotels, holiday homes and sanatoria immersed in verdure, are things you will always remember after a visit to Yalta and the Black Sea coast of the Crimea.

Besides the usual bus, taxi, or automobile means of journeying Yalta, one can also arrive in Yalta by sea from several Soviet Black Sea ports and from Constanta (Romania), Varna (Bulgaria), and other foreign ports. Yalta is beautiful the year around. Even upon visiting it for the second and third times you will still be captivated by its charm and beauty. Yalta has a romantic atmosphere plus comfort, beauty and hospitality, entertainment and excursions, sports and bathing.

The mean temperature for June is 68° F., July averages 75° F., August 74° F., and for December, January and February the mean is between 38° F. and 43° F. Rainfall occurs mainly in winter; summer is usually dry and sunny. The temperature of the sea in summer averages between 77° F. and 79° F. There are about 250 days of sunshine annually and bathing goes on from late May to mid-October. The sea lowers the summer heat, and makes the winters mild. The winter here is short and frost is rare. The climate is Mediterranean.

Arab historians date Yalta from 1153 AD. In 1799, the Russian traveler Sumarokov described it as a fishing village consisting of about 30 houses, a small military post, and a church. By the 1830s the nobility had built about 40 estates in its vicinity. The first structures of its port were laid in 1837. The present-day pattern of its streets dates from the last half of the 19th century. In 1895, Anton Chekhov noted that its comfort and organization was superior to that of Nice on the French Riviera. High-rise buildings now climb up the slopes of the nearby mountains. In the ship passenger port fast hydrofoils provide service between Yalta and Sochi, Odessa, Sevastopol, Evpatoria, and Novorossiysk. The harbor bristles with activity day and night.

Yalta is the major and most popular resort of the Crimea. It became the first climatic resort in Russia in the 1860s. The city is a major center of the Soviet health resort industry. The Soviets have a saying that if you are healthy, visit Yalta and enjoy your good fortune; however, if you are ill visit Yalta and you will feel rejuvinated and your health will be restored.

In tsarist times the nobility regularly visited the fashionable and expensive resort, establishing by the 1880s its future as a resort. Country villas and 70 mansions were scattered around the city. The city also counted some 20 rest homes, 14 hotels, and a 45 bed sanatarium to treat patients with tuberculosis. In 1920, Lenin signed a "Decree on the Use of the Crimea for the Treatment of the Working People." Yalta soon had 18 establishments capable of handling 2,400 vacationers. Former palaces, such as the tsar's Livadia Palace, and those that belonged to princes, dukes and other aristocrats, were turned into clinics, health centers, and vacation homes. Workers and peasants flocked to the Crimea for vacations and health treatments. Sanatoriums, rest homes, and clinics now total more than 170, and Yalta annually receives over 100,000 foreign tourists and more than 2 million guests.

Among the many artists, writers, composers, musicians and singers who have lived and worked in Yalta and its environs, are included: Anton Chekhov, Maxim Gorky, Alexander Pushkin, Fyodor Chalyapin, Isaac Levitan, Vladimir Mayakovsky, Nikolay Rimsky-Korsakov, Adam Mickiewicz, Olga-Knipper Chekhov, Ivan Bunin, and Lesya Ukrainka. The old Tauride Hotel (formerly Rossiya), located along the sea embankment, has received more than its share of famous people. Among those who stayed here were: Anton Chekhov, Modest Mussorgsky, Nikolai Rimsky-Korsakov, Konstantin Stanislavsky, Vladimir Nemirovich-Danchenko, the entire cast of the Moscow Art Theatre who came for Chekhov, Ivan Bunin, Sergei Botkin, Evgenia Mravina, Nikolai Bekrasov, and Valdimir Mayakovsky.

The Chekhov Museum

A visit to Yalta would be incomplete without a visit to the museum located at 112 Kirov Street. It is one of the most famous museums in all the Soviet Union. The great Russian writer Anton Chekhov spent the last years of his life (1899–1904) here. In his "Balaya Dacha" (White Country House), as it was known to his contemporaries, he wrote *Lady with the Dog, Darling, The Bride, The Three Sisters, The Cherry Orchard,* and other works. The house, an elegant white structure, has remained as it was in Chekhov's lifetime. Here much that is linked with the writer's life and work is carefully preserved. The present curator, Hanilo Alla, has served since 1957 when Chekhov's sister Maria died. Maria lived in the house when Chekhov died and was its curator until her death.

The house has nine rooms, four of which are on the ground floor. Chekhov's bedroom was upstairs. A hallway on the second floor contains a cabinet in which is stored some of Chekhov's hats, shirts, the coat he wore to Sakhalin Island, and other clothing. An adjacent room was his mother's bedroom, in which articles of her wardrobe are on display. Olga came to the house in 1898 and lived here until she died in 1919, when she was 83 years old. In Olga's room is a portrait of her painted by her daughter, Maria, around 1899. The room also contains a picture of Chekhov taken just after his wedding in 1901.

Chekhov's wife, Olga Knipper, had her bedroom on the ground floor. She came to the house in 1899 and stayed here until 1900. She returned occasionally when she was free from her work in the theater, usually in the summer. There is a large portrait of Olga in her bedroom done by the painter Shchedrin in 1902–03. Photographs in the room include those of Chekhov in 1903, Chekhov and Olga after their wedding, a photograph of Chekhov in 1899 (the first he gave Olga), and one of Olga given to Chekhov on his birthday in 1903. Olga died in 1959 when she was 91 years old, and is buried with Chekhov in the Novodevichy Cemetery in Moscow.

Some of the other objects in the house include the bag Chekhov used on the journey to Sakhalin, a bell given to him by a prisoner on the island, a wardrobe cabinet used by his mother in Taganrog, a painting of the Istra River by Levitan, a cabinet containing glasses belonging to Chekhov's parents, manuscripts and proofs of Chekhov's last story, *The Bride* (1903), an old wall telephone which he used, and dozens of photographs on the walls and tables.

Surrounding the house is a garden which Chekhov planted, and many trees including peach, cherry, magnolia, palm, plum, and cypress. Chekhov planted many trees himself on his estate. In one corner of the yard is a bench on which Chekhov used to sit and engage in long talks with Maxim Gorky.

Next door to Chekhov's house is the Chekhov Exhibition Center which houses a library of Chekhov's works and rooms for scientific study. There are editions of his works in many languages. Dozens of photographs related to the life of Chekhov are on display. Some of his medical instruments are on exhibit. Playbills and various documents may also be seen.

In September 1901, Leo Tolstoy visited Crimea for the last time and met both Anton Chekhov and Maxim Gorky. Tolstoy recorded in his diary: "Gorky and Chekhov came. I am glad I liked both, especially the former." Gorky, under surveillance by the police, had been denied permission to live in Yalta, so Chekhov invited him to stay at his house in Autka, which was outside the city limits of Yalta. At different times I. Bunin and A. Kuprin also stayed in the house as guests. Other outstanding figures of Russian culture, including the Moscow Art Theatre actors, were guests in the house. Chekhov, a capable doctor, never treated patients in his house, but did make house calls. The sanatorium Yauzlar, where he used to treat tuberculosis patients, has been remaned after Chekhov.

Yalta Museum of Local Lore

At 25 Pushkinskaya Street is the musum of local lore that was founded in the late 19th and early 20th century. It has a vast geological and botanical collection which gives a good idea of the natural features of Southern Crimea. There are expositions on the history of Yalta from ancient times, the struggle for Soviet power in the Crimea, the partisan movement in World War II, and the prospects of future development of the resort area.

Livadia Palace

The former royal residence is a huge palace with approximately 100 rooms. It is located less than two miles from Yalta. Built in 1913 by the architect N. Krasnov, it was the former summer residence of the Russian tsar. The beautiful white palace is built in Italian Renaissance style. It was in this palace in February 1945 that the Yalta (Crimean) Conference was held between the heads of governments of the United States, the Soviet Union, and Great Britain. At the conference President Roosevelt, Josef Stalin and Winston Churchill met to coordinate plans for the defeat of Nazi Germany, and to formulate policies for the postwar world. The palace has been preserved as it was in 1945. The tables, chairs, and beds that were used by the leaders of the conference are carefully tended. Photographs of the "Big Three" are on display. A large map of Europe with lights, arrows, and other map symbols is used by a guide to explain the movement and positions of armies on the Eastern Front during World War II.

The palace is located in the town of Livadia, west of Yalta along the Black Sea coast. A 115-acre park planted with trees, flowers and shrubbery surrounds it.

The Russian tsar Alexander III died in Livadia in 1894 and Nicholas II, the last tsar of Russia, spent several summers there with his family before his overthrow in 1917. The town of Livadia is the largest health resort of general therapeutic and cardiological treatment on the southern coast of the Crimea.

Alupka Palace-Museum

Ten miles down the coast beyond Livadia lies the town of Alupka. Alupka is second in importance only to Yalta as a health resort on the southern coast of the Crimea. Its narrow meandering streets run down to the sea, where the Alupka Palace-Museum (formerly Vorontsov Palace) lies immersed in the lush verdure of a splendid park. The 150 rooms of the palace house a rich collection of works by Russian and foreign artists. The vast collection contains paintings, sculpture and applied art. The palace was designed by the English architect Edward Blore and built in 1828–1846 in English Tudor style with elements of oriental architecture. The crenelated contours of the palace seem almost a replica of the crags of Mount Ai-Petri (4,045 feet) that tower over the town. The palace was built for Count Vorontsov, the Governor-General of Novorossia. Beautiful white stone lions located on either side of a long tier of stone steps guard the entranceway to the palace which resembles that of the Alhambra in Granada, Spain. Onion domes cap the promontories.

The Swallow's Nest

Another turn of the coastline and there appear the turrets and crenelations of a palace which looks like a swallow's nest perched on the rocks overhanging the sea. This snow-white castle of great beauty is built on the very brink of a steep cliff known as Cape Ai-Todor. The castle resembles something out of a Walt Disney movie. This unusual structure is traditionally regarded as a symbol of the Crimea's southern coast. (The hydrofoils which skim along the waters of the southern coast pass beneath the castle.) The castle was built in 1912 in a neo-Gothic style of architecture by the Russian architect A. Shervid. It certainty makes a sea voyage along the Black Sea coast delightful!

Polyana Skazok (Fairy Tale Glade)

A unique outdoor museum is located in a scenic hollow at the foot of Mt. Stavri-Kaya. It exhibits a collection of wooden and stone sculptures by Crimean professional artists and skilled craftsmen. The sculptures represent popular personages from Russian folk tales and those of the world's fairy tales.

Crimean Game Preserve

This preserve is well-known for its pine, beech, hornbeam and oak forests that abound in stag, wild goat, stone marten, wild boar, fox and badger. An excursion will take you to the beautiful Lake Karagol and Uchan-Su Waterfall which drops from a 328-foot high precipice. You will walk the scenic mountain paths—Botkinskaya and Solnechnaya—which afford splendid views of the surrounding landscape. The distance of the preserve from Yalta is about fifteen miles. The guided tour to this site lasts approximately three hours.

Bakhchisarai

The city of Bakhchisarai is located approximately 81 miles northwest of Yalta across the Krymskie Gory Mountains. The name of the city can be translated literally as a "palace amid gardens." The famed Palace of Bakhchisarai was built in 1532–1551 for use as the residence of the Crimean Khans. Bakhchisarai was once the capital of the Crimean Khanate. The fabulous palace of Khan Mengli-Girei has been preserved until today in all of its magnificent splendor. Your tour of it will include the potentate's quarters, the Khan's mosque, and the harem quarters. Here you will see the famous Fountain of Tears of which Alexander Pushkin wrote in his poem "The Fountain of Bakhchisarai." Today the palace houses a museum of history and archeology. From Yalta the tour lasts approximately nine hours.

Intourist Cultural Center

In summer, foreign tourists are invited to attend the Intourist Cultural Center where one can take part in round table talks, listen to lectures, attend special interest gatherings, and see a Soviet film in one of the foreign languages. The Cultural Center is located in the Hotel Yalta, 50 Drazhinsky Street.

Balaklava

This famous battlefield was opened to foreigners in 1989 after having been closed to them since the early 1900s. A visit to it can be arranged in Yalta at the Intourist Service Desk at either the Yalta or Oreanda hotels.

Balaklava is located at the southwestern end of the Crimean peninsula about ten miles southeast of the seaport of Sevastopol. The town is connected by the coastal highway with Yalta. Balaklava is a small seaport, but its name and fame in history is associated with the battle which occurred there on October 25, 1854, during the Crimean War (1854–1856).

The Crimean War found France, Great Britain, Turkey, and Sardinia pitted against Russia. The war stemmed from rival demands over the protectorate of holy places in the Ottoman Empire. Russia threatened Turkey; Turkey declared war; and the British entered it soon afterwards. When the war began practically no one guessed that the main center of action would be a remote, arid, mountainous corner of the Crimea. The peninsula is about one-third the size of Ireland. A chain of limestone mountains stretches from Sevastopol across the southern edge.

Around Balaklava precipices hug the coastline with only a narrow strip of land bordering the sea beneath their heights. In the vicinity grow mulberry trees, cypresses, olives, chestnuts, and laurels right down to the water's edge. Streams of clear water descend from the high cliffs, which ward off cold winds from the north. Former villas and palaces of the aristocracy overlook the sea in the area, and villages are numerous in the vicinity.

In September 1854 a huge armada set sail to wrest Sevastopol from Russia. The fleet consisted of 37 major warships, 100 frigates, 200 transports and lesser ships, and stretched for eight miles. In all 600 ships and an army of 60,000 men set sail. The troops landed at Evpatoria, northwest of Sevastopol, and began a 45-mile advance upon the seaport. Less than two days march north of Sevastopol the adversaries fought a bloody battle at the Alma River and heights. On September 24 the allies crossed the Belbec River north of Sevastopol with the intent of attacking the city from that direction. Instead, Russian fortifications forced the allies to the east of Sevastopol, where they proceeded to capture Balaklava for use as a base of operations against Sevastopol. Balaklava lay on a bay which was an excellent harbor through which to bring in supplies for the campaign. The entrance was via a passageway, through a vertical wall of cliffs 800 feet high, just narrow enough to permit a single ship at a time to enter. Once inside the tideless harbor the ships found a secure haven. The harbor is about three-fourths of a mile long, 250 yards wide and sufficient in depth for anchoring and maneuvering. Dozens of British transports began unloading their supplies for the campaign. From the bay a gap in the surrounding coastal mountains runs northward for three miles and is about two miles wide. The valley and the port of Balaklava would be the objective of Russian forces on October 25th.

The French established their landings and front lines further down the coast near Sevastopol. The land between Sevastopol and Balaklava is barren and mountainous, with little water present. The allied line established itself in almost a semicircle around Sevastopol. The Russians had in that city troops about equal in number to the troops of the allies. Sevastopol lies on a bay about four miles long, into which empties the Tchernaya (Black) River. Cape Chersonese, a mountainous area, lies on the south side of Sevastopol. Fortresses guarded the city on all its approaches. The eastern side of Sevastopol rises in steep hills beyond a semicircle of level land about 500 to 600 yards wide.

The siege of Sevastopol began with each side firing thunderous volleys from their cannons. Gradually the Russians assumed a slow offensive, infiltrated the allied lines, and at times fought small skirmishes with the allies in their rear. Meanwhile, a Russian relief force came through a pass in the mountains north of Balaklava. About two-and-one-half miles north of that town is a plain (Balaklava Plain) surmounted by conical hills extending to the mountains along the seacoast. Here, some units of the allies manned positions, with the Turks holding a number of the hills. The 93rd Highlanders held the mouth of the gorge extending from the plain down to Balaklava. Ten miles beyond on the plain were the British light and heavy brigades of cavalry. On October 25th, the Russians began their attack on this plain, while the main body of Allied troops stood before Sevastopol. The Russians advanced taking hill after hill on the plain, driving the Turks from these backward on the 93rd Highlanders. A Russian cavalry force of 1,500 men then charged the 93rd and the Turks. Volleys from the 93rd cut down the Russians and sent them into retreat. Then the British heavy brigade met the main body of the Russian cavalry sweeping down the plain and cut into it. Together with British Guard units they routed the Russians. Another British force, the light brigade, stood near the end of the Balaklava plain in a narrow valley stretching to the Yaeta pass through which the Russians had entered the plain. Its commander, Lord Cardigan, advanced the light brigade against the retreating Russians which were carrying off the Turkish cannons they had captured. At 1,200 yards, 30 Russian cannons opened up on the light brigade which advanced in two lines through the raking enemy fire. Men and horses fell in the furious charge, but the two lines never wavered. Onward they advanced, overrunning the enemy cannons and sabering their gunners. The light brigade then attacked the Russian cavalry and routed it. Wheeling about, it rode by the silent cannons and charged a force of lancers, decimating them. Thus ended the battle for Balaklava. The exploits of the British forces in this battle, particularly the charge of the light brigade, would hereafter make famous the name of the little Russian seaport of Balaklava. The English poet Alfred Lord Tennyson wrote of that battle:

> Half a league, half a league,
> Half a league onward,
> All in the valley of Death

Rode the six hundred.
'Forward the Light Brigade!
Charge for the guns!' he said.
Into the valley of Death
Rode the six hundred.

Cannon to right of them,
Cannon to left of them,
Cannon in front of them
Volley'd and thunder'd;
Storm'd at with shot and shell,
Boldly they rode and well,
Into the jaws of Death,
Into the mouth of hell
Rode the six hundred.

However the Crimean War did not end on that note. The bloody battle of Inkerman (costly to both sides) was fought November 5, 1854, and the allies continued in pursuit of their objective, Sevastopol. The city finally fell on September 8, 1855, after intense bombardment and a siege that lasted 336 days. The fighting dragged on a few weeks longer, and the war was concluded by the Treaty of Paris in 1856.

During the war medical and hospital service was crude and inefficient. Thousands died from cholera, dysentery, and other diseases. The sufferings of the wounded and diseased were given public attention through the heroic efforts of Florence Nightingale and a group of female nurses working in a hospital on the Bosporus. The war was characterized by mismanagement, inefficiency, and incompetence on both sides.

Viticulture

Crimean viticulture and winemaking is centuries old. Its wines have won many international awards for their aromatic properties and fine taste. The highest awards have gone to wines manufactured at the Massandra wine center—the Crimea's oldest classical establishment of this kind, founded over 150 years ago.

The sun-kissed grapes imbued with the fragrant mountain air and the fresh sea breeze, and the peculiar aroma of flowering grasses impart a unique taste and fragrance to Massandra wines. Kokur, Crimean Maderia, shèrry, Yuzhnoberezhny (South Coast) port and the pride of the entire collection Muscat Bely Krasnogo Kammya (White Muscat of the Red Stone) are excellent choices. You will have the chance to taste and purchase any of these brands when you visit the area. Wine-tasting sessions are held in the Alupka wine and winemaking center.

Restaurants in Yalta

"A fine meal is a must for a fine guest!" This is the motto of catering establishments in Yalta. The city's notable cafes and restaurants include:

Mramorny. Its specialty is Russian cuisine. It offers dishes cooked according to old-time recipes: *rasstegai* (open-topped pastry), *kulebyaka* (meat pies), pike-perch a la Russe, *kvas* (an ancient Russian beverage).

The beach canteens of the Hotel Yalta will treat you to hot Russian pancakes and tea.

Riyeka. Ukrainian cuisine is its specialty. You will be served an enjoyable meal of appetizing *vareniki* (dumplings) and Ukrainian *borshch* (soup) with fritters.

Khrustalny. This restaurant is famous for its Oriental cuisine. Dishes include *shurpa* (Crimean style), tabanan cakes and green tea.

Tavrida and **Gorny Ruchei** restaurants. Specialities are Crimean cuisine.

Rybatsky Stan restaurant and **Espanola** cafe. Fish is the specialty of these two establishments.

Each restaurant offers a wide assortment of Crimean wines and champagne, and pastry.

Evening Entertainment

Those who enjoy Russian folk music, songs and dances are invited to see a performance by the folklore Kalinka ensemble which is well known in the Crimea and Russia.

Ukrainian songs and dances are presented by the Crimean song and dance ensemble Tavriya. Its concert programs are popular.

Those who are keen on classical music will enjoy meeting the Chamber Orchestra of the Crimean Philharmonic. Its repertoire includes music by classical and contemporary composers.

Those who enjoy going to the circus should not miss a visit to the Yalta Circus. Theater goers and music lovers can go to one of Yalta's theaters or concert halls.

There are also many amateur art groups: Bandura Group, folk circus, the Young Pioneers' song and dance ensemble, and folklore groups from other Crimean cities.

The music hall show in the Hotel Yalta is always a favorite with visitors to the city. Tourists enjoy taking part in dance and entertainment programs organized in the hotel's beach pavilion. The hotel also has an electronic games room.

Hotels

Intourist Hotel Complex Yalta. This is an international class hotel with 1,235 rooms. It is situated in one of the most picturesque spots of the Crimean littoral, admist the lush verdure of Massandra Park surrounded by the ancient pines, cypresses, plane and chestnut trees. Overlooking the Black Sea and surrounded by lovely gardens, it is certainly one of the most beautiful hotels in the Soviet Union. Its 13-story building forms an integral whole with the surrounding landscape. Every room offers a splendid view of the sea and the Crimean mountains. Hotel residents have the use of three swimming pools with heated sea water, two for diving and swimming and a special one for children. The sea is just behind the hotel, and an express elevator takes you down to the beach equipped with the latest facilities. There you can rent beach chairs, inflatable mattresses, flippers and diving masks. There are also rowboats, catamarans, watercycles, tennis and badminton courts, and table tennis facilities. The hotel's four saunas have training equipment and cabins opening onto the beach. Visitors can enjoy windsurfing, sunbathing, swimming, hikes to the mountains, and message treatments. There are coaches for aerobics, therapeutic exercises, swimming, and gymnastics. The beach is equipped with two cafes and other places serving ice cream, cocktails, beer and coffee. You can also buy Russian *bliny* (pancakes). In the evenings there is dancing in the pavilion next to the sea and visitors can listen to pop music against the soft murmur of the surf. Car rental is available for those wishing to discover the sights of Crimea and the mountainous landscape. The address of the Yalta is 50 Drazhinsky Street, Yalta 334240. The distance to the center of Yalta is about three-fourths of a mile. The hotel is 63 miles from Simferopol airport and 57 miles from the railway terminal. Telephone: 35-0150, 35-0132.

Intourist Hotel Oreanda. This international class hotel has been in operation since 1896 except for brief periods. In 1984 it underwent reconstruction and then reopened its doors. Built in the style of late Russian classicism on the central embankment at the beginning of Primorsky Park, it affords a splendid view of the sea and the nearby mountains. The hotel has three stories and 119 rooms, and accommodates 230 persons. There are five deluxe suites. Three five-room apartments can be transformed into two- and three-room suites. Two four-room suites can be transformed into two-room suites. The suite on the fourth floor has a sauna and is connected with a roof top rose garden. There is a restaurant with 150 seats overlooking the sea, a banquet hall, an express cafe, disco bar, sauna bath and a swimming pool with heated sea water. The beach is but a short distance away. It is equipped with a medical room, showers, rental service, bar and massage rooms. The service bureau in the hotel offers a variety of excursions in the company of experienced guides, tickets to the theater, circus, concerts, and dances in the seaside pavilion. It will take orders for farewell or birthday parties, receptions for guests, delivery of gifts, flowers, and plane and railway tickets. Also one may hire a taxi, rent a car, and arrange for sightseeing tours at the desk. The address of the Oreanda is 35/2 Naberezhnaya Lenina, Yalta 334240. It is about 60 miles from Simferopol Airport and 58 miles from the railway terminal. Telephone: 32-2034.

Polyana Skazok Camping Ground

The Intourist Camping Ground Polyana Skazok (Glade of Fairy Tales) is a first class camp site which lies amidst a forest on the steep bank of the Yauzlar River. There are three cottages and 180 summer cabins for a total of 390 beds. There is parking for 120 cars. It is located less than two miles from the center of the city. Nearby are the ruins of fortifications once built by Crimea's ancient settlers. Still higher, in the direction of the Stavri-Kai plateau, one can walk the Botkinskaya footpath which gives a splendid bird's-eye view of the forest-covered slopes running down to the sea. Walking down, towards the river, one comes to the restaurant Gorny Ruchei (Mountain Spring) built in the tradition of Ukrainian folk architecture. It is well known for its Ukrainian cuisine, especially *borshch* and *vareniki*. The Polyana Shazok receives guests from June until October. The address of the camp ground is Yuzhnoberezhnoye Highway. Telephone: 39-5218.

Chapter XII.
CONCLUSION

My unwashed Russia, goodbye to you,
Land of slave-and-master race,
And you, phalanxes of official blue,
And you, their obedient populace.
            —*M. Yn. Lermontov*
            Goodbye to Russia

On March 11, 1985, Mikhail Gorbachev was elected general secretary of the Central Committee of the Communist Party of the Soviet Union. Gorbachev was born of peasant parents in the village of Privolnoye in Stavropol territory on March 2, 1931. At age fifteen he began work as a machine operator and in 1952 joined the Communist Party. He graduated with a law degree from Moscow State University in 1955 and in 1967 received a degree in farm economics from Stavropol Agricultural Institute. After 1955 Gorbachev served as deputy head of Propaganda Department of Stavropol Territory, then as second secretary, and later first secretary of the Komsomal Committee of that territory. Between 1966 and April 1970 he served in secretarial posts in the Stavropol City and Territory Party Committees. In 1971 he became a member of the CPSU Central Committee; was elected secretary of that committee in 1978; and in 1979 became an alternate member of the Politburo of the CPSU Central Committee. Gorbachev moved from alternate member to member of the Politburo in 1980.

Gorbachev is an enigma. One often wonders if he isn't more interested in public relations and competing with President Reagan for press headlines

243

than he is in alleviating tensions between the superpowers. Certainly his style of leadership contrasts with that of Chernenko, Andropov, and Brezhnev, his predecessors. The question remains—is Russia better off or worse with Gorbachev in power? Only time will tell.

Gorbachev has a certain flamboyance about him. No doubt he would like to see Russia progress as a nation and rid it of the corruption, waste, bribery, and stagnation in its economy. Gorbachev has promised more and better consumer goods for the Russian people. If he keeps his promise, changes will have to be made in the Soviet system.

There are still many political prisoners in the Soviet Union, but far fewer than in the days of Stalin and Lenin. Some have been released under Gorbachev's policy of "glasnost," such as Andrei Sakharov and his wife, Elena Bonner, who had been exiled to the city of Gorky in 1980. Sakharov was instrumental in developing the hydrogen bomb for Russia during the 1950s, but later turned dissident and spoke out against nuclear testing and the arms race. He won the Nobel Peace Prize in 1975, and in 1980 criticized Russian intervention in Afghanistan before his exile to Gorky. Released in December 1986, Sakharov and his wife went to Moscow where they expressed esteem for Gorbachev and his new policy of openness. Nevertheless, Sakharov told a news conference that a general amnesty was needed for all "prisoners of conscience."

If Gorbachev is to succeed in making the Soviet economy and bureaucracy more efficient, computer technology will need to be introduced into the economy from the lowest levels to the top echelon. Economic planning would greatly benefit from this technology, and assembly-line products could be upgraded in quality, a problem that plagues most consumer products. Much Western computer technology is purposely kept out of the hands of the Soviets. Many, if not most, computers used by Soviet industry are fifteen to twenty years behind those of the U.S. in their performance and technology.

Signs of computer technology are few in the U.S.S.R. Computers can be seen in the airport in Moscow where they are utilized to keep track of ticket reservations, cancellations, and so forth. Few, if any, will be seen in the hotels, department stores, Intourist Travel Agency, or other businesses or public facilities. Clerks, reservations personnel, office workers and others still rely extensively on the abacus to perform routine calculations. The abacus is commonly sold in department stores, Beriozka shops, and hotel lobbies. The military, space program, research facilities, and some other government agencies, however, utilize computers.

Computer technology could greatly enhance industrial production in the Soviet Union. Instead the Soviets are falling even farther behind the West in this technology as rapid advancement in it continues. Russia's failure to incorporate ample computer technology into the economy also comes at a time when there is a slowdown in the country's economic growth. Moreover, it is difficult to foresee any but the most essential application of computer technology in Russia due to fear by the bureaucracy that any extensive spread of computer usage might undermine state security. The fear that hackers or unauthorized individuals might inadvertently tap into classified information or state secrets stored on computers has to be of concern to a government that cloaks much of its activities in a veil of secrecy.

The Russians are clever when it comes to copying or imitating the works or inventions of others. What the Russians themselves do not invent or contrive, but need, they attempt to acquire (namely electronics, microchips, and computers) by outright purchase, blackmail, bribery, or other devious methods.

The Soviet system has not produced the paradise for its people that Lenin envisaged it would. The enormous cost of maintaining its huge military complex is staggering, and drains resources from other sectors of the Soviet economy.

The Soviet bureaucracy determines the kind and amount of goods to be produced. Everything from the number of refrigerators to the number of teachers needed for Soviet schools is planned in advance by the Kremlin. Quality and quantity are terms that seem to have no apparent relationship in the Soviet system. The gulf between the two is continents apart. Those who are members of the Communist party have the privilege of traveling abroad and routinely return from shopping sprees in Paris, London, and Frankfurt with suitcases filled with name brands of items such as shaving lotion, perfume, toothpaste, gum, hosiery, ties, shoes, cigarettes, coffee, chocolates, jeans and other apparel, and similar items of lesser quality or lacking in Russia. One can stand in line at customs inspection in Moscow and Leningrad and watch Russians returning from visits to the West open suitcases filled with an array of such articles.

Russian friends, university students, and other Russians you may casually meet, often want to purchase any such items as the above that you may have available, offering huge sums of rubles for them. A Russian student may offer to buy your camera for five times the amount you paid for it. The tourist or foreigner should be cautioned in this respect for Soviet law prohibits any such transactions that resemble illicit or blackmarket activity, and one can be arrested for engaging in such activity. The person attempting to make a transaction with you may be a police official.

Russia is the natural result of conditions that existed for centuries and led to its expansion and development. Should the present Soviet state cease to exist, the same conditions that helped to propel it to power would not be the basis for launching a new government. Conditions for power change with time. Those conditions which served as the foundation for the tsarist regime have long since passed, and those upon which the present Soviet regime is based are undergoing transformation.

In many ways Russia is a land of mystery. Often what appears to be reality is, indeed, a paradox. Russia is a land of paradoxes. There is a contradiction for nearly every fact. Little can be said about Russia that is true of Russia as a whole. There are always contradictions. What is true about one part of Russia may be totally inapplicable about another part. The Soviet Union is too vast a country and its peoples too diversified to make many general statements about the whole of its territory.

In Russia one senses that everything is conceived, planned, and organized on a grand scale. Think for a moment of those huge state farms, the spacious palaces of the tsars, state economic planning, colossal dams and hydro-electric projects, massive May Day celebrations, enormous rockets, huge tanks, the large assortment and variety of medals and decorations worn by military officers, diplomats, and even civilians on the streets.

A streak of melancholy runs through the Russians. In many ways their character and temperament are a blend of ignorance, boorishness, superstition, cunning, despotism, barbarism, and cruelty stemming from their historic past. A Russian can be naively simple one minute and cold and vindictive the next. There is still much of the peasant in the Russian. The Russian will fiercely devote himself to a cause, to the point of insanity. World War II is a good case in point. Yet the Russian can be delightfully witty, humorous, and flirtatious. The Russian cannot be judged by American or Western ideas and standards. To do so would be an error in judgment. The Soviet conscience is an enigma, especially to foreigners. On the one hand the Soviets blatantly shoot down a foreign airliner, as in the case of a Korean Flight 007, and with the other hand embrace the palms of visiting peace advocates.

Russia is a very bureaucratic country. The bureaus are innumerable and seem endless in their profusion. Bureaucracy seems to be a state of mind in Russia. In the Soviet Union the government owns or controls everything. The system is often as frustrating to the Russians as it is to the visitor. One is often mystified by the logic of the Soviet system.

The state controls all means of production. State economic plans prescribe a planned economy. All resources belong to the state, and their role in the economy is dictated by their availablity and accessibility, not by the demand for them. Nevertheless, Russia is a tremendous industrial power. It is the world's leading producer of iron and steel, and ranks first in the output of petroleum, chromium, manganese, platinum, and some other minerals.

The major difference between Soviet communism and democracy is the degree of freedom permitted the people. Americans take their freedom in stride, revering it as a birthright. In Soviet society its citizens are expected to participate in public service activities. Each year Soviet citizens traditionally volunteer their labor without pay to work for the state in what has become known as a *subbotnik,* or national labor festival. The festival is held to honor Vladimir Lenin and usually occurs before his birthday.

Factory workers, office personnel, teachers, and others turn out to perform labor on farms, clean the streets, plant flowers and trees in public parks, assist in hospitals and in other activities considered worthy of the event. Individuals are not forced to participate in these special activities, but most do so rather than be disdained or chastised by their friends and fellow workers. Donating a day or two of work to the state is easier than social ostracisim by one's peers.

On Red Square, city streets, and in other locations the tourist may frequently see people with red armbands. These individuals are the *druzhinniki* or volunteer law enforcement persons who work without remuneration for their services. They work in their spare time to help the militia mantain law and order.

Activities such as these are in keeping with the spirit and definition of communism. According to the program of the Communist party (October 26, 1985), as printed in *Moscow News,* "Communism is a classless social system, with the entire people owning the means of production, complete with social equality of all members of society [in which] the abilities of everyone will be used with maximum benefit for the people."[4]

On Soviet streets it is not uncommon to see vehicles that are stranded or inoperable because of the shortage of parts or the lack of sufficient mechanics to repair them. Many vehicles are simply cannibalized for necessary parts in order to restore others to operational condition. In several cities I saw autos sitting on blocks along the streets, some with no tires or wheels on them. Many spare parts can be bought on the black market. Gas stations are few in Soviet cities, with even huge cities like Moscow and Leningrad containing only a dozen or so. On major highways gas stations may be fifty or more miles apart. Garages are difficult to find.

The Soviet economy is obsolete. A major handicap is that Soviet economics and ideology go hand-in-hand; they are inseparable. Per capita productivity lags behind that of the West; and since 1977 Soviet labor has been falling farther behind in this respect. Another significant problem with the economy is its management (a more appropriate term would be mismanagement) and the prorities in allocation of resources. Since a substantial part of Soviet resources is lavished on the military, only by changing priorities can the Kremlin expect to get its sluggish economy back on track.

Education is free. There are many kindergartens for children. Secondary education is compulsory. One must pass tough exams to advance into higher education. It costs the state about two hundred rubles per year to educate a secondary school student, more than a thousand rubles to educate a college or university student, and a bit less than a thousand rubles a year to train a vocational school student. Farm students that are sent to study at colleges are provided scholarships by their farms.

Women retire at age fifty-five with an average monthly income of one hundred and thirty-two rubles; men retire at age sixty with the same average monthly income. The lowest monthly retirement benefit for men is fifty rubles. Most women in the Soviet Union have jobs outside the home. Pensions depend on the years of service or work. If one retires before age fifty-five, he or she receives a partial pension. But one can retire before age fifty-five with full pension if that person has had twenty-five years of continuous work or service.

Rent does not exceed 4 percent of the budget of a household. The rent for a three-bedroom apartment with utilities included runs about twenty-five rubles a month. An apartment costs 3–4 percent of the average family income. Food is the big item of expense, generally requiring an outlay of 60 percent or more of one's income.

The average tax is 8 percent of income; the highest is 13 percent. There is a bachelor's tax on males over age 20, the purpose of which is to encourage population growth. Childless married women also pay the tax, which is about 5 percent of one's income. The average family has one to two children. Women receive fifty rubles at the birth of their first child. For the second and third child they get an additional one hundred rubles for each. Women customarily stay home after childbearing until the child reaches one and a-half years of age. The mother does not have to work during that time; her job is secure. A mother with a new child receives a supplemental monthly benefit of thirty-five rubles for one year. There are plans to increase this amount to fifty rubles.

The average wage in the Soviet Union is 192 rubles. Currently, most doctors, engineers, and other professionals average less than two hundred rubles per month, but their prestige is on the rise, and plans are to increase their salaries. It is anticipated that doctors and other professionals will soon receive more income to equal or pass the salary of most other workers. Some doctors and other professionals are currently below the salary of other workers. On the average, men earn higher salaries than women.

A cab driver averages about one hundred and eighty-five rubles; street sweepers (many of whom are elderly women) earn only about eighty-five rubles per month; and trash haulers earn eighty-five to one hundred rubles monthly. On the other hand, factory managers, some lawyers, judges, highly skilled engineers and those in hazardous risk jobs earn from four hundred to one thousand or more rubles monthly.

Nearly every guide encountered in Russia will stress the point that unemployment does not exist in the Soviet Union. Russian guides will tell you that a job is available to anyone requesting employment. That is not to say that the applicant for a job will procure the type of employment or salary he is seeking. Yet some unemployment does exist in the Soviet Union, to include individuals applying for emigration, those refusing service in the military, persons fired from their jobs for personal or other reasons, and those released from jobs due to completion of the project or a reduction in employees. Those refusing work can be imprisoned. Soviet propaganda paints the picture that unemployment is a phenomenon found only in capitalist countries.

Persons refused permission to exit the Soviet Union are labeled by the term *refuseniks*. These individuals frequently find that the only work available to them consists of menial tasks such as collecting garbage or sweeping the streets.

According to the National Federation of Independent Business Research and Education Foundation in San Mateo, California, "the hourly take-home pay in December 1981 was $5.69 for American workers, [and] $1.35 for Russian workers."[5] That foundation also noted that it took a person in Washington, D.C., thirty-seven minutes of worktime to buy 2.2 pounds of beef hamburger, compared to a Muscovite who would have to work two hours and five minutes for the same amount of hamburger in 1981. Also by way of comparison, a color TV in Washington, D.C. which required a worker there sixty-five hours of worktime to purchase, would require his counterpart in Moscow more than seven hundred hours of worktime to purchase. In one further illustration, three hours of worktime would be required to buy a pair of Levi jeans in Washington, D.C., compared to the forty-six hours it would take a worker in Moscow to buy the same jeans.

Income and economic disparity in Russia are actually widening between the masses rather than narrowing as envisaged by Marxist-Leninist dogma. According to an article in *The Chronicle of Higher Education* (1984), which cited a federally funded research project on the Soviet Union by the University of Illinois at Urbana-Champaign, 10 percent of Russia's population controls about 54 percent of that nation's wealth. Further noted was the finding by scholars at that university that productivity by Soviet laborers was on the decline. Display of wealth in the Soviet Union is noticeably lacking compared to that in Western countries. Nowhere did I see prosperous looking suburbs surrounding Soviet cities.

Communism is irrational. Its system opposes change not in accord with state ideology, but without creative change a society stagnates. Communism discourages innovation and individualism. Individualism, a characteristic feature in the West, is suppressed in Russia. Censorship has always existed in Russia. The tsars imposed censorship and the Communists do the same.

Totalitarianism stifles and contravenes creativity.

During the last twenty-five to thirty years, a growing number of dissident Soviet writers and intellectuals have written and spoken out against censorship, and restraints on intellectual freedom in Russia. In return the Soviet press has frequently rebuked and chided these dissident elements for their devionist expression. A huge censorship board represses literary inspiration that does not conform to communist ideology and goals.

The Russians are extremely fond of poetry. In no other country is poetry held in more high esteem than it is in the Soviet Union. Many critics and those familiar with Russian literature consider Boris Pasternak as Russia's greatest poet in the twentieth century. Pasternak was born in Moscow on February 10, 1890. Because his father, Leonid, painted much of his life, and Rosalia, his mother, was an up-and-coming pianist before her marriage, young Boris was encouraged in the arts. He first tended toward music and painting but eventually came to the realization that poetry was in his blood. Still confused about his trade, he entered the University of Marburg to study philosophy, graduating from there in 1913. In 1922 he married the artist Evgeniia Vladimirovan Lourie, who bore him a son, Evgenii. However, the marriage did not last and in 1931 they parted. Three years later, he married Zinaida Nilkolaevna, who gave him another son, whom he named after his father, Leonid. In 1947, after separating from Nikolaevna, he fell deeply in love with Olga Vsevolodovna Ivinskaia, but remained with his wife for the rest of his life. After the publication of *Doctor Zhivago* until his death on May 30, 1960, he suffered much pressure from the government and his peers in the Soviet Writer's Union to leave the country.

His first published poetry was that of *Twin in the Clouds*. Other early works included *Lieutenant Schmidt* and *The Year 1905*. In 1927 he published *My Sister, Life* and *Themes and Variations,* which brought him much attention and fame in Russia. During the great purges of Stalin's era many poets and writers were arrested and sent to concentration camps. Fortunately, Pasternak escaped this fate, perhaps because he had written one poem in favor of communism. However, soon after Stalin rose to power, Pasternak became disillusioned with the Communists' ideals. His greatest work was not a poem but the novel entitled *Doctor Zhivago*, which tells about the life and work of a doctor in Russia from 1903 to 1929. Immediately after its release, it was rejected in the Soviet Union due to its anti-Communist tone. However, Pasternak released it for publication in Western countries and in 1958, just three years after the manuscript was completed, it won the Nobel Prize for Literature. Originally, Pasternak accepted the award, but after much pressure on him by friends and officials of the government, he rejected the honor. The last years of his life were years of constant worry of expulsion from the country or even execution. He managed to supplement his small income by translating works of Shakespeare and receiving royalties from them. While his health was failing in those last years, he wrote *Sketch for an Autobiography* and *When Skies Clear,* his last works until he died of lung cancer after suffering several heart attacks.

After 1900, literary development in Russia passed through three separate phases of development. During the first stage of its unfolding in the twentieth century, Russian literature mushroomed in a great surge of enlightenment and creativity. The new generation of writers and artists rejected the rising tide of materialism and the growth of bourgeois ideas, and sought to redefine the meaning of the nature of man in a more positive and humanistic view. Russian poets, artists, and writers of the early 1900s stressed individual expression over that of the group. Humanism was in vogue and it spurred a renaissance in the creative arts.

Then came the Russian Civil War, which brought about a second and new stage in literary development. From World War I until 1920 Russia had been fighting almost continuously, and once hostilities ended many Russian writers and artists, either out of necesssity or firmly believing in Marxist-Leninist dogma, used their talents to express Bolshevik revolutionary ideals. The Civil War, once ended, provided a rich and fertile background for the Futurists and their literary and artistic criticism of the humanistic movement and the bourgeois establishment. During the 1920s artistic and literary works commonly found expression in what became known as revolutionary romanticism.

Before 1930 Stalin ushered in yet a third step of literary and artistic transformation in Russia. Individual initiative was stifled, and all writings and forms of artistic endeavor were required to conform to Communist doctrine and party directives. Creativity, unless it glorified socialism and the state, was repressed or censored. Nevertheless, writers such as Pasternak and Solzhenitsyn vigorously protested against these measures.

Some of the more internationally known literary works by Soviet dissidents in recent decades include: *Babi Yar* (1967), by Anatoly Kuznetsov; *A No One* (1973), by Nicolay Bokov; George Vladimov's *Faithful Ruslau* (1975); Alexander Solzhenitsyn's *One Day in the Life of Ivan Denisovich* (1963); *Cancer Ward* (1968); *The First Circle* (1968) and *Gulag Archipelago* (1974–75); Andrei Amalrik's *Will the Soviet Union Survive in 1984?* (1969); *Progress, Coexistence and Intellectual Freedom,* by Andrei Sakharov in 1968; *The Life and Extraordinary Adventures of Private Chonkin* (1977), by Vladimir Voinovich; *Going Under* (1972), by Lidia Chukovskaya; and *Doctor Zhivago* (1958), by Boris Pasternak.

Soviet-American relations have frequently suffered, especially in the last two decades, over the issue of human rights. The dissident movement in Russia surged during the latter 1960s and the 1970s. The faster it grew, the more the authorities sought to repress it by arrest, imprisonment, exile, or expulsion. Some dissidents emigrated abroad including many Jews, large numbers of whom left the Soviet Union in the 1970s. Some of the more famous dissidents were simply expelled, as in the case of Solzhenitzyn in 1974. In 1975 the Soviet Union signed the Helsinki Accord, which prompted the founding of a number of monitoring groups inside Russia who kept a watchful eye and records on the number of persons arrested for dissidence or involvement in human rights activities. Anatoly Shcharansky, one of the organizers of a Helsinki group and a prominent dissident, was convicted of espionage, imprisoned, and then released in 1986, whereupon he went to Israel.

The development of a national culture under Soviet ideology is still undergoing transformation. In Russia, cultural education is directed by the goal of Marxist-Leninist socialism. Culture is not considered an aim in itself, but a means of raising the standard and expression of the masses and society. The Soviet Union is a highly literate society. The U.S.S.R. prints more books than any other country in the world.

Television is also a cultural tool and a form of entertainment in Russia. It is also a medium of explaining the party's policy. Most Russians, perhaps 90 percent or more, have access to television, although the state controls all programming. News, documentaries, and sports constitute a large portion of programs aired on Russian television. Information on TV about the U.S. is frequently distorted, taken out of context, and presented with a negative image of the American society. The image of America generally projected on Russian TV is one of rampant crime, much rape, high drug usage, excessive alcohol abuse, poverty, and widespread moral decay.

Marxism-Leninism is the official doctrine of Russia. The state condemns anything that is anti-Marxist. The failure or success of communism rests on the economic and philosophical foundations of Marxism-Leninism. The Soviets have espoused their state socialism as a model for other countries, but after many reforms the shortcomings in their system are as apparent as ever. It is difficult to resurrect a system that operates in such narrow confines that it allows little leeway or constructive change. There are many voices in the Russian bureaucracy, but they all speak a similar ideological tongue. Each bespeaks the promises and dreams of Marx and Lenin, and each seeks to fulfill those promises.

Dissident voices were few on my first trip to the Soviet Union. Today the picture in Russia has improved. In early 1987 dozens of dissidents were freed by Soviet authorities from prisons, labor camps, and places of exile. Not since 1953, when Khrushchev's de-Stalinization drive resulted in the freeing of thousands of political prisoners, have the prospects for human rights in the U.S.S.R. looked better.

Mikhail Gorbachev's policy of "glasnost," sometimes defined as openness, but actually the public debate or discussion of social problems, is a dramatic turnaround from the past. Perhaps Gorbachev and "glasnost" will succeed in bridging the gulf between the rigid bureaucracy and the people. Perhaps not.

APPENDIX
Other Cities and Excursions Recommended for Inclusion in Itineraries

ALMA-ATA

The capital of the Kazakh Soviet Socialist Republic. Situated in the southeast of the republic in the foothills of the northern spurs of the Tien Shan mountain system at an altitude of about 2,788 feet above sea level. Nearby peaks reach 16,000 feet. The population is more than 1,000,000. The climate is extreme continental. The average temperature in January, the coldest month, is 17°F., and in July, the warmest, 75°F.

The city was founded in 1854. It sits aside the ancient Silk Route in the foothills of the Zaili Alatan Mountains. A distinctive feature of the face of the city is the abundance of orchards, among which apple orchards predominate

(Alma-Ata means in Kazakh "Father of Apples").

Alma-Ata has seven theatres, a philharmonic orchestra, a circus, and a sports complex.

Excursions

Sightseeing Tour of the City. Introduces the past and present of Alma-Ata and of the Kazakh people.

Exhibition of the Economic Achievements of the Kazakh SSR.

Central State Museum of the Kazakh SSR. Located in the building of a former cathedral. The exhibits are devoted to the history of Kazakhstan from the ancient times to the present day.

State Art Museum of the Kazakh SSR. Displays paintings, sculptures, works of graphic and applied art of Kazakhstan, as well as of Russian and Soviet art, and Western Europe and Oriental art.

Museum of Archaeology. Has sections devoted to the Stone Age, Bronze Age, Early Iron Age, and the Middle Ages.

Auezov House Museum. The exhibits are devoted to the life and creative work of the outstanding Kazakh writer Mukhtar Auezov.

Exhibition Hall of the Union of Artists of the Kazakh SSR. Displayed are works not only by Kazakh artists, but also by artists from the other Soviet Republics, as well as by foreign artists.

Museum of National Musical Instruments.

Out-of-Town Excursions

Lesser Alma-Ata Canyon. A tour of the Medeo high-altitude sports center and the mudflow control dam, acquaintance with the flora of the Zaili Ala-Tau—a favorite recreation haunt of Alma-Ata's townspeople.

Distance from Alma-Ata: 25 km. Tour duration: 3 hours.

Hotels

Otrar—First class, 5 stories, 360 rooms, Located in city center, 12 km. from airport. Telephone: 33-0045.

Zhetysu—First class, 5-story, 307 rooms (Intourist rents part of space). Located in city center, 12 km. from airport. Telephone: 39-2807, 39-2222.

Kazakh Aul Summer Tourist Camp—30 beds in 14 yurts (traditional Kazakh dwellings). The interiors of the yurts are made of felt and are lavishly decorated with Oriental rugs. Distance from city 25 km. Telephone: 68-8959.

ASHKHABAD

The capital of the Turkmen Soviet Social Republic. Situated in the south of the republic at the junction of the Kopet-Dag mountain range and the Kara-Kum desert. Its population is over 300,000. The climate is dry continental. The average temperature in January is 34°F., in July, 95°F. The city was founded in 1881 as a fort on the site of an ancient settlement named Ashkhabad (City of Love). The V.I. Lenin Kara-Kum Canal—an outstanding waterdevelopment project of the 20th century—passes not far from Ashkhabad.

It is a railway station on a line to Tashkent. The city has many industries, including: shoe factories; wineries; plants producing silk, yarn, and knitted goods; meat packing; and so forth. Ashkhabad is connected by an oil pipeline running 325 miles to Krasnovodsk.

Ashkhabad has an opera and ballet theatre, two drama theatres and a philharmonic orchestra.

Excursions

Sightseeing Tour of the City. Introduces the main attractions of the capital, and the history and present-day life of Turkmenia.

State Museum of History of the Turkmen SSR. The museum houses more than thirty thousand exhibits relating to the archaeology and ethnography of Turkmenia.

Museum of Fine Arts. One of the biggest art museums in Central Asia. Displays Russian icon painting, canvasses by famous Russian, Soviet, and foreign painters, unique carpets.

Museum of Regional Studies. The exhibits are devoted to the history and everyday life of the Turkmen people and reflect the present-day culture of the republic.

Exhibition of Economic Achievements of the Turkmen SSR.

Out-of-Town Excursions

V.I. Lenin Kara-Kum Canal. Acquaintance with the impressive achievements of Turkmenia in the development of desert lands. Distance from city center: 10 km. Tour duration: 3-1/2 hours.

Bakharden Underground Lake. A unique creation of nature. The lake is situated in a cave at a depth of 113 feet. The temperature of water in the lake is 95°F. to 98°F. all the year round. The water is medicinal. Bathing is arranged for tourists. Distance from city center: 110 km. Tour duration: 5-1/2 hours.

Excursion to Nisa. A tour of the ruins of the ancient Parthian kingdom (second to first centuries B.C.). This is one of the most ancient cities within the USSR. Distance from Ashkhabad: 16 km. Tour duration: 3 hours.

Hotel

Ashkhabad—First class, 7 stories. Intourist rents 130 beds. 8 km. from airport. Telephone: 5-7393, 9-0447.

BAKU

The capital of the Azerbaijan Soviet Socialist Republic. Situated on the Apsheron Peninsula, with sandy beaches on the shore of the Caspian Sea. Its population is over 1,500,000. The climate is dry subtropical. The average temperature in January is 37°F., in July 77°F. to 86°F. The city was founded more than a thousand years ago. Baku had Russia's first electrified railway, built in 1926.

In the early twentieth century Baku was widely known as a major center of oil production (51 percent of the world production of oil in 1901). At present, the production and refining of oil still goes on, but other industries such as textiles, metals, and carpetmaking are prominent. Baku, a major industrial center, is also a verdurous city full of sunshine in the southern way. There are several theatres in Baku, including an opera and ballet theatre, two drama theatres, a theatre of musical comedy, a theatre of young spectators, a puppet theatre, and a philharmonic orchestra. The city has a good subway system.

Excursions

Sightseeing Tour of the City. Introduces the achievements of the Azerbaijan people, as well as local attractions, among which is the memorial of the 26 Baku commissars, erected in honor of those who perished in the struggle for the establishment of Soviet power in Azerbaijan.

Excursion to the Old City. Acquaintance with the outstanding monuments of Azerbaijan architecture: the Maiden's Tower (twelfth century), the Palace of the Shirvan Shahs (fifteenth century). A tour of the seventeenth-century oriental bazaar and fifteenth-century baths. A visit to the Museum of Carpets.

Baku Branch of the Central V.I. Lenin Museum.

Museum of the History of Azerbaijan.

Mustafayev Museum of Arts. Displayed are masterpieces of art by Azerbaijan, Russian, Soviet, and foreign artists of different periods.

Museum of Azerbaijan Carpets and Folk Applied Art. The world's first museum of this kind (opened in 1972). Displayed are carpets and carpet products, embroidery, fine fabrics, ceramics, jewelry, carved wood, stone and bone from the ancient times to the present day.

Out-of-Town Excursions

Fire Worshippers' Temple Museum. A historic-architectural monument of the eighteenth century. Distance from Baku: 30 km. Tour duration: 3 hours.

Kobustan Museum-Reserve. Here tourists visit caves used by the primitive man for dwelling 10,000 years ago and acquaint themselves with unique cave drawings and a museum of excavations. Distance from Baku: 70 km. Tour duration: 6 hours.

Zaguiba Settlement. Swimming and sunbathing on the beach of the Caspian Sea. Distance from Baku: 45 km. Tour duration: 5 hours.

Carpet-Weaving Factory in Nardaran. The factory produces famous hand-made Azerbaijan carpets. Distance from Baku: 40 km. Tour duration: 3 hours.

Serebrovsky Oil Production Administration. One of the major oil fields in Azerbaijan. Distance from Baku: 35 km. Tour duration: 3 hours.

City of Shemakha. A tour of the ancient capital of Azerbaijan. A visit to a wine-making state farm, tasting of the famous Shemakha wines. Distance from Baku: 130 km. Tour duration: 10 hours.

City of Sumgait. Acquaintance with a young Soviet city (founded in 1949). Distance from Baku: 40 km. Tour duration: 4 hours.

City of Kuba. Includes a visit to a fruit-and-vegetable growing state farm. Distance from Baku: 200 km. Tour duration: 16 hours.

Mashtaginsky State Farm of Subtropical Crops. Distance from Baku: 30 km. Tour duration: 3 hours.

Hotels

Azerbaijan—First class, 16 stories, 600 rooms. Located in city center 22 km. from airport. Telephone: 98-9842, 98-9843.

Moscow—International class. 15-story, 199 rooms. 2 km. from city center, 27 km. from airport. Telephone: 39-2998, 39-3048.

Intourist—First class, 5 stories, 73 rooms. 25 km. from airport. Telephone: 92-1265, 92-1251.

BRATSK

A town in the Irkutsk Region of the Russian Soviet Federative Socialist Republic. Situated in the south of East Siberia on the Lower Angara River, at an altitude of 1,312 feet above sea level. The population is more than 250,000. The climate is extreme continental. The average temperature in January is 40°F., in July, 66°F. Bratsk lies 3,000 miles east of Moscow.

Bratsk is a young industrial town, with a large aluminum factory and a huge sawmill. From 1954 onwards the town developed rapidly in connection with the construction of the Bratsk Hydroelectric dam. Its reservoir is one of the world's largest manmade lakes. Bratsk has a people's drama theatre, a puppet theatre, and a unique bobsled track.

Excursions

Sightseeing Tour of the City. Acquaintance with the construction and development of the town and with 4.5 million KW Bratsk Hydrodam.

Museum of Regional Studies. The display introduces the history of pioneering the Angara basin.

Sleigh Road Excursion. Narrative about winter sports in the USSR.

Excursion to the Taiga. (15 km. from town center). Acquaintance with the flora and fauna of Siberia and organization of rest and recreation for Bratsk townspeople.

Hotels

Taiga—First class, 7 stories, 104 rooms. Located in town center, 35 km. from airport. Telephone: 4-3979.

Bratsk—(Intourist rents part of space.) First class. 9 stories, 414 beds. Located in town center, 35 km. from airport.

CHERNOVTSY

Regional center of the Ukrainian Soviet Socialist Republic. Located in the southwest of the republic in the Carpathian foothills on the Prut River. The population is over 218,000. The climate is temperate continental. The average temperature in January is 23°F., in July, 66°F.

The city was founded in the twelfth century.

It has a long history of violence. The Tartars sacked it in the thirteenth century and the Hungarians in 1352. The Germans and Russians fought for it in World War II. A university and medical institute are located in the city.

Chernovtsy has a music-and-drama theatre and a philharmonic orchestra. The Burkovina Song and Dance Ensemble here are noted for their traditional folk art performances.

Excursions

Sightseeing Tour of the City.

Chernovtsy in Sports (a thematic excursion).

Museum of Regional Studies. One of the biggest museums of regional studies in the Ukraine.

Picture Gallery and Exhibition of Consumer Goods. The picture gallery displays works by Bukovina artists and is the site of various traveling exhibitions.

Kobylyanskaya Literary-Memorial Museum. The exhibits are dedicated to the life and creative activities of the well-known Ukrainian authoress.

Out-of-Town Excursions

Village of Vashkovtsy. Garas Museum of Folk Art. Distance from Chernovtsy: 70 km. Tour duration: 5 hours.

Town of Kamenets-Podolsky. A tour of the historic-architectural museum-reserve which includes a fortress (twelfth to eighteenth centuries), a former cathedral (fifteenth to nineteenth centuries), and the town hall (sixteenth century). Displayed in the museum are archaeological and ethnographic collections, old manuscripts and printed books, and works of art. Distance from Chernovtsy: 120 km. Tour duration: 8 hours.

Hotel

Bukovina—First class, 5 story, 362 beds. (Intourist rents part of space.) One-half mile from city center. Telephone: 3-8274.

Campsite

Located at a distance of 3 km. from city center. Intourist rents 40 beds on a full- and 40 beds on a half-camping basis. Area provided for 20 tourists' own tents. Parking lot capacity: 20 cars. Telephone: 2-5496.

DUSHANBE

The capital of the Tajik Soviet Socialist Republic. Located in the foothills of the western spurs of the Pamirs in the Hissar Valley at an altitude of 2,690 feet above sea level. Its population is more than 519,000. Its streets are lined with poplars, acacias, and willows. The climate is continental. The average temperature in January is 34°F., in July, 88°F. The city was founded in 1924. For centuries the city has produced exquisite mosaics, wood carvings, and folk art. The city's Firdausi Library contains the works of Omar Khayyam.

Dushanbe has an opera and ballet theatre, the Tajik Drama Theatre, the Russian Drama Theatre, and the Tajik Youth Theatre.

Excursions

Sightseeing Tour of the City. Introduces one of the most beautiful and verdurous cities in Central Asia, and its attractions: a monument to the founder of Tajik literature, Sadriddin Aini; a favorite recreation haunt of the townspeople, the Komsomolskoye Lake; the "Rokhat" chaikhana (tea-house), an interesting specimen of vernacular architecture; the sports stadium; and others.

Museum of History and Regional Studies. The museum's display reflects the history and everyday life of the Tajik people, and the flora and fauna of Tajikistan. Works by Tajik artists are also represented here.

Out-of-Town Excursions

Town of Nurek. Introduces a young Tajik town and the Nurek Hydrodam on the Vakhsh River—one of the biggest in the USSR. Distance from Dushanbe: 75 km. Tour duration: 7 hours.

Varzob Canyon. A picturesque canyon in the Hissar Mountains. Distance from Dushanbe: 56 km. Tour duration: 7 hours.

Hissar Fortress. A tour of architectural monuments of the eighteenth to nineteenth centuries. Distance from Dushanbe: 30 km. Tour duration: 4 hours.

Hotel

Tajikistan—First class, 8 stories, 255 rooms. Located in city center, 7 km. from airport. Telephone: 27-4393.

FRUNZE

The capital of the Kirghiz Soviet Socialist Republic. Located in the north of the republic in the Chu River Valley at the foot of the Kirghiz Range at an altitude of about 2,760 feet above sea level. The population is over 562,000. The climate is continental. The average temperature in January is 22°F., in July, 76°F. Its streets are lined with poplars, mulberry trees, and flowers.

The city was founded in 1825, its former name was Pishpek. Frunze has four theatres, a philharmonic orchestra, and a circus.

Excursions

Sightseeing Tour of the City.

Exhibition of Economic Achievements of the Kirghiz SSR.

Frunze House Museum. The exhibits are devoted to the life of the prominent Soviet statesman and military leader Mikhail Frunze after whom the city got its name.

Museum of History. The history of the Kirghiz people from the Stone Age to the present day.

Museum of the Arts. Apart from works by Kirghiz artists, the display also includes works by renowned Russian and foreign masters. Periodical exhibitions of works of art from the other republics are arranged here.

Zoological Museum. Introduction to the rich fauna of Kirghizia.

Out-of-Town Excursions

Burana Tower. An architectural monument of the eleventh century. Distance from Frunze: 85 km. Tour duration: 5 hours.

Ala-Archa Canyon. A picturesque canyon in the Ala-Too Mountains. Distance from Frunze: 42 km. Tour duration: 6 hours.

Hotel

Ala-Too—First class, 3 stories, 112 rooms. Located in city center, 40 km. from airport. Telephone: 22-6041.

IRKUTSK

Regional center of the Russian Soviet Federative Socialist Republic. Located in the south of East Siberia on the banks of the Angara River at its confluence with the Irkut River. The population is more than 550,000. The climate is extreme continental. The average temperature in January is 6°F., in July, 63°F. Beautiful parks and tree-lined streets add to its appeal.

Irkutsk is a major stopping place on the Trans-Siberian Railway and for planning a fascinating trip to nearby Lake Baikal, known as "The Gem of Siberia." It is the deepest (5,315 feet) freshwater lake on earth. The shores of the lake are lined with many oddly-shaped cliffs, forests, and sandy beaches. Intourist's Hotel Baikal stands on the lakeshore. The restaurant in this modern, three-story hotel serves various kinds of Baikal fish.

In Irkutsk modern buildings stand side by side with older wooden structures decorated with fanciful carvings. Tourists may try their luck at hunting in the nearby forests, which are inhabited with brown bears and red deer.

The city was founded in 1661. During the seventeenth to nineteenth centuries it was the center of pioneering of Siberia. It is often called "Student City," taking its title from its large scientific center.

Irkutsk has a drama theatre, a musical comedy theatre, an organ hall, a planetarium, a philharmonic orchestra, a circus, and one of Russia's best cycling tracks.

Excursions

Sightseeing Tour of the City. Narrative about the pioneering of Siberia, the history and present-day life of Irkutsk.

Museum of the Decembrists. The exhibits are devoted to the Decembrists—the first Russian revolutionaries who rose against czarist autocracy.

Museum of Regional Studies. One of the country's oldest museums of regional studies, it is more than 150 years old. The exhibits are devoted to the history and everyday life of the peoples inhabiting the Baikal basin, and to the nature of Siberia.

Fine Arts Museum. Displayed are works by famous Russian and Western European masters, including Bryullov, Tropinin, the French painter Poussin, and old copies of canvasses by Raphael, Murillo, and Rubens.

Museum of Mineralogy.

Out-of-Town Excursions

Lake Baikal. Acquaintance with the world's deepest lake, its rich flora and fauna. Distance from Irkutsk: 65 km. Tour duration: 7 to 8 hours.

Museum of Wooden Architecture. Acquaintance with peasant estates of the eighteenth and ninteenth centuries. A trip to Lake Baikal. Distance from Irkutsk: 47 km. Tour duration: 7 to 8 hours.

Trip to the Taiga with a Picnic. A full-day trip.

Hotels

Intourist—First class, 9-stories, 290 rooms. Located in city center, 14 km. from airport. Telephone: 91-335.

Baikal—First class, 3-stories, 96 rooms. 70 km. from Irkutsk, 500 meters from Lake Baikal. Telephone: 96-234.

KAZAN

Situated on the left bank of the Volga River, the city has over one million people. Pushkin, Tolstoy, and Gorky either lived or stayed in this city. Kazan University, founded in 1804, has 10,000 students. Lenin was a student here and began his revolutionary activity in the city in 1887. The city is a large industrial, scientific, and cultural center. Its furs are widely known and it is the cinefilm-making center of the U.S.S.R. There are large monuments here to the Tartar poets Musa Djalil and Gabdulla Gukai, and the city is a well-known center of Tartar studies and culture. Among its many museums are:

V.I. Lenin House-Museum. Here the Ulyanov family lived during 1888 and 1889.

Lenin Memorial at Kazan University. It includes the lecture room where Lenin attended lectures, and documents related to the period of his life in Kazan.

State Museum of the Tartar Autonomous Soviet Socialist Republic. Its collection houses over 650,000 items featuring the history of the region from ancient times to the present.

A.M. Gorky Museum. It was opened in 1940 in the house of the former bakery where Maxim Gorky worked from 1886 to 1887. Exhibition rooms are dedicated to M. Gorky and Fyodor Chaliapin.

Fine Arts Museum of the Tartar Autonomous S.S.R. Founded in 1959, the museum holds more than 10,000 paintings, drawings, sculptures, and artworks.

Other cultural features in Kazan include the Exhibition of Economic Achievements; the Musa Djalil Tartar Opera and Ballet Theatre; the Concert Hall of the Kazan Conservatoire; G. Kamal State Academic Theatre; V.I. Kachalov State Academic Bolshoi Drama Theatre; and the Kazan Circus.

Hotel

Kazan—9/10 Bauman Street. Telephone: 2-01-45.

KHABAROVSK

The Khabarovsk is the regional center of the Russian Soviet Federative Socialist Republic, and one of the major cities of the Far East. Located on the bank of the Amur River, its population is over 528,000. The climate is monsoon. The average temperature in January is 15°F., in July, 68°F.

The city was founded in 1858. Modern Khabarovsk is a major industrial center, a transport station on the Trans-Siberian Railway, and has air service to Soviet and foreign cities. Its industries turn out petroleum products, chemicals, metals, lumber, and machinery. It also makes medicinal preparations of ginseng, magnolia vine, and eleutherococus—plants endemic to the

Ussuri taiga.

The city stretches along the Amur River in a pictuesque strip of residential areas and parks for thirty miles. Chekhov was enchanted with the city when he passed through it on the way to Sakhalin. Its 10-story Intourist Hotel is located where the broad Amursky Boulevard meets the park with the V.I. Lenin Stadium.

Khabarovsk has three theatres, a philharmonic orchestra, and a circus.

Excursions

Sightseeing Tour of the City.

Museum of Regional Studies. The history and the present day of the region, and the wonderful nature of the Amur basin.

Far-Eastern Museum of Fine Arts. Displayed are old Russian icon painting, Russian art of the eighteenth and early ninteenth centuries, Soviet art, works of applied art of the peoples of the Far East, as well as works by Western European and Oriental artists.

Hotel

Intourist—First class, 10 stories, 283 rooms. Located in city center, 17 km. from airport. Telephone: 33-7634.

KHARKOV

Regional center, the city ranking second in size (population over 1,570,000) and importance in the Ukrainian Soviet Socialist Republic. Located in the northeast of the Ukraine at the confluence of the Kharkov, Lopan, and Uda Rivers. The climate is temperate continental. The average temperature in January is 18°F., in July 68°F.

Kharkov was founded in 1655–1656.

Kharkov has six theatres, a philharmonic orchestra, and a circus.

Excursions

Sightseeing Tour of the City. Kharkov is a major industrial, scientific, and cultural center of the Ukraine.

Museum of History. Documents and works of art depicting the history of the Ukrainian people, the history of the city from the date of its foundation to the present day.

Fine Arts Museum. This museum's collection is one of the oldest in the country (it is over 170 years old). Represented most fully are Russian and Ukrainian fine arts dating from the sixteenth century. It has the Ukraine's best collection of canvasses by the outstanding Russian artist of the ninteenth century Ilya Repin. The museum has sections of Soviet and foreign art.

Out-of-Town Excursions

Village of Skovorodinovka. Museum estate of the eighteenth century where the celebrated Ukrainian philosopher Grigory Skovoroda lived for some time and where he was buried. Distance from Kharkov: 70 km. Tour duration: 5 hours.

Village of Sokolovo. It was near this village that the First Czechosolovak Battalion fought its first action against fascists in March 1943. Distance from Kharkov: 55 km. Tour duration: 4 hours.

Hotels

Intourist—First class, 5 stories, 137 rooms. 4 km. from city center, 16 km. from airport. Telephone: 32-0508.

Mir—First class, 17 stories, 266 rooms. 5 km. from city center, 16 km. from airport. Telephone: 30-5543.

Motel

Druzhba—First class, 3 stories, 105 rooms. 10 km. from city center, 1 km. from airport. Telephone: 52-2091.

KISHINEV

The capital of the Moldavian Soviet Socialist Republic. Located in the heart of the republic on the banks of the Byk River, a tributary of the Dniester, in the wooded region of Kodry. Its population is more than 500,000. The climate is temperate continental. The average temperature in January is 25°F., in July, 70°F.

The city was founded in 1466.

Kishinev is both a cultural and industrial center. Its industries include a refrigerator plant that turns out 200,000 units a year, and a tractor factory that makes 20,000 tractors yearly. Engineering and chemical works are also prominent.

The city has eight museums, one of which was the home of Alexander Pushkin, who lived here in exile from 1820–23. It was here that he wrote *The Gypsies, The Prisoner in the Caucasus,* and *Brother-Brigands.* The city has many monuments, one of which is of Pushkin done in 1885. One of the most interesting architectural features of Kishinev is the Cathedral of the Nativity.

The capital of Moldavia has an opera and ballet theatre, a music-and-drama theatre, an organ hall, and a philharmonic orchestra.

Excursions

Sightseeing Tour of the City.

Exhibition of Economic Achievements of the Moldavian SSR.

Museum of the History of the Communist Party of Moldavia.

Museum of the Underground Printery of the Leninist "Iskra"

Newspaper. This newspaper played an important part in the development of the Social-Democratic movement in Russia and in the creation of the Communist party.

Museum of G.I. Kotovsky and S.G. Lazo. Dedicated to Soviet heroes of the Civil War (1918–20).

Museum of the Friendship of the Peoples. The exhibits tell about the friendship of more than one hundred nations and nationalities comprising the USSR.

Fine Arts Museum. A rich collection of old Moldavian painting and present-day Moldavian art, works by Russian and foreign masters.

Central Exhibition Hall. Various thematic exhibitions are arranged here.

Out-of-Town Excursions

City of Odessa. Acquaintance with one of the cities of the Ukrainian Soviet Socialist Republic, a major port on the Black Sea. Distance from Kishinev: 200 km. Tour duration: 10 hours.

Recreation Area on the Dniester River. Distance from Kishinev: 35 km. Tour duration: 4 hours.

Recreation Area on the Gidigich Lake. Tour duration: 3 hours.

Visit to a Wine-Making State Farm. Tour duration: 4 hours.

Town of Tiraspol. Distance from Kishinev: 76 km. Tour duration: 6 hours.

City of Beltsy. Distance from Kishinev: 140 km. Tour duration: 10 hours.

Town of Bendery. Distance from Kishinev: 65 km. Tour duration: 6 hours.

Pushkin House Museum in the Vilage of Pushkino. The exhibits are devoted to the life of the great Russian poet Alexander Pushkin during his sojourn in Kishinev in 1820–23.

Hotel

Intourist—First class, 17 stories, 312 rooms. Located in city center, 8 km. from airport. Telephone: 21-7850, 53-2800.

KRASNODAR

Regional center of the Russian Soviet Federative Socialist Republic. Located in the northwestern part of the Caucasus on the banks of the Kuban River. The population is about 700,000. It was founded by the Cossacks in 1794. World War II saw it suffer heavy damage. The climate is temperate continental. The average temperature in January is 28°F., in July, 75°F. The city has oil refining and engineering industries.

Krasnodar (formerly Ekaterinodar) has a drama theatre, an operetta theatre, a puppet theatre, a philharmonic orchestra, and a circus.

Excursions

Sightseeing Tour of the City.

Motor-Launch Trip Along the Kuban River.

Lunacharsky Museum of Fine Arts. Displayed in its twelve halls are canvasses by Russian and foreign artists. Exhibitions of works by local artists and of children's drawings are arranged here.

Museum-Reserve of History and Archaeology. The display introduces visitors to the rich nature of the Krasnodar Region, the history of the Kuban Cossacks, and the present day of the Kuban land.

Out-of-Town Excursions

City of Novorossiysk. A major port on the Black Sea. Along with general acquaintance with the city, the excursion includes a visit to legendary Little Land—the site of a fierce battle for the liberation of the city from the Nazi invaders in 1943. Tourists also visit the museum of the Abrau-Dyurso Wine-Making State Farm (14 km. from Novorosslysk) and taste wines and Soviet champagne. Distance from Krasnodar: 150 km. Tour duration: 12 hours.

Hotel

Intourist—First class, 13 stories, 272 rooms. Located in city center, 17 km. from airport. Telephone: 5-8897.

Motel

Yuzhny—First class, 3 stories, 103 rooms. 3 km. from city center, 20 km. from airport. Telephone: 5-9442, 5-9336.

LUTSK

The center of the Volyn Region of the Ukrainian Soviet Socialist Republic. Located in the northwest of the republic on the Styr River. The population is over 137,000. The climate is temperate continental. The average temperature in January is 23°F., July, 65°F.

Lutsk was founded in 1085.

Lutsk has a music-and-drama theatre, a philharmonic orchestra, and a museum of regional studies. Among the city's attractions are such architectural monuments as Lubart's Castle (thirteenth to fourteenth centuries), the Church of the Intercession (fifteenth century), a synagogue (early seventeenth century), and the cathedral church (seventeenth century).

Excursions

Sightseeing Tour of the City.

Lubart's Castle. A permanent art exhibition displaying works by Ukrainian, Russian, Soviet and foreign masters.

Hotel

Ukraine—Tourist class, 5 stories. Intourist rents 36 rooms. Located in city center. Telephone: 4-3351.

LVOV

Regional center of the Ukranian Soviet Socialist Republic. Located in the southwest of the republic. The population is over 667,000. The climate is temperate continental. The average temperature in January is 25° F., in July 65° F.

Lvov was first mentioned in the chronicles in 1256.

In 1572 the Russian printer Ivan Fyodorov came here and set up his printing press in St. Onuphrius Monastery. During the period of Austrian rule (1867–1919) the city was called Lemberg. Lvov belonged to Poland until 1939. Some sermons are still conducted in Polish in the Roman Catholic parts of the city. The Germans occupied it in World War II. After World War II the city rapidly developed electronic and machinery industries. Today it produces television sets, fork lift trucks, and buses.

The city has many interesting monuments and old churches. In the center of Lvov is Mickiewicz Square on which stands a large monument and statue of Adam Mickiewicz, a great Polish poet. It was erected in 1905. Among the many churches are St. Onuphrius, where Fyodorov is buried; St. Nicholas, built in the thirteenth century; the Dominican, Benedictine, and Carmelite churches (thirteenth to seventeenth centuries); the Benardines church (seventeenth century); the Jesuit church (1635), and a Jewish synagogue (1582). Educational institutions include Lvov University (founded 1661) and the Polytechnic Institute (1872–77).

Lvov has an opera and ballet theatre, the Ukrainian and Russian drama theatres, the Trembita Choir, a philharmonic orchestra, and a circus, and a palace of sports.

Excursions

Sightseeing Tour of the City.

Branch of the Central V.I. Lenin Museum.

Museum of History.

Museum of History of Religion and Atheism.

Museum of Natural History. The flora and fauna of the West Ukraine.

Museum of Ukrainian Art. A rich collection of works of Ukrainian painting, starting from icon painting of the fourteenth century. Applied art.

Picture Gallery. Works by Ukrainian, Russian, Soviet and foreign artists. The gallery contains over 10,000 works of art, some by Goya, Reubens, and Titian. Founded in 1907. It contains Ukrainian art from the sixteenth to twentieth centuries.

Museum of Ethnography and Handicraft.

Museum of Vernacular Architecture and Folkways.

Literary-Memorial Museum of Ivan Franko. The display is devoted to the life and activities of the celebrated Ukrainian writer and revolutionary.

Out-of-Town Excursion

Olessky Castle. The interior of a seventeenth-century castle. Displayed in the museum are West Ukrainian painting and sculpture of the eighteenth century. Distance from Lvov: 72 km. Tour duration: 6 hours.

Hotels

Intourist—First class, 4-stories, 98 rooms. Located in city center, 8 km. from airport. Telephone: 72-6751, 72-5952.

Lvov—First class. (Intourist rents part of space.) Located in city center, 6 km. from airport. Telephone: 79-2270.

Campsite

250 beds on a full-camping basis; area for 150 tourists' own tents; parking lot for 250 cars. 7 km. from city, 16 km. from airport. Telephone: 72-1373, 72-1473.

MINSK

The capital of the Byelorussian Soviet Socialist Republic. Located in the heart of the republic on the bank of the Svisloch River at an altitude of 900 feet above sea level. Its population is over 1,270,000. The climate is temperate continental. The average temperature in January is 21°F., in July 64°F.

Minsk was first mentioned in the chronicles in 1067 as a fortress of the Polotsk Principality.

Minsk is one of those cities of the USSR that suffered most during World War II (1941–45). In Byelorussia every fourth citizen died at the hands of the Nazi invaders, and in Minsk, every other one. Today Minsk is a beautiful modern city, a major industrial and cultural center of the Soviet Union.

Minsk has an opera and ballet threate, a circus, and a philharmonic orchestra.

Excursions

Sightseeing Tour of the City. Acquaintance with the main attractions of the city, a tour of the House-Museum of the 1st Congress of the Russian Social-Democratic Workers' Party and the Exhibition of Economic Achievements of the USSR.

Minsk in Sports. A thematic excursion including a visit to the Olympic Stadium "Dynamo."

State Museum of the Byelorussian SSR. The history and the present day of the republic, the flora and fauna of Byelorussia.

Exhibition of Economic Achievements of the Byelorussian SSR.

Museum of the History of the Great Patriotic War. The exhibits reflect the struggle of the Soviet people against the Nazi invaders, the feats of arms performed by Byelorussian partisans.

Literary Museums of Yanka Kupala and Yakub Kolas—the celebrated folk poets of Byelorussia.

Fine Arts Museum. Widely represented are specimens of Byelorussian folk art, paintings, sculptures, works of graphic and applied art by prominent Russian and Byelorussian masters.

Palace of Arts. Displayed are paintings, sculptures, works of graphic art, photographs, and books.

Museum of Old Byelorussian Culture. Fine fabrics, embroidery, folk costumes, ceramics, carved wood.

Out-of-Town Excursions

Khatyn Memorial. Erected on the site of the village of Khatyn—one of the 186 Byelorussian villages razed by the Nazis during World War II. Distance from Minsk: 59 km. Tour duration: 4 hours.

Mound of Glory. A monument to the Soviet soldiers and partisans who liberated Byelorussia from the Nazi invaders. Distance from Minsk: 21 km. Tour duration: 2½ to 3 hours.

Museum of Soviet-Polish Military Community. Located in the township of Lenino in the Mogilev Region 280 km. from Minsk.

Memorial Reserve of Yanka Kupala. Located in the village of Vyazynka— the poet's birthplace. Distance from Minsk: 45 km. Tour duration: 4 hours.

NOVOSIBIRSK

Novosibirsk stands on the banks of the great Siberian river Ob. The average temperature in January is $-3°F.$, in July, 66°F. It is the U.S.S.R.'s eighth largest city, containing 1.4 million people. The city largely owes its existence to Nikolai Garin-Mikhailovsky, the well-known Russian railway engineer and writer of the second half of the nineteenth century. In 1891-93 he built that part of the Trans-Siberian railway connecting the left and right banks of the Ob.

Novosibirsk today is an industrial giant, a city of science and culture. Its institutions of higher learning include Novosibirsk State University and the Glinka Conservatoire. On the bank of the river Kamenka towers the State Public and Technical Library containing more than five million volumes. It contains rare Arabian and Abyssinian manuscripts and books by Ivan Fyodorov, the pioneer of book printing in Russia.

The city's main thoroughfare is Krasny Prospekt, 6.7 miles long. Akademgorodok (Academic City), is the widely known Siberian branch of the U.S.S.R. Academy of Sciences. It stands on the shore of a large man-made sea formed by the giant Novosibirsk hydroelectric dam.

Excursions

Sightseeing Tour of the City. Introduces the main attractions of the city, its history and features.

State Opera and Ballet Theatre. The "Bolshoi Theatre of Siberia."

The Picture Gallery. Located on Sverdlov Square it has on display works by Ivan Shiskin, Vasily Tropinin, Ilya Kepin, and contemporary Soviet artists.

The Regional Lore Museum. Near the gallery, it will give you a good idea of Siberia's nature and economy, and plans for Siberia's development.

Hotel

Novosibirsk. First class, center of the city.

PETROZAVODSK

The capital of the Karelian Autonomous Soviet Socialist Republic. A port on the shore of Lake Onega. The population is over 240,000. The climate is temperate continental. The average temperature in January is 14°F., in July, 61°F. The city was founded in 1703. Petrozavodsk has the Russian Music-and-Drama Theatre, the Finnish Drama Theatre, and a philharmonic orchestra.

Excursions

Sightseeing Tour of the City.

Museum of Regional Studies.

Museum of Fine Arts. Painting, graphic art, icon painting, and sculpture.

Museum of Applied Art. The history of the development of Karelian applied art, articles of domestic use, costumes, and embroidery.

Out-of-Town Excursions

"Martsialniye Vody" Museum. Acquaintance with the first Russian health resort and a monument of wooden architecture of the early eighteenth century. Tasting of the local mineral water. Distance from Petrozavodsk: 60 km. Tour duration: 3 hours.

Kivach Reserve. A tour of the nature reserve and waterfall. Distance from Petrozavodsk: 85 km. Tour duration: 6 hours.

Kizhi Island. Museum of History, Architecture and Ethnography. An outstanding monument-ensemble of old Russian wooden architecture. An exhibition of old Russian painting (fifteenth to seventeenth centuries). Distance from Petrozvodsk: 67 km. Tour duration: 7 hours.

Hotels

Severnaya—First class, 3-stories. Intourist rents 60 beds. Located in city center. Telephone: 7-6354.

Karelia—First class, 10 stories. Intourist rents 35 beds. Located in city center. Telephone: 5-8897.

POLTAVA

Regional center of the Ukrainian Soviet Socialist Republic. Situated on the right bank of the Vorskla River (a tributary of the Dnieper). The population is more than 279,000. The climate is temperate continental. The average temperature in January is 20°F., in July, 69°F. The city was first mentioned in the chronicles in 1174. Poltava has a music-and-drama theatre and a philharmonic.

Excursions

Sightseeing Tour of the City.

Museum of Regional Studies. The history and nature of the Poltava Region. Among the exhibits are specimens of embroidery, carved wood, ceramics.

Museum of the History of the Battle of Poltava. The events of the Russian-Swedish War of 1700–1721. Displayed are arms of those days, documents, paintings, and works of graphic art dedicated to the battle (1709).

Fine Arts Museum. Ukrainian and Russian art of the eighteenth to twentieth centuries, works of Western European painting of the sixteenth to nineteenth centuries.

Memorial Museums of the Ukrainian writers Ivan Kotlyarevsky and Panas Mirny, and the celebrated Russian writer Vladmir Korolenko.

Museum-Estate of I. P. Kotlyarevsky. After restoration the house again has the appearance it used to have in the eighteenth century.

Motel

Poltava—First class, 3-stories, 102 rooms. Parking lot for 60 cars. 6 km. from city center. Telephone: 3-0024, 3-5747.

PSKOV

Regional center of the Russian Soviet Federation Socialist Republic. Located in the northwest of the republic not far from the Lake of Pskov. The population is over 180,000. The climate is temperate continental. The average temperature in January is 18°F., in July, 63°F. Pskov is one of the oldest Russian cities. It was first mentioned in the chronicles in 903. Pskov has a drama theatre.

Excursions

Sightseeing Tour of the City. Acquaintance with historical and architectural attractions. Among them are the Kremlin (fourteenth and fifteenth centuries), the Troitsky (Holy Trinity) Cathedral (17th century), churches of the fifteenth and sixteenth centuries, etc.

Historical, Architectural and Artistic Museum-Reserve. The history of the Pskov Region, old Russian paintings, frescoes, works of art in silver, Russian fine arts of the eighteenth and nineteenth centuries, Soviet paintings, and works of graphic art.

Out-of-Town Excursions

Excursion to Izborsk and Pechora. A tour of fortresses of the fourteenth and sixteenth centuries, and the Pskovo-Pechorsky Monastery. Distance to Izborsk: 32 km. Distance to Pechora: 54 km. Tour duration: 7 hours.

Pushkin's Hills. Mikhailovskoye. A tour of the Svyatogorsky Monastery (sixteenth century). The great Russian poet Alexander Pushkin was buried in the Assumption Cathedral of the Monastery.
Mikhailovskoye was the Pushkin's family estate. Here tourists visit the house-museum of the poet. Distance from Pskov: 130 km. Tour duration: 9½ hours.

Hotel

Rizhskaya—First class, 8 stories, 260 rooms. (Intourist rents part of space.) Located near city center. Telephone: 2-4301, 3-3243.

PYATIGORSK

A health-resort town in the Stavropol Region of the Russian Soviet Federative Socialist Republic. Located in the North Caucasus on the Podkumok River at an altitude of 1,722 feet above sea level. The population is over 150,000. The climate is temperate continental, warm. The average temperature in January is 25°F., in July, 72°F. The town was founded in 1780. Pyatigorsk ranks as a major health resort due to the abundance and diversity of its mineral springs. The town is the center of the famous Caucasian Mineral Spas health-resort region (Pyatigorsk, Kislovodsk, Zheleznovodsk, Yessentuki). Pyatigorsk has a musical comedy theatre, a summer theatre, and a philharmonic orchestra.

Excursions

Sightseeing Tour of the City.

Lermontov's Pyatigorsk (a thematic excursion). Acquaintance with the town's attractions associated with the great Russian poet Mikhail Lermontov's (1814–1841) sojourn in the town; a visit to the museum "Lermontov's Lodge."

Museum-Reserve of M. Yu. Lermontov.

Museum of Regional Studies. The nature and history of the North Caucasus. The museum's picture gallery displays canvasses by Russian and foreign painters of the eighteenth and nineteenth centuries.

Health-Resort Exhibition. The history of the development of the Caucasian Mineral Spas health-resort region.

Out-of-Town Excursions

Mt. Elbrus Region. A high-altitude climatic resort. A center of mountain skiing. Tourists have an opportunity to go by ski lift to an altitude of 10,171 feet to enjoy a panoramic view of Mt. Elbrus—the highest summit in Europe (18,510 feet). Distance from Pyatigorsk: 170 km. Tour duration: 12 hours.

Dombai Valley. A high altitude climatic resort. A mountain skiing center. Distance from Pyatigorsk: 225 km. Tour duration: 12 hours.

Health-Resort Town of Zheleznovodsk. Distance from Pyatigorsk: 25 km. Tour duration: 4 hours.

Hotels (Intourist rents part of space)

Mashuk—Tourist class, 4-stories, 262 beds. Located in city center, 30 km. from airport. Telephone: 5-3431, 5-2245.

Pyatigorsk—Tourist class, 5-stories, 118 beds. Located in city center, 30 km. from airport. Telephone: 5-6670, 5-2470.

Motel/Campsite

Volna—First class, five 2-storied lodges for a total capacity of 85 beds. The camp site has 25 summer houses, 28 tents, area for 35 tourists' own tents, and a parking lot for 60 cars. 38 km. from airport, 10 km. from city center. Telephone: 5-0582.

RIGA

The capital of the Latvian Soviet Socialist Republic. Located on the banks of the Daugava River not far from its influx into the Gulf of Riga of the Baltic Sea. The population is more than 850,000. The climate is transitory between oceanic and continental. The average temperature in January is 24°F., in July, 64°F. Riga is one of the oldest cities in the Soviet Baltic Republics. It was founded in 1201. Riga is a major seaport. Riga has an opera and ballet theatre, a drama theatre, a philharmonic orchestra, the Dome Concert Hall, and the Dzintari Concert Hall in the town of Jumala.

Excursions

Sightseeing Tour of the City.

Excursion Through the Parks and Gardens of Riga (arranged in summer for separate groups of tourists).

Literary Riga (a thematic excursion).

Museum of the Revolution of the Latvian SSR. The exhibits introduce the history of the Latvian people's struggle with czarist autocracy for the establishment of Soviet power.

V. I. Lenin Memorial Museum. Memorial Flat of V. I. Lenin. The exhibits are devoted to the life and activities of the founder of the Soviet state.

Museum of Red Latvian Riflemen. The Red Latvian Riflemen were active in the October Socialist revolution of 1917.

Museum of History of the Latvian SSR. One of the biggest historical museums in the USSR. The museum is housed in the Riga Castle built in 1330.

Latvian Ethnography Museum. The oldest museum of this type in the USSR (founded in 1924). The museum's collection includes monuments of rural architecture and domestic life of the sixteenth to nineteenth centuries.

Museum of Natural History of the Latvian SSR.

Observation Tower of St. Peter's Church. The tower's height is 236 feet. The church is an architectural monument of the thirteenth century.

Museum of the History of Medicine. The history of medicine of various peoples. An exhibition of space medicine.

Museum of the History of the Theatre of the Latvian SSR.

The Dome Cathedral. An outstanding architectural monument (built in 1211). The interior features carved wood and stone and splendid stained-glass panels. There is an organ in the cathedral.

Museum of Foreign Art. Masterpieces of classical, ancient Oriental, as well as modern Western and Oriental art.

Fine Arts Museum of the Latvian SSR. Founded in 1905. Displays works by Latvian, Russian, and Soviet masters of sculpture, painting, and graphic art.

Janis Rainis Museum of the History of Literature and Art. Materials on the history of Latvian literatue, theatre, music, and cinema. Exhibits devoted to the life and creative work of the celebrated Latvian poet Janis Rainis.

Out-of-Town Excursions

Salaspils. A memorial complex dedicated to the memory of tens of thousands of people of different nationalities who perished at the hands of the Nazis in the Salaspils concentration camp during World War II. Distance from Riga: 17 km. Tour duration: 3½ hours.

Resort-Town of Jurmala. One of the well-known USSR's health resorts. Distance from Riga: 20 km. Tour duration: 3½ hours.

Town of Siguida. Acquaintance with the history and present day of the town, architectural monuments of the Middle Ages, the Gauja National Park; a visit to the local museum of regional studies. Distance from Riga: 58 km. Tour duration: 7 hours.

Town of Ogre. Picturesque scenery in the Daugava and Ogre River Valleys. Visits to special interest sights and lunch at an out-of-town restaurant. Distance from Riga: 40 km. Tour duration: 7 hours.

Saulkrasti. Scenic beauties of the Vidzemskoye seashore. The excursion's program includes a visit to a collective fishery, rest on a beach, and lunch at an out-of-town restaurant. Distance from Riga: 48 km. Tour duration: 7 hours.

Town of Ainazi. Museum of the history of high-seas navigation, a visit to a collective fishery, and lunch at an out-of-town restaurant. Distance from Riga: 100 km. Tour duration: 7 hours.

Hotel

Latvia—First class, 26 stories, 365 rooms. Located in city center, 16 km. from airport. Telephone: 21-1781.

SAMARKAND

Samarkand is located in the Uzbek Soviet Socialist Republic. The city lies in the Zeravshan River valley at an altitude of 2,300 feet, and has a population of about 520,000 people. Founded in the fifth century B.C., the city is about 2,500 years old. Here kingdoms emerged, flourished and quickly died away owing to the fame and prosperity of the city that attracted conquerors. Alexander the Great conquered it in 329 B.C. Genghis Khan destroyed it in 1220. Tamerlane, a Tartar leader, conquered the city in the fourteenth century and made it the capital of his empire. The Tartars brought to the city their plunder and tribute paid to them.

In the eighth century Samarkand became a center of Moslem culture. Many mosques, minarets, and Muslim schools *(medresehs)* are found in the city.

Samarkand is really two cities—the old and the new. Ancient trade routes connected the city with China and India, one of which was the famed "silk road." The new city was built after 1868, the date of the Russian conquest. Many mausoleums and old tombs can be seen.

Samarkand's industries include wine making, shoe manufacture, machine building, carpet and rug weaving, silk weaving and spinning, and canning and processing of agricultural goods. The city developed rapidly beginning in 1896 when the Krasnovodsk-Tashkent railway reached it.

Samarkand has both Russian and Uzbek theatres, including an opera and ballet theatre.

Excursions

Sightseeing Tour of the City. Introduces the past and present of Samarkand and the Uzbek people.

Registan Square. A good example of city planning. Around it are many of the city's celebrated *medresehs* or Muslim schools, including the Ulug Beg (dating from the early 1400s); Shirdah (early 1600s); and Tilla Kari (mid-seventeenth century).

Bibi-Khanym Mosque. Built in the fourteenth and fifteenth centuries. A Chinese wife of Tamerlane is credited with building it. This crumbling mosque has a huge archway.

Gur Emir Mausoleum. Built in the fifteenth century. It is the resting place of Tamerlane and his grandson Ulug Beg.

Ulug Beg Observatory. An astronomer, mathematician, and philosopher, Ulug Beg made many discoveries in this largest astronomical observatory of the Middle Ages.

Shah Zinda Mosque. Dates from about 1350.

Out-of-Town Excursions

Intourist arranges trips from Samarkand to Pendjikent, a town in the valley of the Zeravshan River in nearby Tajik Soviet Socialist Republic.

Hotel

Samarkand. 11-story Intourist hotel, 154 rooms.

SHAKHRISABZ

A town in the Uzbek Soviet Socialist Republic. Located in the foothills of the Zeravshan Range at an altitude of 2,159 feet above sea level. The climate is continental. The average temperature in January is 33°F., in July, 82°F.
The town was founded in the thirteenth century.

Excursions

Sightseeing Tour of the City. A tour of the monuments to the past. Among them are the remains of the Ak-Sarai Palace (1380–1404), the mausoleum of Jehanghir (fourteenth and fifteenth centuries), the Chor-su covered market typical of Central Asia (fifteenth century), a town bath (fifteenth century), a mosque, and other ancient structures.

Khujun Handicraft Factory. Carpets and the traditional headdress of the Uzbek people—tyubeteikas (skullcaps worn in Central Asia)—are made here.

Silk Spinning Mill.

Winery.

Out-of-Town Excursion

A trip to the recreation area. Tea-drinking. Distance from Shakhrisabz: 22 km. Tour duration: 3½ hours.

Hotel

Shakhrisabz—First class, 2 stories, 63 rooms. Located in city center. Telephone: 38-61.

SHEKI

A town in the Azerbaijan Soviet Socialist Republic. Located in the northwestern part of the republic on the slope of the main Caucasian range at an altitude of 2,215 feet above sea level. The population is over 55,000. The climate is warm. The average temperature in January is 33°F., in July, 73°F.

Sheki, one of the most ancient towns of the Transcaucasia, is about 2,500–2,600 years old. Sheki has a drama theatre. The city is renowned for its pottery, jewelry, silk, chased utensils, and carpets.

Excursions

Sightseeing Tour of the City. An excursion along the main streets and squares of the town, a trip to the recreation area, a visit to one or two museums.

Museum of Regional Studies.

Museum of the Combat and Revolutionary Fame.

House-Museum of M.F. Akhundov. Dedicated to the classic of Azerbaijan literature. Akhundov was a well-known nineteenth-century playwright and philosopher.

Palace of the Sheki Khans. The architectural monument of the eighteenth century.

Hotel

Sheki—First class, 9-stories. Intourist rents 32 rooms. Located in city center. Telephone: 24-88, 36-75.

SMOLENSK

Regional center of the Russian Soviet Federative Socialist Republic. Located on the banks of the Upper Dnieper. The average temperature in January is 16°F., in July 63°F.

Smolensk is one of the most ancient Russian cities. It dates back to 863. The Smolensk Drama Theatre is one of the oldest in the country (inaugurated in 1780). The city also has a puppet theater and a philharmonic.

Excursions

Sightseeing Tour of the City. Includes a visit to the amusement and recreation park (built in 1872), where a monument to the Smolensk defenders from Napoleon's army in the battle of August 4–5, 1812, is located, and the Garden of Memory of the Heroes of the Patriotic War of 1812 and the Great Patriotic War of the Soviet Union. A tour of historical and architectural monuments: the Cathedral of the Assumption (seventeenth and eighteenth centuries) and the King's Bulwark (seventeenth century).

Historical, Architectural, and Artistic Museum-Preserve. The history and culture of the Smolensk Region from the ancient times. Decorative and applied art of the sixteenth to nineteenth centuries. An exhibition of works by well-known Soviet sculptor Sergei Konenkov.

Art Gallery. Works of Russian, Soviet, and Western European art.

Planetarium.

Out-of-Town Excursion

Museum of Folk Art "Teremok" in the township of Flenovo. Displayed are lace, embroidery, carved wood, paintings, fragments of architectural ornaments, and articles of domestic use. Distance from Smolensk: 18 km.

Hotel

Tsentrainaya—First class, 5-stories, 336 beds. (Intourist rents part of space.) Located in city center. Telephone: 3-3604.

Campsite

Khvoiny—15 km. from Smolensk, 15 bungalows for 100 beds; 25 tents; area for 100 tourists' own tents. Parking lot for 100 cars. Telephone: 3-4906.

Hotel/Motel

Phoenix—First class, 202 beds. 14½ km. from Smolensk. Telephone: 2-1488.

SOCHI

A city in the Krasnodar Region of the Russian Soviet Federative Socialist Republic, the USSR's biggest balneal, mud cure, and climatic resort. Sochi has 200 days of sunshine a year. Bathing lasts from May until November. Located in the North Caucasus on the Black Sea coast (length along the coastline, almost 150 km.). The population is over 300,000. The climate is subtropical steppe. The average temperature in January is 43°F., in July, 70°F. to 82°F. Sochi is a major seaport. Many gardens and parks dot the city.

The ancient Romans knew Sochi and the waters of its springs. The first sanatoria were built in the city in 1902. Along the seacoast of the city is Riveria Park, which contains the Alley of Writers with its many busts of Soviet and Russian writers, and trees planted by Soviet and American astronauts.

Intourist's motor route "The Great Caucasian Ring" extending for 3,200 km. (Moscow-Kharkov-Rostov-on-Don-Krasnodar-Sochi-Sukhumi-Tbilisi-Ordzhonikidze-Pyatigorsk-Rostov-on-Don-Kharkov-Moscow) passes through Sochi.

The city was founded in 1838, the resort in 1909. Sochi has several theatres, a philharmonic orchestra, and a circus. The country's finest theatre, music, and dance companies come here on tour.

Excursions

Sightseeing Tour of the City.

Sochi, a City of International Friendship (a thematic excursion).

Sochi, a Garden-City (a thematic excursion).

Dendrarium. Hundreds of species of trees and shrubs representing the flora of the Black Sea coast of the Caucasus and different countries of the world grow here.

Excursion to Mt. Akhun. (1.12 km. above sea level) An observation tower gives a good view of Sochi below and the Caucasus Mountains. Russian and Caucasian cuisine are served at the Akhun Restaurant on top of the mountain.

Excursion to the Dagomys Tea-Growing State Farm. Acquaintance with the development of agriculture, tasting of tea. (Dagomys is the home of Russian tea.)

Museum of the History of the Resort-City of Sochi.

Memorial Museum of N.A. Ostrovsky. The exhibits are devoted to the life and creative work of the noted Soviet writer.

Exhibition Hall. Works by Russian and Soviet artists, exhibits from Leningrad's Russian Museum, Western European art of the thirteenth to nineteenth centuries.

Out-of-Town Excursions

Yew-and-Boxtree Grove. A unique relic grove. Distance from Sochi: 20 km. Tour duration: 11 hours.

Lake Ritsa, the Resort-Town of Gagra. Distance from Sochi: 120 km. Tour duration: 11 hours.

City of Sukhumi. The capital of the Abkhazian Autonomous Soviet Socialist Republic. A seaport, a popular health resort of Georgia. Distance from Sochi: 150 km. Tour duration: 12 hours by motorcoach or ship.

Health Resort of Pitsunda. A wonderful corner of natural scenery of the Black Sea coast. Distance from Sochi: 80 km. Tour duration: 8 hours.

Novy Afon. A resort town. A visit to a karst cave. Distance from Sochi: 140 km. Tour duration: 11 hours.

Park of the "Yuzhniye Kultury" State Farm. Subtropical plants of the Caucasus. Distance from Sochi: 20 km. Tour duration: 3 hours.

Hotels

Dagomys Tourist Complex—Includes the hotels "Dagomys" (27-stories, 1,015 rooms), "Olympiyskaya" (8-stories, 231 rooms), and the "Meridian" motel (six 2-story buildings, 115 rooms, a covered car park). 20 km. from city center. 43 km. from airport. Telephone: 32-1600, 32-2595.

Intourist-Kamelia Hotel Complex—First class. Includes the hotels "Intourist" (4 stories, 97 rooms) and "Kamelia" (11 stories, 180 rooms). 31 km. from airport, 7 km. from city center. Telephone: 99-0590, 99-0292.

Zhemchuzhina—International class, 19 stories, 953 rooms. 33 km. from airport, 2 km. from city center. Telephone: 92-2388, 92-4355.

Intourist also rents part of space at the hotels "Caucasus," "Khosta," "Leningrad," "Moscow," "Sochi-Magnolia," "Priboy-Gorizont," as well as at the tourist hotels "Svetlana" and "Frigate" and at the sanatorium "Zarya."

STAVROPOL

The center of the Stavropol Region of the Russian Soviet Federative Socialist Republic. Located in the North Caucasus. The population is over 260,000. The climate is continental. The average temperature in January is 25°F., in July 72°F. to 77°F.

The city was founded in 1777. Stavropol has a drama theatre founded in 1845, a philharmonic, and a circus.

Excursions

Museum of Regional Studies. The history and the present day of the

Stavropol Region—an important agricultural area of the country. Among the exhibits are works of ancient art, ancient weapons and coins. Of world significance are paleontological exhibits, such as a skeleton of the southern elephant, which became extinct more than a million years ago, a skeleton of the fossil rhinoceros, a collection of petrified imprints of insects of the Tertiary Period.

Museum of Fine Arts. Works by Russian and Western European artists of the seventeenth to nineteenth centuries, an exhibition of works by Stavropol's artists, traveling exhibitions formed out of exhibits from the leading art museums of the country as well as foreign museums.

Out-of-Town Excursions

Strizhament Nature Reserve. Strizhament is a mountain (2,730 feet) whose plant life is representative of the flora of all the natural zones of the Stavropol Region. Distance from Stavropol: 20 km. Tour duration: 3 hours.

Teberda and the Dombai Valley. Famous high-altitude climatic resorts, nature reserves of the North Caucasus. Distance from Stavropol: 245 km. Tour duration: 2 days.

Excursions to Collective and State Farms of the Stavropol Region. Distance from Stavropol: 20 to 165 km. Tour duration: 3 to 7 hours.

Hotel

Caucasus—First class, 6-stories, 300 rooms. (Intourist rents part of space.) Located in city center. Telephone: 3-2366, 3-9561.

SUZDAL

A town in the Vladimir Region of the Russian Soviet Federative Socialist Republic. Located 26 km. from the city of Vladimir and 220 km. northeast of Moscow. The climate is continental. The average temperature in January is 12°F., in July, 64°F. Suzdal is one of the most ancient Russian towns. It was first mentioned in the chronicles in 1024.

Excursions

Sightseeing Tour of the City. Acquaintance with attractions of the town where about 100 architectural monuments have survived; a visit to the local museums.

Cathedral of the Nativity of Our Lady. Frescoes of the thirteenth to seventeenth centuries, works of decorative and applied art.

Arkhiyereyskiye Palaty. (Bishop's Chambers). A unique monument of Russian residential architecture of the fifteenth to seventeenth centuries. The museum's exhibits reflect the history of Suzdal, old Russian icon painting (icons of the thirteenth to seventeenth centuries), and interior decoration of the seventeenth century.

Former Convent of the Intercession. Narrative about the life of nuns.

An Outer-City House. An exceptional specimen of stone residential architecture of the seventeenth century.

Museum of Wooden Architecture and Rural Life.

Carved Wood Exhibition at the former Church of Resurrection.

Out of Town Excursion

Village of Kideksha. A former place of residence of the founder of Moscow, Prince Yuri Dolgoruky. The Cathedral of St. Boris and Gleb—the oldest whitestone structure of North-Eastern Rus (1152). Distance from Suzdal: 4 km. Tour duration: 1½ hours.

Hotels

Suzdal—First class, 2-stories, 404 beds. (Intourist rents part of space.) 4 km. from town. Telephone: 2-1137.

Pokrovskaya—First class, 13 rooms, and 32 beds in log cabins. 4 km. from town. Telephone: 2-0131.

TALLINN

The capital of the Estonian Soviet Socialist Republic. Located on the shore of the Gulf of Finland of the Baltic Sea. The population is over 470,000. The climate is transitory between oceanic and continental. The average temperature in January is 27°F., in July 63°F.

The first written mention of Tallinn dates back to 1154.

Tallinn is a treasure trove of fine monuments of medieval architecture.

Tallinn is actually two cities in one. The old city (Toompea) is located on a limestone plateau, while the principal part of Tallinn is built on the lowlands along the coast. Modern Tallinn is a seaport and industrial center. Kadriorg, a large city park, contains a cottage built by Peter the Great in 1714. The walls and towers of the old city date from the thirteenth to eighteenth centuries. The fortified gates, towers, and bastions give the city a medieval appearance. The old Oleviste church (thirteenth to sixteenth centuries) has an imposing tower and spire which overlooks the city.

Tallinn has six theatres and a philharmonic orchestra.

Excursions

Excursion to the Old City. A tour of the Toompea Castle, the city wall and towers, and Town Hall Square.

Excursion to New Residential Districts.

Museum of Ethnography in Rocca-al-Mare (in summer). A tour of monuments of wooden architecture.

Kadriorg-Pirita Recreational Area including a visit to the Mariamagi memorial complex dedicated to the struggle of the Estonians for the establishment of Soviet power, the fine arts museum, the song field where imposing song festivals are held and the yachting center.

Fine Art Museum. Housed in the Kadriorg Palace (eighteenth century). Estonian art, Western European painting.

Museum of the Theatre and Music. Estonian art of the theatre and music. A collection of old musical instruments.

Museum of the City. Tallinn from the ancient times to the present day.

Kiek in de Kok (Peep into the Kitchen) Gun Tower. One of the old city strongholds. Displayed in the tower is a collection of medieval weapons.

Monastery of Dominicans. An architectural monument of the fourteenth century.

Town Hall. Acquaintance with the history of the city's administration. Built in the fourteenth to fifteenth centuries, the two-story structure has an elegant tower and spire on it.

Lodge-Museum of Peter the Great (early eighteenth century). Visits are arranged only in summer.

Naval Museum. The history of Estonian navigation and fishing from the ancient times.

Museum of Applied Art.

Out-of-Town Excursions

Town of Parnu. Distance from Tallinn: 125 km. Tour duration: 12 hours (with an overnight).

City of Viljandi. Distance from Tallinn: 147 km. Tour duration: 12 hours (without overnight stay).

Town of Tartu. (Distance from Tallinn: 187 km. Tour duration: 12 hours (without overnight stay).

Hotels

Viru—International class, 22-stories, 458 rooms. Located in city center, 6 km. from airport. Telephone: 65-2070, 65-2081, 42-1514.

Tallinn—First class, 5 stories, 113 rooms. Located in city center, 7 km. from airport. Telephone: 44-1504.

Olympia—International class, 26-stories, 424 rooms. (Intourist rents part of space.) Located in city center, 7 km. from airport. Telephone: 60-1768, 60-2346.

Campsite (Intourist rents part of space)

Located 8 km. from city center, 10 km. from airport. 100 beds in summer cabins. Parking lot for 150 cars. Telephone: 23-8786.

TASHKENT

The capital of the Uzbek Soviet Socialist Republic, which lies in the central part of Central Asia. Ranks fourth in size (population, about 2,000,000) in the USSR after Moscow, Leningrad, and Kiev. The city is located in the Chirchik River Valley at an altitude of 1,575 feet above sea level. The climate is continental. The average temperature in January, the coldest month, is 30°F., July, the warmest, 82°F.

Tashkent is one of the most ancient cities of Central Asia. It has existed for over 2,000 years. In the Middle Ages Tashkent was on the crossing of caravan tracks from Europe to Asia. Today Tashkent is considered one of the most beautiful cities of the USSR. It is a major tourist destination. The city has nine theatres among which is the Alisher Navoi Opera and Ballet Theatre (architect, Alexei Shchusev). The building of the theatre took into account national traditions and is an architectural attraction of the city. A severe earthquake hit it in 1966.

Every two years the traditional cinema festival of the countries of Asia, Africa, and Latin America is held in Tashkent. Its slogan is "For peace, social progress, and freedom of the peoples."

The city gives one the impression of a vast flourishing garden, so green are its streets lined with tall plane trees, poplars, acacias, oaks, elms, and maples standing among the irrigation ditches, locally called *aryks.*

The heart of the republic's scientific life is the Uzbek SSR Academy of Sciences with its dozens of research institutes. The city's large public library, named after Alisher Navoi, a well-known poet of the past, contains four million volumes. Tashkent is a major industrial center, most prominent in engineering. Textiles and agricultural machinery are manufactured here. Surrounding the city are fields of cotton, vineyards, and orchards.

Excursions

Sightseeing Tour of the City. Introduces the history of Tashkent and the republic, with the Uzbek people's achievements in all spheres of life. Apart from seeing the present-day architectural attractions of the city, the tour includes acquaintance with the monuments of ancient Uzbek architecture—

the Kukeldash Madrasah (sixteenth century), and the Jami Mosque (fifteenth century).

Branch of the Central V.I. Lenin Museum. During the excursion, tourists are introduced to the life and activities of the founder of the Soviet State, Vladimir Ilyich Lenin, and to the revolutionary movement in Uzbekistan.

Exhibition of Economic Achievements of the Uzbek SSR.

Museum of the History of the Peoples of Uzbekistan. This display is devoted to the history of Uzbekistan from the ancient times to the present day.

Museum of Applied Art of Uzbekistan. State Museum of Fine Arts. The museum displays exhibits describing the development of art of the classical and medieval periods, the Uzbek applied art, modern fine arts of Uzbekistan, Russian painting and sculpture, as well as Western European and Oriental art.

Out-of-Town Excursions

Leninsky Put (Lenin's Course) Collective Farm. Acquaintance with the republic's agriculture and the development of its main branch—cotton growing. Distance from Tashkent: 30 km. Tour duration: 3 hours.

Chimgan and Ak-Tash Recreation Areas. Acquaintance with the organization of rest and recreation for the working people of the republic. Distance from Tashkent: 95 km. and 75 km. respectively. Tour duration: 9 hours.

Tashkent Sea. Acquaintance with the successes of Uzbekistan in irrigation. Distance from Tashkent: 50 km. Tour duration: 6 hours.

Hotel

Uzbekistan—First class, 17-stories, 479 rooms. Located in city center, 10 km. from airport. Telephone: 33-3959.

TBILISI

The capital of the Georgian Soviet Socialist Republic. Located in the southeast of the republic on the banks of the mountain river Kura at an altitude of about 1,558 feet above sea level. The population is over 1,066,000. The climate is temperate continental. The average temperature in January is 33°F., in July 75°F.

The first mention of the city dates back to the fourth century.

Tbilisi has seven theatres, a philharmonic orchestra, a circus, and Intourist's cultural center.

Excursions

Sightseeing Tour of the City.

Thematic city sightseeing tours.

Historic-Revolutionary Places in Tbilisi.

Tbilisi in Literature.

Tbilisi in Sports.

Tbilisi in Architecture (the Metekhi Cathedral, thirteenth century; the Narikala Fortress, fourth century; the Cathedral Church, sixth century; modern housing developments).

Old Tbilisi (a tour of the old city; houses and a cathedral of the fourth century).

Dzhanashia State Museum of Georgia. The republic's biggest repository of historical exhibits.

Tbilisi Branch of the Central V.I. Lenin Museum.

Fine Arts Museum of Georgia. Paintings, works in repousse, jewelry, and other masterpieces of Georgian art beginning from the fourth century.

Museum of History and Ethnography.

Museum of Georgian Vernacular Architecture and Folkways.

Art Gallery. Periodical exhibitions of works by Soviet and foreign artists.

House-Museum of the Bolshevist Underground Printery. The printery operated from 1903 to 1906.

Museum of the Friendship of the Peoples. The display tells about the united family of the peoples of the USSR.

Out-of-Town Excursions

Town of Mtsaheta. From the fifth to the second half of the fourth century B.C. Mtskheta was the capital of Iberia—the ancient Georgian state. A tour of the Dzhvari and Svetitskhoveli Temples (sixth century). Distance from Tbilisi: 70 km.

Gori. An old town, the home of Joseph Stalin (his house-museum is here). The tour includes visits to Mtskheta, the Dzhvari Temple, and the cave town of Uplistsikhe (sixth to first centuries B.C.). Distance from Tbilisi: 118 km.

Village of Pasanauri (includes visits to Mtskheta and the Dzhvari Temple). A tour of a castle of the sixteenth and seventeenth centuries. Distance from Tbilisi: 100 km.

Village of Kazbegi and the Krestovy Pass (17,858 feet above sea level). The birthplace of the prominent Georgian writer Alexander Kazbegi. (His house-museum is here.) The architectural attraction of the village is the Tsminda Sameba (Holy Trinity) Temple (fourteenth century). Distance from Tbilisi: 118 km.

Intourist also arranges one- and two-day excursions from Tbilisi to the cities of *Ordzhonikidze* (the capital of North Ossetia), *Borzhomi* (a mineral spa), *Bakuriani* (a center of mountain skiing), and *Telavi* (an ancient town that has historic-architectural monuments from the sixth to the nineteenth centuries).

Hotels

Iveria—First class, 22-stories, 288 rooms. Located in city center, 22 km. from airport. Telephone: 93-0695, 93-0488.

Adzharia—First class, 22 stories, 300 rooms. 2 km. to city center, 25 km. from airport. Telephone: 36-2716, 36-9822.

Tbilisi—First class, in operation since 1915, 5 stories, 115 rooms. Located in city center, 22 km. from airport. Telephone: 99-7866, 99-7829.

Hotel/Motel

Ushba—First class, 4 stories, 68 rooms. 11 km. from city center, 30 km. from airport. Telephone: 51-4922, 51-1681.

TELAVI

District center of the Georgian Soviet Socialist Republic. Located 180 km. from Tbilisi, the capital of Georgia, in the Alazani River Valley. The climate is temperate continental. The average temperature in January is 32°F., in July, 73°F.

The famous Kakhetian wines are produced in Telavi. The town was founded in the first century B.C. In the eleventh and seventeenth to eighteenth centuries it was the capital of the Kakhetian Czardom. Telavi has a drama theatre.

Excursions

Sightseeing Tour of the City. Acquaintance with the local attractions, including the palace of Irakli II; a visit to the museum of history and ethnography and the art gallery.

Out-of-Town Excursions

The Ikalto Monastery (eighth to ninth centuries), **the Alaverdi Cathedral** (eleventh century), **the Dzveli Shuamta** (fifth to seventh centuries) and **Akhali Shuamta** (sixteenth century) **Monasteries.** The Ikalto Monastery, the academy founded it in the eleventh century, is where the great Georgian poet Shota Rustaveli was educated.

Hotel

Kakheti—First class, 258 beds. Telephone: 34-06.

ULYANOVSK

Regional center of the Russian Soviet Federative Socialist Republic. Located on the Volga in its middle course at the influx of the Sviyaga River into the Volga. The population is over 500,000. The climate is extreme continental. The average temperature in January is 7°F., in July, 72°F.

The city was founded in 1648. Its former name was Simbirsk.

The founder of the Soviet State, Vladimir Ilyich Ulyanov (Lenin), was born in Simbirsk on April 22, 1870.

Ulyanovsk has a drama theatre.

Excursions

Sightseeing Tour of the City. Acquaintance with the history of Ulyanovsk and its present day and with those places in the city that are associated with Lenin.

Lenin Memorial. Dedicated to the life and activities of Lenin. On the territory of the Memorial are the *House-Museum of the Ulyanov Family* and the *Museum of Gifts Presented to Ulyanovsk, the hometown of Lenin.* A film about Lenin is shown at the Memorial.

House-Museum of V.I. Lenin. Lenin spent his childhood and adolescent years in this house.

Secondary School No. 1. Here, in the former gymnasium, Lenin was educated.

Fine Arts Museum. Works by Russian, Soviet, and foreign artists; traveling exhibitions.

Art Gallery "Lenin in Fine Arts."

Museum of Regional Studies.

Motor-Launch Trip along the Volga.

Hotel

Venets—First class, 23 stories, 988 beds. (Intourist rents part of space.)

Located in city center. Telephone: 9-4595.

URGENCH

The center of the Khorezm Region of the Uzbek Soviet Socialist Republic. Located in the southwest of the republic on the bank of the Amu Darya River. The population is over 100,000. The climate is extreme continental with the average temperature in January 23°F. and in July 83°F. The city sprang up in the second half of the seventeenth century. Urgench has a drama theatre.

Excursions

Narimanov Collective Farm. Acquaintance with the region's agriculture and everyday life of the villagers. Distance from Urgench: 40 km. Tour duration: 4 hours.

City of Khiva. Acquaintance with one of the most ancient cities of Central Asia (Khiva was founded in the sixth to eighth centuries). Its historical and architectural attractions include madrasahs, mausoleums, and other structures of the fourteenth to nineteenth centuries. Distance from Urgench: 32 km. Tour duration: 6 hours.

Museum of Khiva.

Museum of the History of Khorezm of the Soviet Period.

Museum of the History of Medicine of Ancient Khorezm. Among the exhibits are outstanding works by the scientists and physicians of ancient Khorezm ibn-Sina and Biruni.

Museum of Applied Art. Repousse work, carved wood and ganch (a kind of gypsum), marble, and carpets.

Museums of Natural History. The flora and fauna of the Khorezm Region.

Hotel

Khorezm—First class, 2 stories, 63 rooms. Located in city center, 5 km.

from airport. Telephone: 6-5408.

UZHGOROD

The center of the Transcarpathian Region of the Ukrainian Soviet Socialist Republic. Located in the foothills of the Carpathians on the Uzh River on the border between the USSR and Czechoslovakia. The population is over 96,000. The climate is mild. The average temperature in January is 28°F., July, 75°F.

Uzhgorod is one of the most ancient cities in the Ukraine. It was first mentioned in the chronicles in 903.

Uzhgorod has the Ukrainian Music-and-Drama Theatre, a philharmonic orchestra, and an Intourist cultural center.

Excursions

Sightseeing Tour of the City. Acquaintance with the past and present of the city. A tour of the central squares, a medieval castle, the Mound of Glory, the Avangard Stadium.

Museum of Regional Studies. The history and nature of Transcarpathia. Articles of bronze, embroidery, carved wood, ceramics, manuscripts, and old printed books.

Fine Arts Museum. Has sections of Russian, Ukrainian, Soviet, Western European art, and the Transcarpathian school of painting.

Museum of Vernacular Architecture and Folkways. Located by the medieval castle. Transcarpathian village of the eighteenth to early twentieth centuries.

Out-of-Town Excursions

Town of Mukachevo. Acquaintance with the region's industry and agriculture and its natural scenery. Distance from Uzhgorod: 45 km. Tour duration: 3 hours.

Veretsky Pass. One of the most scenic spots of the Carpathians. Distance from Uzhgorod: 120 km. Tour duration: 10 hours.

Nevitskoye. Acquaintance with a recreational area of the working people of Uzhgorod, a visit to the Verkhovina international youth tourist camp and to the ruins of a medieval castle. Distance from Uzhgorod: 15 km. Tour duration: 4 hours.

Hotel

Zakarpatye—First class, 14-stories, 309 rooms. 2 km. from city center. Telephone: 9-7504, 9-7140.

VILNIUS

The capital of the Lithuanian Soviet Socialist Republic. Located in the southeast of Lithuania in the valley of the Neris River—the right side tributary of the Neman River at an altitude of 328 feet above sea level. The population is over 500,000. The climate is temperate continental. The average temperature in January is 23°F., in July, 53°F.

The first mention of Vilnius in the chronicles dates back to 1323. Vilnius in Lithuanian means "Amber Land." Its setting is one of rolling hills. The city has both an old and new district, with the old quarter lying below the ruins of Castle Hill. More than two dozen Roman Catholic churches in addition to those of Protestant, Orthodox, and others are found in Vilnius. The old churches present a variety of architecture, many of which were built in the seventeenth century. Napoleon visited and admired the small St. Anne's Church in 1812. From 1377 until 1710 the city suffered repeated invasions and was beset with a plague in 1588 and a fire in 1610. Beginning in 1915, Germans, Russians, and Poles took turns occupying the city. In 1944 the Russians seized it from the Germans.

Vilnius has an opera and ballet theatre, a puppet theatre, a philharmonic orchestra, and the Palace of Sports.

Excursions

Sightseeing Tour of the City. Introduces the history and present day of Vilnius, new residential districts of the city, its architectural and sculptural monuments.

Lithuanian SSR Museum of the Revolution. This display is devoted to the history of the revolutionary movement in Lithuania, the struggle of the

Lithuanian people against the Nazi invaders, and the working people's achievements in the national economy.

Lithuanian SSR Museum of History and Ethnography. Introduces the history and culture of the Lithuanian people beginning from the Stone Age.

Museum of the Vilnius Castle (the Castle of Gediminas). The castle of Gediminas (the founder of Vilnius) is the only tower of the upper castle ensemble (fifteenth century) that has survived to this day. The display reflects the history of Vilnius castles.

Fine Arts Museum. Displayed are works of Lithuanian art of the nineteenth and twentieth centuries. The museum has several branches: the Art Gallery, the Palace of Art Exhibitions, the Section of Folk Art.

Lithuanian SSR Museum of Atheism.

Cathedral of Sts. Peter and Paul. An architectural monument of the seventeenth century.

Out-of-Town Excursions

City of Kaunas. Acquaintance with one of the most ancient cities of Lithuania, with its attractions. Kaunas has many interesting museums, including the Museum of History, the Museum of the Ninth Fort (the Nazis tortured to death tens of thousands of prisoners-of-war and civilians in this fort during World War II), the Kaunas Castle (fourteenth century), the Fine Arts Museum, the Gallery of Sculpture and Stained Glass, the Museum of Works, and Collections of A. Zmuidzinavicius. Distance from Vilnius: 100 km. Tour duration: 1 day (without overnight stay).

Town of Trakai. The ancient capital of Lithuania. A visit to the museum of the town's history. The museum is housed in the Trakai Castle (fifteenth century). Distance from Vilnius: 25 km. Tour duration: 5 hours.

Museum of Folkways in the Village of Rumsiskes. The most interesting specimens of vernacular architecutre and rural life of the late eighteenth and early nineteenth century are gathered here. Concerts of a folk music ensemble are arranged in the museum. Distance from Vilnius: 80 km. Tour duration: 7 hours.

Village of Pirciupiai. Like the village of Oradour-sur-Glane in France or Lidice in Czechoslovakia, the village of Pirciupiai was razed by the Nazis in 1944. The exhibits of the local museum depict these events. Distance from Vilnius: 44 km. Tour duration: 6 hours.

Town of Druskininkai. A health resort. The house-museum of the prominent Lithuanian painter and composer Mikaloius Ciurlionis is in this town. Distance from Vilnius: 165 km. Tour duration: 15 hours.

Hotels (Intourist rents part of space)

Vilnius—Tourist class, 4-stories, 86 rooms. 9 km. from airport. Telephone: 62-3665, 69-1394.

Gintaras—First class, 5-stories, 197 rooms, 1½ km. from city center, 6 km. from airport. Telephone: 63-4496.

Neringa—First class, 4-stories, 34 rooms. Located in city center, 9 km. from airport. Telephone: 61-0516.

Turistas—First class, 7-stories, 120 rooms. Located in city center, 10 km. from airport. Telephone: 73-3002, 73-3106.

YAROSLAVL

Regional center of the Russian Soviet Federative Socialist Republic. Located on the Upper Volga. The population is over 600,000. The climate is temperate continental. The average temperature in January is 13°F., in July, 64°F. Yaroslavl is one of the most ancient Russian cities.

Yaroslavl's history began with the Slavic settlement of Medvezhi Ugol, which was located on its site in the ninth cenutry. Yaroslavl the Wise conquered the city in 1010 and gave it his name. The city became part of the State of Muscovy in 1463. During the seventeenth century it was a significant trading center, but with the rise of St. Petersburg in the eighteenth century it lost much of its importance. Today the city has chemical and rubber industries and a huge oil refinery.

Yaroslavl has some of the oldest churches in Russia, including the Church of the Dormition (1215) and those of the Transfiguration of Our Saviour Monastery (1216–18).

The Yaroslavl Drama Theatre, named after F. G. Volkov, is the first Russian national theatre (founded in 1750).

Excursions

Sightseeing Tour of the City. Includes a tour of architectural monuments of the sixteenth to eighteenth centuries and of new residential districts.

Historical and Architectural Museum-Reserve. Founded in 1864. Displays icon painting and applied art of the sixteenth to nineteenth centuries, as well as exhibits relating to the history and present day of the region.

Fine Arts Museum. Portrait painting of the eighteenth and nineteenth centuries, a collection of works by prominent Russian masters, works by Yaroslavl artists. The museum has a *Section of Old Russian and Applied Art*. This section is housed in the building of the former Metropolitan's Chambers (seventeenth century). The display includes Yaroslavl painting of the thirteenth–eighteenth centuries, and titles of the seventeenth to nineteenth centuries.

Church of Elijah the Prophet. An architectural monument of the seventeenth century. Frescoes of the seventeenth century and a wooden iconostasis of the eighteenth century.

Out-of-Town Excursions

Museum-Estate of N. A. Nekrasov in the village of Karabikha. The exhibits are devoted to the life and creative work of the progressive Russian poet of the nineteenth century. Nekrosov was a famous Russian poet and writer of the nineteenth century. Distance from Yaroslavl: 16 km. Tour duration: 3 hours.

Town of Rostov. Historic-Architectural and Fine Arts Museum. The Museum is located on the territory of the Rostov kremlin (seventeenth century). The display includes icon painting of the fifteenth to eighteenth centuries, works of applied art porcelain, and finift (painting on enamel). Distance from Yaroslavl: 54 km. Tour duration: 4 hours.

Town of Pereslavl-Zalessky. Museum of History and Fine Arts. Located on the territory of the Goritsky Monastery. The display includes old Russian icon painting, sculpture, painting of the eighteenth to twentieth centuries. The tour includes a visit to the Cathedral of the Assumption (eighteenth century). Distance from Yaroslavl: 130 km. Tour duration: 9 hours.

Museum "Fun Boat of Peter the Great". An early eighteenth-century ship with typical rigging. Distance from Pereslavl-Zalessky: 3 km.

Museum "Cosmos" in the village of Nikulskaya. The exhibits are devoted to the world's first woman-cosmonaut Valentina Nikolayeva-Tereshkova, who was born in that village. The history of cosmonautics. Distance from Yaroslavl: 27 km. Tour duration: 1½ hours.

Hotel

Yaroslavl—First class, 5-stories. (Intourist rents 90 beds.) Telephone: 2-1258.

YEREVAN

The capital of the Armenian Soviet Socialist Republic. Located on the bank of the Razdan River in the Ararat Valley at an altitude of 3,000 feet above sea level. The population is over 1,000,000. The climate is continental, dry. The average temperature in January is 17°F. to 10°F., in July, 82°F. to 93°.

The Caucasus Mountains surround Yerevan on three sides. Nearby Mt. Arart (16,966 ft.) and its snow-covered peak were known in biblical times. It is known as the traditional site of the resting place of Noah's Ark.

In the autumn, grapes, peaches, and apricots ripen in the Ararat Valley, while cornfields take on a golden color.

Armenia is a sunny republic and one has only to spend a few days in the area to acquire a tan. The gem of this "land of mountain rivers" is Lake Sevan, one of the loveliest high-altitude lakes in the world. Greatly impressed by its beauty, Maxim Gorky likened it to a piece of blue sky set amidst the mountains. The climate and mountainous air are beneficial to the health of the local inhabitants. There is one centenarian to every 3,000 Armenians.

The Armenian Academy of Sciences oversees numerous research institutes in the city. The many highly developed industries in the city include chemicals, synthetic rubber, precision instruments, machine tools, and electronics.

Since many of Yerevan's structures are built of a rosy colored rock material called tuff, the city is often called "rosy city."

Yerevan is one of the most ancient cities in the world.

It was founded in 782 B.C. as one of the fortresses of the mighty Uratu Kingdom. First settlements on the territory of Yerevan sprang up in the fourth to third millennia B.C.

Yerevan has the prominent Spendiarov Opera and Ballet Theatre, three drama theatres, a philharmonic orchestra, and the House of Chamber Music.

Excursions

Sightseeing Tour of the City.

Museum of the History and Revolution.

Museum of the History of the City of Yerevan.

Picture Gallery. Widely represented are works by Armenian artists from the Middle Ages to the present day, as well as Russian and Western European art.

Matenadaran. A major repository of ancient manuscripts and miniature books.

Erebuni Museum. The museum is located on the territory of the Old City (Erebuni is the old name of Yerevan), where the remains of the palace of the Urartu King Argishti I as well as of temples, fortress walls, the water supply system, and other structures have survived. Displayed in the museum are bronze and iron tools used by the people of Urartu, weapons, earthenware, and jewelry.

The "Armenian People in the Great Patriotic War of 1941–45" Museum.

Museum of M. Saryan. Displayed are dozens of canvasses of the famous Armenian artist.

House-Museum of Khachatur Abovyan. The exhibits are devoted to the life and activities of the renowned Armenian thinker and writer of the nineteenth century.

House-Museum of Ovanes Tumanyan. Dedicated to the life and creative work of the great Armenian poet.

Museum of·Modern Art. Works by Armenian artists are represented here.

Children's Picture Gallery.

House of Folk Art. Exhibits of works by the best folk craftsmen are arranged here.

Exhibition of Economic Achievements of the Armenian SSR.

Out-of-Town Excursions

Town of Echmiadzin. Zvartnots. In Echmiadzin, tourists visit one of the first Christian churches on the territory of the USSR, as well as the cathedral church (fourth century) with a museum and the Ripsime Temple (seventh century). Zvartnots is a historic-architectural monument of the seventh century. Distance from Yerevan: 22 km. Tour duration: 3 hours.

Garni-Ghegard. Garni is an antique temple of the first century (the Sun Temple). In Ghegard, tourists visit a cave monastery of the twelfth and thirteenth centuries. Distance from Yerevan: 38 km. Tour duration: 4 hours.

Oshakan. Tourists visit the church (seventh century) of the Oshakan Village where the creator of the Armenian alphabet, Mesrop Mashtots, was buried. Distance from Yerevan: 70 km. Tour duration: 4 hours.

Amberd Fortress. The remains of a palace fortress of the ninth and tenth centuries, a church of the thirteenth century. Distance from Yerevan: 70 km. Tour duration: 8 hours.

Lake Sevan. One of the largest mountain lakes in the world. A visit to the Sevan Peninsula and churches of the ninth century, with a rest stop on the shore of the lake. Distance from Yervan: 30 km. Tour duration: 3 hours.

Dilizhan and Agartsin. Dilizhan is a health resort. Agartsin is a monastery complex of the thirteenth century. Distance from Yerevan: 120 km. Tour duration: 8 hours.

Town of Tsakhkadzor (the "Canyon of Flowers"). A big sports camp and the Kecharis Monastery (twelfth century). Distance from Yerevan: 70 km. Tour duration: 6 hours.

Sanain, Adkhpat, Odzun. A tour of unique historical monuments of the fifth to tenth centuries. Distance from Yerevan: 250 km. Tour duration: 16 hours.

Sardarapat. A visit to the memorial erected in honor of the heroes of the Battle of Sardarapat (1918) and to the museum of ethnography. Distance from Yerevan: 70 km. Tour duration: 6 hours.

Metsamor. In the village of Metsamor tourists visit the remains of an ancient observatory (third to first millennia B.C.) and copper-melting furnaces of the same period. Distance from Yerevan: 55 km. Tour duration: 5 hours.

Hotels

Armenia—First class, 7 stories, 227 rooms. Located in city center, 13 km. from airport. Telephone: 52-5393.

Ani—First class, 14-stories, 336 rooms. Located in city center, 13 km. from airport. Telephone: 52-3961.

Dvin—First class, 14-stories, 297 rooms. Located in city center, 12 km. from airport. Telephone: 53-6348.

Motel

Sevan—First class, 109 rooms, parking lot for 50 cars. 75 km. from Yerevan, 100 km. from airport. Telephone: 42-13 (from Yerevan—using code number 82-2230).

ZAPOROZHYE

Regional center of the Ukrainian Soviet Socialist Republic. Located in the southeast of the Ukraine on the banks of the Dnieper. The poplation is over 800,000. The climate is temperate continental. The average temperature in January is 23°F., in July, 75°F.

Scythian tribes occupied the area nearly 6,000 years ago. Many serfs from central Russia fled here during the fifteenth and sixteenth centuries and called themselves Cossacks ("free people"). Built near the Dnieper rapids, Zaporozhye became a Cossack fortress.

The city was founded in 1770 as the Alexandrovskaya Fortress.

The city was given its present name in 1921 and started to grow rapidly in the 1930s when the Dnieprovskaya Hydrodam was built.

Abundant electricity together with nearby deposits of coal, manganese, and iron ore led to the growth of large-scale industries in Zaporozhye. By the time of World War II the city was producing one million tons of steel a year. Today it makes over five million tons annually. Zaporozhye saw heavy fighting and damage in World War II but was rapidly rebuilt after the war. The small Zaporozhets car is made here.

Zaporozhye has a music-and-drama theatre, a circus, the Glinka Concert Hall, the Oktyabrsky Palace of Culture.

Excursions

Sightseeing Tour of the City: Zaporozhye, a major industrial center in the south of the Ukraine.

V. I. Lenin Dnieprovskaya Hydrodam

Excursion to the Khoritsa Island and the Zaporozhsky Oak-Tree. The island lies within the city limits and is a recreational area. The excursion introduces tourists to the history of the Zaporozhye Cossacks. In the city suburbs, tourists are shown the oak tree, now 700 years of age, under whose crown, according to the tradition, the Cossacks held their meetings.

Excursion Around the Khortitsa Island. A fascinating motor-launch trip. Tourists are acquainted with the history of the island, of the Zaporozhye Cossacks and with the way recreation is organized for the townspeople.

Fine Arts Museum. Displayed are works by artists from the Zaporozhskaya Region, the Ukraine, and the other republics of the USSR.

Hotel

Zaporozhye—First class, 11-stories, 278 rooms. Located in city center, 30 km. from airport. Telephone: 33-3184.

Campsite

(Intourist rents part of space)

22 km. from city center, 12 km. from airport. Telephone: 34-8232.

Notes

[1] Boyce, Ronald R., *Geographic Perspectives on Global Problems: An Introduction to Geography* (New York: John Wiley & Sons, 1982), p. 184.

[2] Thompson, M. W. *Novgorod the Great* (London: Evelyn, Adams and Mackay, 1967), p. 9.

[3] Longworth, Philip, *The Cossacks* (New York: Holt, Rinehart & Winston, 1969), p. 4.

[4] Anonymous. "Programme of the Communist Party of the Soviet Union," *Moscow News,* Supplement to issue No. 44 (3188), (1985), p. 4.

[5] Anonymous. "What's the Difference," *National Federation of Independent Business Research and Education Foundation* (San Mateo, California, 1982). (Poster).

INTOURIST MOTOR ROUTES

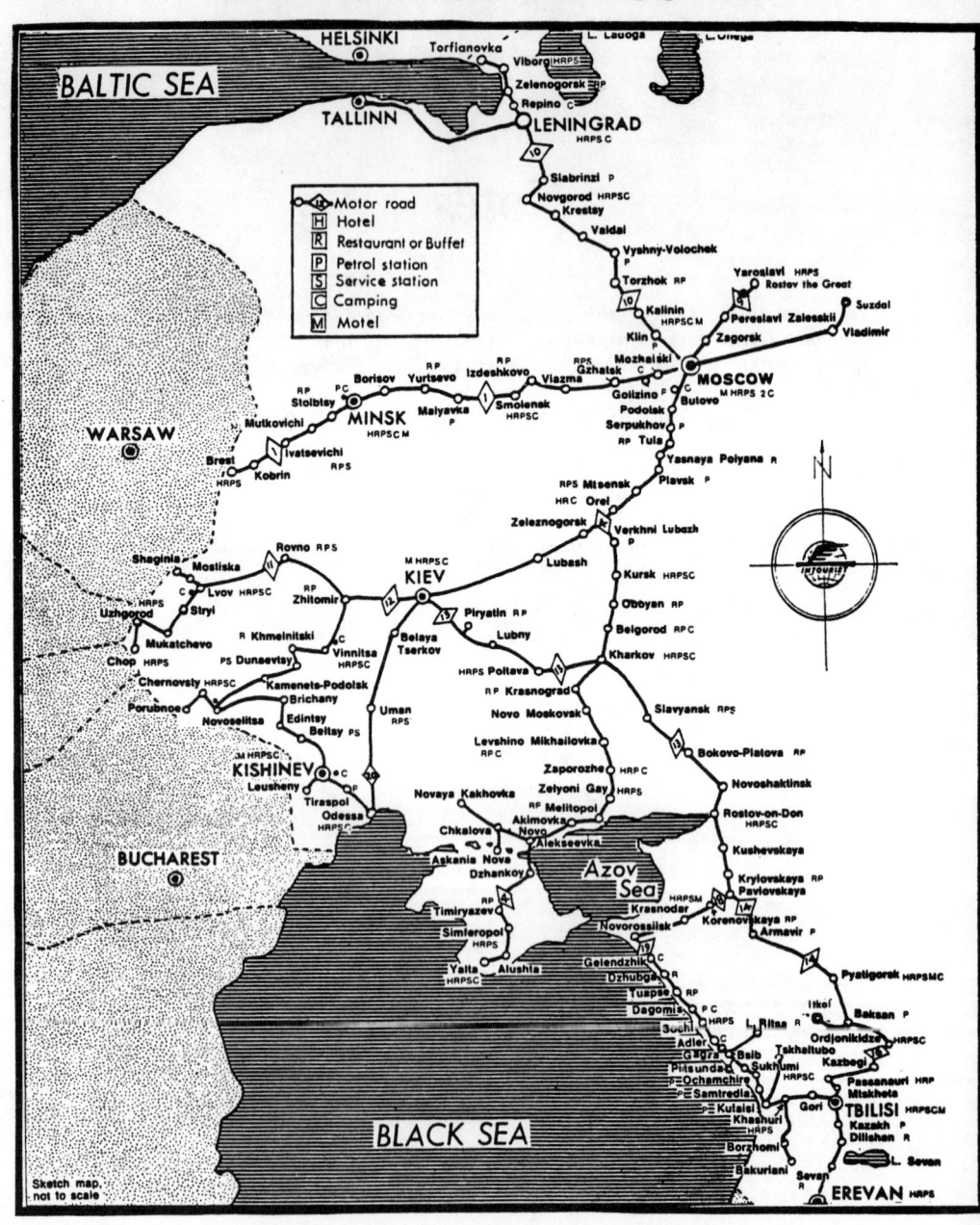

BALTIC SEA

HELSINKI
Torfianovka
Viborg HRPS
Zelenogorsk RP
Repino C
TALLINN
LENINGRAD
HRPS C
Siabrinzi P
Novgorod HRPSC
Krestsy
Valdai
Vyshny-Volochek
Torzhok RP
Yaroslavl HRPS
Rostov the Great
Kalinin
HRPSC M
Peresiavi Zalesskii
Suzdal
Vladimir
Klin
Zagorsk
Mozhaiski
RP
Borisov Yurtsevo
Izdeshkovo
Viazma RPS
Gzhatsk P
MOSCOW
Stolbtsy PC
Smolensk
HRPSC
Golizino P
M HRPS 2C
Butovo
WARSAW
Mutkovichi
MINSK
HRPSC M
Malyavka
Podolsk
Serpukhov P
RP Tula
Brest
HRPS
Ivatsevichi
RPS
Yasnaya Polyana R
Kobrin
RPS Mtsensk
Plavsk P
Shaginia
Mostiska
Rovno RPS
Zheleznogorsk
HRC Orel
Verkhni Lubazh
Lvov HRPSC
KIEV M HRPSC
Lubash
Kursk HRPSC
Uzhgorod HRPS
Stryi
Zhitomir RP
Piryatin RP
Oboyan RP
Mukatchevo
Khmelnitski R
Belaya C
Lubny
Belgorod RPC
Chop HRPS
Vinnitsa HRPSC
Tserkov
Kharkov
Chernovsty HRPSC
PS Dunaevtsy
HRPS Poltava
Kamenets-Podolsk
Porubnoe
Brichany
Uman RPS
RP Krasnograd
Slavyansk RPS
Novoselitsa
Edintsy
Novo Moskovsk
Beltsy PS
Levshino Mikhailovka RPC
Bokovo-Platova RP
KISHINEV M HRPSC
C
Zaporozhe HRP C
Novoshaktinsk
Leusheny
Tiraspol
Novaya Kakhovka
Zelyoni Gay HRPS
Rostov-on-Don HRPSC
Odessa HRPSC
Akimovka
Melitopol
Chkalova
Nova Alekseevka
Kushevskaya
BUCHAREST
Askania Nova
Azov Sea
Krylovskaya RP
Dzhankoy
Pavlovskaya
Timiryazev
Krasnodar HRPSM
Korenovkaya RP
Simferopol HRPS
Novorossiisk
Armavir P
Yalta HRPSC
Alushta
Gelendzhik
Pyatigorsk HRPSMC
Dzhubga C
Itkol
Yuapse RP
Baksan P
Dagomis C
L Ritsa P
Ordjonikidze HRPSC
Sochi HRPS
Adler
Baib
Tskhaltubo
Kazbegi
Pitsunda
Sukhumi HRPSC
Ochamchire
Passanauri HRP
Samtredia
Mtskheta
Kulaisi
Khashuri
TBILISI HRPSCM
Gori
Kazakh P
Borzhomi
Dilizhan
Bakuriani
L Sevan
Sevan
BLACK SEE
EREVAN HRPS

Legend:
- ⬡R Motor road
- H Hotel
- R Restaurant or Buffet
- P Petrol station
- S Service station
- C Camping
- M Motel

Sketch map, not to scale

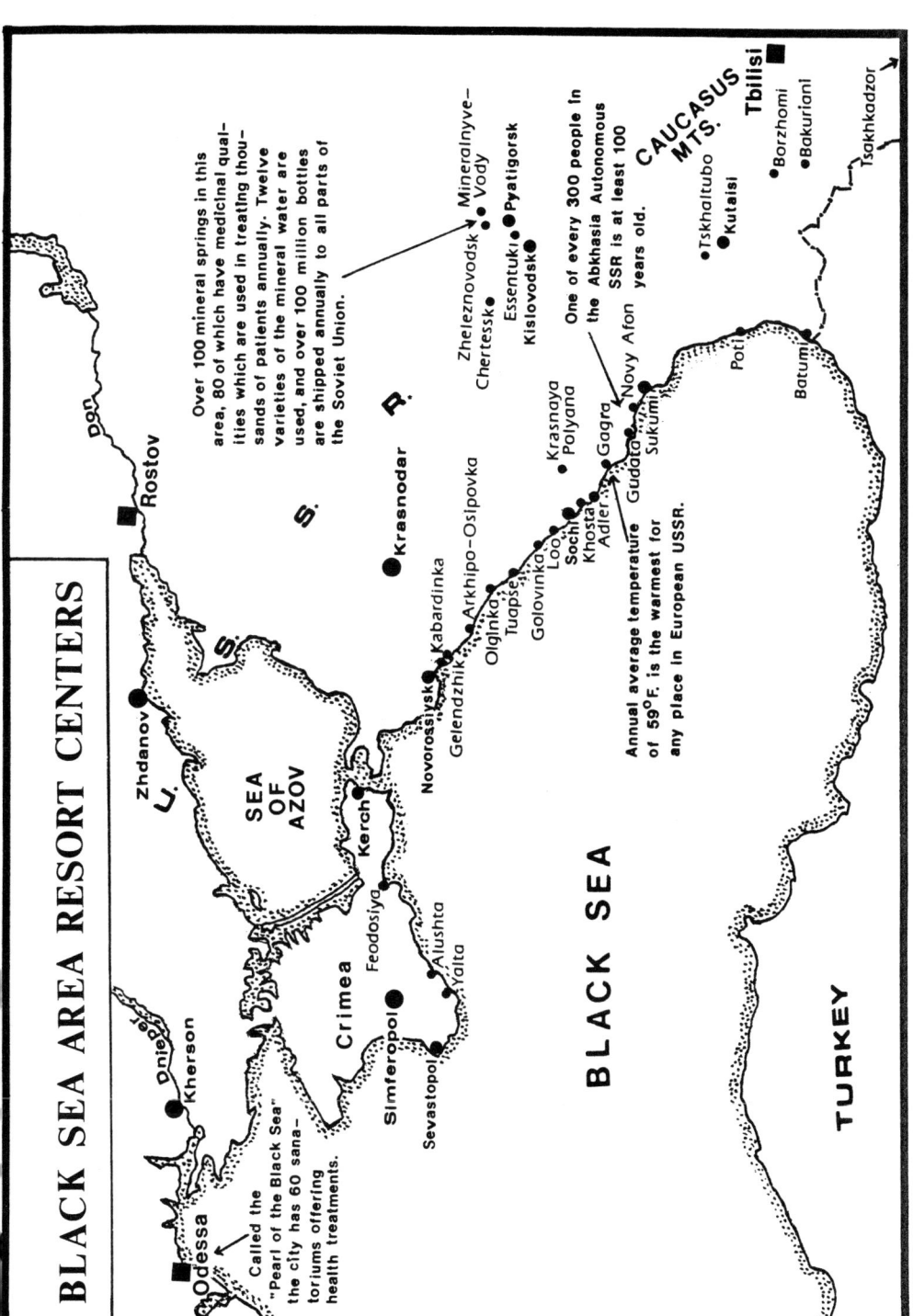

BLACK SEA AREA RESORT CENTERS

Over 100 mineral springs in this area, 80 of which have medicinal qualities which are used in treating thousands of patients annually. Twelve varieties of the mineral water are used, and over 100 million bottles are shipped annually to all parts of the Soviet Union.

One of every 300 people in the Abkhasia Autonomous SSR is at least 100 years old.

Annual average temperature of 59°F. is the warmest for any place in European USSR.

Called the "Pearl of the Black Sea" the city has 60 sanatoriums offering health treatments.

TURKEY

BLACK SEA

SEA OF AZOV

CAUCASUS MTS.

Crimea

Tbilisi

Borzhomi
Bakuriani
Tsakhkadzor

Tskhaltubo
Kutaisi

Poti
Batumi

Novy Afon
Sukumi
Gudata
Gagra
Krasnaya Polyana
Adler
Khosta
Sochi
Loo
Golovinka
Tuapse
Olginka
Arkhipo-Osipovka
Kabardinka
Gelendzhik
Novorossiysk

Mineralnyye-Vody
Pyatigorsk
Essentuki
Zheleznovodsk
Chertesske
Kislovodsk

Krasnodar

Rostov

Don

Kerch
Feodosiya
Alushta
Yalta
Simferopol
Sevastopol

Zhdanov

Kherson
Dnieper
Odessa

315

Bibliography

Allworth, Edward (Editor). *Ethnic Russia in the U.S.S.R.: The Dilemma of Dominance*. New York: Pergamon Press, 1980.

Auty, Robert; Oblensky, Dimitri, and Kingsford, Anthony. *An Introduction to Russian Language and Literature*. Cambridge: Cambridge University Press, 1977.

Baron, Samuel H. (Editor). *The Travels of Olearius in Seventeenth Century Russia*. Stanford, Calif.: Stanford University Press, 1967.

Billington, James H. *The Icon and the Ax: An Interpretative History of Russian Culture*. New York: Vantage Books, 1966.

Boyce, Ronald R. *Geographic Perspectives on Global Problems: An Introduction to Geography*. New York: John Wiley & Sons, 1982.

Brandes, George. *Impressions of Russia*. New York: Thomas Y. Crowell Company, 1966.

Carmichael, Thomas N. *The Ninety Days*. New York: Bernard Geis Associates, 1971.

Daniels, Robert V. *Red October: The Bolshevik Revolution of 1917*. New York: Charles Scribner's Sons, 1967.

"Economic Inequality on the Rise in the Soviet Union". *The Chronicle of Higher Education*. December 5, 1984.

Erlich, Victor. *Gogol*. New Haven: Yale University Press, 1969.

Evans, John L. *The Kievan Russian Principality: 860–1240*. Orlando, Florida: Associated Faculty Press, Inc., 1981.

Ewen, David. *Encyclopedia of Concert Music*. New York: Hill and Wang, 1959.

Fichelle, Alfred. *Russia in Pictures*. Translated by Laetitia Gifford. London: Gerald Duckworth and Company, Ltd., 1956.

Florinsky, Michael T. *Russia: A History and an Interpretation*. New York: The Macmillan Company, 1947.

Gregory, James S. *Russian Land Soviet People*. New York: Pegasus, 1968.

Grey, Ian. *The Horizon History of Russia*. New York: The American Heritage Publishing Company, Inc., 1970.

317

Herberstein, Sigmund. *Description of Moscow and Muscovy, 1557.* Edited by Bertold Picard and translated by J. B. C. Grundy. New York: Barnes and Noble, 1969.

Hindus, Maurice. *Mother Russia.* Garden City, New York: Doubleday, Doran and Co., Inc., 1942–43.

Hingley, Ronald. *A New Life of Anton Chekhov.* New York: Alfred A. Knopf, 1976.

Hooson, David. *The Soviet Union: Peoples and Regions.* Belmont, Calif.: Wadsworth Publishing Company, Inc., 1966.

Howe, Sonia E. *Some Russian Heroes: Saints and Sinners.* London: Williams and Norgate, 1916.

Huxley, Michael (Editor). *The Root of Europe.* New York: Oxford University Press, 1952.

Jorre, Georges. *The Soviet Union: The Land and Its People.* Translated by E. D. Laborde. New York: John Wiley & Sons, Inc., 1967.

Kaiser, Robert G. *Russia: The People and The Power.* New York: Atheneum, 1976.

Kaser, Michael. *Health Care in the Soviet Union and Eastern Europe.* Boulder, Colorado: Westview Press, 1976.

Keefe, Eugene; Boucher, Arsene A.; et al. *Area Handbook for the Soviet Union.* Washington, D.C.: U.S. Government Printing Office, 1971.

Levine, Irving R. *Travel Guide to Russia.* Garden City, New York: Doubleday & Company, Inc., 1960.

Lindstrom, Thais. *A Concise History of Russian Literature.* Volumes I and II. New York: New York University Press, 1966, 1978.

———. *Nikolay Gogol.* New York: Twayne Publishers, Inc., 1974.

Livermore, Gordon; and Schulze, Fred (Editors). *The U.S.S.R. Today: Perspectives from the Soviet Press.* Columbus, Ohio: The Current Digest of the Soviet Press, 1981.

Longworth, Philip. *The Cossacks.* New York: Holt, Rinehart, and Winston, 1969.

Lydolph, Paul E. *Geography of the U.S.S.R.* New York: John Wiley & Sons, 1977.

Magarshack, David. *Chekhov.* Westport, Conn.: Westport Press, Publishers, 1970.

———. *Pushkin.* New York: Grove Press, Inc., 1967.

Magocsi, Paul R. *The Shaping of a National Identity: Subcarpathian Rus', 1848–1948.* Cambridge, Mass.: Harvard University Press, 1978.

Mallac, Guy de. *Boris Pasternak: His Life and Art.* Norman, Oklahoma: University of Oklahoma Press, 1981.

Mellor, R. E. H. *Geography of the U.S.S.R.* New York: St. Martin's Press, 1964.

Pares, Bernard. *A History of Russia.* New York: Vintage Books, 1965.

Parker, W. H. *The Soviet Union.* Chicago: Aldine Publishing Company, 1969.

Paxton, John (Editor). *The Statesman's Yearbook, 1985–86.* 122nd edition. New York: St. Martin's Press, 1985.

Payne, Robert. *The Life and Death of Lenin.* New York: Simon and Schuster, 1964.

————. *The Three Worlds of Boris Pasternak.* Bloomington, Ind.: Indiana University Press, 1961.

Platenov, S. F. *History of Russia.* Bloomington, Ind.: Indiana University Press, 1964.

Putnam, Peter (Editor). *Seven Britons in Imperial Russia: 1698–1812.* Princeton, N.J.: Princeton University Press, 1952.

Rayfield, Donald. *Chekhov: The Evolution of His Art.* New York: Harper and Row Publishers, Inc., 1975.

Riasanovsky, Nicholas V. *A History of Russia.* 4th edition. New York: Oxford University Press, 1984.

Rogger, Haus. *Russia in the Age of Modernization and Revolution, 1881–1917.* New York: Longman, 1983.

Rydel, Christine (Editor). *The Ardis Anthology of Russian Romanticism.* Ann Arbor, Michigan: Ardis, 1984.

Schopflin, George (Editor). *The Soviet Union and Eastern Europe.* New York: Facts on File Publications and Muller, Blond and White, 1986.

Seaton, Albert. *The Russo-German War 1941–45.* New York: Praeger Publishers, 1971.

Shabad, Theodore. *Geography of the U.S.S.R.* New York: Columbia University Press, 1951.

Shoemaker, M. Wesley. *The Soviet Union and Eastern Europe: 1983.* Washington D.C.: Stryker-Post Publications, 1983.

Sholokhov, Mikhail. *The Don Flows Home to the Sea.* Translated by Stephen Garry. New York: Alfred A. Knopf, 1946.

————. *And Quiet Flows the Don.* Translated by Stephen Garry. New York: Alfred A Knopf, 1946.

————. *Harvest on the Don.* Translated by H. C. Stevens. New York: Alfred A Knopf, 1961.

Showers, Victor. *World Facts and Figures.* New York: John Wiley & Sons, Inc., 1979.

Simmons, Ernest J. *Chekhov: A Biography.* Chicago: The University of Chicago Press, 1962.

Sumner, B. H. *Peter the Great and the Emergence of Russia.* New York: Collier Books, 1973.

Stephenson, Graham. *Russia from 1812 to 1945*. New York: Praeger Publishers, 1970.

Sturley, D. M. *A Short History of Russia.* New York: Harper and Row Publishers, Inc., 1964.

Thompson, M. W. *Novgorod the Great*. London: Evelyn, Adams and Mackay, 1967.

Todd, William Mills III (Editor). *Literature and Society in Imperial Russia, 1800–1914*. Stanford, Calif.: Stanford University Press, 1978.

Troyat, Henri. *Tolstoy*. Garden City, N.Y.: Doubleday and Company, Inc., 1967.

Twain, Mark. *The Innocents Abroad and Roughing It*. New York: Literary Classics of the United States, Inc., 1984.

United Nations Educational, Scientific and Cultural Organization. *U.N. Statistical Yearbook, 1985*. Louvain, Belgium: Imprimerie Ceuterick, 1985.

Werth, Alexander. *Russia at War*. New York: Dutton and Company, Inc., 1964.

"What's the Difference?" *National Federation of Independent Business Research and Education Foundation*. San Mateo, Calif: 1982. (Poster).

Jude Wanniski, "Save Perestroika With Monetary Deflation.", *The Wall Street Journal* (May 16, 1990).

Andrei Kuteinikov, "Soviet Society--Much More Unequal Than U.S.", *The Wall Street Journal* (January 26, 1990).

Index

33; language, 44, 84–85; mail service, 29; medical service, 29–32; population, 17, 20; press, 58; prostitution, 61; Protestantism, 86–87, 91; religion, 81–92, 125, 140, 141–143; safaris, 33; skiing, 33; tax, 232; television, 236; temperatures, 16, 18; transportation, 19–20, 79–80; wages, 232; writers, 58, 62, 64–65, 93, 107, 109, 114, 192, 193–202, 211, 213–216, 250, 251
Russian Civil War, 159, 161, 172, 179, 186–187, 251
Russian Museum, 109–110
Russian 62nd Army, 174, 179
Russo-Turkish War, 205

Saint Ann's Church, 55
Saint Basil's Cathedral, 50, 55; Museum, 74
Saint George Monastery, 132
Saint Isaac's Cathedral, 94, 96–98, 118
Saint John the Baptist Church, 66
Saint Petersburg *see* Leningrad
Saint Sergius Monastery, 83
Saint Sophia Bell Tower, 131
Saint Sophia Cathedral, Kiev, 143–145, 148, 155; Novgorod, 128, 130–131, 132, 134
Saints Peter and Paul Cathedral and Fortress, 94, 95, 96, 106–108, 118
Saint Vladimir's Cathedral, 149
Sakharov, Andrei, 244
Saltykov-Shchedrin Public Library, 101
Samarkand, 285–286; excursions, 285–286; hotel, 286
sanatoriums *see* health resorts
Seamen's Club, 213
Sea of Azov, 195, 218
Sergius (Saint), 82
Seventh Heaven Restaurant, 47
Shakhrisaba, 286–287; excursions, 286–287; hotel, 287
Shcharansky, Anatoly, 252
Shchek, 139–140

Sheki, 287–288; excursions, 287; hotel, 288
Shevchenko State Academic Theater of Opera and Ballet, 151
Shevchenko, Taras, 150–151
Sholokhov, Mikhail, 183, 186–187; and *And Quiet Flows the Don,* 183; and *Harvest on the Don,* 187; and *Seeds of Tomorrow,* 187; and *The Quiet Don,* 186; and *Virgin Soil Upturned,* 187
Siberia, 18, 19
Simferopal, 228–229, 237–239
6th Army, 172, 174, 175
Slavs, 21–22, 125
Smolensk, 288–289; campsite, 289; excursions, 288–289; hotel, 289; hotel/motel, 289
Smolensky Church, 83
Smolny Cathedral, 103
Smolny Institute, 103
Sochi, 289–291; excursions, 290–291; hotels, 291
Socialist Revolution, 53, 56, 94, 98, 103, 104, 105, 107, 110, 114, 161, 186
Sophia (Princess), 62
Soyuza, 58
Spaso-Evfimiyevsky Monastery, 69
Sports Palace, Kiev, 152; Odessa, 220
Sputnik, 46, 47
Square of Fallen Heroes, 175–176, 179
Square of the Potemkin Sailors, 217
Stalingrad *see* Volgograd
Stalin, Joseph, 41, 89, 162, 172, 174
Starov, Ivan, 111
state farm, 159–170
State Historical Museum, 55
Stavropol, 291–292; excursions, 291–292; hotel, 292
steppe, 14–15, 164
Stroganov Palace, 103
Summer Garden, 10
Summer Palace, 110, 118
Summer Palace of Petrodvorets, 112–113
Suzdal, 127, 292–293; excursions, 293; hotels, 293